12/20/14

MW01235606

To: Val, ___

Best to
you

Billy L S___

Search-Rescue-Escape-Evade

The Story of a K9 Search Team

Billy L. Smith Sr.

authorHOUSE®

AuthorHouse™ LLC
1663 Liberty Drive
Bloomington, IN 47403
www.authorhouse.com
Phone: 1-800-839-8640

Published by AuthorHouse 09/05/2014

ISBN: 978-1-4969-3852-7 (sc)
ISBN: 978-1-4969-3851-0 (e)

Library of Congress Control Number: 2014916003

Preface

This a novel about an average 50 year old man winning the "biggest lottery ever" and goes wild for a year with his best friend. Then "Charlie" decides to give back to society by forming the best Search Team ever. When duty calls, they are asked to search for a kidnapped U.S. industrial executive in Peru by friends from the old days, the Viet Nam era. The U.S. State Department won't touch an attempted rescue; Peru is in a political turmoil, yet "Charlie" thinks money can buy anything. But the victim's employers want their man "out" without raising any dust. There is also an unknown "Mystery Man" in the background who seems to appear when least expected who "makes things happen." Some think he is from the CIA.

This is a novel, a pack of lies, figments of an old man's imagination and none of this ever happened. All the characters are fictional and the names are made up. Some of you may say "I remember that," but you know nothing and will say nothing.

Billy L. Smith Sr.

As you read this book, think about the movie actors Ward Bond or Wilford Brimley being "Charlie" and telling you a story around the camp fire.

All the women are beautiful and the men handsome, except "Charlie."

This is the first of three novels about "Charlie." Please enjoy them all. I need the money.

Chapter 1

If you have ever been in a Holiday Inn Bar, you have been in them all. At 2:00 in the afternoon when the bar tender was unlocking the door, I was walking by. "Why not!" I said as I walked in.

While sipping on a stale, overpriced beer out of a tall glass, a couple of other people walked in. They all appeared to be regulars from the greetings given by the bartender. I just sat there with nothing to do. My traveling partner was still in bed. I guess he was suffering with the world's biggest hangover.

We had been boozing and whoring for almost a year. We had gotten lucky and won the "BIG LOTTERY" of 83 million in Texas the year before. I had kept my mouth shut, went to a lawyer, made sure my wife of 40 years, our grown kids, and all the grandkids were taken care of for life.

Immediately thereafter I went bumming, in style. A big motor home with two drivers so we could keep that sucker rolling. We had a hard time finding two female drivers with the right type of license.

My lawyer made me run everything through him. "Big tits do not a bus driver make", Max the Mouth Piece yelled at me. I have to say that Max is one of the few honest lawyers I have ever known. He charges the shit out of me, but he keeps his word.

"And why not? You ever have seen them drive a bus?" I asked. But I knew he was right.

"Yes, I have" he screamed. "And I am still trying to settle everything with the two guys that the two blonde bimbos ran over making the turn off IH-10

a couple of days ago. It is a good thing the drivers were not hurt. I had to promise them a new pickup each for a signed release from them. They are at the dealers right now picking them out. Do you know the price of a new Ford Diesel?"

I noticed that those veins in his neck stick out a lot when he talks to me.

Here I am 60 years old and he talks to me like my daddy would if he were still alive. He is right though. I knew I was too drunk to drive that big Greyhound looking thing. Bart was in the back puking, so what were my options? Let one of the bimbos drive the bus? I can't even remember where we found them.

One of them told me she used to live with a truck driver, so that had been good enough for me. Away we went, out of the parking lot of a "Gentleman's Club," up on the west bound ramp of IH-10 on the eastside of Houston, Texas. We made it across town okay. The Bimbos did okay while I was in the back trying to make myself a vodka martini. I gave the one driving instructions to take us to the Wal-Mart on the west side of Houston. I told them we had to stop and get supplies for a trip Bart and I had planned. That is when things turned to shit.

"Get off here", I hollered as I felt the bus swerve to the right. ...There was a terrible sound on the right side of the bus. Even Bart stopped puking cheap wine long enough to open the bathroom door.

"What the fu__!" Bart said over the screech of metal. And then a second screech and grind as the bus made a skidding stop.

I looked outside. There was the remains of a pickup smashed against the cement guardrail. I got out and looked. Here came two very pissed off individuals in hardhats... looking directly at me.

I knew the drill. Say nothing. Called Maximillian Guerra, Esquire, Attorney At Law. I ran it down to him what had happened and he hung up and told me to stay in the bus and not say a word. He called back and wanted to know EXACTLY where we were. I told him we were on an exit west of Houston and the two guys banging on the door had hard hats on that said "International Lighting Company, INC". Houston. There was blood in their eyes. Mine.

"That's great!" yelled Max the Mouth Piece. "What do you mean 'GREAT', ", I said.
"The owner of the company and I went to college together. Let me make a call" and he hung up.

I left the phone on and waited about fifteen minutes and the phone rang. "Yo", I said.

"Charlie, ask out the door if either one of the guys trying to get in is named Steve Riley" said Max in a very tired voice.

"Yo, ...any body named Steve Riley?" I shouted over the crowd noise. Several of his buddies had shown up too.

"Yeah, I 'm Riley. What's it to you Shit Head. How did you know?" The biggest of them all shouted back.

"Yup, there is a Steve Riley here" I said in the phone to Max. "Put him on" he said.

"What? You want me to go out there?" I said. I then noticed that the two bimbos were leaning out the window on the driver's side giving all the boys an eyeball of tits. At least it kept them off Bart and me.

"NO! NO! NO! Just hand him the phone through the door. Any cops showed up yet?" Max asked.

"Nope"

"Yo! Steve. Its for you." I said "What kind of shit is this? You know my name and now you trying to tell me I am wanted on the phone. What kind of shit is this?" As he took a large piece of two-by-four and attempted to pry open a window.

"He don't wan...." I started to say.

"I have his boss on the phone on conference call.... tell him it is Ben Price calling and please talk to him".... groaned Max.

"Hey, Ben Price wants to talk to you." I said. And then all of a sudden things got quiet. Steve Riley looked at me strangely...took the phone and walked away from the bus towards the front and stood in the lights with one hand over his left ear while talking. After a few seconds, he came back...tossed the phone back up to me in the bus and said, "You got a deal".

"He said you got a deal. What deal?" I asked. That was when I was told I had just bought two new pickups.

A few minutes later, I felt like we could open the door of the bus without being dragged out and stoned. I opened the door and five or six guys all wearing hard hats and T-shirts with "International Lighting Company, INC Houston" got on. All of them were scoping out the bimbos while Bart and I got off the bus and walked over to the Wal-Mart parking lot. As luck would have it, a taxi was dropping someone off. Bart and I jumped in and said "Hyatt Regency, please."

The driver turned and looked at us. It was 7:00 AM and we looked and smelled like bums. I handed him a $100.00 bill, he smiled and away we went.

So, the next day Max called me about hiring two drivers. The bus had minor repairs that could be fixed in a week in Dallas.

He hired me two drivers alright. Not bad looking, a little rough around the edges, quiet types. Great drivers, but they did not smile. He made me promise that Bart and I would leave the "hired help" alone. We did. They were gay and we didn't know it until we had been on the road for about a couple of months later when we got the bus back. Bart comes up with a black eye he never did explain.

"That sorry piece of shit, signed a years contract with them two at six figures and per diem," I said to Bart Duffy, my traveling companion. Max was looking after my best interest. I got to admit they were good at their jobs...the bus was always clean inside and out...and they were Johnny on the Spot. Good mechanics too. Maybe, Max knew what he was doing after all.

My "partner in crime" was an old Navy buddy of mine... we had both been with Inshore Warfare Group Pacific. We were not SEALS in any way shape or form...those guys were good.... we were not sea going sailors either. In fact we had been "McHale's Navy" type all the years we were in the Navy, but we kept the brass happy by doing things that were "not Navy" when the others could not find rules to follow, so they left us alone. The Navy Department gave an audible sigh when we Bart and I retired. No ceremony. No nothing. I just threw the wife and three kids in the station wagon and headed back to Texas.

We trained dogs in the Navy. Oh, did I not mention that? Well, I did. Met Bart Duffy while doing hair brained things with dogs and parachutes at the Navel Test Station, El Centro, California. Bart was the Master Chief of the Parachute loft. We used an R4D to jump out of a plane with a dog strapped to us. Bad idea. We had the dog in a safe strap, but Bart figured with our weight and the weight of the dog, air temperature being hot and thin that we needed a better idea.

"O.K. Chief, what you got in mind," I said.

Now, Bart was the Chief Rigger too. He knew his business, but I did not recognize it at that time. We were both young bucks who had all the answers in those days and I bet we looked like two Bantie roosters standing there, trying to impress each other.

Bart suggested we use a bungee cord. One end attached to the harness and one end on the dog's hoisting sling. When we jumped, the dog was strapped tight to our chest. Both of our arms were placed over the top of the dog that was strapped crossways in front of us. We did not have a reserve chute since it was supposed to be strapped to the chest where the dog was. So, we would "static jump". This means we would have the ripcord attached to the aircraft and when we jumped, the chute would be pulled open.

The plan was this: after we jumped, the chute would open. After the chute opened and we stabilized, we would release the "quick-connects" and allow the dog to be eased down on the bungee cord, which was about thirty feet long. The objective was that the dog would reach the ground first. By landing first, the dog would take the pressure off the chute and jumper, long enough to make a softer landing in an old T-type chute.

"Chief Duffy, that sounds like a great idea. Lets try it" I stated in my best "military voice".

Away we went to the parachute loft. We rigged up the dog's harnesses with a few modifications, along with the harness we were going to use. The chute was packed with special care. The bungee cords were folded back and forth and secured with the correct size thread. We dangled in the tall

9

parachute loft over and over to make sure that everything was correct. Chief Duffy's Parachute Riggers were real pros. Stayed up all night making sure we could do it the next morning since it was going to be a calm day. Calm days in El Centro were rare for that time of year. But the "weather guessers" said it would be a good day. Chief Duffy's boss was the Air Operations Officer (AirOps) and he made arraignments for the R4D aircraft that the Air Force called a DC-3.

We were all set for the jump the next morning at dawn. All of Duffy's men and my team slept on the long riggers' tables with our heads on the chute bags. Our dogs slept on the floor beside us.

The dogs were German Shepherds. Nothing special in the breeding. In fact they were "rescued" from several places. Pounds. Backyards. And mine was a stray named "Hobo" or just "Bo" for short. "Bo" was a black shepherd with a large white patch on his chest. Solid as a rock and brave. Could not ask for more. I picked him up off the streets in National City, California at the back of a Shoney's Big Boy at 14th and National Ave. He was hanging around, probably eating out of a trash can for a living when I drove in. The kids and I were down there getting a special treat when we spotted the dog.

"BO" looked at us and we looked at him. The kids made some comment and I told them not to pet strange dogs and all that. When we came out, he was still there. He sat there as we got in the old pickup and watched. "Bo" caught my eye and something happened.

"Well, if you want to go, get in," I said and with that "Bo" jumped from the ground over the side of the old ragged '60 Chevy pickup and looked in the back window at the kids. I know he smiled a little smile. But hell, we all know dogs can't smile, don't we? Anyway, we went home.

The next day, "Bo" went to the Coronado Vet Clinic and was given all the shots a dog would need to be a working dog. "Bo" was supposed to be taken to the Military working dog kennels and processed. The U.S. Navy at that time did not use the DOD Kennels in San Antonio. There "dogs did not meet the Navy's needs" was the official reasons. The truth to the matter was the asshole running the place, some chair bound USAF major, who had been stationed at Lackland (Medina) all his career except once when he got transferred to Italy someplace. To inspect veggies for the "O" Club. This man turned out to be a wart on society's ass.

But "Bo" never did officially go the kennels in Imperial Beach Radio Communications Station. He lived with the family and slept with the kids on the bed.

Back at El Centro we got up early and went to the flight line for a briefing. Three teams would jump with dogs. One team member was a Photographers Mate, Second Class named "Casey" (what else) Jones. Casey was going to photograph everything he could and had lined up a few of the assigned base photographers to use the long lenses out on the test jump area to make moving pictures.

Now, remember this is back a long time before VCR cameras were even thought of. These were big and bulky type cameras. But Casey would do it.

"Bo" and the others dogs had been strapped into their canvas "jump suits" and then after being airborne, they were strapped to us with the help of Bart Duffy's crew. "Bo" went along with everything real well. All three of the dogs were very "sociable" dogs and had no problem with all the noise.

To the best of my knowledge this was the first time any of the dogs had ever flown. They did just great.

The takeoff was at dawn,very dramatic looking with the blue flames from the Pratt & Whitney 1300 engines belching blue flames as the "Gooney Bird" struggles to get airborne. Dawn was coming up over the dessert and we were a little chilly. The dogs are laying up over the wing spars so the engine sync "wall" will not be on top of us.

Finally the throttles start coming back to cruise speed and we can see out the square windows while setting on canvas folding "troop seats", which meant we must be getting close. The Test Range rules state that it must be full light to make an experimental jump of this type. And since the pilot was also our Air Ops. Boss, we waited till dawn.

The three of us are setting there, trying to look calm as we look at each other every so often. Here I am, the Team Leader, "what the fuck did I get us into this time?" thoughts going through my head. But the idea is great. While we were in Viet Nam a few months before, we wanted to be "inserted" to do some "blood tracking" for a sniper team. But the Hueys were noisy and I was not in the Infantry. But that is how we went in country. A place where myself and the two other dog handlers just "dropped away" from an Army "leg" Company sized patrol and lay in the bush while they went past. The "shooters" dropped off with us along with the spotters and a couple of automatic weapons men we had hand-picked from an Army group we knew. I do not think anyone except the First Sgt. even knew we were there or when we dropped out. We were dressed in OD fatigue uniforms and looked like the rest, except we had no flashings or markings of any kind. Just like we wanted it, we were "just there".

I have to say our U.S. Army counterparts were great people. They helped with logistics (dog food and supplies) and even brought the beer to the hooch so we could drink. We never left our dogs unattended.

After making that long walk into the bush the next morning, I said, "There has to be a better way."

So now comes the bright idea of Charlie Gray, that's me, to have a "parachute dawg team." So the idea was born.

Now, you have to understand that you do not go and do things like this on a whim. The U. S. Navy has "channels" and official paperwork to do. So we did it.

I wrote (or Frankie Roberts, the Yeoman wrote) a long mega page "proposal" to the Commander of the Naval Air Forces Pacific Fleet, a three star admiral in charge of all navy airplanes (see, we are thinking of transportation too) in the Pacific Ocean. The very last page of the proposal I wrote "Unless otherwise directed, I will commence this experimental canine program under the direction of ComNavAirPac (Code 049) as soon as possible"...submitted: Charles P. Gray, Senior Chief Petty Officer, USN.

I took the finished document to the "Code 049", a Navy Commander named Johnson. Commander Johnson was an old "war horse" who had done several tours in Viet Nam on carriers in the mid-60, He was a real live hero, an A4D driver. This job he had as Code 049 was a reward. So he did not get excited about the "petty shit" as he always said.

We invented a "Take-Your-Boss-To-The-Chiefs-Club-For-Lunch- Day". So off the Chief Petty Officers' Club we go.

"Commander Johnson-it-is-so-nice-you-could-join-us" attitude with our Dress Tropical White Long Uniforms on. Smiling a lot, my co-worker in this deal was a Chief Aviation Machinist Mate by the name of Howard Mueller. And we looked so "neat and pretty" in our "dress canvas".

"How come you two are in Dress Whites?" Commander Johnson observed looking out the corner of his eyes at us. "You two hoodlums don't own a pair of Dress Whites. Who did you steal 'em from?"

"Oh, that's a good one, Sir. But since we are on ComNavAirPac Staff, we must make a good showing, right, Sir?" Howie said.

"Humph! You guys with the dogs are here because the Boss said to take you in. No one else wanted you. One of you were "squiring" the C.O.'s old maid sister-in-law at the last base you were stationed...and he was going to shit can all of you if the Admiral had not seen the dog program a few weeks before.... and what you guys had done in 'Nam. And that's another thing...how did the Navy get involved in all of this anyway? This is supposed to be an Army deal"

"Well, Sir, here we are at the Chiefs Club...we can talk about it inside", I said as we drove up to the guest parking area. Howie jumped out of the back seat and opened Commander Johnson's door for him while I parked the car.

After I parked the car I went inside, Howie and the Commander were at the bar having a drink while waiting for a table. Howie would normally have a beer, but today he was drinking a Martini with Commander Johnson. Commander Johnson was explaining the finer techniques of making the perfect Martini to Howie when I walked up. Oh, and Howie was playing the role. He was very attentive and hanging on every word, while going through the motions of making a Martini and nodding the head. I sat back and listened, but drank a coke.

After about three martinis, neither one of them was feeling any pain. The table was ready and we ate. And of course they had a few more martinis. By the time the meal was over Commander Johnson and Chief Petty Officer Howard Mueller were, what is the technical term..."shit faced".

As we were walking away from the table, we ran across Vinnie Rideout.

Now, Master Gunnery Sgt. Vincent Rideout is a hell of a Marine's Marine. I had been with him at several duty stations and our kids played together. But when he had been drinking, he was a bear to get along with.

Vinnie came over to Naval Air Station North Island for lunch from Marine Corp Recruit Depot, San Diego about once a week. The Chief's Club had good food and he could go home from there that night with a minimum drive to The Strand Housing area for senior enlisted men. And today, Vinnie was "steaming on all boilers".

"What the fuck you squids doing in ice cream suits?" he laughed real big and slapped me on the back. "You look like a bunch of pussies dressed like that." and roared with laughter. Vinnie had only seen us in OD green utilities, which made us look like "grunts" except we had "U.S. Navy" above the left breast pocket.

"Commander Johnson, may I present Master Gunnery Sgt. Vincent Rideout. Vinnie is an old friend of ours from "in county". He helped us, how would you say, procure necessary logistic support from our friends in the Army."

I was hoping it would help the situation by trying to be formal. But, alas, never to be.

"Commander", Vinnie said in his best drill field voice...."these two fucking squids are the only ones I allow in my compound...they can steal a loaded round from a 105 while being loaded....hah hah hah..."

I went out the door to get the car from the parking lot. I drove to the front door and poured Commander Johnson inside the front seat. I went back inside to get Howie but could not find him. He was gone. Vinnie was gone and I had a "shit faced" senior staff officer in a U.S. Navy sedan in front of the Chiefs Club, which is a "NO NO " in itself.

I found Howie and Vinnie back at the bar. Howie was trying to explain to Vinnie how to make a martini. About every other sentence, Vinnie would say, "Fuck you, squid". I knew it was about to happen. A fight.

I got a few of the others to distract Vinnie and I scooped up Howie and took out the keys to the...it's gone, "the fucking car is gone", I said out loud.

I sat Howie down on the patio chairs and went to look for the car and Commander Johnson. I went around the corner near the Beach Front and there was the car, in the sand up to the axles, with Commander Johnson passed out at the wheel. The Base Police were coming around the bend by the end of the airstrip, but had to wait for taxing planes.

"Oh, shit" I thought, "Now what?"

About that time, the side door to the Chiefs Club bangs open and out comes Vinnie and two Staff Sergeants who were in the club. They stop and look at what is happening. Without a second thought all four of us jumped into "action stations." I shoved Johnson over and started the car. Vinnie and the two Staffs went to the front of the car and pushed. The car only had to go about one car length and it was on hard surface.

Just as the car got on hard surface, I turned the wheel and hid the car behind a series of Dempsey Dumpsters setting outside the Galley Entrance to the Chiefs Club. The Base Police drove buy, and did not even look where we had been, but it had been a close situation.

I jumped in the car, drove around the corner and picked up Howie, who for all practical purposes, had passed out. I got them all in the car and headed out. But to where?

I drove Commander Johnson home since he lived on base. When we got to his quarters, I got him out and helped him inside. I knocked on the door and Mrs. Johnson came to the door. She just opened it and stepped outside.

"Oh, Leon", she said "what have you been doing out with "those" enlisted men?" as she turned to her daddy, a retired four stripper from the old Battle Ship Navy.

"Four Stripper" is a term used for a Navy Captain, and very senior Captains were often Commodores. The old gentleman smiled and nodded not saying a word.

"Chief?" he finally said as we placed Commander Johnson in his easy chair, "What happened?"

"I think it must be the Hong Kong flu shots, Commodore", I said. "We went to lunch and he didn't feel well, so I brought him home."

"Hmmm..... Chief, just how many "Hong Kong Flu Shots" did he have?" asked Captain Jonathan Prebble Dahlgren, USN (retired) with a slight twinkle in his eye and an almost curled up corners on his lips.

"About twelve, Sir" was all I could say.

"Thank you, Chief, Mrs. Johnson and I will carry on from here." as I was steered towards the door.

"Very good, Sir" as I walked on the battleship gray porch of the senior officer quarters.

"Chief". "Yes, Sir?"

"Some things never change do they?" the Captain chuckled, as he looked over the railing of the porch towards the sedan in the drive. Howie, who was in the back seat, had his head back and his mouth open. Passed out. "Sir?"

"When I was a young Gunnery Officer on the Old Indianapolis, I was invited to a "social event" by the Gunnery Department Chiefs...down in Panama.... took me three days to sober up...was in 'hack and harness' for thirty days over that...the only difference was they brought me back to the ship in a wheel barrow...those were the days" as he signed and looked away to some unseen time. "Yes, Sir"

'The Indianapolis was sunk in '45...last capital ship of the line to...."

"Yes, Sir. I know. Going from Guam to Australia...my father was Chief Gunner's Mate Daniel Grey, Chief Master

19

At Arms...he survived.... sharks got the rest" as we looked in each other's eyes.

The old Captain nodded as I walked away and went to get in the car. A slight wave was exchanged from the porch as I backed out. But I still had to get Howie home.

I was still driving around the base with a dunk chief in the back of a Navy sedan that was "borrowed" from the staff motor pool for official business and now overdue. What now?

I then noticed the Commander's hat with all the gold braid on the bill...called "scrambled eggs".... lying on the seat beside me. "I have an idea" as they say in the cartoons.

I took the senior officer's hat with "scrambled eggs" and put it on Howie s head. The dress whites of chiefs and officers appeared to be the same if you did not look too hard.

I reached over the rear seat and grabbed Howie and made his head "flop" forward. Slammed the hat on his head and threw a trip ticket log on his lap as if he was reading it. I eased up to the gate and the Marine popped a salute as we drove through. I bet they thought that this was a very senior officer to have a chief petty officer as a driver.

I drove to Coronado Avenue, made a right turn and away to Strand Housing we went. A few minutes later I pulled into Howie's driveway and got him out.

"Okay, now what have you assholes been up to?" asked Joann, Howie's gorgeous wife. A tall blonde and the most charming lady in the world...most of the time.

"I think it is Hong Kong flu...."

"Bull shit, he had Hong Kong flu last week when you brought him home drunk...and the time before that is was Asian Dingy Fever or some shit..."

"Well, you ain't gong to believe this....but...."

"You fucking "A" I ain't going to believe this shit, Charlie Gray...get your ass out of here..."

And with that I left. I backed out of the drive and went across the street to my house. Put on a new set of dress whites and went back to the base to return the car. You would be surprised how dirty one gets wrestling drunks.

The next morning Howie and I were "standing tall before the man" as they say. Commodore Johnson was a little upset. ...and hung over.

"I have never been so humiliated in my life...my father-in-law, Commodore Dahlgren, said not to say a word to either one of you...and I had to promise. Between him and my wife, they were on my ass all morning at breakfast... her daddy kept mentioning the "old Indianapolis Gunnery Department"...I don't know what that means...he has been acting strange lately....." as he answered the ringing phone.

"Yes, Sir Captain....(It was the Chief of Staff) .....I am sorry I missed the staff meeting ...Yes, Sir....I know.....Yes, Sir......I became ill while eating lunch and had to go.....my hat?.....was in your car this morning......?....I will be right over...Yes, Sir!....."

Billy L. Smith Sr.

"Commander, before you leave could you sign a little routine document here concerning a training program......" as I handed him the prepared folder.

"Yes, yes, yes.....here let me read it." as Commodore Johnson perused the pages. With a quick flick of the wrist he grabbed the U.S. Naval Academy pen off his desk and signed the documents.

Howie and I were still standing in his office when he ran across the street to the Chief of Staff's Office.

"Thank you, Sir!" we said in unison. The jump was approved.
And we smiled.

Chapter 2

A blast of cold air rushed through the plane when the cargo door on the left rear was opened by Parachute Rigger Second Class Tommy Ricks, acting as Jump Master for this trip. I jerked to an "awake" position and "Bo" stood up too. I scratched his head as we turned on a north -south heading on an approach to Area W28, the jump zone.

"O.K., Asshole. You said you could do it. Now lets see you do it." Tommy looked down at the dessert below and was talking into the Inter Communications System, a microphone and headset commonly called an ICS. He stepped back from the door and faced forward where we were. Tommy gestured to "Stand-Up" by raising his extended arms up with the palms up like the Choir Director at church would do. Next, he made a "Hook-Up"" gesture towards the wire or static line running from front to rear of the aircraft.

We had discussed everything at a plane side briefing prior to takeoff. We wanted to "stand-up-hook-up" in a minimum of time because we would have the dogs strapped to our chest. Their own weight pressing against our bodies would be somewhat uncomfortable to say the least. We anticipated that we might get some resistance from the dogs. Well, all except old "Bo," I knew he would be okay.

We planned to place both arms on top of the dogs jump sling about shoulder high. This would help us hold the dog down when we jumped and the chute opened. This would also keep the dog from flying into our faces. Once the chute opened and we stabilized, we would unhook the dogs and let them ease down to the end of the bungee cord. We only wanted to be suspended in the air a total of one minute after the opening shock until we hit the ground. Once the chute opened, we would release the "rocket fittings" and slowly lower the dogs to the end of bungee cord, I thought.

I was worried about "Cup Cake", Howie Muhler's dog. She was a mean bitch and that was all there was to it. Jessie Long and "Sam", "Bo" and I would be okay. And the dog we had to leave behind because he was vomiting would have been OK also, but we had to leave both the handler and dog on the ground. The handler, Frankie Roberts, who had written the whole plan in one day, was disappointed. Frankie understood he had to do it. He would be with Bart Duffy at the drop zone to help us with the dogs once we were on the ground, especially Cup Cake.

Before Tommy made a gesture to "Stand in the Door" several of Bart Duffy's riggers helped us hook up the dogs to our harnesses. The handlers knelt down low and bent over. The Rigger would make sure the "rocket fittings" were secure and then the handlers would stand up straight with the dogs in the "jump suits". The handlers then would "hook up" and "walk" to the door. Shuffle is a better word. Place there arms over the top of the dogs and jump, we thought.

All of this took place with a very short time, less than a minute. The idea at the briefing was that we would all stand and walk to the door and go out as a "stick". All of this had to be timed so we would arrive over the jump zone when we "marked on top".

Cup Cake decided enough was enough. She tried to eat the Rigger helping Howie, and even tried to eat Howie. Now remember, Howie is locked to this dog and her head was only a few inches from his face when locked in. She was trying to get out of the "jump suit". Howie is "Hooked up" and the jump zone is coming up fast. It was briefed that for any reason the handler didn't want to "go" that he would set down flat on the floor. This would be a signal that he was "N.F.G.", No Fucking Guts is what we teased each other about, but that was for safety reason.

Jump point was coming up fast. Howie was supposed to be number one in the stick with Jesse in the middle and me last.

With Cup Cake acting up, I thought that Howie would sit down and Tommy would unhook him. Howie was throwing his head back as best he could while trying to avoid Cup Cakes snapping jaws and push down on harness at the same time.

The alternating yellow lights started flashing, meaning "Stand in the Door," and get ready. Tommy was trying to plug his ICS back in so he could talk to the pilots. It had come unhooked while Howie was "dancing" with Cup Cake.

All of a sudden Howie ran to the door and jumped with Cup Cake trying to eat his lunch. Jesse went out right after Howie as he should have done. Instinct and training made me follow the other two.

As I was going out the door, I noticed the other two chutes had deployed or were in some stage of making a routine opening.

"Good", I thought as my own chute eased open. Bart Duffy had made extra-long static lines so we would have an easy opening. He is a jewel, thinks of everything.

After we were stabilized and the plane had flown away, all that could be heard was the gentle "pop" of the silk above my head and someone yelling. It sounded like Howie.

I looked to my left and, yup, there he was, yelling at the top of his voice, "...you fucking bitch, you bite me again and I drop kick your ass all the way back to San Diego...ouch! mother fucker!" He was trying to reach the retro rocket fittings to release Cup Cake down the bungee line. Each time Howie would try and reach the left fitting, which was by Cup Cake's head, she would bite him. Still, he was able to get the fittings opened on both sides.

Now, the original idea was for the dogs to be GENTLY lowered down the bungee line. And by this time, Jesse had released the fittings and lowered his dog to their landing position and was ready for touch down. Each was swinging gently and looking down preparing to land.

Well, all except Howie and Cup Cake. Cup Cake was fighting so hard and biting Howie, he just released the fittings and said: "There, you fucking cunt...I'll take care of you on the ground" and started to prepare for a landing.

One little problem occurred we had not "briefed for". A bungee cord is like a big rubber band and when Howie just dropped Cup Cake, she was mad. When she hit the end of the bungee cord, Howie was going down and she was coming up. When she reached the top next to Howie, she bit him on the ass and then went down again. "Boing" could be heard, I swear, just like the cartoons. Back came Cup Cake, still mad, she made it as high as his boots this time and got a toe of the left boot in her mouth. She hung on for a split second and Howie, in the meantime, was still saying all sorts of words his mother didn't teach him. Cup Cake was still going up and down but not reaching Howie now.

However, the landing was coming up in less than 10 seconds and I had to pay attention. At least Cup Cake couldn't get to Howie now and I had problems of my own. Since I was last in the string, and not paying attention, I had drifted over to the edge of the cleared landing zone. I was going into a brushy place and was going in fast.

I had an uneventful landing, Bo was great. He came to me wagging his tail and jumping around like a kid just off the Hammerhead ride at the carnival. There was almost no wind and my chute fell on top of me. I ducked under the edge real fast and unhooked "Bo" from his "jump suit". I was about fifty yards outside the jump zone and I heard yelling from Howie and barking I recognized as being Cup Cake's deep roar.

I popped my chute off and called "Bo" to me. I was looking around trying to get a direction of travel towards Howie and Cup Cake. I followed the noises and came on the funniest site I have seen.

Howie is tangled up in the risers of the chute trying to get loose with Cup Cake trying to bite him. Bart Duffy and his crew were driving up in a Dodge Power Wagon and didn't know what to do. Still, what they did know was that they were not going to get out of that truck with a big German Shepherd acting crazy.

The chute had fallen straight down on Howie. He did not have time to duck from under the chute canopy since Cup Cake was trying to bite him. Ever time Cup Cake made a run at Howie, he would "feed" her a hand full of risers. Cup Cake would take the risers in her mouth and thinking it was Howie, play tug of war with them still attached to the harness. Howie would then fall head over asshole trying to get untangled.

By the time I finally stopped laughing, Jesse had seen what was going on and ran up to Howie. Jesse grabbed Cup Cake by each side of the jump suit and held her. I ran over to Howie, finished collapsing the chute and cut him out of the risers he was tangled in. Somewhere in all this mess Frankie, the dog handler we had to leave behind, showed up.

In less than two minutes it was all over. Cup Cake was out with the other dogs playing in the bush. And all of us were rolling in the face powder dust roaring with laughter. The safety team in a second Dodge Power Wagon ambulance drove up and just stood there wondering if we had all gone crazy.

"At least we got it on film", I managed to get out between laughs. "That is why we were trying to tell you not to jump, but to "go around." We did not get the jump on film." one of the voices to one side said.

After we got back and had washed a little dust off, we de-briefed.

It seems while were in the aircraft just prior to jumping, Tommy's ICS had come unplugged while wrestling with Cup Cake. He did not hear the "Abort" call from the cockpit. Howie seen the yellow lights flashing and knew within five seconds they would turn to steady green, or should have. With Cup Cake in a minor snit over the whole deal, Howie decided not to wait around, and of course we followed.

While we were de-briefing and still laughing at the incident, a loud bang could be heard at the door to the Parachute Loft as it was jerked open. In comes the Air Ops Officer, who had been our pilot for the deal. He was mad and read everyone the riot act as best he could without laughing at what had happened.

"Didn't you guys learn anything in Jump School at Ft. Bragg?" he yelled as he slammed out the door.

Howie looked at all of us and then at Bart Duffy and said "we never went to no jump school...didn't think we would need it......gravity gets us down and we had this cord tied on to the airplane...chute had to open"

"What?" screamed Bart Duffy "You guys never went to Jump School? "Another beer, Pal?" snapped me back to reality at the Holiday Inn in Louisiana and the present.

"Yeah, why not", I said.

About this time the swinging door to the Holiday Inn Bar burst open and in came the cutest little thing I had ever seen.

Chapter 3

All the lights were on in the bar. The two bartenders were restocking and getting ready for the night. The other patrons in the bar were talking among themselves. No throbbing music or twirling lights, just a nice place to get out of the heat.

The young woman that entered the bar was walking in strides much too long to be lady-like. She was dressed in a riding habit that I recognized as being associated with a ritzy "hunt club," or maybe they were riding jumpers. Race horses maybe? I did not know, but she looked good in the high stable boots that come to the knees and the riding breeches, as they were called. Very petite, you could say. I could not tell how old she was, but she was no girl, she was definitely a grown woman. Like any man, I had to check the upper torso. Very nice. She had a T-shirt on with some company logo, and had a "sports bra" type gear on, no jiggle. Damn, I bet they looked good "unharnessed".

About that time Bart Duffy stuck his head in the side door by the electronic slot machines that are legal in Louisiana. I saw him in the back bar mirror and gave him the "yo" sign with a nod of a head. He came in and sat on the bar stool next to me. The one bar tender had stopped and was looking at our newest guest too, frozen in midair and motion. Everyone one was looking. She was a sweetie.

This newest guest in the bar was not a raving beauty. She was not in any way different from any of the other women you meet daily, but yes, she was different.

You could tell she was letting her eyes adjust to the dimmer lights inside the bar after coming in out of the blazing Gulf Coast mid-afternoon sun. She was looking for someone and the patrons in the bar were helping her "look".

All of this took place in about ten seconds, then she moved to the rear of the large room, across the typical Holiday Inn bar dance floor where a man was seated alone. We had not even seen the man. He must have come in while I was in the john.

The bar tender noticed Bart and came over to us. Bart just motioned to the bar tender by pointing at the draft I was drinking indicating "the same". The bar tender went back, got a fresh glass and filled it. When the bar tender came back, Bart asked "who is that?" in a very soft voice since it was quiet in the bar. The bar tender shrugged his shoulders and indicated "who knows".

"I've never seen her before" he said, and walked away to do whatever bar tenders do.

Bart and I could watch her across dance floor out the corner of our eyes without being obvious. We looked and enjoyed what we saw.

The man she was talking to was no gentleman. He was a short,

stocky, graying older caucasian male. He looked like a dork in fact. My first thought was a junky. He never rose when she approached and never offered her a seat. From what we could see she was talking with both hands to her side, a very composed lady.

"Oh, well" I said.

"A spinner", said Bart referring to her short frame.

"Yup," and we both laughed a small chuckle by lifting our chests a little. The bar returned to normal.

We sat there in silence for a full minute, both of us trying to hear what the man and woman were saying, but we only heard a small noise indicating they were talking in a very low voice.

"Bart, we got to get our shit together. We been running hard for almost a year. We ain't done shit but just run and play. I just talked to Max the Mouth Piece this morning and we have spent almost $300,000 on shit....nothing we can write off and now we are getting to the point we need to pay BIG taxes. Or rather I am."

Bart just sipped his beer and looked at me in the back bar mirror, glancing at the young lady.

"Max says I got to attend this meeting tonight and make a donation to the Home for Unwed Kitty Cats or something. Black Tie here at the Holiday Inn Main ballroom. 8:00 PM. You going with me?"

"Nope" "Why not?"

"Going home" Bart stated. "Why?"

"Tired of running hard. You know, I don't even know the date. " "I looked at my Indeglow Timex watch and said it is the 18th." "Hmmm. What month?"

"July . No August. Isn't it?" and we both laughed.

Bart looked around and saw a newspaper lying by the bar maid's station where they people up drinks. He caught the bar tender's eye and said "May I look at the paper?"

"Sure, but it is yesterdays" the bartender noted.

"Thanks, just wanted to see the baseball scores" as Bart went to the end of the bar and picked up the paper.

"July" he said.

"Hmmm. Like I said, it is time to get our shit together and get clean. This is my last beer. No more booze." I pushed the empty pilsner glass away and nodded to the bar tender. He came over and I handed him a twenty and said "Keep it". He raised an eyebrow and walked away.

"Got any money?" I asked Bart.

"Yup" he stuck his hand in his pocket and came out with several hundred dollars in assorted denominations, straightened them out, and folded them. "Use the company credit card and buy yourself a ticket back to San Antonio. Can you get home from there?"

"Yup."

"Coming back?"

"I'll let you know" said Bart, and he walked toward his room without turning back.

I felt sad. My best friend had just left and I was all alone.

"Hey, I got several million bucks to spend" I said to myself. "How can I be lonesome with that kind of pesonality." I laughed at my own joke.

I started to stand up when the young lady started walking back across the dance floor. She turned to the right and walked behind me as I stood up. I turned, watching the "action" as she walked away when suddenly, she stopped and turned to me and said "YOU, have anything to say?"

All I could do was shake my head in a negative manner. I did get a look into her set of "bedroom eyes". Hell, it wasn't just one bedroom, it was the whole motel. She spun around and left out the side door by the slot machines, turned right and went towards the pool.

I slowly walked out the same direction and didn't see her as I am sure she was walking much faster.

I walked up to the suites that Bart and I had rented on the third floor. We each had separate rooms. Bart was walking out with a small suitcase we had bought at some airport somewhere. Looking sad, head down, which was very unlike him.

"You taking the car?" I asked. "If you don't mind?"

"Of course not. Anything else? Need any money?" He just shook his head and walked off.

Marla, the driver we had hired last year, took his bag and walked with him towards the Chevy Van we had bought here last week. He looked old.

"Well, so do I." I thought. I guess if I didn't have the money I had, no decent woman would have anything to do with me. "Peso-nality" I said aloud as I closed the door to the room.

"Shit, tonight's deal is black tie."

I promised Max the Mouth Piece I would show up. I called the front desk to see if I could rent a tuxedo this late.

The front desk was very helpful as they should be. Of course we tossed around twenties like a champ when we tipped. Marla was taking Bart to the airport and would not be back for a couple hours. Oh well, cabs run all day too.

"Can you get me a cab or something, Ma'am? Marla took the car to the airport" since they all knew who we were and who Marla was.

"I can have the courtesy car available to you, Sir, if you want." "Yeah, that will be fine...how long?"

"Right now if you like, Sir" the sweet voice crooned on the other end. Not a New Orleans Southern accent, but very pleasant type voice, perfect for this type of work.

"Okay, let me shower and I will be right done."

About a half hour later I went down to the front desk and stood to one side as a guest was checking in. From the back room came a lovely lady. I recognized the voice from the desk clerk who I had talked to. Except she wasn't the desk clerk, but rather the corporate manager of Holiday Inn New Orleans, Inc., owner of several "properties" as they like to call them, in the New Orleans area. A real lady, you could tell.

"Our driver, Sammy, is tied up with tonight's banquet. So, if you don't mind I will take you to where ever you want to go. I understand you want to rent a tux. I know of a place that I would recommend." she said in a very refined voice.

"Yeah" I mumbled. I stumbled over words like a High School kid. "That's great".

A real lady, class all the way. Vanderbilt? Vasser? Ah, some hoitty toitty eastern prep school for proper young ladies probably.

Still, when we shook hands she looked you right in the eye, and had a very firm hand shake. Not like a man gripping each other, but firm an honest grip.

"Excuse me a moment, please. I need to shut the office and get my purse. I will be just a second?" and returned to the area behind the desk.

"Class. All the way, class".

A few moments later, she walked out a side door and walked towards me.

"I'm sorry, my name is Amber Ames, I am the property Manager for Holiday Inns of Greater New Orleans. We have several properties I oversee and this is the central office" as she lead the way.

I followed like a puppy.

We went to the parking lot and I started looking for the regulation green and white Holiday Inn Airport shuttle bus, but none was to be found. Instead I followed Amber to a Ford Explorer 4x4. She used the automatic door opener and "clicked:" the doors open as we approached. I opened the door and got in.

Amber said "I hope you don't mind me taking my car, I am leaving a little early and have no intentions of coming back. What I will do is I will let you off at Lakeside Mall and then Sammie will come get you when you call? Is that Okay?" she said was we roared onto IH 10 East.

"Sure, that okay with me." as if I had a choice.

She maneuvered the big Ford through traffic like a Le Manes road racer. After a few miles we turned north towards the South Lake Yacht Club. I knew where we were because Bart and I had rented a whole yacht for a supper cruise about a week before. I had no idea who was on board, we just invited everyone.

A short drive and a few lights we were at the Lakeside Mall, very upscale and very expensive looking. Even with the almost unlimited funds I had available over the last year, I still wore Levi's, boots and cotton western type shirts. Oh, Bart and I had bought a couple of suits. I simply do not remember where we left them, what a waste. Now we are getting right and no more booze, none.

Amber Ames drove the big Expedition into a parking spot that was not designed to be entered into at 50 mph.

"Oh, I think I will run up with you. I have not seen these folks in such a long time." Amber said as we got out of the vehicle. As I was admiring the truck, as most men would, I noticed a red and gold USMC sticker on the rear window. She noticed me looking at the sticker but said nothing.

We walked in the mall and entered the caverns of shopping. I never did like them, but Amber acted like she knew where she was going so I followed. Up an escalator and down more rows of small shops that looked like big bucks. After what felt like a two and half mile hike at the least, we came to a shop with tuxedos and formal dresses in the window and entered.

When we walked in there were several customers and clerks in the store. Out of the back came a woman dressed in a man's tuxedo. It had been modified in some way but it was still a man's tuxedo.

39

"Amber, Darling" the woman cooed as we walked towards her. "Such a long time. I missed you at the last couple of meetings".

"I know, I should go, but things come and ...." explained Amber. They embraced like old friends and turned to me.

"Ginny, this is Mr. Gray, a guest at the Holiday Inn. Mr. Gray, Ginny Collins, an old friend."

"Call me, Charlie, Ma'am, my father was Mr. Gray"

They chatted a few more minutes, when a second person, a man, came out of the back wearing a similar type tuxedo and walked over to Amber. They greeted each other in a similar manner while I was looking at a counter containing fancy shirts and cummerbunds.

While Amber and the man chatted, Ginny came over to me. "Charlie, how may I help you?"

"Oh, I guess I need a monkey suit for tonight's big do"
"Oh, you are coming tonight?" Ginny gasped.
"Yeah, I will be there with bells on", I tried to sound enthused.

"Good, good good. It is such a worthy cause, isn't it" as Ginny placed her hand on top of mine in a sincere way.

"I'm all a quiver, Ginny" I said.

Ginny looked at me for a long time and then removed her hand.

"Stella, would you mind helping Mr. Gray, please?" as he walked away, off to the rear of the store.

Amber was looking in my direction and had a puzzled look on her face as Ginny went to the back of the store where a small office could be seen. Stella came over and we discussed tuxedos. She did the normal measurements but you could feel that she had a keen eye and knew what she was talking about. Stella went to the back, to what may have been a storeroom.

When Stella returned she had a frown. "Mr. Gray, I have some very bad news. Due to big M.S. Gala tonight at the Holiday Inn....."
"Wait a minute.....a big what and where?' I stammered. "Multiplescorouses...I can't even say it right....you know....
M.S....effects the nerves and all....it is the Gulf Coast Chapter...big to do every year. New Orleans has it this year. I think Houston has the next one. Ginny and Amber are big movers and shakers in the organization." Stella waited for my reactions to no Tux to rent.

"Well, what do you suggest, Miss Stella? I am supposed to go."

"Well, do you have a dark suit? That would be acceptable with a white shirt and tie....we do have tuxedos for sale, but the price is sooooo high now." she apologized.

"I'll take one, break it out lets get it ironed." I said as I was looking towards Amber, trying to get her attention. I caught here eye and she nodded so slightly at my gesture. I knew she was a real lady all along.

As she walked over, I said "Miss Amber, I think I fuc __up... I mean I made a mistake I need to correct it" I said like a little boy caught with his hand in the cookie jar. I explained what I had said and that did not mean to say anything bad, I was just trying to make a funny remark.

There was a long silence as we stood and looked at each other. She almost giggled, but the composure came back. "I'll be right back", Amber said and went to the rear of the store.

In the meantime Stella came back and asked what type of Tuxedo I wanted. I stated I wanted a plain regulation monkey suit, none of the hippie looking ones I seen in the window. Stella giggled and went to the back and came out with a tuxedo. She said it was some French dude's name and I said "Fine. I will take it. Wrap it up."

"Mr. Gray, we need to tailor this tuxedo. It is the finest to be had. Would you mind stepping this way to the fitting room. Oh, and by the way, we are supposed to ask. Will this be a credit card?" she asked with a raised eye brow.

"Do you take out of town cash?" I asked while looking her straight in the eye.

"Well, of course we do......but you are talking about almost a thousand dollars...this is Friday and the banks are closed...where you going to get..."

I reached into my old jeans and pulled out a wad of bills. I honestly did not know how much was there, but I figured if this was not enough, there was an ATM someplace.

"Figure up the bill and we will see," I said, just as Ginny walked up to me. "Oh, Mr. Gray, er ah I mean, Charlie. I thought you knew this was for the M.S. Gala tonight." said Ginny Collins.

"No, Miss Ginny. I was just invited to come and..."

"Well, we had better hurry. Oh Stella, are we going to be able to fit Mr. Gray?" as she started pulling shirts and ties out of boxes.

"Oh course, Ginny" Stella calmly said....."From the skin out" and blushed a little.

About an hour later, we left the mall and we were driving back to the motel. Amber had decided to wait for me after all. As we were driving away I apologized again. "It does start at 8:00 PM doesn't it?"

"Yes, the cocktail party starts at 7:00 with a silent action in the Bayou room." Amber recalled. "Oh, you do have a ticket don't you?"

"Uh, no, Max didn't..."

Amber slammed on the brakes of the Expedition and just missed a small station wagon pulling out of a mall parking slot.

"Asshole" she said under her breathe, and continued with "They are $250.00 a piece, but I think I can get you in...after all you did just spend a big chunk getting a tuxedo and all.......I am glad you did it...Stella works on a commission.....where did all these people come from?" as we waited to turn right on Airline Blvd.

In a short time, we were back at the motel. Amber dropped me off at the back and drove off after she told me I could pick up my ticket at the Front Desk.

Stella was bringing the tuxedo and all the stuff with her to the room. I told her I needed to be dressed "from the skin out"...could she help me out? She blushed a little, I thought it was cute to see that from a grown woman. I continued, "Well, you know shoes, socks and all, shirt and all the doo dads that go with it." Stella said she would be at my room at about 6:45 or so,
and that was the best she could do. I said great, "I will be there."

I went over to my old set of hiking boots and got a couple of bills out of the lining for "walk-a-round" money. I never even wore the boots. They were just my bank.

Chapter 4

After I completed checking my money in the boot-bank, I went to the sitting room and turned on the TV. I went behind the bar in the room to check if there was any coke and noticed the booze had been replaced and the glasses we used last night were washed and cleaned. I made note to tell Maria, the maid, to clear it out and replace it with soft drinks and water. No more booze, I was serious. Well, except maybe...no, none, I was done with that.

I was jolted back to reality when the phone rang. It was a soft "dingle- dingle," not like most phones where the tone is rude.

"Ah, must be Stella" as I looked at my watch, "nope" I said aloud on the second ring and picked up the phone.

"Mr. Gray?" a soft voice cooed in the phone. "Yes?"
"Mr. Gray, there is a bank messenger here. Said he has a package for you and needs your signature. May I send him up?"

"Sure, send him up. Who is the package from? I ain't expecting no package."

After a few seconds she said "A Mr. Maximillian Guerrara, Sir." "Oh, Okay, send him up"

I went over and opened the door just a crack for the messenger to get in when he came. A few minutes later I heard a knock and yelled "Come in."

Around that time two of the biggest anythings I had seen in a while entered the door. Both were in uniform and armed. They checked the bathroom door as they came by and looked at me.

"Are you Mr. Charles P. Gray?" asked the one with arms bigger that my ex-girlfriends thighs.

"Yes I am." I responded, becoming a little defensive.

"Sir, I am required to see positive identification and get the password prior to giving you this package." he stated in a very professional voice.

This was not some everyday "rent-a-cop" here, something was up. There were only two or three people in the whole world who knew I had a password, and since this is from Max the Mouth Piece, it must be real.

I showed "Thompson" my driver's license and told him "Bowl Weevil," which is pronounced "Bo'weevil".

Being satisfied with my identification and the password, I was handed a large cardboard envelope. They stood there like stone statues.

"Thompson" showed me an attached piece of paper I was supposed to sign. I read the notes attached, one of which was checked: "Wait for Answer," which is what they were doing.

I signed the receipt and opened the envelope. Inside the envelope was another envelope from Max's office. I open it up and there was a check made out for $500,000.00…

"What?" I half shouted, "That mes'kin has lost his rabbit ass mind" and I walked over to the phone. It rang just as I reached for it.

"What?"

"Er ah, Mr. Gray? There is a lady here with your Tuxedo and…" "Yeah, send her up, thanks" and I broke the connection.

I dialed all the numbers to Max' private line and Shirley picked up the phone with a simple hello.

"Shirley, this is Charlie? He has lost his…" I faded out as Shirley spoke.

She explained to me as a lawyer and my CPA that this was the best way to go, the non-profit 501(c)3 organization we had formed with the remaining 25 million dollars has got to be used. The interest alone over the last year had…

blah blah..blah...for a few minutes. I see why Max married her, smart lady.

"All right if you say so.." I said as I looked at "Thompson" and his mutated friend wearing a rent-a-cop uniform. "Yeah, I'll call her one day... Anything else?...Nope...nope.....just pay'em.....Nothing official...As of today, no more booze.... nope....nope...he went home...I dunno, but leave him on salary and also keep his credit cards paid until you hear different... Okay, will do...I have an idea...I will need to talk to you and Max together...No, no... no more booze and no more three o'clock in the morning phone calls...Nothing, just need to talk...you guys be home this weekend or wait till Monday?...Okay I'll wait till Monday...I don't know...Marla has the car now, use her car phone . She can find me...yeah... same hotel....Okay, see ya later." and I ended the conversation.

"Okay, guys, nothing else," I said as they both snapped a very snappy salute. "Wow,"   I thought, remind me to keep this company's name. They are sharp and professional.

The two messengers turned to go out the door and almost ran over Stella coming in loaded with boxes. They quickly bent down to help with the dropped boxes and brought them into the room for her.

"Who or what were they?" she said looking back towards the door.

"Messengers brought me a letter". I figured she did not really want to know.

48

"Well, here I am. You had better get dressed. I know I am a little early, but I have to take Amber's dress to her. She had some alterations done."

"Uh huh, look, Stella I need to take another shower and freshen up and little..and....er ah...."

"No problem, I will be back in a fifteen minutes. Want me to call before I come back?" she said as she made her way towards the door.

"No NO No, just come in. Here, I will give you the key to the other door and you can let yourself in. I will be here in the bedroom, just holler when you get here."

I took a real long shower, just standing there, soaking hot shower. Even if I just had a shower only an hour or two before, I was sweaty from the New Orleans summer heat.

I dried myself off and walked out to the bedroom naked to get underwear to from my..."oops," I said. Stella was standing next to the bed taking the new tux out of a plastic zipper bag.

"Oh," she said and averted here eyes and turned around. I tried to get back to the bathroom and ran into the door jam hitting my eyebrow. "Mother fu---" I said and then remembered that a lady was present.

"Shit" I said as I got back to the bathroom.

"I thought you heard me come in, I did yell," Stella shouted.

"Nope, not with the water running, give me a second and let me get some pants on," no answer.

I went to got a T-shirt and clean underwear out of the drawer. I felt a little moisture on the eyebrow.

After I put them on I went into the bathroom and looked. A swelling! Not what I needed. I knew it was a bad omen. I got a moist face towel and pressed on the eyebrow. Removed it and could still see blood starting to ooze. I went back to the bedroom and saw the door shut to the living room. I put on the trousers and put pressure back on the eyebrow. Then I put on the pants.

I called out, "Okay, I'm decent," but no answer.

I went to the living room and looked out, the hallway door was open or ajar, but no Stella. "Okay, Gray. You screwed up another beautiful friendship. She ain't gonna understand it was an honest accident." I thought out loud.

About that time I heard the front door open and a swish of petty coats. There is no other sound in the world like a swishing petty coat or an 870
Winchester being racked open and closed. "Charlie?"
"Yo, come on in. Thought you had run off. Say, about just a minute ago...I am...."

"Don't worry about Charlie" she said not looking at me."No big thing". "You DID peek didn't you?" We both laughed.

"Hey, I went and got some ice. Let me see." and removed the towel.

"Here, I can fix that" and she consulted the contents of her purse. After rummaging around a second, Stella put something on the eyebrow. "There, that will do."

I looked at the eyebrow in the dresser mirror and didn't see anything.

It felt "tight" from the swelling, but it was no longer bleeding. I did not have my glasses, so I put them on. The eyebrow did touch the frame, but it was okay.

At that point I noticed Stella. She was dressed in a light blue formal.

It had all the "girl stuff" on it. Her hair had been in a bun, but was now, how do you say...down on the shoulders. She had on very tiny little earrings, and her horned rimmed glasses were gone too. I guess she had on contacts, no person could have natural color in the eyes like she did, a very deep shade of blue. "Oh hell, Charlie, get your mind off it. She ain't going to have anything to do with an old man anyway" I thought.

"What's was that stuff"

"Super Glue stuff" she said as she inspected her handy work on the eyebrow.

"Believe it or not I used to work in a Small Animal Clinic. We used super glue to close wounds a lot of times, works great." She said as she put materials back into one of two bags she had.

I had been standing there with my hair standing straight up and holding my pants up with one hand. I was trying to put the suspenders on so I could at least preserve some modesty. With a flick, Stella turned the waist band out, attached the suspenders front and back and had them hanging by my side. On went the white shirt and in a few seconds the studs were in and the cuff links attached. The cummerbund was cinched up and placed correctly. Now the tie did present a problem, as it was not a pre-tied model.

I sat on the chair all motels have in their rooms and she stood behind me and tied it with a flash of hands. I felt the front of her dress on my neck.

"Naw, man. What are you thinking. She is just a nice lady trying to help an old fool get a monkey suit on. Get all them thoughts out of your mind."

"Oh, dear. I gotta run. The silent auction starts in 10 minutes. I'll see you down there." and with that Stella was off like a deer in the woods. Nice lady. Wonder what her last name is."

I combed my hair and put the jacket on. I looked at myself in the mirror again. "Yo! Dude, who are you tonight?" I thought that I should go to the bar and tell them I wanted mine "Stirred, not shaken."

Oh, well. You can put a tuxedo on a monkey. But when you get through, you still got a monkey."

I tucked the check into my inside pocket and walked to the front desk. When I got there, a group of well heeled persons were entering the Front Lobby and going down a red carpeted hall to the Bayou Room. Remembering that I needed a ticket to get in, I went to the Front Desk and gave them my name.

"Yes, Sir Mr. Gray, Miss Ames said to give you this envelope."

I opened the envelope with a lone ticket inside with a little yellow "sticky" note that said "I will collect for these later. A.A."

I stuck them in the pocket with the check and walked down the hall. I waited as the line moved through the doors. It seemed everyone knew everyone else but me. I gave the ticket to the youngster at the door with a hippie looking tuxedo and entered.

When I got inside I saw the bar and groups of people standing around. I went over to the bar tender who recognized me from the two weeks I had been staying here and he started to make a Stolies Vodka Martini with two olives over ice. "No, just orange juice for me", I said. He looked at me and I shrugged my shoulders a slight amount. He nodded like he understood. Who ever said that people do not communicate any more.

I stood looking around the room not knowing a soul. This was supposed to be a "silent auction." It sure was, you could not hear a thing. I felt like a whore in church with all the rich folks standing around. The only one I knew was the bar tender and he was busy.

I was looking across the room when I saw Amber Ames. She was near the head table talking to a handsome young man with a clipboard. The long black dress she had on had a slit up the left side to her naval. With one long and very shapely leg sticking out. You could just get a peek at the inside thigh of the other leg when she strode away. Amber looked around the room for a few minutes as if looking for someone. She caught my eye and gave a little wave with just the tips of the fingers as she walked near, but did not stop. She continued on around the room and went back to talk more with Mr. Handsome. Both of them looked like they were about to panic.

I listened to the piano player a few minutes and decided I had better go to the men's room before the banquet started. I still had fifteen minutes to kill anyway.

When I returned to the Bayou Room, people were taking seats at different table. A couple of waiters were bringing in extra tables and setting them up in back. When they finished I took a seat at a table with four people. It was set up for eight, so we had room. It was also near the kitchen. I liked it here. I could lean my chair back against the wall. The people at this table never said much. Just looking around, waving at different folks as they came by.

After a few minutes there was a "tinkle, tinkle, tinkle" on the side of the glass with a spoon. A very distinguished gentleman was standing at the dais at the head table.

"Ladies and Gentlemen...I was hoping our guest speaker was going to show up, but we can't find him. Does anyone here know Mr. Weevil." He pronounced it as "Wee-vill".

"Who the hell would ever name a kid "wee-vill?" I laughed to myself. "Mister Wee-vill has not made it yet, but I was assured by Mr.

Maximilliam Guerrera that...."

"Who?" I thought, "did he say Max the Mouth Piece's name?"

I sat as still as a deer in headlights, listening to what the fancy dude was saying.

"...that Mr. Wee-vill is a guest here at the hotel. But Miss Ames has checked her listings and no one with that name has checked in. However, we shall continue with this delicious food provided by the Holiday Inn Banquet Facilities." and he sat down.

After a few minutes I saw Amber Ames walking towards the side exit. I got up and walked toward the same exit and walked out as she was coming around the corner going toward the Front Desk.

"Amber, please. Miss Ames. Wait."

She kept walking and said "Charlie, I have a major disaster on my hands. Our guest speaker hasn't shown up and I have to find him. That man that was on the speakers stand is my boss. There are TV critiques and newspaper reporters out the ass.....and oh, hell, what do you want, Charlie?"

"I think I am the person you are looking for." I stated a little ashamed. "What? Your Bo Weevil?" She talked like I was a spoiled little brat. "Well, no I ain't exactly, but the foundation..." I stammered.
"Charlie, you're a nice fellow and all but..."

I took the check out of the envelope and held it where she could read the '"GREATER NEW ORLEANS M.S. FOUNDATION" and "FIVE HUNDRED THOUSAND DOLLARS" printed on a long legal sized check.. In the upper right hand corner was a little cartoon of a bowl weevil eating a leaf.

I smiled as she stood there slightly bent at the waist reading the check and looking at me. I was standing there looking down the front of her dress.

When we all got through looking, she stood up and said. "Er ah er ah, Charlie, that check is for $500.000.00."

"Yes, Ma'am. It sure is. Max Guerrara is my lawyer. The name of the foundation is the Bowl Weevil Foundation. My daddy called me Bo'wevil most of my life." I pause as I folded the check back. "You still want it?"

Amber Ames reached down and gave me the biggest smooch I have ever had, right on the lips.

Chapter 5

Amber Ames scooped me up took me to the Head Table where I had to set there and try to eat. I looked over the crowd while the guest speakers were talking and spotted Stella. She was at a center table. She was being "squired" by an average looking businessman. Without starring, I was trying to figure out her age, maybe 45 or 50 years old. I think "genteel" and old world ambiance came to mind. I did notice she had a large name tag on her shoulder that looked liked the ones on the people at the Head Table. I think she was some type official with the Gulf Coast M.S. Society or whatever it was called.

I ate the peas and dabbled with the chicken, buttered some bread and sipped coffee. This meal sucked and I was in hoc for $250.00. Oh, well, I guess this is called high society.

About that time I heard my named mentioned by a speaker, the man with the clip board, who Amber was talking with before the shindig started. I was asked to come forward and was met by Amber and Clipboard. We stood together and had photos taken. I gave Amber the check. And then all of a sudden I was left at the speaker's microphone alone... and I had to go bathroom real bad.

"Ladies and Gentlemen, (it got quiet) I am a very fortunate man. I 'hit the big one' as they say. I did all the things that you would dream of doing 'if I hit the big one' and now I am tired. I realized in this hotel bar this afternoon, that I had wasted a year of my life and drinking and whoring, partying, (laughter) and spent more money than the average person sees in a life time. Today is the first day of a new life. (applause) I would like to give back to society, but I will not be a patron of M.S. even though you have a wonderful organization. There are areas where I can better serve. I am forming a non-profit organization for training canines, dogs if you will, to assist law enforcement. I hope to be able to hire and train the best cadre available in the world. To assist at no charge, any law enforcement agency that asks, either by furnishing them a dog or by assisting them when a canine is required."

With this, I will ask the good Father that gave the Benediction to step up here and say a small word for this program. Father?"

With that I stepped off the raised platform, went out the side door and to the men's' room. I now know how Forrest Gump felt at the White House.

After a few minutes the guests started easing out of the Bayou Room and walking out the front. Either that or to the bar which had the loud music. I felt like a third wheel, so

I was walked towards the rear entrance when Amber called to me from down the hall.

"Charlie! Oh Charlie, wait up."

As I turned around Amber and "Clipboard" were walking arm in arm towards me. Each had a drink and acting very cozy.

"Charlie, come to the Executive Board Room with us. We have some papers for you that we need to sign that Mr. Guerra sent us." Amber said as she and "Clipboard" walked past me to a door I had not noticed.

When we entered there were a half dozen or so people in a large meeting room standing around with drinks. A private bar had been set up and a waitress was taking drink orders from whoever was "empty."

When I walked in, they applauded and came over to shake my hand with the routine bull shit that goes with giving a $500.000.00 check to a group of assholes like this. I hated to tell them I didn't even know about it until this afternoon. These same people would not have even stopped to talk to "Charlie" this time yesterday when I was wearing a pair of Levi's and a Wal-Mart shirt. But here I am, wearing a $1000.00 monkey suit and they think I'm a hero.

I would not have done that unless Shirley Guerra hadn't told me I needed to do it "for tax purposes". No doubt it is going to a worthy cause, but if I had my shit together, I would have come up with this canine idea earlier.

I wish Bart was with me. We could have gone out and had some kicks. Naw, I'm on the wagon now.

As I walked in the door I noticed a woman on the far side of the room with her back to me. I almost recognized her, but from where? Dressed in an all white dress with white shoes, she was standing with her left arm across her front, her left hand holding up her right elbow. In her right hand a glass of white wine. I noticed she was standing with her weight on her left foot and the right heel tucked into the instep of her left foot. I don't know how to explain it, like a model does, very feminine, a tiny little thing. I had the feeling her white shoes were uncomfortable or she didn't like them.

She was smiling as she talked to "Clipboard." What a nice smile.

"Yes," I almost said aloud. I raised up a finger and almost pointed at her, then caught myself. It was the young lady in the bar, this afternoon with the riding breeches.

I was going to say "Hello" to the mystery lady, but I was cut off by the waitress who asked "May I get you a drink, Sir?"

"Oh yeah, orange juice please. Straight, over ice" I said and waited for her to take the few steps back to the bar where a bartender had already started on the orange juice.

I still had my back to the Mystery Lady in white. She was about four or five feet away when I heard her tell "Clipboard" that if he ever put his hands on her or tried anything "cute" again, "I'll kick you in the balls in front of your fancy friends."

"Whoa!" I thought. This lady is not to be trifled with. I just smiled at the waitress when she bought the drink. The Mystery Lady was walking out the door when I turned around. "Clipboard" was standing looking towards the door. He turned towards me and I nodded and raised the glass of orange juice.

"Who was the young lady you were talking to a moment ago?" I asked. "The one that just left.....I have seen her around several times today and never knew her name"

"That, Mr. Gray, is Cassandra Malloy Phillips. She works for me. I own the Lake Front Polo Club, she is the manager, very good with children and horses and things. Her program for M.S. Children,s Fund is known all over the U.S. and Canada. Does marvelous things with..." he was saying when he was distracted by Amber coming up and taking his arm.

"Did you meet Sassy, Charlie? She is one of my best friends. We work together on the M.S. programs for children. Quite a girl, don't you think so, Stan?" Amber chuckled as she placed her arm on "Stan's" shoulder.

"Well, well, well" I thought. Ol' Stan is playing in both courts, or trying to.

After a few more minutes, Amber and Stan were all but undressing each other with their eyes. He had his arm around her waist, raising it up to press under the arm where the softness of the breast begins. Nothing overt, but well, you know...

I left. I walked back up towards the front and I guess out of habit, into the bar. It was quiet. By that I mean there is no music playing, it looked it was intermission. The bar was crowded. I walked in and decided to just keep going. I was walking out towards the back by the bar where Bart and I had sat earlier in the afternoon, when a delicate little hand came out of the dark and said, "Mr.Gray, how are you?" It was the Mystery Lady. I mumbled something. The two guys one each side of her did not smile or act friendly. They just looked at the Ol Dude in the Monkey Suit.

"You did say you wanted to talk to me over dinner didn't you?" and with that she squeezed my arm tightly.
"Oh, yes Miss Phillips I did, but since you are ...er ah..." I mumbled. "Good, you said you would meet me here. Thought I had been stood up. So, I 'll see guys later," she said in a very coy manner and slid off the bar stool and took my arm.

"Thanks for rescuing me from those two Bozos. " she said as we walked out, "they are always trying to get a girl in bed, with one or with both of them"

"I'll leave you here Mr. Gray, you don't have to take me to supper, just teasing you. My car is parked over there," indicating the rear of the motel, and she walked off.

"Miss Phillips, I would love to take you to supper, but I don't know where to."

"Naw, that's okay. I want to stop at a couple of places and visit with some friends," and with that, she disappeared towards the rear parking lot.

I must have stood there a full fifteen seconds looking in the direction she had gone when the two young men came out of the bar. They started walking in the same direction as the Mystery Lady, as I came to know her in my mind. They just gave me the "go to hell" look and kept walking towards the rear parking lot.

"Oh, well, ain't none of mine," I thought to myself as I turned to walk to the elevator and my room.

I was still hungry since the "dinner" sucked. I think a good breakfast at IHOP, Waffle House or someplace was in order. It wasn't even ten o'clock and I was ready to call it a night. You stop drinking and look what happens? Your social life goes to hell. Just thinking of drinking made my palms sweaty. Hmmmmph! wonder if I will get the shakes and all too? I had noticed that my face was puffy. You know how it gets when you drink a lot of booze, wrinkles, puffy eyes and fat starts setting in. Well, I had that look, time to get my shit together.

I had to walk back to the main lobby to get to my room because all the exits had been locked for security reasons. As I walked past the lobby I noticed Stella was carrying several large boxes and bags. She was having a little problem trying to get through the crowd and all.

"Here, let me help you" I said and started trying to take the boxes to ease the load.

"No, that's okay Mr. Gray. I'm very capable. Thank you, but." and she dropped them. I scrambled to pick them up for her while she was still saying she could do it. We finally got the boxes picked up and started to walk again to who knows where.

"Stella.? Did I do something to offend you or make you angry?" I asked, as we walked out of the side lobby door.

"Oh No Mr. Gray, nothing like that. I just have to get this stuff loaded in my car and then... " she said as she sat the assorted bags and boxes on the trunk of a four door Toyota. Stella opened the door and placed all the boxes in the back seat, placed her purse in the front seat and prepared to get in the car.

"Wait a minute, Stella. What is this?" as I stood there looking at her, she was fussing around the car, "you calling me 'Mr. Gray' and only a few hours ago, you and I had no secrets." I tried to chuckle and get a smile concerning the incident in the bedroom, "I don't understand."

"Mr. Gray, a few hours ago you were 'Charlie' and I was 'Stella" the Shop Girl, who brought you a tuxedo over because you said you did not know how to put one on. All I wanted to do was help someone, not because it was my job. Now, I find that you are 'MR. GRAY,' the guy that gives away a half a million dollars and I am still Stella the Shop Girl. You have probably have more tuxedos than Ginny and Sam have in their shop." she said and looked at me for the first time since I saw her in the Lobby.

"Wait a minute, Lady Bug." I noticed tears in her eyes when she looked up at me, reflecting in the bright lights in the parking lot. "Yeah, I gave away some money, but you heard where I got it, public record. You were in the Bayou Room when I got up to make an ass out of myself before all those big time dudes." I was still standing a double arm's length away from her.

"No, I had to leave for a second to get Amber's dress. Oh, I have to get home." she started to fumble in the car for her purse. I took my handkerchief out and handed it too her. She took it. It was a big red farmer model."

Stella looked at the handkerchief for a split second and I am sure she noticed it. "I know, it don't go with a tuxedo does it?" I said as I took it back.

We stood there in awkward silence. "Stella, I was about to go for breakfast. Please come with me?...Please? I need to go to the room and get out of this monkey suit, but if you have a second or better still, come with me while I change, " and with this she looked at me and almost bolted. "What did I do now?"

"Oh, nothing, Mr. Gray, Charlie" and she smiled a little secret smile. "I'll have to go change too, maybe meet you somewhere or something." She was still wearing the pretty blue dress.

"Stella, I have a car and driver available to me 24 hours a day. I don't drive, I have a driver. I was advised by my lawyer it is cheaper to hire a driver than to take a chance of getting involved in a law suit if I have a wreck. You know where my room is, you must have other clothes, you may change there. I don't know what is wrong. I don't intend on meeting you 'somewhere later.' There it is, What do you say?"

"Okay, let me get my bag" and with that we started towards my room. "Er, aaah... Charlie? May I just meet you there in a few minutes? You know, walking through the lobby and all."

"Sure, sure, I understand. It is some of the OTHER folks that may not see you in a few minutes" as I walked off.

"Strange reactions from her," I thought. Oh well, some girls need to keep up appearances about going to a man's room with a suitcase, as it should be.

About ten minutes later, I had changed clothes. I threw the monkey suit in the closet and put all the little doo dads in a sack. I had on a comfortable pair of fresh pressed jeans and a shirt. Felt like a human being again, and there was a knock.

I opened the door and let Stella in and took her plastic hang up bag that had "Collins' Boutique" in big bold letters.

"Here, use this as I opened the bedroom door to the suite. I will put you gear in here." as Stella walked in with the swish of the petite coats from her pretty dress. I closed the door and went to watch TV while she was changing. Here it is, 11:00 PM, sober watching TV. Maybe I do feel better. It was first time my tummy felt right in a long time.

I took the TV control and clicked on the TV. It came on just as a CNN Reporter was finishing up about an American Executive being kidnapped and held for ransom in Peru. The major export company "has no comment and is working through the United States Department of State to resolve the matter, back to you Ed..." The CNN Atlanta desk came on line and I clicked over to an old movie.

My mind started thinking back to Viet 'Nam, early 1971.

It was hot and sticky in the briefing hut, called a Butler Hut. Folding chairs and young boat crews laughing and talking, trying to make everyone else think they were just as calm as everyone else. Charlie Green and Steve Ford were standing off to one side of the briefing room quietly talking. "Attention on Deck" rang through the small briefing hut and all noise stopped as the men stood at attention. A group of four men came in making long strides to the front of the briefing area.

"At Ease" was given when all were in place. "Please have a seat".

All the green clad boat crews sat and watched as the briefing officers unloaded their brief cases and charts.

About that time three men in flight suits came in and stood at the rear of the hut. Chief Petty Officer Charlie Gray was standing at the front. He recognized one of them as a crewman from HA(L)-3, Helicopter Attack (Light) Squadron 3, a very good gun ship unit of the U.S. Navy.

After a few seconds, the briefer were ready and looked around. About this time they noticed Chief Gray, Master Chief Ford of SEAL Team 7 and the three aviators in the rear.

"Gentlemen I am Commander Tischner, Riverine Force Command. I don't think I recognize some of you here. Mr. Calvin, can you introduce the other members?" he gestured.

"Yes, Sir. I am afraid I don't know them by name, but I did know they were coming," gesturing towards Charlie Gray.

"Yes, Sir. I'm Chief Charlie Gray, Team Leader, Inshore Warfare Group and canine handler for tonight's operation." as I turned to Steve.

"My name is Ford, SEAL Team 7," and let it go at that.

They looked at the aviators in the back as everyone turned around to see them for the first time. They introduced themselves in order. Now all eyes went back to the front of the hut.

"Okay, let's get started. Tonight, Flotilla One and Nine will move out to Duong River inlet and meet at Xray Three with the Army's Monitor Fleet for refueling. In the morning, once you have refueled, you will move along the main channel as if you are on a normal Market Garden Patrol. Stop a few boats if need be and try to keep it looking routine. Late tomorrow afternoon, three boats from Flotilla One will return to the Monitor that is on station and take on SEAL 7 and Inshore Warfare Teams with canines. Once they are aboard these boats, Flotilla One will move up river to a point designated on your maps and wait for further orders from the Airborne Commander. A point will be designated where SEAL Team 7 will be inserted using standards methods. Inshore Warfare Teams will be inserted if and when called for by the SEALS. Use three boats for this operation, all three will run full throttle while the third will throttle back and insert the Teams. In this way the enemy, who will be listening, will not know, we hope, know that one boat has dropped out for about thirty seconds to insert teams. SEAL 7 will be in charge of the operation, so keep as close as you dare to take them out if they run into trouble. The helicopter units will remain at the Monitor in a "ready" position to help as needed. However at dawn the next morning, the HAL-3 Teams will sweep the area and monitor the frequencies noted in the briefing packages we have here for you. Same with all the boats, any questions?"

There were a few technical questions from the boat crews concerning operations within the Riverine Squadron.

Attention was called again and the briefer left. Very professional group, knew their shit. I feel real comfortable working with these people.

I walked back to the rear of the hut and introduced myself to the three aviators from HAL 3."I think I am suppose to get a ride with you guys to Ben Tuey, can do?"

"Can do" was a standard answer and they also offered Steve a ride back to catch a flight to Hotien where his group was located in the Delta. "I have a ride, thanks," he said. "Rode up with 'Thunder Bumper,'" and they all shook their heads like they knew who "Thunder Bumper" was. I did not know who "Thunder Bumper" was, but it was very common to refer to an airplane driver by his radio call sign.

The objective of the operation was to put a SEAL Team in and try to ambush a Viet Cong Cadre Leader and messenger or payroll officer would be perfect. "Shooters" or snipers would wound the messenger and use the dogs to blood track back to their hidey holes, underground bunkers and supplies. Not the first time we had done this, worked good each time.

The bedroom door snapped open and Stella walked out. "What's wrong, Charlie? You look like you are in a trance or something. Don't do that, it's scary."

"Sorry, I was just thinking about something, ready?"

"You sure you feel okay?" she asked with real concern as she touched my forehead.

A nice gentle touch, soft and, "Aw man, there you go again. Get off that shit."

"Yeah, let me call Marla and see if she or the other one is going." I stopped and picked up the phone and called Marla's room. In a second the phone was answered by someone I didn't know, there was so much noise I couldn't hear if it was a male or female. "Hello" Marla said. "Hey, knock it off a minute," with her hand over the mouth piece. "Yeah, who is this?"

"Marla? It's Charlie, need a ride. Can you do it?"

"Oh man. I thought you were at the Ball downstairs. Belle and I are having a party here…shit, okay. I think I can do it, give me a minute and I'll run down there and talk to you." said Marla and she hung up.

About thirty seconds later she was at the door knocking. She and Belle had the suite above us.

I opened the door. There was Marla, dressed in a party get up and about half shit faced.

"Yo, Charlie I am so sorry, but I didn't know you would go out tonight. Shit…"

"Hey Marla, don't worry about it, we can get a cab." I said.

"You sure? Here are the keys Let the 'Bimbo' here drive, you have before. Hee hee heee," she said with a silly giggle.

"Marla. Miss er, ah…Stella, is not a bimbo, but she…"

"Fuck, I'm sorry lady, I didn't know." and she just melted onto the floor, in the door way, completely passed out.

"Well, I guess we don't have a driver, unless the "Bimbo" wants to drive." I offered Stella the keys.

With a genuine deep throated laugh, Stella took the keys and gestured "what the hey."

I called back up to Marla's room and in a short time several of Marla's friends came down to help her back upstairs.

Marla was no small woman, six feet tall and dressed out at a good 200 pounds. Her friends had a little problem, but they got her upstairs and I guess all was okay. I never did see the other one, Belle was it? I should check on that one. I can't remember the last time we seen her. What does she look like? Come to think of it, why do we still have two drivers, we gave the bus away.

That was the most I had ever heard Marla say at one time in the year she worked for us.

Chapter 6

On Saturday, the next morning, I was setting in the living room, when I heard the front door open with a slight tap tap tap.

"Room Service," it was Maria, a very nice, grandmotherly Hispanic lady. All the beauty and grace was still there, even though she was many years past her prime. I always enjoyed talking to her, and most of the time in Spanish.

"Buenos dias, Senora. Como esta? Shhhh, mi ruka is en otro quatro." She knew there was never another woman in the bedroom. It was a running joke, but she giggled anyway.

There never was anyone with me, and once she asked why. Her son was the bar tender at night downstairs when they had a band and she knew Bart and I liked to Rock and Roll.

I always told her since she was no longer available, my heart was broken and there could never be another woman for me, in Spanish of course. It was a big laugh between us. Since it was a big apartment, another housekeeper would come in and help. A young girl, she could not speak English and later asked Maria if it was true. She said "No," it was a joke.

"Que? No pachunga a la noche? Maria asked.

"Nope, no party, In fact I want all the booze taken out and only orange juice, grapefruit juice and bottled water in the refrigerator. Same with Bart's rooms we are on the wagon now."

"I am glad. Every morning we come in and there is such a mess, all the beer and alcohol bottles…I worried about you and Senor Bart." she said with a shy smile.

"Maria, I have an idea. How would you like to come live with me? Take care of my house and run the whole house for me?" I asked.

"Senor Gray, I am not that type of woman, and am a good woman and I do not wish to speak of it." and she turned as if she was leaving.

"No, no, no, Maria." I jumped up and walked towards her, "Nothing like that. I mean a job, you will be the housekeeper. You can hire your own staff. You will be the jefa de todos los casa."

"Oh, I am sorry, well…" she said as she patted her hair, "that is another thing."

"Whatever you make here, I will double it and furnish you with a van. Will you think about it?" I asked sincerely.

"I will consider it, but where is the house to be located? I didn't know you owed a home here." Maria said as she went behind the bar to start cleaning.

"I don't, not yet, but I am going to try and find one in the next few days." I replied.

"We shall see…Let me think about it." Maria mumbled.

I was still dressed in my pajamas and a robe. One of the few things I had "upgraded" in my life style for some reason.

I got up and walked over to the coffee pot for a refill when Amber walked by, stopped and turned around when she saw me standing there.

"Good Morning, Charlie. How you doing this morning?" she said in a very cheery manner. She was dressed in a "cover up" I think they are called, what women wear when they have a bathing suit on and don't want folks to look at them. She was dressed as if she was on the way to the pool.

"Good Morning Amber. May I offer you a cup of coffee?" I responded. Sorry I had not combed my hair or shaved.

"No, just on the way to the pool for a quick dip while it is still not crowded. Being Saturday, the kids will be swarming the pool. Come join me" she said as she moved the housekeepers' cart from in front of the door.

She also acknowledged Maria and Carmen in the room too.

"Naw, I don't even drink the stuff, much less play in it," I attempted to inject some humor.

"Well, you should. Look out the window here, a very nice pool, the best of any of our properties" as she moved over to the edge of the room and slid open the doors to the balcony.

Hmmmph! I did not even know they had a pool or balcony by my room. I wonder what else I had missed.

"Amber, you are a business woman, MBA, some fancy eastern school. I need some business advice." I said.

"Charlie, I do NOT have an MBA in Business. I have a Bachelor's degree in Marine Engineering, Annapolis, '88," she said looking me.

I know I choked on the sip of coffee. I did a double take and starred like a dummy.

"Surprised, Charlie?" She said with a chuckle in her smile, eyes shining. "Charlie? Say Something."

"I don't know what to say. It just took the wind out of me. I was thinking Vasser, George Washington or something like that."

"Nope, but I tell you what, let me go take a little swim and I will meet you for breakfast downstairs. That is, if you are not still full from last night," she said, peeking over the top of the sunglasses she was wearing. "I see Stella's car is still here" She glanced towards the closed bedroom door. "Stella? Er, ah..." I stuttered.

"Well, oh never mind. None of my business anyway, see you." she said as she tried to leave, but Maria was standing at the cart, blocking her way while she was getting towels off the cart.

"Hey, wait a minute. Let's eat up here, more private and I like my breakfast here. Is that Okay? In my room ?" I half yelled.

"Okay with me, in about an hour. Bye Stella," she flounced out like she had a secret.

"Marie, do you see anyone here?" I asked.

"I don' see nothing or hear nothing, Senor Charlie. I will be back to do the other room when you finish with your shower. I will use the other door. Time for my coffee break." as she walked out the door.

A half hour later, I had shaved and showered. Put on clean Levi's and walked out on the balcony.

Down below, Amber swam a steady crawl from one end of the Olympic size pool to the other, then on her back in the opposite direction. On one pass she was swimming on her back and noticed me just above her.

"Charlie, call down for breakfast. I will be there in fifteen minutes, just a few more laps." she said in a quiet, normal tone.

I gave her a "thumbs up" and went to the phone. I talked to Ruben and told him I need a hearty breakfast with all the trimmings. I knew he would do it as when he brought the breakfast up. It was always good for a twenty.

There was a coffee pot and toaster in the room on the bar, so he always sent fresh bread along with the homemade bread, a specialty of the house.

Fifteen minutes later, I had the door open to the hall when I heard Maria enter from the hall to the bedroom. I heard Amber's voice while she talked to Maria, but could not hear what they were saying. Amber bounced in the room and looked around.

"I'm starving. Where is the chow?"

"I called down and they said it would be right up."

Amber was dressed in warm up pants and a light weight summer jacket. Amber had her hair styled so that it could be shaken out, blow dried, and be ready for a party, tight curls and all that stuff. She may or may not have still had the bathing suit on, but she was an attractive woman to start with.

With both doors open, I heard the elevator bell ding and the rumble of a cart coming down the hall. In a few heart beats a large covered food trolley appeared and Ruben brought it straight in. He was surprised to see Amber in the room, but did not say anything. The table was set and the food was placed on the table in the candle lit warmers. I shook hands with Ruben as always with a twenty dollar bill folded discreetly in the palm, and he departed and shut the door. I bet this was going to be good gossip in the kitchen when he got back.

While Amber was filling her plate, Marie motioned from the bedroom for me to come there. I got up and went to the bedroom and shut the door. Maria said that Amber asked if another woman had been here. Maria told her that she did not see anything. She just turned away and smiled while continuing to make the bed.

"Okay, Okay, Okay," I thought. "What is this?" Amber could not even care about things like that, not as far as I was concerned. I guess she was just nosey.

During the course of the breakfast, Amber talked almost constantly. She was on a roll and feeling good.

She said she was a little country girl from West "By Gawd" Virginia, and raised in a small town where her daddy drove a "coal bucket."

"What's a 'coal bucket?" I asked.

"It is a large dump truck that carries coal from the mines to the loading area." She continued to say she had been "raised in Rangoon."

"Burma?" I asked.

"No, West Virginia, north central part of the state, graduated from high school and went to Blue Field, that is in West Virginia, also to a two year college to study to be a nurse. I lived with my Grandmother there, worked in a dinner and department store and was happy. One day I decided I wanted to apply for the Air Force Academy or something. I just knew I was not going back to Rangoon. There was something in life for me besides being a mother to ten sniveling kids and die young without ever seeing anything. SOOOO, I applied for the Naval Academy and was accepted. Was I surprised?"

"Upon graduation I was commissioned a Second Lt. in the United States Marine Corp, the sticker you were looking at on my truck, and posted to Quantico, Virginia. While I was there I met my husband. Harry."

"I didn't know you were married." I said.

"I'm not," she continued, "I'm a widow. I was married to an FBI Agent stationed at the National Academy, that's the school local cops go to at Quantico, " between bites.

"He was out following the "yellow brick road," that's a jogging course that crossed the Interstate and was hit by a car skidding on the ice, over the guard rail and was hit by several other vehicles, messy..."

"I was in Saudi at the time, a Provost Marshall Captain in charge of POW logistic support on Swartzkoffs' staff when Harry was killed. Why am I boring you with all of this?"

"Not boring, Amber, thanks for sharing."

Amber continued to eat and acted as if she was thinking. "Oh, what did you want to ask me about business? Remember my degree is in Marine Engineering." she said with a chuckle.

"Amber, I was a dog trainer for thirty years prior to hitting the lottery. Narcotics dogs mainly, never had much, except a good time. So now I want to do something, like having a training facility for training law enforcement in the proper use of canine. Cost nothing, other than their time and effort.

Have a breeding program and the best inside training areas you can think of. What do you think?"

I looked up and Amber's fork, with food on it, it was halfway up to her mouth from the plate. She was staring at me.

"Where?" she said as she put the fork down on the plate. "Where what?" I returned.

"Where will the kennel be?" she said.

"I dunno. Some place her in the States, Europe. I don't care. I guess the States someplace. Why? Interested?" I teased.

"Big time. You know, my daddy was a coon hunter in West Virginia and Ohio mostly, but he did well for himself. I have chased many a dog through the woods at night. When I graduated, my boy friend and I had a big fight over going coon hunting or to the Prom Night dance. We left about 10:00 PM and caught up with my daddy and his friends over on Spivey Ridge. I still remember that night. Got three..." she faded off. "Any children?" I asked.

"Huh? Oh no, no kids. Maybe some...Nah, I don't want any kids." she said and went back to eating.

"How serious are you?" I asked. "'Bout what?" she said. "Learning how to train dogs my way." I said in a straight voice. "Depends on where and what it pays" Amber responded.

"It will pay as much as make now, possibly more, if you pass the test." "Now, what kind of test is that?" she perked up.

"Physical, mental, drug screening and background." I stated flatly. "Well, that lets me out" she said.

"How"

"I have M.S. I'm good for another 5 years, maybe 10 if I keep my health up. That is why I swim and exercise so much." she said with a little sad note.

"Amber, I have only the same time left too. Males in my family don't last long."

"I saw you swimming and you look good to me. Better than half the pukes in the world. If you want out for that reason, that is good enough for me. But a doctor will have to tell me you are 'out.'"

"Oh, I can do it. No problem, but over a period of time, I will start going down hill."

"How about the rest? Any dope? Can you pass a urine test?" "Nope, not if the medications I take now counts."
"No, I am talking about marijuana, cocaine, heroin and 'speed,' stuff like that." I replied.

"Oh no, never. Well, I took a few puffs while I was in college at Bluefield, but that is it. Nothing since then," Amber stated, "and that was marijuana".

I asked, "Can you pass a heavy duty background check?" "Every Day and twice on Sunday" she snorted.
"How well do you know Sassy?" I asked.

"Known her the ten years she has been here. In fact, I helped her get the job she has now. You know she works for Stan out at Lakeside Polo Club?" Amber said.

"Are you and Stan an 'item,' the two of you?" I questioned.

"No, oh no, good friends and before you ask, 'no' I have not slept with him" Amber said defensively.

"I didn't ask that did I?"

"No, but the look on your face did." "You have a boyfriend?" I wondered.

Amber did not look at me and I didn't press it. I offered her a fresh cup of coffee and found there were fresh little sugar coated pastries in one of the warmers. I could not remember what they were called, but you can only get these special kinds in New Orleans, at the Morning Call Restaurant.

I drank my coffee and we moved to the living room portion of the suite. Amber sat on the couch and put her long legs on the coffee table, just relaxing.

"I have a boyfriend, lover or whatever you want to call him. Do I have to tell you about him to be considered for the job?" she asked.

"Amber, I will not do the background. I have someone that will do it for me. You can tell me or omit whatever you so desire. But when I feel I have been deceived, then the deal is off. I do not care what you tell me, but it is what I find out. Does that make sense to you?"

Amber nodded in an affirmative manner.

"I am going to spend $500,000.00 on each team member. If they have something in their background that is so horrible that they do not want me, not the other team members, to know about. Then I can justify in my own mind a good reason not to spend a half million dollars on them." I stated in a "matter of fact" manner.

"Now, you do what you think is best." as I went to get another cup of coffee. With a long sigh, Amber started her story.

"He lives her in New Orleans, regular military, a Marine Major at the Naval Reserve Center, a classmate of mine from the Academy. He is married and we got involved in Quantico after Harry was killed. I was assigned to Marine Corp Barracks Quantico. Johnny had just been brought up on charges for not ordering his men to go into an area that a German gas detector unit had declared a "hot" area for nerve gas while he was in Iraq. They were going to court martial Johnny, but then they would have had to bring out the fact that nerve gas was used in the Gulf War. While he and I were at Marine Corps Quantico, we went for a casual drink, then it got to be dinner and you know the rest. He has a wife in Cherry Point someplace and I was a new widow. Bing Bong." Amber never raised her eyes from the glass of juice she had been nursing like a cocktail. I never looked directly at her either.

"So Johnny got sent here after an Administrative hearing and I followed. He is still married and of course he was reduced 200 numbers, which means he will never get a promotion. Our relationship is not overt. I live here on the property in fact, in the same unit as this one except on the other end. We get to see each other when we can."

"But there was gas there, it was proven."

"I know," she said. "But Uncle Sam's Misguided Children" did not see it that way. While I was going through my yearly physical last year, they discovered M.S. I am taking medication, but for all practical purposes I don't have any signs, yet." she added.

"I will be very hard and demanding work," I warned her.

For the first time, she looked up at me and straight in the eyes, just like yesterday afternoon.

"I am a Marine"

"Good enough for me".....I said.

Chapter 7

Sunday mornings at a Holiday Inn were the same as any other day. I was getting tired of the dining room food there, same menu, same food,

same cookie cutter atmosphere. So, I walked down the street a block or so to Denny's and had breakfast. On the way back I walked to the rear of the motel to look for the van. When I reached the back lot where we normally parked I saw the van parked about where Stella's car had been. Great, wish someone had told me. I wonder where the keys are? I walked to the lobby and asked if there was any mail or messages, not really expecting anything, but it gave me something to do.

When I approached the desk, a young college age man came from the back and stated he had some mail and a message or two.

When he returned, the car keys were in with a couple of messages. One of the messages said "I returned the van, but you were not in your room. Call me sometimes. S.D." Well, "S.D." had to be Stella, but I did not know the last name.

I wonder where I had gone last night? I had not gone to any place except....oh yeah, Wal-Mart. Went to get toilet articles and couple of sets of underwear, I took a cab. The old man driving the cab always waited and brought me back, nice old dude. Whenever I need a cab I always call Crescent City Cab Company and ask for number 12. It seems like he is always on duty and of course I always gave him a good tip.

I walked back to the desk and asked if Miss Ames was available. The young man informed me that she had left the property for the Polo Club and excused himself to answer the phone.

I could hear him talking in the backroom as I walked away, "Mr. Gray, you have a call, you can take it right over there." indicating the house phone near a large sofa.

"Charlie, Stella. I hope you don't think I am being too forward calling you early Sunday morning, but...but I just wanted to make sure you knew your van was back in the parking lot." she stumbled.

"No, I am so glad you called me. Your note said..." and I looked around, there were several people in the lobby and of course you hate to talk in public like that. "Stella, why don't you come by for breakfast," I chuckled. " It seems I am always inviting you to breakfast."

"Okay, I can be there in about twenty minutes. I have just left St. Charles Cathedral and am heading towards home. I live near you, so how is that?" Stella asked apprehensively.

"Sure, I'll get Marla, she can drive us. You wanna come up to the room or..." I didn't know what to say.

"Of course. See you in a few minutes," and she hung up.

I called Marla's room and did not get an answer, but I had told her earlier that the weekend was open for her. She had said she and Belle were going out with friends somewhere, I think the French Quarter, over the weekend. Of course, she had passed out at my door on Friday night. Oh, well. I guess Stella can drive the van. Hmmm, I wonder what her last name is?

I was walking up the steps from the outside entrance to the second floor when I met Maria, the Housekeeper, coming down from the third floor. I was still on the landing by the entrance door to the second floor when she called my name.

"Senor Gray! Senor Gray, up here!"

I looked around and finally looked up the stairwell to the third landing. It was about ten o'clock in the morning, the normal time Maria made the rounds to the suites. I noticed she was gesturing for me to come up the steps in a mysterious manner. I looked around and went up to the third floor.

"Mr. Gray, does the two women in the suite on the third floor work for you?" she asked in a small voice.

"Yes, yes they do, they are my drivers. Why?" I asked.

"Come with me. I was coming to your room to talk to you anyway. I don't think you will like this, but you treat me nice and well...maybe if I work for you." she was saying as we walked into the third floor hallway and directly to the rooms Marla and Belle occupied. "This could get me fired, but I don't care. You need to see this," as she opened the door with her pass key.

When I walked in I could smell the marijuana smoke, no doubt. After thirty years of chasing dope and being around it, there was no doubt.

"Okaaaaay," maybe one of her guests I thought, but when I went to the ash trays and saw ten to twelve "roaches" and in the trash can where several baggies had the corners cut out, it left little doubt.

"How often is it like this?" I asked Maria.

"Every morning you been staying here, every morning," she said sadly, "and look at this." She indicated to a small tray that every Holiday Inn room has to hold the ice bucket: A mirror, a single edged razor blade, and a straw. The edge of the mirror that goes into the plastic frame had a small amount of white powder. I pressed my thumb on the mirror and attempted to pick up a sample, which I did. I rubbed my thumb and forefinger together fast and using pressure, the friction produces heat. I waited a second and then smelled my finger, it smelled like "wintergreen" and my finger was slightly numb, cocaine!

That rips it. I could almost forgive marijuana in the room. I would have pissed tested both of them and if they had refused I would have fired them on the spot, but cocaine, nope, not on my payroll, not a chance.

I thanked Maria with my eyes and walked out and went to my room. I picked up the phone and looked at my watch. Max the Mouth Piece would still be at Mass on Sunday morning and then go to the Golden Coral for breakfast.

The answering machine picked up on his "Bat Phone" and I explained what had happened and I wanted those two off the payroll now, fired. If the contract was still in effect, pay it off. I did not want those two anywhere near anything I owned. I knew the "Bat Phone" would automatically page Max and he would get the message.

I called the front desk and asked who was speaking. The young man told me his name was "Robert." I identified myself and asked him if the suite upstairs was on my account. "Is that correct?'

Robert came back a few minutes later and said "Yes, Mr. Gray, all of their room expenses have been billed to your special account. Direct billing to Guerrara, Inc., in Texas I believe."

"That is correct, Robert, but as of right now, there will be no more charges to that room and after tonight, I will not, I repeat I will not be responsible for their bill. Any questions?"

"No, Sir, very clear." He said. I also told him I wanted Miss Ames to know about this ASAP. "Find her."

"Any questions on that, Robert?"

"Very clear Sir. I shall let Amber, I mean Miss Ames know at once."

I have known several people who have cleaned up their shit from cocaine and heroin. These are the people that are strong willed and can lay it down when they decide to. Good people who made a bad choice, but the cure rate for drug rehabilitation programs are 93-97 % FAILURES. Drug rehabilitation is the biggest flim flam this country has seen and who pays? YOU DO, in your health insurance payments every month where you work. Thanks to the bunch of assholes that hung around LBJ in the '60's, we now have a mega million dollar industry called 'rehabilitation.' Now whenever one of the little bastards get in trouble with dope, they run to some rehab center and cry "King's X...I need help," and with my money. Prisons are full of them. If the programs are so good, then why did the Federal government close down Lexington, Kentucky?

I was still steaming when there was a knock on the door. I jerked it open and there stood Stella.

"Charlie, my God, what is wrong?" she said with fear in in her voice as she stepped back from the door. I looked at her for a minute and swallowed, took a deep breath and mumbled "Nothing, come on in. I'm sorry, I was thinking of something else."

"You frightened me...I...you didn't...I don't know what to think," she said as she entered the door.

"I'm sorry, Stella." I explained what had just happened and I apologized for being upset. I was upset with myself more than anything. Bart and I had been doing "our own thing" so much I could not see what was going on under my very own eyes. Just like some parents not paying attention to their kids, and the kids jump the track.

"Please have a seat. May I get you some coffee or a glass of juice?" I checked the refrigerator at the bar. I see where Maria had taken all the booze out and had replaced it with assorted juices. Cranberry juice? I don't think so.

"Well. You ready for breakfast?" I asked as we walked towards the door? "Charlie, I have already been to Confessions once this morning so I guess I had better 'fess up' to you too. After Mass I was so hungry, I drove through a McDonalds and had an egg and biscuit just before I called you, but I will go with you if you are hungry." she said with an angelic smile.

Billy L. Smith Sr.

I laughed real big and said "I had just walked in from Denny's when you called me". We both had a good laugh with that one.

Stella and I went down the side steps and out to the parking lot. She took the keys and started the van and was backing out when she asked "Where to?"

"It's a nice Sunday morning. Let's drive around. I'm thinking of buying a house and need to look at the lay of the land."

Stella pulled out of the drive and onto the Interstate. She was a very modest driver and I am sure it was due to the fact that it was a strange vehicle, much bigger than her little Toyota. I got to looking around in the van's front cubby holes. The van only had 1200 miles on it in two weeks. Bart and I had been to every "slop chute" in the New Orleans area and no place else. I had a hunch that I would find what I was looking for, and I did find it. Wrapping papers, a couple of baggies, several roach clips, and a hash pipe with marijuana smell.

Stella was looking with wide eyes but saying nothing. "Stella, pull off to that roadside park, please." which she did.

I got out of the car and started looking. I shook down that van so well that I bet my old Field Training Officer Carl White at the L.A.P.D. would be proud of me. I dumped all I could find in the trash cans and we got back on the highway.

"Know where a car wash open on Sunday is located?" I asked dryly.

Stella had not said a word but had helped me pick seeds off the floor and from between the seats.

Without a word, Stella took the next exit and turned right. After a few blocks we came to a "Mr. Car Wash." We pulled up and I asked the young lady taking orders to fill the gas tank and for the "Special". She advised me that it would about a half hour and there was coffee in the waiting room.

We walked in the side door and Stella was looking at all the different "grabbers" hanging on the wall while I waited for the gas ticket. In a few minutes, the gas ticket came in and I paid the bill. I noticed that I was running low on cash and I had better make a withdrawal from my "boot bank."

We walked into the lounge. It was empty since most of the people were walking around or watching the men wash the cars through the steamed up window.

"So you want to buy a house?" Stella asked while setting there in a very "proper" manner, legs crossed at the ankles and back straight.

"Yeah, about 500 hundred acres and a house, I will build if I have to. I want a big house for lots of guest. Even a second house for guest and of course houses for my hands working there, and of course a kennel".

Stella asked about the kennels and I explained to her about what I wanted to do, with training dogs for law enforcement. She looked interested, but asked no questions.

"You want to build here in Louisiana?" she asked.

"Oh, I don't care. I will know when I find the right spot. You know anything about dogs?" I inquired.

"Well, I have a Chihuahua, does that count?" as I chuckled. "It's a dog, it counts." I said.

After a pause she asked "You want a recommendation? I mean on who to contact about buying land?"

"Sure, you know someone?" I asked.

"Yes, Stanley can help you I bet. Stanley, you met him Friday night. He was the M.C. at the Banquet, Stanley Hines." she said.

"Stanley? Oh, yes Stan. Okay, I never knew his last name, was with Amber or whatever." I said.

"I wish he was with Amber, Amber has a boyfriend, I think. Never really seen him, but just have that feeling sometimes...No, I think Amber and Stanley would make a nice couple, but Stanley is in love with someone else and I think she is...not up to his standards. Stanley could have any girl in New Orleans, in fact several has set their caps for him, but no. Stanley is a very successful broker you know, Hines and Associates. His grandfather started the business a long time ago and Stanley went to Yale School of Business, graduated with honors..." as she smiled off into the distance.

I sat there and watched Stella. There was something I didn't understand. I had worked around crooks and convicts for many years. You develop a sixth sense about some things, but something about her story didn't ring true.

After a few moments of silence the van was pulled up front and five or six men with towels were wiping and drying. We waited a few minutes and the man that appeared to be in charge of the crew came over to me and asked me what kind of odor I would sprayed in the van. I told him "New Car" and offered to shake hands with him as I said thanks. He automatically stuck his hand out and then hesitated, but took it. In my palm was a twenty dollar bill. He recognized the feel and smiled a broad smile.

"Gracias, Amigo" I said in Spanish. "Con mucho gusto, Senior"
"De nada. Es para otros composinos tambien. Verda?"

"Si, Senor. Yo se." He tipped his hat to Stella, not in a subservient manner, but as a gentleman would, honoring a lady. I think that is one of the reasons I like the Spanish culture so much. If you are polite and respectful, they are extremely polite in return.

In a short time, the van was ready. They were very surprised when Stella got in the driver's side. In Hispanic culture, the man always drives. Due to the age difference, they probably though that "she must be his daughter." As we drove off, they gave a little wave and a smile.

"You said Stan may be able to help me?" I asked continuing the conversation about the proposed training facilities.

"Oh, yes...Stanley is very good about that" she smiled.

There she goes again with "Stanley this and Stanley that." Just like a mother would.

"Where is Stanley's mother and father from?" I asked. "They still alive?"

"Oh, yes, Stanley is adopted and he knows it, and he has only known Stan senior and Katie as his real mother and father." She made a turn back on Lake Road. "You want to see Stanley?"

"Sure, you know where he is on Sunday Afternoons?"

"Up where he always is on Sundays, at the Lake Side Polo Club. Stanley has a well-bred string of polo ponies, they are playing this afternoon at 5:00 PM."

There she goes again with "Stanley." I wonder if she could be the...Noooo way. She could not be that much older than "Stanley" I would guessed.

We drove to the Lake Side Polo Club and started to enter the grounds. A police officer in uniform was directing traffic on the highway and a security guard was stopping cars at a gate just off the highway.

"Yes, Ma'am. May I help you?" the Security Guard asked very politely. "Yes, we are here to see the match." Stella said.

"Are you a member? I don't see a vehicle pass on the vehicle and this gate is for members only."

"I'm sure if you check with Stanley Hines he will allow us to use this gate," she smiled.

"Stanley Hines?" he said. "Okay, just a moment please," and he unfolded a cellular phone and dialed.

"May I have you name Miss?" The Guard asked after a few moments. "Stella Dunn, he knows me." she said out the window.

"Dunn" I thought. That's it, been trying to figure out how to ask her. Hee, hee. I turned to my right and smiled at myself in the van's door glass.

"Ms. Dunn, do go in. Mr. Hines asked you meet him at the Club House Patio Bar."

"Thank you" and she drove through the gate. "Good Ol' Stanley" she said more to herself.

We drove down a well-manicured path lined with the type of trees you see in Louisiana with moss hanging down and came to a large parking lot full of Lincolns, Cadies and big cars. It looked like the kind of place where you would want to make a commercial. Off towards the polo field, I guess that is what they call them, I had never been to one before, was a large glassed-in building with a "patio" on the field side. White coated waiters and waitresses were walking among the tables. It looked like the men were in "sports attire," polo shirts (what else) and slacks. I was dressed in Levi's and a denim shirt. Stella had on the dress she wore to church that morning and there I was again, the fifth wheel.

As we walked up to the Patio Bar, "Stanley" came out and met us. He hugged Stella and shook my hand, acted like old home week. Very nice man I thought, not a snob as I thought this crowd would be.

Stella and I spent the afternoon watching the match and "Stanley" ride his five or six ponies in the ground, but I was impressed. I enjoyed hearing the leather squeak and smell the ponies sweat. I even went out to help the replace the dirt clods between chuckles. They had a name for them, but I forgot what it was.

One thing that surprised me more than anything, I saw Sassy handling Stan's polo ponies. Well, she was directing the stable hands. She was so petite and tiny. She didn't go around the ponies. She often just ducked under them. I was thinking of a grasshopper jumping around, but they accepted her and it appeared to me she knew her business. She checked hooves, bumps and scraps from the game, and it was a rough game. More than I appreciated it to be.

I noticed Sassy was leading a pony back towards the stables that was limping. She was walking backwards and watching the pony with a professional eye. About halfway back, a man carrying a black bag came up and she greeted him with a hug. He was much taller than she was and it was a little comical, but after a few seconds, attention her was turned to the pony. Then I noticed something unusual, Stan came up and spoke to the man who I guessed was a vet. The man shrugged his shoulders and turned and walked away. I could not hear any conversation, but I was guessing that Sassy was having a strong conversation with Stan, who turned on his heels and walked back towards the picket line where his horses were standing.

After the polo match, we left and started back towards the hotel. We had had a great day, a fun day. We were a little sunburned from having a "bar room complexion" for the last year.

We were driving back towards town and talking about the game and "Stanley" when Stella made a statement that almost made me "flip out." She said off handily, "I'm so proud of my son."

I then she realized what she had said. Her hand went to her mouth and she looked at me and tried to cover the story up, but it didn't work. Stella was driving and I told her to pull over into a convenience store parking lot. Then she started sobbing the biggest sobs I had ever heard. I let her cry and just sat there. What else could I do?

After a few minutes I went in the Circle K Store and bought a box of Kleenex and a couple of bottles of drinking water. I came out and offered both to Stella. She took the Kleenex and dabbed at her nose.

"Will you drive please?" she said.

Without a word I got out of the van and walked around to the driver's side. Stella, being much smaller than I was, slid over to the passengers seat and was just staring.

"Except for my mother, Stanley Senior and Katie, no one else in the world knows."

"Your secret is safe with me, Stella, this I swear," I said very softly. I didn't want to look at her, but I wanted to say something. I was sitting there thinking. She was older than I thought, I thought fifty maybe, tops.

"Can I talk about it with you, Charlie?" she asked.
"Sure....now?" I asked. She just shook her head.
I attempted to put the van in gear but couldn't. Stella told me I had to step on the brake for the gear shift lever to work. "Shows you how much I drove the new car. Before I came into the lottery money, all I ever had was a ten year GMC stick shift pickup. Now I can't even get this one in gear. Ain't that a bitch?" I chuckled a little.

The van jerked forward and I had to get it under control. I went to the highway, pulled on and started back towards the motel. I guess it is sort of like riding a bicycle, you never forget.

Somehow, we made it back to the motel. I parked and locked the van. Stella got out and came up to the room. She looked tired, very, very tired and she walked like she was in a daze. I guess after 30 some odd years of holding a secret it would take a little wind out of you. I did not say a word that did not need to be said.

"Charlie, I need to go home for a minute...feed the dog and check on things at the house, mainly get out of these clothes. I feel gritty." she said.

"Well, I have a shower here and..." I let it fade away.

"No thanks. I will be back in about an hour, I promise. We need to talk...or at least I need to talk. Okay?'

"Sure, no problem, will be waiting here for you. Let's see, it is eight PM. You should be back by nine or so? I'll order some sandwiches up if you like?"

"I'm not really hungry, but go ahead if you want," she said as she walked out the door.

What a hell of a day.

Chapter 8

After Stella left, I went in the bedroom I normally did not use and noticed a pile of neat folded laundry on the bed: t-shirts, underwear and socks. Hanging on the corner of the chair were several hangers with freshly pressed shirts and new Levi's. In a different little cluster of clothing were the three or four "track suits" I had bought earlier yesterday, thinking that I will get on a health kick and start doing some exercise.

A note was pinned to one of the shirts. In a very pained printed message, Maria had said she had washed and ironed, or rather, had someone iron the clothes and hoped that she did not offend me. "Offend me? Maria, you are a Sweetheart first class" I said aloud.

There was enough underwear and socks on the bed for three people. What did I miss being shit faced half the time?

I was freshly showered, shaved, hair combed and wearing my new track suit with just socks. Maybe next time I will get a pair of tennis shoes. I do not think cowboy boots go too well with this outfit I called down for a dozen assorted fancy little sandwiches and a gallon of milk. Ramon was not there on Sundays, but I talked to a young lady who cheerfully said that she would bring them up in about half an hour.

I sat in the overstuffed chair holding a cup of coffee and had intended to relax for a moment.

I flicked the TV on and ran the through the channels. There was an old 'Nam movie playing, *The Deer Slayer*. For some reason I stopped there and half-assed watched it as I tried to relax, waiting for Stella to come back.

My head went back and I must have snoozed a little.

There is no sound in the world like the swish of pettie coats, the sound of an 870 shotgun having a round jacked in the chamber and the steady "whop whop whop" of a "Huey" helicopter, like the sound I was hearing on TV.

We were back in the Delta on board Riverene 1's boats, me with "Bo," and Huey Muhler with "Cup Cake." Three boats were running full bore up a side canal when a helicopter from HAL-3 flew low overhead searching where we were going to for bad guys. With as much noise as we were making, Ray Charles could hear us coming, but that was the idea. The Boat Coxswain was called "Running Bear" or just "Bear", a full blooded Mohawk from New York, he motioned to get ready. The young Gunner's Mate on the forward M60 was covering the bank as we approached the insertion point. "Bear" slowly pulled the throttles back, allowing the other two boats to get ahead. Just as the bow of the boat touched the bank, myself and Howie with the two dogs were out in ten seconds along with two other team members who were our "shooters" or folks who were there to protect us. Howie and I did not normally carry anything but side arms, due to having to handle the dogs. Other firearms were too bulky and we could not do too much anyway. Still, we had learned to be deadly accurate with a Colt .45 caliber ACP, snap shooting from the hip.

As the boat was pulling away and "Bear" slowly applied throttles to catch up to the other boats, we moved about twenty feet into the bush up a small trail and "went to ground" to see what was in the area. We had received a "Yo" from the HAL-3 crew that this area appeared to be "cold," or not currently occupied. That was the reason we got off at this spot. "Bear" and the Hal-3 crew had been talking while we were running up river to make sure we were at the right spot.

The term "Yo" that we use today came from "Nam. It can mean almost anything: an exclamation, a greeting, an attention getter or a command to execute a move, for example. There is a great deal of history behind "Yo." "Yo" was also a reward given out until someone lost "Yo."

As the sound of the boats faded, we stayed very still to listen. "Bo" and "C.C." (Cup Cake) were excellent for this type of work. Unlike most dogs today who have all the hand signals and commands, our dogs were taught "down" and "stay" by placing our hand on the top of the shoulders and applying pressure. The dog would go to a "down-stay" as any other dog and if we wanted a "dead dog down", giving us the lowest profile, we placed our hand on the top of the head and applied pressure. The dog was required to stay "dead dog down" no matter what, even with people walking around us. We would practice this at our training facilities in Imperial Beach California around the old coastal gun emplacements we used as offices. I laugh when I see young dudes running around today trying to speak something they call "German" or "Dutch" or whatever. The Germans and Dutch also laugh at them, all the way to the bank. Most of them know jack shit about working a dog that is not in some "ring sport rule book." I guess today there is no practical use for it.

It was full dark a few minutes after we got there. We assumed a circle position in a small clearing. If you will picture a clock, the dogs were placed at the "12" and "6" o'clock positions. This offered us the benefit of the dog's keen sense of smell and hearing if someone moved near us. If the dogs did hear something, they "scratched" on the handlers leg or arm gently. Some dogs like C.C. would nuzzle Howie's arm, but "No Bark" was the rule. The shooters were in the "3" and "9" o'clock position. Everyone's feet were to the inside of the circle with feet touching. If you needed to get someone's attention, you kicked very gently to get there attention. You just had to move your foot. The toe would be in the ground with the heel up. Just wiggle the foot and kick the person next to you twice. The answer back was one kick.

We had a new hand held transmitter on this trip too. Smaller than the PRC-25 which you wore on your back and had an antenna that caught on everything in the bush. These new transmitters were smaller and would fit in a holster on your chest. They had three channels and a microphone with a clip that could be extended to your shoulder or web gear. The "press to talk" or PTT mike, could also be a speaker. But we had the "twiggets" disable that quick. You listened to the radio with a small cord that ran to an ear piece. What will modern science think of next?

Our plans were made with Steve Ford and his SEALS to "wait until called for" on our common frequency.

We knew we would be there all night, so we settled in. Howie and one of the "shooters", a new kid from Rock Springs, Wyoming, had the first two hours. After which, we would relieve them.

For all practical purposes, the night was uneventful. "Bo" did wake me up once when he moved to standup and piss. I let him go to the end of the leash and "do his business." "Bo," being a dog, had to scratch the ground to tell all of the other little doggies in the world that this was his spot. With a gentle correction I brought "Bo" back and placed him on my left side. The reason a dog always works on the left is to insure your "gun hand" or right hand in my case, is free in case you need it. That is still true today.

We heard noises on the river and talking during the night. We also heard voices walking towards the river as well. I think they were across the river, but you know how sounds carry at night.

We had shifted the watch back and forth all night, two hours on and two hours off. I was "not really asleep but just resting my eyes" when Frankie Roberts "kicked me" awake. My eyes popped open and I kicked back gently one time. I slowly raised my head to look around. I could guess from the sky that it was close to dawn, but I could not see the watch I had on and I was not going to show any light. I wish someone would invent a watch that would light up in the dark. The GI watches we had were supposed to "glow in the dark," but I mean a watch that you could push a button and a small bulb would come on so you could see the numbers, Right! "Never gonna happen GI!"

I reached down and tuned on the radio. In a few moments things were about to happen.

"Dutch Boy - Candle" "Candle- go".
"Candle, Dutch Boy will start making things happen in a few. When we give you the word, move down the trail south, approximately 300 meters. You will spot a log across the trail with a stick leaning on it. Stop there and wait if you have not heard from us again. At that point you will be about thirty feet from a clearing. Just wait for us to call."

Howie clicked the microphone twice to indicate he acknowledged the transmission.

We allowed ourselves to get a little bit more light before we moved out. We wanted to be able to see "trip wires" and anything else.

It took us about half an hour to move the three hundred meters. We did hear voices coming from our left, there had to be a parallel trail. We heard them last night and decided they were on the other side of the river, but maybe not.

"Bo" and I were on point or up front ahead of the others about 50 feet and Frankie was "ass dragging," or bringing up the rear. Howie was in the middle "counting". "Counting" is where you count the number of steps you take using beads as a calculator. Every one hundred steps, you drop a bead. The Counting Beads look a lot like Rosary Beads. This way you can estimate how far you have traveled.

Two "clicks" went off in my ear piece. I froze and put "Bo" in a down-stay. I looked around and saw the team had stopped.

Keeping my attention forward and on "Bo," I did not see anything. However, two "clicks" meant "stop" or "danger" and you always followed that order. "Bo" was looking forwarded with his ears flickering backwards every few seconds, but there was nothing to be concerned about.

My ear piece had a sound like an "open" microphone, but nothing was said for a few seconds and then it would turn off. This was normal, it gave you a chance to stop moving and pay attention. Again, an open mike and Howie was softly whispering, "You see a log ahead?" I shook my head side to side but did not take my eyes off the trail, "according to my count, we have gone way past 300 meters."

"Candle-Dutch Boy, hold your position. You are on the wrong trail. Out." "I ain't on the wrong trail," I thought. "…you are." But I did not say anything. I had faith in Steve Ford and his SEALS.

"Candle-Dutch Boy, you are in a good position if you are where I think you are. "Bush up" for the day and I will advise you. I did not take a picture, acknowledge." It was Steve Ford's Philly accent.

"Understood – out," Howie replied.

"Did not take a picture" meant that Steve did not see the person he wanted through the scope and that he did not fire.

For the first time, I turned around to look behind me. I noticed that Frankie was making a circle motion with his finger straight up and then patting the top of his own head. This meant "look at me" or "follow me." I nodded my head in an affirmative manner and Frankie Roberts, who had been a soda jerk in Calhoon, Georgia 18 month ago, was now leading a combat patrol in Viet Nam.

113

We all turned around, but kept our spacing. Then we moved back down the trail where Frankie and then Howie went into the jungle. I passed "Cowboy" McGuire, who was the fourth team member, who was now rear guard. We moved about 100 yards to a large stand of mango trees which made a natural "fort" for us.

Dog handlers always wear four canteens, three for the dogs and one for the handlers. I took a canteen cup and filled it with water and allowed "Bo" to drink. After "Bo" had a full cup, I drank. Howie and I moved about fifty feet apart, on each side of the mango trees and went to "ground" behind several large roots sticking out of the ground. Everyone was reaching for the meals-ready-to-eat packages we had in the side pockets of out BDU's. The handlers also carried MRE's for his canine too.

After we shared our meals and made sure we picked up all paper and buried it, we tried to sleep. Even when "Bo" had to scratch, it was quiet. All the gear he had on was leather or made from braided nylon parachute cord. No noise was the key thing.

After a short period the radio ear piece came alive with "Candle this Dutch Boy, we just took one picture and are moving out. We thank the bogies are coming down your trail, out." We could hear them breathing as if running or moving under strain.

Since all members of the team had a radio, we came alive. In less than five minutes, it could have been an hour, since our nerves were so "wired up," we heard a "jingle jingle jingle" coming from the direction we had just come. It sounded like troops moving at high speed down the trail we were just on, and then they stopped.

"Shit" I thought, did they see some signs we had left? Had Cowboy left "sign" and not wiped out all the tracks?

The blood was pounding in our ears and we were all as still as the trees. "Bo" was on my left side and he reached over and scratched my right arm since I was laying on my right side with my left hand on his back. I was scratching him behind the ear acknowledging I understood what he was telling me. His ears were up and he was alert and watching the bush towards the trail. I could not see Howie, but I am sure he was going through the same thing. I wish we had put out the Claymores we had with us, but we did not, so stillness is the best cover we had.

In a short time we could hear a large throbbing motor… from the river? Yes, a "Monitor" was coming up the river. A Monitor is a large, heavy duty armored landing craft used by the Army. I hoped they were not coming in to land where we got off. The Army has strange ways of doing things. Just before they turned into the shore, they raked the area for five minutes with 20mm and 40mm weapons to "clear an area". Right, they hosed down everything. I heard the "jingle jingle jingle" go back up the trail and a distinctive "glug" of water in a canteen. A half drank canteen would give a "glug" sound that carried over a long distance. That was a good sign that we have "rookie troops" running around. No seasoned members would tolerate a "glug."

In a short time the throbbing of the large river craft could be heard. The splash of the bow making its way through the water was audible and sounded like it was coming towards the bank.

"Stay down" I said over the radio since we were spread out. I did not have to tell them.

In a short time we could here men talking, English words. A loud voice yelled "Move out" and we could hear loud music being played on a "boom box." "Funky Tiiiimmmmmmeeee" carried thought the Delta as our U.S. Army moved through the jungle. I would have bet a month's beer ration that it was an element from the 25th Infantry.

The slow throb of the engines on the Monitor indicated it was staying in place.

"Candle the Calvary has arrived," Steve Ford said in a sarcastic voice. "Yeah, we heard them. Now what?" I asked.
"Come on back south down the trail you were on and meet up with us. We are on the edge of the clearing. The "legs" (army Infantry) are going to the 'ville."

"On our way"

We moved back out in normal order to where the company size patrol had moved. There was no doubt the

U.S. Army was here, candy bar wrappers, MRE's, and some equipment that Charlie can use.

When we reached the edge of the clearing, I was the first to meet with Steve. He and his platoon were in a casual "defensive circle" and not saying a word. All communications was done with American Sign Language in many cases. A brilliant idea, we spoke in soft words.

Steve briefed us on the village ahead of us. The Army was to go past the village and look for hidden holes. But Steve had not told the Army he had been watching the village for 24 hours and felt the hidey holes were very near where we were standing. People had been coming to this side of the village and were not coming out. There were a hundred people somewhere near us. Look at the amount of acreage, pigs, grain storage bins and houses, enough for a hundred people. No one in the fields and no one in sight. So where were they? In the ground?

"Charlie, think you can find the caves?" Steve asked. "Don't know, but we will try. Howie what do you think?" "Steve, you said you took a picture, you kill'em?"

"Nope, leg shot with a Swift 222 caliber. He did a double back flip but was helped off the playing field. He had come out of that hooch over there and was standing on the porch talking to the village people when he walked down the steps. That is when Eddie took his picture. Don't know where he went. I know he didn't come out the back way where the "legs" went. He had to come this way, over between the sheds and the main hooch. So here we are."

"Okay, can you show us where exactly the guy was when you greased him?" Steve and Eddie took us about three hundred yards to the village and showed us where he thought he was. Eddie's spotter was there and agreed tacitly.

The house looked as if it may have been an old European Planter's House from the days of French Indo China. An area near the front porch had a scuffed and a dark stain that looked like blood. The house had been "cleared" by the army when they went by, but Stevey had a couple of his troops look at it too, just to make sure.

Howie and I brought "Bo" and "C.C." and pre-scented them on the dark spot. At that time, we did not understand that blood was scent specific, we know better thirty years later, but back then we thought a blood track was a "blood track." Both "Bo" and "C.C." started across the yard area to the east side of the village several hundred yards away. "Bo" went towards a hooch, as if he wanted to enter. A slight correction and 'Bo" came back to me. A couple of Steve Ford's SEALS Team 7 went in and "cleared" the hooch. The hooch was about the size of an American two car garage, probably a stowage room from the outside, but not a residence. The men came out and shook their heads like they were saying "Go ahead, all clear."

"Bo" and I entered the hooch, which was dark and steamy and getting worse the higher the sun rose. "Bo" walked around the room several times and stopped, looked up at me and then went "down" real slow.

"Strange," I thought, "I had not seen that before." I walked over to "Bo." As I approached, something under my foot felt different. The dirt I was walking on did not feel the same. I stopped. I motioned to Frankie to get out. My first thought was I had stepped on a mine.

After looking around a few seconds, I moved my foot and nothing happened. "Bo" was still "down" and waiting for me. I eased over to him and felt the same thing as before under my feet. I stomped my foot and there was a hollow sound.

I called Frankie back in and by that time Steve was with him. I eased back out the door with "Bo" and explained to Steve there may be a door under all the piled up mats and baskets.

A short time later the U.S. Army came back through on the way to the Monitor. Our HAL-3 helo was overhead and said they had not seen any movement for about five clicks in any direction.

Bad news, this is a work day. Where are the people? This is not a Market Day or Holiday, "bad vibes" as the hippies were saying in that day and time.

The Army left with all their glory and we were there alone. Steve had radio contact with Running Bear and the Swift boats through "Tea Kettle Actual," the HAL-3 chopper.

Steve and I looked around and made notes that this place was NOT a regulation farmer's village. An Army Intelligence Captain from the "leg" unit was asked to stay with us for the rest of the day as an advisor. I have to say that Army Intel folks have some sharp people. It is their infantry draftee dope smoking pukes I have problems with.

Here is what the three of us came up with, and remember Steve Ford was in charge that day.

A. No People
B. No water buffalo for plowing, no water buffalo droppings, none seen in 24 hours either.
C. No signs of children, a big give away
D. Wounded high cadre official did not leave the village.
E. One of Steve Ford's men said the ground had not been plowed for a while and this was planting season and there were no boats along the river which is the "highway" for farmers. "Running Bear" said they had not seen anything all morning which is rare.

"CC" was off her leash and went over to a small shed that tools may be kept in and whined and went "down."

"Yo" Howie said and indicated towards "C.C." "Cup Cake don't lie." I half said aloud.

In a few seconds, the shed had been moved or tilted over and a trap door was found. Not a rare thing the Vietnamese had been using holes in the ground for mega-centurys to "hide" their crops from invaders. However, this hidey hole had a couple of long trenches running north to south, and they were deep, like for walking.

When Steve looked in the hole he said "Nuc Maum", a Vietnamese sauce used as a seasoning for everything, made of fish guts, terrible smelling stuff. He backed up and asked one of the men to check the hooch's and see if there were any breakfast fires. In a few minutes one of the SEALS came back and said there were no signs of breakfast fires, or cooking utensils, or anything that made this look like a normal village.

We looked at each other. "I'll call it in." Steve said to no one in particular. Steve got on the radio and relayed through "Tea Kettle Actual", the chopper flying several thousand feet over our position called back to his command for instructions. After a long conversation I noticed the HAL-3 chopper coming back our way.

"You guys may want to move out, Charlie, "Bear" has an ETA of fifteen minutes and will give you a ride. We are going to plant a few surprises and let a couple of 'Sandys' work this place over."

A "Sandy" is a very large single engine propeller driven attack aircraft used by the Navy and Air Force. It can carry its own weight in ordinance.

With that, we moved in "battle order," as they say, back down the trail to the river. After a few minutes of waiting for "Bear" and crew to pick us up, we could hear the drone of the boats and small arms fire, "tap tap tap."

"Charlie?" "*Tap tap tap*," it was getting louder, "They must be getting closer."

"*Tap! Tap! Tap! Tap!*

"Charlie?" Then I heard the sound of an old French rifle bolt being cycled to put a round in.

"Charlie, you were dreaming," said Stella's voice. "Wake up. If you don't stop watching these old war movies, it will give you night mares," she stated as some young lady in a white waiter coat wheeled a food trolley in.

I jumped up. Looked around for Steve and Howie... they were not there. The young lady smiled at me and was waiting for the tip. She knew one always came from this room. I felt for my wallet and forgot I had on my jogging suit. I went and got my wallet out of the other bed room, tipped her and she left.

Chapter 9

After the room service waiter left, Stella and I sat around nibbling sandwiches and drinking milk. Saying nothing and not looking at each other. She was sitting on the couch with her feet curled up under her. She was wearing a matching short set and had a pillow over her legs. I guessed that the air conditioner was blowing on her legs and brought her a light blanket from the bedroom. The sofa or couch, I never know which one to call them, it had small throw pillows which she placed under her back.

I did notice a few things in my old ways. She had good looking legs and any woman that wears a Wonder Bra with a low cut blouse like that one had no business getting upset when old men look at their chest.

After a long silence, Stella spoke." I was fourteen when Stanley was born, almost fifteen, but I was fourteen when he was conceived. I was a young girl here in New Orleans area and was trying to learn about feminine things., flirting and all. I had developed early, so I thought...a boy living close by... I thought I was in love with him and we went too far, he was sixteen. It's funny, but Stanley was conceived in the stable tack room at the Polo club. Not the one there now, but on the same spot where the present stables are. The old ones burn down in 1960." Stella sat and nibbled a corner of a sandwich. She reminded me of a little mouse.

"My father worked at the Polo Club" she continued. "He was a grounds keeper. I came by one day after school and met..." She gave a long pause, "Stanley's father." I didn't say a word, she needed to speak.

"Oh, Charlie lied and I have been telling lies for thirty six years until this moment. Stanley Senior is Stanley's father. I was fourteen, he came to the stables where I was petting the horse after school one day and asked what I was doing. I told him I was only petting the horses and he said to come with him and I was trespassing and that was against the law. I told him my father was Berry Dunn. He stopped and said that was even worse, he would have to fire him for 'allowing this to happen,' could not live in the house on the Polo Grounds that was furnished with the job. We would have to sleep in the streets tonight. I panicked, didn't know what to do. He said come with him to the tack room. I did and he..."

Stella started sobbing softly. What could I say, I wanted to go over there and put my arms around her and just...well, comfort her, but I didn't dare do that. Stella did not need that right now...I guess, I didn't know. I just sat still with my head down. I wanted to cry too.

After a few minutes, I went over to the sink and got a box of Kleenex from under the counter. All Holiday Inns have them in a little dispenser. I brought them to Stella, she had stopped crying. I took the glasses she was wearing, she had taken them off and had her head in her hands. I cleaned them off, I didn't know if they were dirty or not, I just needed something to do.

I went and got a glass of water for Stella. She took a little sip, put it down, and continued. "I was wearing shorts. He told me to take them off, he ordered me. I didn't know what to do. I took them off and he took off my panties, started kissing me, putting his finger in me. I still remember the cigar smell to this day. After a few minutes, he had me laid over the feed sacks and forced my legs open. I remember the rough sacks was hurting my back and bottom. The stack of sacks were just right for him to...you know. He dropped his pants and I remember..." She paused for a while and continued, "I remember him panting. For some reason it reminded me of a freight train, huffing and puffing."

She took a drink of water, put her glasses down and looked at me for the first time. "After he fucked me, and that is all I can call it, fuck. What a dirty word, and I felt dirty. I don't recall how long it lasted, I know I had this sticky stuff running down the crack of my butt. I don't remember any pain, I was told as a young girl that if you were a virgin, there was blood and pain on your wedding night. I wanted to wipe, but didn't have anything. He stood up when he got through. I think it lasted about ten or fifteen minutes. From what I know now I think he climaxed twice and I got to see this...thing, penis he had stuck in me and I thought how ugly it looked. I know my butt was raw."

"After he got through with me, he told me to get dressed and he wanted me to come hug his neck. Funny thing, I did it and wanted to do it, I don't know why. I put my panties and shorts on and he told me that if I didn't tell anyone, Daddy would not be fired. I never did until now."

I remained silent. There was nothing for me to say.

"In a few weeks, I knew something was wrong. In those days, you didn't talk about teenage pregnancy, rape and unwed mothers, except behind closed doors. There must be something wrong with 'those type of people' from the way their voices always dropped. I was in the eighth grade. I didn't have anyone to tell the story. I was going to Catholic school at St Thomas, it's gone now, combined with Our Lady of the Lake. I knew I couldn't go to confessions and say anything. In those days, I was scared to death of the priest and sisters. They reminded of football players that spoke German," she laughed a little, "but I was pregnant."

"School had just started and I was starting to show. I wanted to wear coats to school and in November it is still hot here. Finally, my mother walked in on me by accident in the bathroom while I was bathing. My secret was out." Stella said as she paced the room.

"Long story short, I was sent to a 'girls home' run by C.Y.A. in Baton Rouge. When I came back, I was in the ninth grade then. First year in high school, and everyone knew."

Stella walked over to the window and looked out to the swimming pool, opened the balcony doors and watched one man swimming in the pool, closed them and came back in.

"Want another glass of grapefruit juice?" she asked me.

"Sure," I said and I handed her the glass. Stella went to bar area, poured the grapefruit juice and handed it to me. Our fingers overlapped and touched for just a second. Maybe she left her hand there just a second longer than needed, trying to tell me something? I felt something I had not felt in a long time, electricity...

"Naaaaaah, Man! Get that shit out of your mind, you are as crazy as a run over road lizard," I thought.

"One day, just before the baby was born. I told one of the sisters at the C.Y.A. home who the father was and that I was raped. Before this, I didn't even know what the word meant. She didn't believe me, said I was going to hell for being a 'fornicator and a liar.'"

"When the baby was born, I never got to see it. Stanley was taken from me. My mother was there for the birth, but I don't remember much. I was kept doped up."

"After a few weeks, I was up and about and was given chores to do. Since I was so small, I was given light housekeeping duties in the records office. While I was cleaning, I found the records of the adoption for a baby boy to 'Stanley F. Hines and Katy Broussard Hines,' on the day that my baby was born. I was the only girl to give birth that day, or even a few days before or after."

"After I came back here, I went back to St. Thomas for a year. No dates in high school, no boys. Except one time I remember when a couple of boys asked me to go for a ride with them. I was so happy. Without thinking I just jumped in the car. We went out by the lake and they wanted me to go skinny dipping. I was told 'all the girls that go with us have to skinny dip to make sure they are girls. We don't hang around no queers' I ran back to the yacht club and got a ride home with a girl that bussed table there. My folks were furious with me. I tried to tell them and they didn't want to hear it. My dad told me he didn't want no girl that got 'knocked up' hanging around and stuff like that."

"Ever get married?" I asked

"Yes, didn't last. I couldn't have sex with him. Oh I did, but I kept thinking and smelling cigars and my hips rubbing on the feed sacks. Well...it was repulsive. I hated to even think about what he was doing to me. I was being raped all over again ever time we had relations." she said.

"But I loved him."

"I hate to be rude, but you tell me you have not had a normal sex life. Ever...uh...climax?" I asked.

She shook her head negative and hung her head down.

It was 2:00 AM when we finally stopped talking. We were nodding out and just closing our eyes. Somehow I went to the opposite end of the couch and was just sitting there. She was on the opposite end. She got up to get a fresh glass of milk and sandwich and just sat down next to me. We had light conversations about everything in the world and enjoyed ourselves.

Stella put her head back on the back of the couch and went to sleep.

I gently laid her down, put a pillow under her head, placed the blanket over her and went to the other room to just lay down for a minute.

It was full daylight when I jerked awake. I went to the living room and Stella was still asleep. I could wake up quick enough, but I looked at my watch and it was 9:30.

"Shit. I wonder if she has a job or anything."

"Stella. Stella, you had better wake up. It's 9:30…Stella." She woke up, stretched like a kitten and smiled.

"Good morning Charlie. I am sorry I went to sleep, not a very good date am I? Haven't had much practice." She looked around for her glasses and put them on.

"You have to work this morning?" I asked.

"No silly, its Labor Day" as she headed for the bathroom.

I made coffee and was about to pour a cup. Then the door opened from the hall.

"Buenos dias, Senor Charlie. Como esta?" Maria said in a happy voice. "Esta muy..." and she stopped in mid sentence as Stella walked out of the bedroom. She turned around as if doing something at the bar. "Pardon, Senora." and she walked out to her cart.

The door was standing open and she stood there with her back to us.

"I do have to go home. Take care of the dog and all. Can you give me a call or something, sometime?" she said.

"Sure, I would like that. Please give me your er, ah..." I stammered looking for the little pads that every Holiday Inn has on the phone table.

Just as I bent down to look for the paper, Stella, mousy little Stella, reached up and gave me a kiss on the cheek and said, "Thanks for a wonderful evening, Charlie Boy," and then went "grrrrrr" like a tiger. I was so surprised. I just stood there as she walked out and said in a light voice. "Good Morning, Maria. Have a nice day."

Maria just stood there looking at me like my mother use to look, arms crossed over the chest, head slightly tilted up and her eyes cut at a 45 degree angle.

Here came the good part, Amber walked by the open door on her way to the pool as Stella walked around Maria's house cleaning cart. Stella gave her a little finger tip wave and says "CIO" as she skipped to the stairwell door. I was looking at the door where Stella just went out, along with Amber and Maria who was still giving me the "Momma Mia" look.

Then Amber says in a very "I know what you been doing" voice, "Well, Good morning Charlie," and slowly sauntered toward the swimming pool.

Chapter 10

After being looked at by Maria like I had been a "bad boy" for about ten minutes, I left the room and decided to go to Wal-Mart to buy some sneakers. "Nope, ain't going to Wal-Mart, I am going to Lakeside Mall. Where there are some real stores. Got a choice, don't have to buy just what they want you to buy."

I looked at my driver's license and was surprised to see it was still good for a year. I guess I can drive myself. I had not had a drink in three days, no shakes, no hangover, nothing. What a bummer.

I wonder if this is going to be the best I am going to feel. I went back to the Front Desk and "Robert" was on duty.

"Robert, I'm Charlie Gray. You take care of that little matter for me?" I asked, referring to Marla and Belle's account.

"Oh, Yes Sir! Let's see, yup they checked out last night about midnight, didn't say a word."

"Good" I said since I was expecting some trouble, but I guess it worked out okay.

I walked to the parking lot and discovered the van had four flats, and a broken window or two, the sides had been scratched as well.

"Spoke too soon I guess." I thought.

I went back to the Front Desk and asked about a rental car. Robert advised me that Enterprise was close and they would deliver to the motel.

"Get me a set of wheels sent over will you. Call me in the room when it gets here. I will give them an American Express Card if they want."

"We can take care of that Mr. Gray, you are a 'Golden Service Customer.' We just charge it to your Executive Service Account. What type of vehicle do you want?"

"Oh, I guess a Ford Diesel Pickup will do." I said to Robert.

"Oh, you must be teasing, but I can get you Lincoln Towncar, very reasonable. I have a friend that works there. Shall I do that?"

"Yeah, sure. Will they bring it over for me or do I have to get a cab?"

"Oh, they bring it. In fact, my friend Reginald will be the one bringing it down" Robert stated.

I nodded and walked away. "Figures he had a friend name Reginald," I thought and went to the room.

Maria, was just finishing up and was leaving. She didn't look at me or anything. I think she was pissed, don't know why. I wonder if she knows something I don't know? "I got four flats on my truck or van. I guess Marla and Belle did it." I told Maria.

"You should see the room. Miss Ames, she will file criminal charges on them. They trashed it," she said in a wonderful Spanish accent.

"Good, put their ass in jail." I said. "Maria? Why are you angry with me? I can tell." "Senor Gray, I am not angry with you," she said without looking at me.

"Maria, look at me. Was there a pillow and blanket on the couch?" I said as she looked back at the now clean room. "And wasn't my bed just wrinkled on the top as if I laid down?"

Maria looked at me and nodded. "Well, nothing happened, nothing." I stated as Maria smiled.

The phone rang and Robert told me the car was down there, but Reginald needed my signature on the rental contract. In a few seconds a neat young blonde haired "beach boy" looking man came up with a clip board, copied the credit card info and I signed the contract. I was given the keys and was told the car was parked under the front entrance portal.

Maria came out of the second bedroom with a arm full of towels. As I went by I kissed her on the cheek and "Adios, me corozone"

"Boboso" she said as she wiped her cheek. She said something like "get out of here" in Spanish, and I went down the back steps listening to her laugh.

I walked to the Front Desk and gave Robert my "twenty dollar" hand shake. His hand shake was soft and clammy.

"Oh wasn't he just gorgeous?" he bubbled, "Reginald, you know." "Uh yeah, I guess. If you like that type." I kept walking.

The car was a nice soft white, all the whistles and bells, lots of class. I got in and pulled out into the traffic and started for the Mall. I blew the exit and had to drive another mile or so to find a crossover that came back that way. I finally made it to the mall and went in the Sears' Automotive entrance.

After I got into the main part of the mall I found a direction map with an arrow that says "You are here" with a red arrow. I looked at that map like a nanny goat looking at a wrist watch.

"Good Morning, Mr. Gray" said a very pleasant voice. I looked around behind me and across the small passage was Cassandra Malloy Phillips.

"Good Morning, Ms Phillips" as she offered her hand, "How are you? And, what a pleasant surprise."

Which it was. Could this be the same lady that had me walk her out of the bar at the motel the other night?

She looked like "Suzy Homemaker" this morning, not the little trollop she was playing that night. However, she did leave alone and with style, and that counts. Besides, none of my business what she does. She is a grown woman, very grown, very much a woman.

I explained that I was looking for a place to buy a new pair of sneakers as we walked down the Mall's main passage.

"Well, there is a Foot Locker right here, I bet they could help you out," she gestured towards a store with several sale clerks dressed in referees shirts.

"Say, I appreciate your help…er, ah…you in a hurry?" I asked as I noticed she kept easing away from me down the hall.

"Yes, I need to get back. My daughter may be home and I need to talk to her before she goes to work." she said as she looked at her watch.

"You bet, take off. I guess I will see you around. Take care of the girl" and with that she went toward an exit.

"Very nice lady, worrying about her little girl like that," I thought as I went in the store and bought my sneakers..

I walked through the mall for half an hour and decided I had had enough of too many people. I don't know how City folks survive, but crowded places are not for me.

I walked out of the mall and drove back to the motel. When I entered the room, I noticed the little red light on the phone was blinking, telling me I had a message. I dialed in the correct numbers and received several messages. One was from Max Guerra, my lawyer, saying that "Yogi", his legal assistant would be in town tomorrow to discuss a few legal matters and had a few papers for me to sign. Stella called and said she would call back later. I wish I could have gotten her phone number.

"Yogi" Berra is a girl. Well, not a girl now, but she had went to high school with my daughter. I watched her grow up, get married and make a career for herself as Max's Legal Assistant. If fact, Yogi had done 99% of the work on the trust funds I had set up after I received the "inheritance money." Yogi was six feet tall or better with long blonde hair, very attractive and had a million dollar smile. She would turn heads walking down the street. The only thing she ever regretted about being over six foot tall was not being able to buy shoes, and Yogi was a "clothes horse" too, always dressed. Her husband was an Environmental Safety

Engineer for a major chemical company in the Houston area, a real great guy.

I tried on my new track suit and put on the sneakers I just bought. Well, I guess I am going to have to do some walking and exercise to get my self back in shape. I might even buy myself a few cans of "Slim-Fast." Yuck, but I need to get rid of what it took me thirty years to put on.

I picked up the phone and called the Front Desk. Maybe someone can tell me if I can hire a private Physical Fitness Instructor to work with me every day until I can get back in shape.

"Front Desk, Robert speaking, how may I help you?"

"Sorry, Robert, I'll call back," I said. "Very bad idea, I don't need any of his friends. I can see Amber tomorrow."

"Well, I guess today is as good as it gets to start working out and walking," I said aloud. I decided that a T-shirt would be all I needed to wear with the jogging pants. "I don't think I am ready for the shorts and all."

I walked downstairs and walked along the sidewalk towards the next major crossover for the highway. As I approached the corner I heard a horn honking. I looked around and saw a Ford F250 going the opposite way and woman waving. "I wonder who she is waving at?" I thought.

The pickup made an illegal U-turn when the light turned green and came to the curb where I was walking. The window went down and I recognized the driver as being Sassy Phillips.

"Well, good to see you so soon again, Miss Phillips." I said "I can't stop here, I going to pull into the next driveway by those apartments. You have a second?" she smiled.

"Of course, be right there." and started a fast walk, damn, almost a jog, to where she turned into a group of apartments. When I got there I noticed another woman in the truck with her.

"Mr. Gray, this is my daughter, Rebecca." she said.
"Rebecca, my name is Charlie Gray, just Charlie will do." she smiled and said hello. "Well, how about calling me 'Sassy.' I'm just a country girl from Oklahoma. I got the name when I was a kid. I couldn't say "Cassandra," which is my real name. So it ended up being 'Sassy,'" she explained with a very pleasant smile. I noticed she had freckles that blended in with the deep tan on her face, a tan from working years in the sun a lot.

"When you said you had a daughter at home, I was thinking about a little girl," holding my hand out about waist high. I looked at Rebecca and said "Rebecca, I see where you get you charm and beauty from, a beautiful mother".

Rebecca was looking out the passenger window, but turned towards me and looked without response, then returned to staring out the passenger window.

"Oops," I thought, "We have a little brat here."

"She is not a happy camper right now. Her car was giving her trouble, so she took it to her father to repair. He got it about half way repaired and his girlfriend came out and insisted they had to go somewhere. So I had to go get her. I will go home and she can take my truck to work." Sassy said.

"What I stopped you for Mr. Gray, sorry, Charlie." We both laughed about the similarity to the tuna commercial of years gone by. "What I was going to say is there is a hunting field trial next week in Pearl River. I thought maybe you would like to attend since you like labs."

"Are you inviting me, Sassy or am I suppose to go by myself." I asked.

"If you like, you can ride up with me. I guess you would need to know where the place is wouldn't you?"

"Yes, a lot easier to watch." she laughed.

"Where are you staying, Charlie?" And got her purse opened as if looking for a pen.

"I have a room at the Holiday Inn right over there," pointing back where I came.

"Oh, yes I know Amber Ames, the Manager very well. Okay, tell you what. I'll get back to you and give you the details. I'm off this next weekend and I think it would be fun. How about that?" she said as she put the pickup in gear as she prepared to leave. "Great, I'll pick you up where ever you say." I said.

"You may not want to put my dog in your car. I 'm running a dog. He will be a little wet"."

"Maybe not. Give me a call and we can work out the details." I steeped back from the pickup. "See ya, Rebecca," I said without seeing a response.

"Will do, see you." and she drove off.

Sassy did a 180 degree turn in the large lot and went back out on the street. When she made the turn, I heard the tires squeal as she accelerated. I also noticed that on the truck it had a heavy duty receiver hitch on it for a large trailer. "Wonder if she has a large boat?"

I was sweating after walking the four blocks. I guess I had a lot of bad stuff in me to make me sweat like that, but this was the way to do it, walking, and I was going to walk and get in shape...Right after I stopped at the Dairy Queen for a ice cream cone.

When I got back to the room, the little red light was blinking again. One was a recorded message from Stella and one from of all people, Yogi. What a sultry voice she had. It sounded like one of the voices on phones sex lines that I... er, ah...that I had been told about.

Yogi said for me to be up early, sober and be ready to take her to breakfast at "0800 hours." She liked to use European time since she had been overseas when her dad was in the Navy in Naples. In fact, she went to local Italian schools. She spoke Italian like a native when she was a child. It would be good to see her again.

I finally had a phone number for Stella. I called her and she answered after three or four rings.

"Charlie," she said. "Let me call you back. I am standing with a towel wrapped around me. I am in the shower."

"Yoooooooooooo!" I thought, "Okay, no problem."

I got in the shower and stood there like a duck in the rain for a long time. When I turned the water off, I could hear the phone ringing in the bedroom. I grabbed a towel, wrapped it around me, walked over and answered the phone, it was Stella.

"You ain't going to believe this..." but I told her I have a towel on now. We both got a chuckle out of that.

"Can I come over?" she asked shyly. "You know, just to talk again? I haven't had anyone to talk to in a long time, and well...We have no secrets now as they say."

"Of course, any time. Come on over, how long will it be?" I asked. She said about ten minutes. I had better hurry then. I went back in and shaved while I was standing there naked and looked at the steam covered mirror, what a scary sight.

"Boy, you look like Donald Duck. All gut and ass!" I said. "But starting tomorrow, that will change."

As I was standing there shaving, I was wondering what was up with Stella. "Not a bad looking woman, forty five years old or so, straight hair hanging down, bangs cut just above her eyes, very little make up. Has a nice figure I guess. Except for the blue ball gown she had on the other night, that is all I remember...Oh, yes! She has beautiful blue eyes, when she wears her contacts. The big glasses she has with dark lenses, orange I think."

There was a knock on the door. I answered it and there was a lady standing in the door. "Yes?" I said, smiling, she must have had the wrong room. "Stella?!" I said. "Stella?" "Hi Charlie, you like it?" the person standing there said.

"Stella?" I yammered again. "Uh, uh Stella?" I stepped back as if inviting her in.

Standing in MY room was a gorgeous creature. She had red hair and a haircut like J.R.'s momma from the Dallas

TV series had when she played Peter Pan. Mary Martin! Yeah, that was it. A Pixie cut I think it was called. Gone was the mousy looking little Stella and here stood a...a...I do not know what you would call it.

"Come in Stella. What have you done?" I said meekly.

"Went shopping. I felt so good when I left, so relieved, so something. I went shopping, haven't been shopping in years. I know I maxed out two credit cards, but I don't care. Look!" she demanded.

"I am looking. I don't believe what I am seeing. Stella?

She was wearing a white blouse like the ladies in Mexico wear, kinda low. Hell, I could almost see her nipples. And a skirt of some type, just a regular skirt, not too short, but for a lady her age, just right. Hell, I ain't a clothes critic, but it was real nice and I liked what I saw.

"Come over here and have a seat, please." I was almost bowing like some sissy dude in the movies.

She sat down on the couch where she had been before and I sat in the stuffed chair. When she sat down I saw a flash up her dress that was white. Oops, I saw her panties. I won't look, much.

Did she do that on purpose or..."Naaaaaah, what did I tell you about that?" I said to myself.

144

Stella was just bubbling over, happy.

"Charlie, after we talked...you know, about Stanley and all and what happened to me. You did not treat me like dirt or call me a whore or any bad names. I feel so much better. I can't explain it. Today is the first day of my new life."

Chapter 11

The next morning, Yogi Bera showed up at the Holiday Inn like she said she would. She called the room and I met her in the lobby. Yogi was dressed in a business- type dress and carrying a brief case.

"When did you get in?" I asked.

"I went to Baton Rouge and stayed with Jeff's folks. Had an easy drive over, only two hours from here to Baton Rouge. Come on, you are taking me to breakfast." she said and grabbed my arm.

"How is Jeff by the way? You know I have not seen him since...When was it?" I was thinking.

"Oh, who cares? I'm starved." Yogi whispered in a deep throaty voice as she grabbed my arm. I didn't have much choice about the matter either. When a six foot woman grabs your arm and says "Let's go," you had better be ready to un-ass wherever you are standing and start walking.

Just as we turned and crossed the lobby, I heard a door close behind us and Amber Ames said, "Good Morning, Charlie."

"Good morning, Amber. I would like you to meet my legal counsel, Eve Lynne Bera. 'Yogi,' this is Amber Ames, the Manager of the Hotel."

"Yogi? What a charming nick name." Amber said in a manner I had not heard before. I felt Yogi's grasp on my arm tighten and then relax.

They shook hands very politely and I explained we were on the way to the dinning room for breakfast. I also asked if she would like to join us, but she said she had a few things to take care of from over the weekend, especially "your two girls' room expenses."

Yogi spoke up and said she would talk to her later on that matter since she handled Charlie's legal affairs for her boss, Max the Mouth Piece.

"Good, I do look forward to chatting with you later on the matter," as we walked off. "Eve Jackson," I called her by her maiden name. "I have never seen this side of you. What is wrong?" I asked.

"I'm sorry, Charlie. Something about her just rubbed me wrong." she said as we were being seated by the morning waitress at the Holiday Inn Dining Room.

"You two are alike, both fire eaters." I chuckled.

Yogi and I discussed a few legal matters, taxes and an investment program, Shirley, my CPA and Max's wife, wanted me to get involved in.

"I dunno Yogi, doing the stock market thing is like shooting craps and I ain't lucky. I like houses and land, something I can see."

"Charlie, you know the money you gave to the MS Society last week? That was just the interest on the investments Shirley made for you. If we don't hurry, you are going to be paying taxes out the wah-zoo according to Shirley, think about it."

Yogi continued, "And also, the little 'party' you have had for the last year has the books in a mess. I have tried to keep a lid on things for you, but you and your friends traveling around the world doing a survey of the 'texture and color of the female topless dancer's nipples' ain't passing muster with Shirley. That is why I am here." she continued to unbraid me.

"Stop." I held up my hand like a traffic cop. "Yogi, I have taken the pledge. No more booze. Bart went back to San Antonio last week. We went on the wagon before he left and I have not had a drink since last. Oh, I think it was Friday afternoon and I am not going back there again." I said sincerely.

"Right, Charlie!" she said as the breakfast was served. "The check is in the mail and I promise not to...you know the rest."

After breakfast dishes were removed and during our second cup of coffee, Yogi excused herself and went to the ladies room. When she returned she leaned over and whispered that there was a cute little "red head" in the side office talking to Amber.

"I heard you're named mentioned," she said, "so I had to stop, woman's thing I guess. She looks like a hooker to me, and you a married man."

"Yogi, you could not be further off base. That is Stella." I said and I explained everything to her. Except the private story she has shared with me. "I'm going to try and hire her as a full time Administrative Assistant. I talked to her last night about it, and we cut a deal. She said she would think about it and she has a degree in secretary stuff. You know, the same thing you did while you went to college."

Yogi looked at me but did not say anything for a while.

"Okay Charlie, maybe it is a good idea. I will let Shirley know. What kind of 'deal' did you work out with her?" I questioned the way she said "deal."

I gave her the salary range we had discussed and added, "Look Yogi, I ain't sleeping with her and I don't plan to sleep with her." I did not add the part about her not liking sex and how she was repulsed by the idea.

"Okay Charlie, new subject. You know Robert Perez?" she asked. "He has been trying to get hold of you for the last few weeks. We kept telling him we didn't know where you were. He did not believe us."

"Bobby Perez...Yeah I know him, works for Customs. He is a dog handler, been there for a while too." I stated, "You get a phone number?"

"Yup, it is in the package here for you to go through." Yogi indicated to some papers on the table.

"Look, Yogi, let's go up to the room. We can talk better there. Plus, 'I gotta go pee.'" I said, trying to sound like Forrest Gump.

I signed the check and asked if Ramon could send up coffee and some little pastries to my room. While we getting ready to leave, Ramon walked to the kitchen door and gave me a big thumbs up and asked how many. I told him six or eight folks may be there.

Yogi and I walked out of the restaurant and started through the lobby as Stella was coming out of the motel office.

"Morning Stella, you get the stuff we need for the office?" I asked.

"Good morning," Stella said looking at Yogi. I made the proper introductions and kept walking. "No, I didn't get anything...number one. Nothing was open when I left last night and two, how am I going to pay for the stuff?" she said as we walked to the elevator.

I reached into my front pocket and handed her roll of bills. "Here, this should cover things to get started. I want steno-tablets for everyone. Also a couple of packages of long yellow tablets, you know the legal size, a package of pens, the good kind."

"And keep receipts for everything," Yogi chimed in. "Stella, if we are going to work together, you are going to have to take care of him. Receipts, receipts and more receipts."

"I know, just like a man. Women have been looking after them for years. So I guess because he has a lot of money. I will have to help him keep track of it." They looked at each other and gave a knowing nod.

When they walked into the room, Charlie asked Stella to get in touch with Amber and ask her if she could come up for a meeting. Stella grabbed a folder of stationary from the table and started making notes.

While Stella was calling Amber, Yogi and I sat down at the table and broke out some legal papers. Yogi explained what each of them were for and Charlie signed them. In about ten minutes, Yogi started stuffing papers back in a very expensive briefcase as if she were getting ready to leave.

"Charlie, I going to go down to an Office Max near here to get supplies, anything special I need to get?" Stella asked.

"Yeah, look around, we are going to set up the other suite across the hall into an office if we can get Amber's' heart right. We will need desk, tables, chairs, the whole nine yards. Think about it and we will need. Also, computers, we will need one for me and you and lap tops for each of the troops we hire. You know anything about computers. Stella?"
I asked.

"Er, ah, yes ...I do. I...er...ah." she stammered.

"Charlie you are asking me to spend money like...like it's going out of style." Stella stood, awed.

"This ain't nothing. Wait till we get a full head of steam up. Also, call the dealership where we bought the van and tell them to come get it repaired. I think I seen a card in the glove box when you and I were out driving the other day. Call that dude and tell him to come get it and have it fixed A.S.A.P.

There is a sticker on the rear saying where I bought it if you can't find the card. Got it?" "Got it." she said. "I'm gonna like her, she is sharp." I thought.
"Yogi, where are you staying tonight?" I asked.

"Well, I was going to Jeff's folks tonight in Baton Rouge...." Yogi stated.

"Nah, I would like you to stay here, need you. We are going to form a company and you are going to be a principle. I will need your advice on this matter. Can you do it?" I asked.

"Well, yes. Sure, if you need me."

"Good. Done deal, I have an extra bedroom here or you can have Bart's room. " "I'll take Bart's room and...er, ah..."

"I don't blame you, but I was hoping I could brag about having a six foot tall blonde staying in my room. Improve my image."

"Charlie, you could have a homosexual billy goat in your room and it would improve YOUR image." and we laughed.

I looked at Stella and she just stood there. "You back already?" I chuckled. "Here are the keys to the car and I think there is gas." I said.

"I would rather take mine, easier to park at the mall." She went out the door.

When Stella went out, I went over to my "boot bank" and checked what the balance, the side pockets were empty.

"Charlie, what are you doing", Yogi asked.

"Oh, I keep a little spare change in the sides of these boots. Easier than going to the bank, all I have is an American Express Card. Sometimes I need cash." I answered.

"You have a Visa Gold card with no limit. Where is it?" Yogi stated.

"You mean this thing? Never have used it, said I have to have a PIN number. Can't remember what it was, lost the paper it was wrote on."

"Give it to me." Amber went over to the phone and dialed a number. "Nina Jackson, please," she said when someone answered.
"Nina? Yogi...No, I'm in New Orleans with Charlie Gray...Yup, that Charlie Gray... " they talked for a moment, "Look, can you get me a new PIN Number for his card. He has not used it and he needs to start...Okay, I'll wait.... Good, got it." She wrote it down on a piece of paper. "Okay Nina, tell Mom hello and call Jeff for me and tell him I will be home when I get there....Okay, bye."

On Friday, we had all the nuts and bolts in place: phone lines for computers, direct lines for office phones and fax's, a copy machine. Bart's rooms were emptied and replaced with office furniture and we were rocking and rolling. Stella started bringing her Chihuahua, "Chico" to work. Chico would just sit on the couch and bark. We also had three rooms down the hall rented "just in case"

On Monday, I got in touch with Bobby Perez in El Paso and learned he had been in a terrible crash, lost his wife and daughter. An eighteen wheeler was going too fast on an overpass curve and overturned. The liquid he was carrying caught fire. Bobby was thrown out, the others were not, terrible. It happened about a year ago.

I invited Bobby out for a visit, my treat. He did not say it, but I suspect he was burned. He mentioned that he had been in the hospital until about a month ago and he was not working. He was a very handsome man according to the reactions of the girls, small thin moustache and dark complexion, good manners and well dressed. I told him I would have someone meet him at the New Orleans International Airport.

"Okay, will do. I'll buy my own ticket, I ain't no charity case." he said. "Okay, pal, but you do want me to meet you, right?" I asked.

"Sure, but if you don't come, and send someone, how will I know who to meet?"

"Just look for the best looking red head you have ever seen" I said to him knowing that Stella was close enough to hear. "Send me the flight info when you get it, Okay?"

"Good show, see you Friday, and Charlie?....Thanks" and hung up. "Your sweet, Charlie." Stella said.

I did not tell her a thing concerning what Bobby told me about Marta and Michelle, she would learn.

"Well, you had better watch that 'Mes'kin,' and keep a half hitch on your knickers. You know what they say about Latin Lovers." I said jokingly to her.

"Really? Are they like that, Charlie?" She stopped what she was doing.

"You know Charlie, while I was at Office Max, a man actually flirted with me. I had a feeling…I can't understand it. A strange feeling, felt nice." she said with a certain dreaminess.

"Stella, you are a pretty woman, a good looking red head. Don't ever forget that." I earnestly told her.

She blushed and returned to what she was doing.

"To be as old as she is, she sure is naïve. Ain't been around much." I thought as I watched her out of the corner of my eye.

"By the way, will you pick him up for me on Friday? Bring him back here and just make him feel comfortable?" I asked.

"Well, if that is what you need. What am I supposed to…you know, Do? You said he might…Charlie I don't…you know." She said.

I laughed and said that he was a perfect gentleman and she had nothing to worry about. Just take him to his room and tell him the three of us will go out to supper tonight. "Anyone like Cracker Barrel?"

"Oh, by the way, while you were on the phone, Sassy Phillips called and left a number." She said as she placed the "While You Were Out Memo" on my desk and left the room, walking briskly.

I returned the call to Sassy. She said we needed to leave her house about 6:00am on Saturday for the Field Trial and to meet her at her house. Sassy explained that I needed to drive about 500 yards past the main entrance to the Polo Grounds and turn right at the first drive. She would have the outside lights on.

'You bet, I'll be there with bells on." and hung up.

"Well, T.G.I.F. and in about ten minutes, I have to leave to go pick up your friend Bobby Perez from El Paso." She looked at her watch. "When he gets here, what you want me to do with him?"

"Give him one of the rooms down the hall. I'm going to the auto dealership and talk to them while you are gone. Anything need to be done?"

"Nope." She said and looked around.

"Well, you're going to dinner with Bobby and me?" I asked. "Well, no…I, ah…you got old times to talk about and all, I guess."

"I would like you to be there. Besides, you been working hard, and I owe you." I smiled at her.

"Well, I will need to go home and change…Okay, will do."

"By the way, where do you live? I know one thing, you ain't been spending much time there have you?" I turned to start turning off equipment.

"No, sure haven't. In fact, I brought some stuff up to the room on the end. Been staying there next to the one Yogi had, but since she went home, I guess I will too for the weekend."

"Well, make sure Bobby gets one of them, and I don't care if you use it if you want to. That is what we got them for. In fact, we have this whole little corner here now don't we?" meaning the two suites and four regular queen-size rooms.

"Stella, why don't you like Sassy? She seems real nice to me. Amber likes her and you like Amber." I asked as we were leaving the room for the parking lot.

"I dunno, Charlie. I guess it is because of Stanley. Stanley is head over heals in love with her and well…she…I dunno. I'll talk to you later, I don't want to be late picking up Bobby for you." and she walked off.

Chapter 12

I got back from the car dealership about 8:30 that evening and there were two messages on the answering machine in the office. One said Bobby had arrived and was in one of the rooms down the hall. The next message was from Stella saying that she and "Roberto" were going out to supper and would not be back till late, so I went to bed.

I got up at 0430 and had some juice and coffee and drove out to Sassy's house. As I drove in, she was putting dogs in a nice all stainless steel Jones 6 dog trailer. Now I saw why she had a heavy hitch on the truck. I stopped about halfway down the drive and noticed the trailer had inside lights for the dogs to enter the trailer and outside "work" lights.

The pups came out of the kennel on a heel and did not break until they were told to "take a break", until released.

I do not know how many dogs Sassy had all together, but the two that I saw get in the trailer were impressive.

Big, broad chested dogs from what I could tell from the outside lights.

I parked my car where she indicated and she asked if I would like to come in for a cup of coffee. "No," I told her, I had better not. "I get to drinking coffee and have to go pee every ten miles."

We entered the truck, started down the road and hit the interstate heading north at a good speed. I noticed that she was pulling the Jones Trailer at a steady at 75 mph.

When we got off the interstate there was a slight rain. Sassy tried to put the brakes on too quickly and we slid through a red light. As luck would have it, no one was coming the opposite way.

Watching a "retriever field" trial dog work will show you every move that needs to be made when working a scent discriminating dog. With slight modifications, no matter what the breed, you will have a dog searching. The secret is to have the basic retriever training on the dog. The dog must be brave and bold, you cannot train out "gun shyness" or a "scary-fearful" behavior in a dog.

There are different tools to be used but the idea is the same. Some have rubber or plastic retrieving dummies or a wooden buck. The idea is to be at a "sit-stay-heel", watch the dummy fall, no matter where it comes from. If you throw it or have a second person throw it, the dog will watch "where" it falls and then go toward it and return with it. It is a simple game of fetch, very simple, but people will not do it. They want to put bangles and bobbles on a dog and call it training.

Another issue is selection of the dog, not the breed, grant you. There are breeds I like better than others, but I also select the right dog for the job. The further we get away from the basics, the less we find a good dog for the program.

I want a dog to have his head "up" or "down" when searching, dog's choice, not to follow a "man-made rule." These were rules made by man to make HIM look better in his own eyes. In sport tracking that is apparently okay, but in real time, all "man rules" must end. When a dog is in the wild and chasing prey, they do not run up to the hole and "sit" and look for someone to say "good doggie". They dig, scratch, and they try to get the prey out of the hole.

We watched the dogs go in the water and cross the lake to the far bank, "searching" for the duck in this case, and return the exact same route to the handler. We are talking a distance of several hundred feet for the dog to travel.

These same dogs can be trained easily, in just a few days, for any scent work you want them to do, if you have the basic retrieving drills in place. There is an exception of course and that is the issue of explosives. You will need to modify the alert the dog gives since the "finding" is usually fine, but the "alerts" may cause a problem.

You can always put the "whoa" on a dog, you just cannot put the "go" into one.

Also, do not believe the person that tells you a Labrador Retriever will not do bite work. You will find out that they will, but they are "dirty." They do not play by the ring sport rules.

The Egyptian Pyramids are a marvel of the world, but what would they look like if built upside down, standing on the pointy end? They would fall over. Training a dog is the same way. You need to have a nice broad base that you can build on. That base will be "come-sit-stay-mark-back-out." Again, no matter what you want to train a dog for, once you get these down, you can train for anything. If a dog fails high up on the pyramid of training, then you can go back down a couple of steps and try again. That is why you need to have a broad base to work from.

Sassy ran three dogs that day and two of them did great, a good showing, and qualified for a "fun trial" coming up in the Bayou State Club. The third pup had a bad day. She did not come back the same way she went out, called "bank running," but that happens no matter how good you are.

That evening while we were driving back, we stopped at a restaurant to eat supper, nothing serious, just talking "dog." I told Sassy of the plans I had and how we would run it. She listened while I talked and did not make any comments until I was through.

"What will it pay? Sassy asked.

I gave her a figure and the side benefits. She raised her eyes and thought it was a good salary.

"Can I be considered?" she asked.

"Yes, when I start hiring, you will be given a chance to interview. Right now I only have two people on the payroll: Bart Duffy and Stella Dunn." "Stella? But I don't know this Bart guy."

"Something wrong with Stella?" I asked, noting how she had said Stella's name. "She is good at her job."

"Well, Stella sure don't like me. Called me a slut and whore more than once. Was going to tear her head off, but Stan stopped me. You would think she was his Momma the way she jumped all over me. I think she is jealous, but she is too old for him. I told her to leave the Polo Club Bar and sober up once. All I was doing was dancing with him one night when the crowd was light. The Polo Club had paid for the band. Why waste it? I'm a big girl and know what I want" "Stan is kinda sweet on you isn't he?"

"Yeah, I guess. He asked me to marry him about six months ago. We had a thing going, but I don't need the "wife" shit. Just got out that scene a few years ago. I am happy with my life. Some folks don't like it, but they will just have to live with it. He hasn't given up and I have been told he is not seeing anyone else. Stan is nice enough and of course he is part of the 'New Orleans Old Money.' I know

Stella was really pushing Amber his way. Amber and I are friends…" She let it drift off.

It was almost 9:00 o'clock in the evening when I got back to my room. I went across the hall to the office area just to look. I could hear the band down in the club going "boom de-boom de-boom." There was a note from Stella that said, "Charlie, we are going to go downtown New Orleans and have a real nice supper. See Ya, SMD." There were little hearts and "x's" on the note. "Hmmmm, not like Stella, but she sounded so happy." I thought.

I went across the hall to the rooms and clicked on the TV to see what was on. There were 99 channels and nothing good on. I watched the History Channel for a while. Hell of a way to spend a Saturday night, alone and sober.

Three weeks later on a Monday morning, I had scheduled a meeting for a planning session. I invited Amber, Bobby, Stella and Sassy to attend and do some chalk board planning. Roberto Javeiar Perez-Mendoza was on the payroll now, his knowledge of dogs more than justified his salary. I had not heard from Bart Duffy so I had Stella call one or two people who might have known where he was. I checked with Shirley, my accountant, to see if he had been using his Bowl Weevil Foundation credit cards. I was told he had used them several weeks previously to buy a plane ticket from New Orleans to San Antonio on Continental Airlines and nothing else. However, the currents month's bill has not come in.

"Shirley, do me a favor let me know next time they are used. I am worried about him and I thought he would have called. I have Stella trying to contact one of his kids." I asked concerned.

"Charlie, I got Dale Powell on hold", Stella said in a stage whisper. I nodded at Stella and raised one indicating "hold on one minute".

"Mr. Powell, may I ask you to hold on a second while Mr. Gray finishes another call? Thank you very much," she said. I nodded, indicating that I understood. Stella was on a portable phone from her desk and as she walked by Robert standing at the copy machine she "goosed" him. I was looking from a different direction, but the mirror on the wall where a dresser had been when this was a motel room and not an office, showed their reflection. I didn't see it happen, but I saw Bob jump as she went by. I knew he was "goosey" if you poked him in the ribs. He jumped and Stella giggled like a high school girl. Boy, did I create a monster, but Bobby was happy too.

Dale Powell was a Deputy Sheriff in the county where Bart Duffy lived and was friends with Bart. Dale informed me that Kay, Bart's wife, was dying of cancer. She had only found out a few weeks before Bart left with me, but did not want to call him. Dale said Kay were in the cancer ward of a hospital in San Antonio and gave me a phone number to the room where she was. I thanked Dale and made a few minutes of small talk before I hung up.

I dialed the number and a man answered the phone. I said this is Charlie Gray and may I speak to Bart Duffy.

"Yo, Charlie" a small and flat voice said. "Bart?" I asked "Yeah…she's dying Charlie." and he started sobbing like no human being can describe. Words cannot be made to explain the feeling you have when hearing your friend sob like this.

There was nothing I could say, nothing I could do. This sobbing went on for a full five minutes.

I was on the speaker phone and did not realize that the others had come from the other rooms to the door and were just standing there. Stella had a tissue up to her eyes. Amber just stood and looked at the phone. Robert walked out of the room and I heard the room door softly click. He had been there not too long ago and did not want to go back.

"I should have been here for her, Charlie. Instead I was out trying to re-capture youth and I…" he started sobbing again.

"Charlie, this is Alicia," a very small voice said. "Charlie, this is not a good time. Just leave us alone. I think you have done enough. Just leave Daddy alone." and the phone connection was cut.

I was stunned, "My Gawd, what have I done? What did I…." I looked to the others for support.

But they were leaving the room. I was responsible and had to take the heat.

I did the automatic dial for Shirley's and Max' private line. Max picked up and I explained about Bart and Kay. He listened as I explained that I wanted everything that could be done for Kay and Bart. "Max, I know you got connections at that hospital. Make it happen." I said. "And call me back, keep me up to speed." Max acknowledged and hung up.

I felt like shit.

Robert came back into the office, shut the door and just stood there as tears ran down my face. "What have I done?" He said nothing.

The first time I saw Bobby Perez after he arrived, after Stella left him alone long enough for us to talk, I was sad by what I saw. Bob had been burned on his left side where the acid and fire had stuck to him when he was thrown out of his car. The skin was scarred, but he had most of the use of his left hand and arm. He showed me how he could not close his fist completely, but did not seem to bother him. His left ear and the left side of his face were disfigured as well, but he was still a great looking man and his smile was worth a million dollars, and Stella did not seem to mind. If Bobby was in the room when she walked in? She just went to a high glow and so did he. I cannot describe it any better.

Robert talked about the wreck. I knew his wife and daughter, wonderful human beings. Bobby told me it took him a while but he has learned to live with it. "Stella is a big help too," he added as he turned to lay his hand on Stella's hands which were on his shoulder from behind. Robert was setting in a chair. He did not go any further than that. I also felt that he had finished and did not want to talk anymore. So he stood up and left the office and went to the hall. Stella walked with him and after a few minutes I noticed she was back at her desk. I did not know where Robert went.

Needless to say, there was no meeting that morning. I walked out of the office, into the hall, and over to my room. I had not noticed, but Sassy was standing down by the elevator smoking a cigarette and seated on a small bench. She had not said a word during this last ten minutes of the ordeal and heart wrenching sadness.

She followed me into the room and took the car keys from me that I had picked up off the dresser and led me down the stairs, more or less. We walked over to the car and she "clicked" the doors open. I got in with her and she drove away.

Sassy drove towards New Orleans proper, but not in a hurry. She just drove down side streets I did not know or think I would care to know, but we came out on a beautiful flower covered circle. The street was paved with bricks and there were flowers carefully groomed along the sidewalks. Large trees covered the streets and were curved where large trucks had hit the limbs and kept them trimmed back. It was very relaxing.

Sassy parked the car on a side street and we got out. Not a word had been said for the last 45 minutes since we had left the motel. I looked at the houses. They were old but extremely well preserved, exclusive turn of the century houses.

"I used to live in that house, Charlie," she said pointing to one particular house. "Lived there for ten years. Rebecca was born there and I use to bring her to this very bench and watch her play as a child," she said as she lit a cigarette. "But I can never come back to this house, to this era, it's gone. She said as we got up to stroll to nowhere.

"And I am glad. I played the perfect housewife. Made sure the party was perfect and then after everyone went home, I was called a whore, bitch, slut and accused of sleeping with one or more of the guests. Sometimes he hit me." she said as she folded her arms and stared at the house.

"But I left this golden lined hell hole and I come here ever so often to celebrate my freedom and it makes me feel good. I see the fancy grill work as bars."

"Why did you bring me here?' I asked, talking for the first time since we arrived. We had started walking back towards the car, her arm was tucked in mine as we walked.

"I dunno, Charlie. I just call it 'my place.' To come and relax and remember what used to be. Now if you like it can be 'our place.' I always feel better after I come here. I hope you do." She said when we got in the car.

I did feel better. She just told me that money could not buy everything. Sassy is a hell of a woman.

Chapter 13

The days were getting cooler as we started getting closer to Thanksgiving. The Bayou Country is always nice but those days were bright with sunshine that makes you want to do something outside. Robert had caught on and took charge of getting us land and a kennel built. We could start training facilities, jumps and obstacle courses at the same time.

Robert was given complete authority and control of the project since he knew what needed to be done. The kennel floors needed to be "glass slick" with a one inch drop for every three feet of length. This meant that an eighteen foot long and four foot wide kennel would have a six inch drop going towards a drain. This insured that the kennel could be kept as clean as possible. The hoses plugged into a water supply overhead using a short four foot hose.... there would be no dragging hoses in and out of a run. Inside the kennel proper was a four by four kennel house with a sliding gate where a dog can be isolated when required.

Robert put a lot of thought into making this kennel.

Over the outside kennel runs, Robert was having a roof built over the whole kennel that was open on all sides. This kept the overhead sun off the kennels, but allowed for a breeze. In the Southern states, heat is something that needs to be considered whenever building kennels.

Robert had bought 500 acres of sugar cane land next to a major bayou with access to a large lake. We could use this for "water work" with all the dogs. However, the land was diverse so we could have plenty of good tracking.

Amber gave notice to the Holiday Inn folks and planned to continue with them until they found a replacement. Amber said that the management company had been good to her and she was not going to cut them loose without notice.

Amber worked day and night. She did her hotel work in the day and at night did what she could with the Bowl Weevil Foundation. Amber was tasked with the physical fitness and firearms training of the team. She and Robert were working together designing a training course for the canines and for the people. It was her responsibility to come up with automatic weapons and side arms we might encounter while doing an operation.

Even if we never used them, it would still be fun to do.

I had only one rule for her, I did not want any involvement with "gun nuts," paramilitary, "I'm against the world" groups and such. Amber was in complete agreement and suggested that when it came to the weapons, we lease them from a collector instead of going through all the ATF jumps to get a license that was needed to have certain weapons. With all the anti-gun groups running around, we did not need it. Amber was also looking into building a state of the art gun range, but had run into EPA problems. She suggested that we use a range that was already in place.

"Great idea, start looking around, but I don't want our name involved with bad actors. Okay?" I said very firmly.

Stella had put the office into shape. She had bought mainframe computers, laptops, printers and all the other goodies needed to run a proficient company. We all had a pager and cell phones.

But we still had one problem, vehicles. I thought that would be the easiest, but I was wrong.

I had asked Sassy to come and work for with us on several occasions. She had not refused, but she was hesitant. The bottom line was that she enjoyed working at the Polo Club and was in charge. She needs to be "in charge" I guess after all the years of being "controlled," and she was good at her job.

We had been given an extended "guest" membership at the Lake Side Polo Club for our group. We had all the privileges except voting rights at the club. Which was okay with me, as I never planned on attending business meetings anyway.

Stanley Hines had called me and asked if I was trying to hire Sassy away from him. I was up front with him and said, "You bet, but she won't do it."

"I don't think she will leave here. We have an agreement and friendship." Stan said.

I noted the way "agreement" was spoken, but kept my own council. I bet Sassy did not know about this.

Back to vehicles, I still had to buy or lease vehicles. My plans were to allow each person to select their own vehicle if they could justify why they wanted it. Stella had heard me discussing this idea of vehicle leasing several times but has said nothing.

"Stella, have you decided what type of vehicle you are going to submit for?" I asked one day.

"Er…I..er…No I hadn't." She said. "I didn't think it included me. You know, since I am going to only be in the office." she said. "Oh, Yeah?" I snorted. "Who made that rule?"

"Well, no one in…I only thought since I am not going to be a handler or whatever, it did not include me."

"Stella, you are wrong, but I have contacted every 'slick Willie' car dealer around and they all have a wild idea I am going to pay big bucks since it hit the Times-Picayune Newspaper I donated a few buck to MS. Since you showed me how to look on the computer on-line service for car leasing, well…I know what is right. You got any ideas?"

"Yes, I do. Let me make a few calls." Stella said firmly in a manner I had not heard before.

A few minutes later Stella came in and told me to grab my hat and go with her. Since I was not involved in a major management decision and only playing a video game, I decided to go.

We drove several miles north of the motel to a small town between New Orleans and Baton Rouge, and made an exit toward a dealership that you would not even notice unless you lived in the area. Since it was before noon, we were the only "lookie-lou's" as customers in the auto business were called.

When I drove the big Towncar into the parking lot, a man walked out dressed like a typical car salesman, white shirt and tie with a Panama straw hat. A nice middle aged man with a sincere smile watched us walk up.

"Hi, I'm Art Nelson owner of …Stella?" he stared at Stella. "Hi Art, how are you doing?" she beamed at him. "Wha…How…ah, how are you?" is all he could get out.

Stella had toned down, I guess you could say, her red hair to a softer color red. I would call her a roan if she was a cow pony. I think strawberry blonde may be a way of putting it. I know that it looked a lot nicer. Stella had also toned down the clothes she wore too. Nice business suits and dress sets. I do not know much about ladies clothing, but I liked what she was doing now.

Art and Stella gave each other a hug, sorta, and Art just looked at her.

"This ain't the frumpy lady you knew a few months ago Pal," I thought as we walked in to the showroom to get out of the late fall showers that were spitting.

"When you called this morning to see if I was here…I'm sorry I couldn't talk but I was having a sales meeting. That's why I told Margie to have you just come see me. I had to let a few folks go. Business has been down this last quarter. Hey, come on in." We walked back to a private office.

"I'm sorry, I didn't remember your name, Sir." he said, turning to me.

"Charlie Gray, Art. Yeah, Stella will knock your socks off won't she?" as Stella blushed. I was enjoying this, one of her old boy friends I bet. "Hee, hee, hee." I laughed.

For the first time Art looked at me out of the corner of his eye as if to say, "okay, who is the old dude?"

"Let me make some fresh coffee. I'll be right back." He said as he hurried out the door, almost running.

"I'm proud of Art. He started here as a salesman and now he owns it." as she spun around quickly making her skirt stand out a little, only for a split second, giddy girl stuff.

I didn't say a word for a long time as she walked around the office walls looking at the baseball sponsors plaques and "High Sale for the District," normal stuff like that.

Art burst back into the room with a small tray and three cups of coffee, packets of sugar and creamer.

"Stella, how can I help you and Mr. Gray?" he said as he sat down behind his desk.

"Oh, not me Art. Charlie here wants to buy or lease a few vehicles." she gestured towards me.

"A couple?" He showed real interest in me.

"Yeah, I do. Need to know the best route to go. Need for you to crunch a few numbers for me. Can you do that?" I said as I pulled my Purina P.M.I. baseball cap off.

"Sure, let's get down to it," Art said as he took a pad from his desk.

Stella was so distracting to Art by just being there that at one point I had thought of asking her to step out of the office. She did nothing but just sat there, crossing and uncrossing her legs, joining the conversation as my

"Administrative Assistant" should have done. She also had a note pad and wrote items down as we covered them.

Once we had agreed on what I wanted, Art said he would have to "crunch the numbers" and get back to me. "Could I come to your office later today or tomorrow with final figures on this deal, Charlie?" he asked.

"Sure! Sure! Sure! Take your time. Get with Stella here and make a date, she will handle the schedule if you don't mind?" I said.

"Wish I could make a date, but I am a married man." We all laughed at the little joke.

"How is Raynell, Art?...and of course your son. I see he played baseball last season." Stella said looking at the baseball plaques.

"Ryan is fine, great kid, going to be an athlete too. Raynell is at her mother's in Memphis. She had a stroke several months ago and she is there helping out. Nobody but Ryan and I at home now, so I am a house husband or whatever it is called." He said as we walked out the door.

After the normal departure handshakes and hugs, we got in the car and headed back south towards New Orleans.

"I didn't know you knew him. You really took him down didn't you? He was really looking at you."

I stated as we pulled the big Towncar out into traffic. "Old boyfriend?" "Nope, ex-husband".

We drove back towards New Orleans in silence. Stella had a knowing little smile on her face, but said nothing for ten minutes.

"Raynell's daddy used to own the dealership. When Art went to work there, she worked in the office and now he married the boss's daughter." she laughed.

"What's funny about that?" I questioned Stella.

"She is a cow." She laughed really hard about that. I laughed too, don't know why, but Stella was enjoying this.

As we drove I wondered if Robert was at the new kennel site. I asked Stella if she new a short cut to get there coming from this direction. She directed me down different roads until we reached the kennel building site and I saw Robert standing in front of the old plantation house which had brush and vines growing all over the front. It had broken windows and the porch was falling down.

I drove up to where they were standing and Stella and I got out. Stella walked over to Robert and was standing beside him. I do not think she even realized she did it. She and Robert greeted each other without saying a word.

I was introduced to the contractor and we talked a few minutes about the estimate. He showed me a clipboard he was holding and told me it was a rough guess on bringing the house "up to code."

We looked at the pages as he explained what he was going to do. I nodded and said "It sounds great but you will have to satisfy young Robert there. Robert…Robert, Yo!" as he and Stella were just looking at each other a few yards away.

"Oh, yeah Charlie. Sorry, we were discussing something….er…Yeah, what do you need?" he blushed.

We ended the little chat and were ready to leave.

"Bobby, anything on the boat dock and boat house yet?' I asked.

"I am having to deal with a couple of politico types. I think they have their hands out. What shall I do?"

Robert said as he kicked a little dust in the ground. "Mordida?" I asked.
"Si, possible."

"Cuanto?" I asked about how much.

"Un mil dolores. Yo no se" Robert said as he looked at me.

Give the son of a bitch a $500.00 donation to his favorite charity in cash. If he balks on you, we will find someone to run against him and beat his ass. "Capeche?"

"Si, jefe." Robert laughed as Stella and I got in the car.

I rolled down the window and asked Robert, "How long do you think it will be before we can move in, Bobby? Best Estimate?"

"Oh, a realistic date will be 1 April for a turn key operation. This guy is supposed to be real good. His brother is a cousin to my wife's people." He laughed.

This is a running joke in South Texas, about who your "Primos"(cousins) are.

I was rolling up the window when an old car came driving up. I cannot even tell you what kind, it was in pretty bad shape. It looked like an old Plymouth Fury with the big fins. In the car was a woman about twenty five or thirty years old, hard to tell. In the back were two small children wrapped in a blanket. They were a sad looking lot. The woman had on a Levi jacket with a T-shirt that was dirty, just dirty. I noticed the two children were eating a baloney sandwich with nothing on it and drinking water out of a one liter Coke bottle.

There were boxes scattered over the back seat and the trunk lid was tied down with a piece of cord. At that time I did not understand what I was seeing.

"You the foreman here?" she asked.
"No, I'm not the foreman. He is over there by that building someplace" Robert answered. "He hiring any

hands?" she asked with her hands in her back pockets and swinging here dirty hair out of her face as she looked over towards the building site where the new kennel was going to be.

"I don't know. You will have to ask him." Robert said.

"Thanks," she said as she walked to where Robert had pointed. "You kids stay here and be good while I'm gone, you hear?"

I looked at the children and neither one had made a move since she stopped. The position of the sandwich was still just barely up to their lips.

These were preschool children. I couldn't tell if they were boys or girls, but one did not have a shirt on that I could see. I leaned over into the car and I could smell urine very strong. The other child was wrapped up tightly in a ragged dirty blanket.

In a short time the young lady, I still could not tell how old she was, came back. She looked real "hang dawg" is all I can say, very sad.

She started to get in the car and I asked. "Young lady?" as she turned to me. "You get a job?"

She just shook her head and would not look at me and kept going to the car. "You want one?" I asked.

All of a sudden she looked up at me and said after looking at all of us for a long time. "Doing what?"

Robert answered a little too quick, but not meaning anything by it said, "Does it matter?"

"What do I have to do?" again questioning the authenticity of the offer.

Robert and Stella both looked at me. "Maintenance, here on the place. You live near here Miss...er...Miss?" I was fishing for a name.

"Pat, Patricia Cox. Yeah, I live down on Bayou La Rose." she said.

"What's the address?" I asked.

"Ain't no address. We just camped out down there, got a little cardboard shack for me and the kids." She said as a matter of fact.

I just stood there. I didn't know what to say. What was the best way to handle this? "Well, do I get the job? I can't get no food stamps or anything because I ain't got no address. Mister, I need this job. I'm broke...spent my last three dollars getting kids a sandwich and stuff. I spent all morning picking up cans to get that. My gas gage is broke, and I ain't real sure I can get back to where I'm staying." she said in desperation.

"You got the job. Ready to go to work?" I asked.

She nodded and started to have tears in her eyes. She reached down and grabbed the tail end of a dirty T-shirt and wiped her eyes.

"Robert, see that she and the kids get to the motel and well... We can start from there." I said.

"Look, Mister. I ain't much, but I ain't no whore and I ain't starting with you," as she glared at me. "Not yet anyway."

"Good, but you need a bath and the kids need a bath. Robert will take you to your place and pick up whatever gear you have and bring it to the hotel," I said.

"I ain't got nothing there. I have to bring it all or someone will steal it. What about my car?" she asked.

"It will be okay here, no one will steal it. What have you got in the car you want to take with you?" Robert asked.

She got the kids out of the car and put them in Robert's four door Ford diesel pickup. She went through several boxes and took a few items out with her. The children were clinging to her and would not let go. It was a pitiful scene.

I motioned to Stella to go with Robert and...and what was her name? Ah yes, Patricia Cox.

Stella got in the truck and they left for New Orleans, about half an hour away.

After they drove away, I went over to the foreman of the job and told him what I had done. I asked if he could put her on the payroll and I would reimburse him her salary.

"Mr. Gray, I am sorry, but I can't do it. I work only union craftsmen and I get these type showing up to ever job and my insurance won't cover her either. I wish I could help, I do, .but..." he did look concerned.

"Okay, Whitey, I understand. I just thought...Yeah, business is business." I said and walked off.

When I got back to the hotel I saw that Robert's truck was there, but I did not see Stella's car. I went up to the office suite and looked in. Robert was there going through messages when I walked in.

"Where are they, Bobby? " I asked.

"Stella went to buy them some clothes. One of the kids didn't even have any underwear on and messed in the blankets coming back. Stella went somewhere to get them a couple of pair of panties and shorts or something, I dunno. She just ran out saying something about withdrawing from the 'boot bank.' You know what she was talking about?" Robert looked at me with a puzzled look.

I smiled and knew it would be okay. Stella was on the job.

"By the way, here is a message on the answering machine from Sassy Phillips, wants you to call." Robert said as he tossed the messages back on the pile on Stella's desk.

"Okay, thanks" I said.

"Oh, here is one from Amber, said she was flying to Rangoon. That's in Burma?" "Nope, West Virginia, that's where she was raised. Funny, thought she would have said something." I thought as walked to the phone.

I called Sassy but did not get an answer. However, when the answering machine came on I just said "This is Charlie" and hung up. I hate those damm things anyway.

In a short time Stella came back in with a load of packages. I could tell she had been to Wal-Mart by the blue plastic bags. No one in this world can hide a Wal-Mart bag.

Stella came in her office while I was standing in the middle of the room reading a fax and talking to Robert. She did not say a word. She just walked in, reached in her desk and got a key out and went across the hall to my room. Then went in the bedroom door and to my dresser.

Robert and I were standing in such a manner we could see everything. He looked at me and I looked at him, shrugged my shoulders and watched as Stella went and got two undershirts out.

"Night gowns" she said as Robert and I both nodded like we knew that.

In a flash, Stella had gone down the hall. Robert and I still holding the papers we were reading as we went to the hall and watched as Stella enter one of the rooms we had rented.

"Oh, well Bobby. I think we just saw a woman with a mission." I also noticed a dining room waiter rolling a food cart towards the room.

Robert and I had stayed late going over estimates and projected cost. When I looked outside and saw that it was getting late and I asked Robert if he wanted to eat supper with me. I was fixing to call down for a steak.

"Yeah, I guess. I thought Stella would be back by now. Yeah, why not?" Robert said.

We called down to the restaurant and ordered. Robert and I continued to do minor work when the food cart rolled up to the suite door across the hall. We just dropped what we were doing and went to eat. I didn't realize how hungry I was.

After we had finished eating, Patricia Cox and her two little girls came in the room. The kids were scrubbed and each of them were wearing one of my t-shirts for a night gown. Their hair was combed and I think had been trimmed. Pat was wearing a new pair of jeans and a western shirt of some type. I knew her hair had been cut because her bangs didn't hang down in her face.

The children were clinging to Pat as she sat on the couch and they were just staring at me. Patricia was smiling and I noticed that Stella had changed out of her business skirt and blouse and into a casual pair of pants of some type.

"Hey, kids. You like some ice cream?" I said as I walked towards the small kitchenette in the room. I got no response, but I continued talking to them. When I got the ice cream and started walking towards them with a couple of bowls and spoons, they climbed all over their mother and making small animal sounds I had never heard a child make.

"Mr. Gray, I had better take them to the room. I'll give them the ice cream there if you don't mind." she said.

I placed the ice cream carton and bowls on the counter and stepped back to give them plenty of room. Pat took the ice cream and started out the room and said "Come on, Jenny and Jody, we will go down to our room."

The children climbed over the back of the couch, which was sitting in the middle of the suite, and ran after their mother, like scared animals.

After they left, I said half aloud "I wonder what I did?"

"You didn't do it, Charlie. It is a long story. Pat shared some of it with me. There has been a recent incident concerning their mother that may have left a bad impression on the kids." Stella said sadly.

"I had to wash the kids hair three or four times with 'Rid,' they had head lice. I think that Pat did too. I noticed the bottle was empty when I went in to get the kids clothes. I put the clothes in a plastic laundry bag. I took their clothes, all of them and put them in the dumpster. I will have Maria spray the room every day. I told Pat what we had to do. I robbed the bank Charlie. I hope you won't be too mad at me. You can take it out of my pay." Stella said holding a mug of coffee in both hands while sitting on the edge of the big chair, staring at the floor.

I walked over to Stella and patted her on the shoulder, walked out into the hall while the waiter came back and took the dishes away.

"Now what?" I said to no one.

Chapter 14

The next morning "at coffee", as we had learned to call our morning meetings, we learned that Amber's mother had passed away from a long-term illness none of us knew anything about. All of us were sad and had feelings for Amber.

"Are any of us going to go the funeral?" Stella asked.

"Stella, why don't you check with someone downstairs to see if any information is available." I asked in a slow soft voice.

"Poor Amber," I thought, but she has a large family there.

Stella came back in the room with her note pad, as she always had these days and announced, "The funeral will be in Nestorville, West Virginia at 2:00 PM tomorrow at the Community Church or something like that. I have a phone number for Amber in West Virginia if you would like it".

"Yeah, see if you can get her on the horn. " I asked Amber.

In just a few minutes, Stella had Amber on the phone and brought the speakerphone over to the table we were all setting around.

"Hello, Amber." I said and after a few minutes, "Amber, I going to put this on the speaker phone if you don't mind, so we can all talk." I pushed a few buttons and nothing. Stella came over and did it right so we could all hear and speak. "Click" went the speaker.

"Hi everybody..."

"Yo, Amber," most of us said. There was Robert, Stella, Maria who had just come in, myself sitting there, and Sassy was there too. I didn't see her come in since my back was to the door while I was on the speakerphone, she said nothing.

Those present said all of the right words and Maria crossed herself while we were talking. "May we attend the funeral? Or is it private, Amber" I asked.
"Of course you can, but it is going to be tomorrow. Can you get a flight out? Amber asked. I looked at Stella who shrugged her shoulders.

"Yeah, we can figure something out. We will meet you at the church or funeral home at 2:00 PM?" I asked trying to get the directions straight. "Hey, you and Stella work that out, okay. We will see you tomorrow."

Stella took the phone with the long card away with her and placed it back on a side table...and after she placed herself on "hold". Stella went into "her office" as she called the main room of the suite, to continue talking to Amber.

As a group, we had only been together for a short period of time. The last four months seemed longer, but we were family. I still could not get Sassy to come into the fold. However, she did oftentimes show up and had coffee with us, or me, which was a welcome relief.

Sassy had deep-rooted hatreds, for people, for men, and especially herself. Her presence often affected the light mood of the group while we are in a meeting. Watching the group from the end of the table where I normally sit, I see this, I see Sassy's moods. However, I am not a shrink and I could be wrong, but after a few years of experience, I had learned something.

I do not mean she was a "wet blanket" on a fire. She did "shuck and jive" with everyone and yet, there is something, way down deep.

"Who wants to go?" I asked after we hung up. No one spoke.

"I don't do funerals too well, Charlie", Robert stated. I nodded and understood. He had been to a couple too recently His wife and daughter, last year around this time...

"I can't leave my critters overnight. I have to be home to take care of them. My daughter won't be there," Sassy said. "But, I would love to go. Amber is a friend of mine."

"I'll take care of them, Sassy," Robert said. "No problemo."

Sassy looked at him in surprise, but let the emotion fade quickly. ."Okay, I'll go. How much will it cost for the...?"

"Don't worry about that. The Bowl Weevil Foundation can spring for the trip." I thought if Shirley, the CPA. I hope she wouln't scream too loud. "Stella?"

"Well, Charlie, let me think on it," she said as she was walking around the room with her portable phone.

"Oh, hello Amber, Stella. Look, we are trying to put this together. Where is the nearest airport we can fly into? ...Ouch, that is two hours away. Do you mind if I call you back? I don't want to disturb your family...You sure? ...OK, I understand... Yeah, okay. Thanks, Amber."

"Maria, you want to go?" I asked.

Maria was shocked that she was even asked.

"Maria, you are part of this 'family,' dysfunctional as it may be, and remember when we get closer to the first of April. You need to let me know if you want to come to work with us, but right now, do you want to go? As it stands right now, I have no idea when we will leave or be back, but it will be short and sweet."

"Yes, I want to go. If you don't mind."

I stood up to get a cup of coffee and as I walked by her. I stopped and put one arm around her shoulder and gave a little hug, without saying anything and walked back over to the table. She and Amber were close, not just an employee-employer relationship.

I could hear Stella in the other room talking to someone and heard her mention names. In the mean time I called the assistant manager for the Holiday Inn and asked if anyone wanted to go to West Virginia to the funeral. In a few minutes, they came back with the number. Two wanted to go and with Maria that was three, I was four, Sassy five, and Stella was a "maybe," a total of six at the outset.

"Charlie, I need to call Shirley for approval and also get the airlines on the phone." Stella said.

I held my hand up like a traffic cop saying "stop." I looked at Stella and said, "When I give you a job. I give you the responsibility and the authority to get it done. I trust your judgment. Now just get it done," she smiled. We had had this conversation before at this table about being "responsible" and "authority."

I had a sign on my desk that said "a job half done is never done." I wish I could remember the gentleman from Kansas that said that. It impressed me so much I used it as a motto sometimes.

"Robert, you and Sassy need to get together on the details. You know where she lives and all?"

"Nope, but we can go out there if she can show me." said Stella. "I'll be on the pager." He and Sassy walked out the door.

"You are on two hour stand-by to move out." I yelled as they went towards the fading steps.

"Okay." "Slam" went the stairwell door.

Maria walked out the door and said she was going to go home and get ready. She left a phone number on the note pad by my chair and said she would soon be back. I suggested she bring an overnight case, just in case.

Patricia Cox and the two little girls walked in the door of the office. The two children had not said one word in my presence and that bothered me. I guess they could talk. I had asked Stella how old they were and she said six and eight or something like that. They were so small. "Malnutrition" was all she said.

Stella came in and said she had "leased" a plane from Atlantic Airlines. A Swedish made twelve passenger model that could get us into a small airport at Philippi, West Virginia, about twelve miles away from where we wanted to go. Amber made arrangements to have us all picked up. She was not going to be able to meet us as she was making arrangements of course. When we were expected to be in Philippi, she had not talked to the pilot, but the person at Atlantic Airlines said he would call back with a recommended departure time.

"Did I miss anything?" she asked herself. "Oh, yeah, I'm not going Charlie. I will stay here with Robert and of course Patricia and the kids," she quickly added. "You know I don't like funerals either...Do you mind?" as she came over to me and took my chin in her hands, just for a second.

"Naaaaaaah! Man! What have I been telling you about things like that, she is just being nice." I thought.

"Sure, Stella. No problem." as Patricia stood there with a question on her face. "Come on in Patricia, we were talking about a funeral in West Virginia. A member of our little family here lost a loved one, Amber, whom you have not met yet.

We have chartered a plane to go up there for the day, maybe overnight. You will be okay here and stay if you like." I said.

"You mean you are going to rent a whole big ol' jet to take you way up there?" she asked amazed at what she had heard. "You must be a rich man, Mr. Gray"

"Charlie"

"Oh, okay. Charlie," Patricia said.

"Pat, I have been blessed. I done a lot of bad things and now I am trying to get something right for a change and as far as leasing a plane? It is cheaper than trying to buy six or seven tickets and then rent cars, a pure matter of economy." I stated to her.

"Mr. Gray, I mean, Charlie. What can I do to earn my keep? Me and the kids here do appreciate what you have done. All the new clothes and stuff and Stella bought me these new clothes and under..." she stopped." And other stuff." she said.

"Patricia, you said you were working for me, right?"

"Right, but..." she said

"This means, I'm the boss. Right?" "Yes"
"Then your job will be to stay here, take care of the kids and help Stella while I'm gone. Can you handle that?"

"Yes, sir"

"Pat, how old are you?" I asked. "I am going to need for Stella to get all this info and send back to our office. You know, you and the kids, for insurance. You have birth certificates?"

"I'm 24 years old, almost. I was 15 when Jody was borned. She was borned at home, so we don't have no birth certificate on her, I don't think. She was born Butte La Rose at my aunt's house. She is a mid-wife and we didn't need no regular doctor or nothing. Jenny was borned at Lafayette General."

"Stella, while we are gone. Why don't you check this out?"

"Got it. I understand," she interrupted, "Can do." I looked at Stella. It was hard to believe this was the mousy woman from the tuxedo shop a few short months ago as she stood there with her weight on one foot and her hip stuck out to one side. She looked good and with Robert, well, she said she was exercising and swimming.

"I am still going to get me one of them exercise people, whatever they're called." I reminded myself again. "One of these days."

"Patricia, why don't you come in here with me and we can start on the information we need." Stella said as she went by Patricia. She bent over and picked up the smallest of the two little girls, but as Stella placed her on her hip to carry her away, her little head swiveled around and she watched me like a hawk. The older one followed Stella when she was called.

"Where is your husband, Pat?" I asked.

Patricia hung her head down. "I ain't got no husband. Maurice and I just "jumped the broom" when I was 14. He just run off about a year ago, said he was going to New Orleans to get a real good job on a river barge or something. And said that he would send for us. We never heard nothing so I came looking for him about a week ago and here I am." she said as she finally looked up.

"Do you want us to help you find him, Patricia? It is up to you."

"I dunno what to do. I have no money, my family can't help none. My step-father, or I should say "my mother's husband," he is always coming around and wanting to kiss on me and all. Said if I don't 'do-it' with him he will kick us out. I didn't know what to do and he hollers at the kids all time, chases them out of the house whenever he comes over to...you know." she said. "So I left, at least Maurice didn't holler at the kids and he only hit me when he had been drinking, or if'en I didn't have his supper ready when he came home from the mill, just regular stuff."

I didn't say a word. Stella was standing at the door and looked at me.

"Well, you got a family now." I stood up when and walked around the desk and put my arms around her to give her little hug. When I did, I heard the same little animal sounds from the two girls. The youngest that Stella was still holding, was trying to "climb" up her body.

"It's okay girls, don't be scared," she said to them as she went to them, but they never took there eyes off me.

We met the pilots from Atlantic Airlines at the Executive Air Terminal at New Orleans International Airport. We went by and picked up Maria and Sassy. As I was driving up to Sassy's, I saw Robert's truck and the lights in back of the house in the kennel area were on. It was a chilly morning, Stella had a parka on that I suspected belonged to Robert and with rubber boots on up to her knees. She was washing down kennels. I bet she had never washed a kennel in her life, but she was doing this one.

The dogs were all quiet and "housed up" in their dog houses to be out of the way. The pens were regulation 4 x 16 x 6 foot high with a covered top. Sassy used barrels that were secured to the fence with large hose clamps for dog houses. These were very good dog houses, up off the ground and made of plastic. This means that they can be cleaned easily and in the winter you can take a piece of 3/4 inch plywood and put a front on the barrel for a wind break and a method of holding the hay on the barrel. Simple, easy and effective, these can be used in Southern states where the winters are mild.

Sassy came out of the house and brought a carry on bag with her in case we stayed overnight.

The two from the hotel staff were to meet us at the terminal at 0545

"Sorry, I wasn't ready Charlie. I hope we won't be too late?" Sassy said as she jumped in the back of the Towncar.

"I have all the faith in the world, young lady. They will not leave without us."

I saw Robert walking out of a garage side door with a stack of dog food pans in his arms and flicked the lights at him. His arms were full, so he just raised his head a little in acknowledgement.

We parked the car in the Executive Terminals' private parking area and went inside to meet the pilots. I saw the aircraft parked just outside the terminal and a Flight Attendant was loading something onto the plane.

When we walked in, a pilot in a neat pressed uniform and cap came up and said,"Mr. Gray?"

I acknowledged and said we were ready. A second young man in a blue kaki colored uniform took all out bags and placed them on a cart he had.

"Whenever you are ready Mr. Gray we can depart" the Captain said. "What is the weather like where we are going", I asked.

"Little foggy right now, but I think it will be okay when we get there. I want it to be VFR (Visual Flight Rules) when we land. There is a couple of 2,000 foot mountains on either side of the runway. They could bite us if we are not careful." He said and smiled.

"Captain, there is nothing at that place worth taking a chance on. You know what I mean?" I said lightly.

"Sure do Mr. Gray, I didn't get these grey hairs from being stupid." We both laughed as we walked towards the plane.

The rest were on the plane when I got on and we taxied out for a routine flight. There were a few bumps over Kentucky, but nothing dramatic. It was a nice aircraft. I made a mental note to keep these folks in mind when we started doing our traveling in the future, they had a bathroom on board too.

Maria was sitting next to me across the aisle. They were single seat accommodations, not side by side, and I swear we flew a thousand feet higher the way Maria was lifting up on the arm rest. Maria was a "white knuckle flier." I did not know it but this was her first airplane ride, but she sat there with as much dignity as possible.

We landed at the Philippi airport with no problem on a beautiful fall day. There was no "terminal," but we taxied over to where several folks were standing beside a hanger and fuel truck. In fact, there must have been several dozen cars.

As we taxied up to the hanger, a man with a set of paddles directed the aircraft to a halt and the pilots cut the engines. The flight attendant open the exit hatch and we exited the plane.

A man and woman walked up to us and introduced themselves as Amber's kin. I do not remember how they were kin, but they sure were nice folks. They kept looking at the aircraft like they wanted to look inside, so we walked up to the aircraft to help get the bags out.

The pilot said he would like to fly out and go to Clarksville since he needed JP fuel, which they did not have here. I told him I did not know when we would be ready to go. The funeral was at 2:00 and then I did not know what would happen. The pilot said that if we could not get out of here by 5:00 PM, he looked over his shoulder, then we should consider staying the night. The mountains were a little too close for a night takeoff and he did not have radar behind these mountains.

"Okay, done deal." I said. "What time then tomorrow?" I asked the pilot.

"Considering the fog this time of year…why not make it about noon for sure. I will be here as soon as we can. I have your pager number and cell phone. If any changes come up, I will advise you." the pilot stated.

"Sounds good. Noon will be a good time and if you come early I bet one the Hattfileds or McCoys will call on us." we chuckled and shook hands.

The pilot and co-pilot made a routine takeoff and we watched as they cleared the far mountain with no problem.

All five of us, plus Jimmy and Molly, got in a van with Mt. Olive Baptist Church on the side and headed towards Nestorville.

The funeral was what I call "country," very nice and sincere. All the folks had known each other for years and when one of the fold leaves. They were really missed, it was not just a ceremony.

Amber was there with her family members. She caught my eye and smiled at me.

After the funeral at the graveside, I noticed that it was clouding up. "Ain't going to fly out tonight," I thought.

I called the pilot and confirmed that tomorrow would be a good day.

We all went back to the motel in Philippi and checked into a nice motel and we looked around for a place to eat. I gave each of the two ladies that worked at the Holiday Inn cash money, told them to have fun and bring receipts back. They looked at each other and said they were going to a Country-Western Bar across the street from the motel in a strip shopping mall. Sassy said she had promised a man she met at the funeral she would meet him or something. I don't know, she is a big girl.

"Maria. Looks like you got a date with "un viejo pendajo." "You are not an old fool, Charlie" she said kindly. "Solomente un viejo, Maria," I replied.

Since we did not have a car...and there were no taxi's in Phillipi, we walked across the street to the Embers Restaurant. It looked good and they were having the "Tygart Valley Soil Conservation District Meeting" according to a banner outside, with a speaker from "Anderson-Broaddus College" as a speaker.

Maria and I went in and were seated. She was a charming lady and you enjoy being with a woman like that. After the meal, I walked her to her motel room door, which was three down from my room and we said good night. For some reason I leaned over and gave Maria a kiss on the check, nothing to it, just a friendly peck and said "Good Night." I caught myself and said.

"I'm sorry, Maria. I,...er..." I sputtered.

"I have not had a man in my life for many years, Charlie. Don't worry about it." she said in a coy voice and walked inside.

"Naaaaaaah, get out of here," I told myself.

The next morning about 0800, the pilot and I got in touch with each other. He informed me there was no way he could get to Phillipi, or even try due to the light snow at altitude and the rain and sleet on the runway. I told him we would wait and asked him about his best estimate of departure. Steve, the pilot, advised me we would have a small window sometime around 5:00 PM and we could try it then. I advised him that the whole deal was up to him...I was in no hurry and not complaining about paying the "down time" fee his company was charging.

About that time, I saw Sassy walking by the window. I opened the door real quick and said "Yo, Sassy!" as I was talking to the pilot. She came back to the door, entered, and shut the door. The heavy coat she had been wearing yesterday was slung over her shoulder and was dry. Sassy waited until I got finished talking to Steve.

"Sassy, we will not leave at noon today, bad weather. We may get a chance at 5:00 this afternoon. Sorry," I said.

"Good. I will be in my room, I need some sleep anyway." She walked away smiling a far away smile.

I woke up Maria. I advised her and asked if she would call the other two folks who came with us. I did not even know their names and Maria said she would.

As I put the phone down, it rang immediately. It was Amber.

"Good morning, Charlie." she said in her up beat manner. "Want some breakfast?" "Sure", let me get Maria. Where are you?"

"I'm at my house. I will be there in...ten minutes or so. How's that?" "Can do." and I called Maria.

Maria said she did not want breakfast and would walk down to the lobby for coffee and juice later.

When Amber and I had finished breakfast, we went driving around the countryside. Central West Virginia is beautiful with the mountains and valleys and the slow pace of life we all yearn for.

"Stop," I said as we drove on one of the side roads that Amber was telling me about from her childhood days. "I seen a sign back there, can you back up please?"

Amber put the pickup in reverse and we eased backwards. "Stop" I said again. I was looking at an old sign that said "For Sale."

"You know this place?" I asked

"Yes, but I don't remember who owns it. But the real estate agent is a cousin of mine." Amber said and was amused when I laughed.

"What's so funny," she demanded jokingly. I explained about Robert Perez and the joke we had about his cousins.

"Oh, yeah, you guys told me once before" she said. "You know where I can find this real estate agent?"
"Yeah, he is buried in the same place my mother is buried." she said without cracking a smile.

"Okay," I said as we drove off.

"His wife was at the funeral, in fact you spoke to her. The one with the 'child bearing hips,' the one with the big ass." she giggled.

"I didn't notice" I lied. "If someone told her to haul ass, would she have to make two trips?"

With that Amber pulled back on the road.

"Amber, what do you think about having a summer training facilities? Or a place where can train in the winter?"

Amber thought a moment and said "Sure, I guess. I just don't know enough right now to comment. I know that my daddy use to run coons all around this part of the country." She lost her sophisticated accent for the warm West Virginia twang.

I grabbed the phone and called Stella. She was giggling like a school girl when she answered the phone. "Stella?'

"Yeah, Charlie." A voice in the background said, "That ain't Charlie you little imp." "Yes it is. Here talk to him." Stella made a loud "tee hee hee" sound.

"Hello, who is this?" said Art Nelson, the car salesman and ex-husband. "Who the hell is this?" I said.

"Click"

I called back and Stella answered, "Charlie, you would have paid a million dollars for this scene." Stella said with roaring laughter and coughing. " He came in here and, and…and…" she continued laughing. "What? Whaaaat do you want Charlieee?" she laughed.

"Well, I was thinking of talking to a sane person when I called. Guess I was wrong." Stella started all over again. "When wheeeeen you yelled at him, he grabbed his… hee heeee…hat and took off like a scalded dog…hee heeeee."

I finally got her settled down and told her we might spend another night in Phillipi due to weather. She said she would contact the motel too about Maria and the other two employees being gone one more day from work and Amber said she had done that.

"How is Patricia and the kids?" I asked.

"Fine, she has wiped down and waxed everything in the place. Just keep telling me she wants to earn her keep." Stella said in a serious manner.

"Fine, leave her be. I like that, and she feels like she is doing her part. I guess that I will see you when I get there." I said.

"Okay Charlie, Robert and I have been taking care of business," she said. "I bet you have," I teased.

We hung up as we were entering town. I think this will be our summer home, Philippi, West Virginia.

Chapter 15

I was hard to believe we had been together for nine months. Bart Duffy was back and we had filled out our teams with Samantha Joann McGee and Emil Dupree, a French Citizen.

So that gave us Amber, Robert, Bart and I ready to go. Sassy has not made a decision yet and her time was running out. Stella, who said she had never been very active, had started jogging and working with weights. We would see.

Samantha McGee was called Sammie, of course. She was a Chemical Engineer graduate from Georgia Tech who had until the first of the year, worked for Dow Chemical Company in some capacity. Why she was on a "sabbatical" was unknown, but her background check was beyond reproach. She was "married," but not living with her husband. Her husband's last name was different from hers. She had not changed her name when they got married. I guess that is okay nowadays, but I think it is dumb.

Sam is a soft spoken woman in her thirties, but do not expect me to know ages without looking on the employment contract or asking Stella, I do not care. I have always been more concerned with production. "Results" is the only goal I will accept. I liked her, she was nice.

Sam would let this foolish old man make statements without correcting me in public, but I have learned to recognize the look when I am saying something that is not correct concerning, oh, for example, the chemical reaction of explosives when subjected to heat.

Samantha was harder to get to know, but after you discover her dry sense of humor, you will love her to death as all of the members of the "Bug Brigade" call themselves now, since they could not remember what a "bowl weevil" was. I tried to explain to them that bo'weevils are a type of bug that eat cotton plants. In fact the Bowl Weevil Foundation's logo is a cute little bo'weevil eating a cotton leaf and smiling. Most people look at our letterhead and think we are a pest control company of some sort. That was a good cover if we ever needed it. In fact, I needed to have some magnetic signs made for the vehicle doors, just in case.

Emil Dupree, a citizen of France according to his documents, was a very nice man in his early 40's maybe, well-built and muscular. I think one of the ladies, Amber I think, called him "Fabio," whoever that was.

Emil came to us on a strong recommendation from Robert Perez, who had met him several years ago at the U.S. Customs Canine School in Front Royal, Virginia, as an exchange student from French Customs. His last assignment was training drug detector dogs for Cuba. Unbeknownst to me, in 1998 Cuban Customs started using French dogs and really enforced "Zero Tolerance." Emil was sent to Cuba for that project. I do not know what breeds they used.

Emil was hard working, very polite to the ladies without being hokey and worked well with the men.

On a hot spring day, he had his shirt off working in the water around the new boat house clearing choke weeds from the water. Patricia Cox, who was living in the Trainers Apartment over the kennels with her two little girls, was helping him drag limbs on the bank. I stood there and watched them work. Then I started watching Pat who was just staring at Emil. Emil raised up for a minute to stretch a tired back. "Ain't he purty, Charlie?" she whispered to me.

"Yeah, I been thinking that too, Patty," I teased her as she blushed when she realized what she had said.

That was when I noticed a tattoo on his chest that said "Legio Patria Nostras." My first thoughts screamed that this was a prison gang tattoo.

"Ah, shit, how could this happen," I said aloud. Pat turned to me with a questioning look on her face.

"What?" she asked.

"Oh, nothing…I was just wondering why we didn't do this when we had the heavy equipment here." I said.

I turned away and went back to the ATV we used as our "ponies" to ride around the grounds for working. I had to get this checked out. I had seen that tattoo before, but I could not remember where. "Jeez, what a crock."

I rode the four wheeled drive ATV back to the kennel where I noticed Bart and Robert talking by the field training course.

Bart and Robert were discussing the scent boxes laying on the ground. Both of them were masters at passive alert training.

The boxes they were using were 12" x 12" x 4" deep with a 4" hole drilled on one side in the center. The object of the boxes being made was to allow the for them to be placed in different places, ease of transport and also a milk crate can be placed upside down over the 3/4" plywood boxes to insure the dog, during training, cannot see in the box. This way, the dog must use his nose. When the dog reaches the correct scent box, they are given the command "sit" and after a slow count of three they are rewarded. We only use "Kong Balls" or "Kool Kongs" as reward toys. They are easy to use and have less of a tendency to pick up odors from the ground or the surrounding area. Another reason why they are used is because they are tough and with a little care… they will last a long time.

The discussion they were having was the merits of making an initial "find" and having the dog do a "re-find". A "re-find" is where a dog must look at an object, such as a scent box, and "sit" a second time to receive the reward, a Kong Ball in this case.

We stood there and talked a while when we got to the point of using "oil of anise" as the very first scent item to train for. This is an old timers' retriever dog trick. You place a couple of drops of oil of anise on an object, like the rope on a Kool Kong and toss the object for the dog to find. After a few times of this, you change objects, place the oil of anise on a new object for the dog to find. Except this time, it has been hidden out of the dog's sight, such as in a scent box, like the ones we had been talking about. When the dog finds the scent, a command of "sit" is given and the pup is rewarded. After a few short repetitions of this, the dog should indicate that a scent has been detected and "sit" on his own.

"Passive alerting" is a good method to train a dog, but the maintenance training time is high in order to maintain proficiency. No matter what the breed or what scents, they will be trained to detect, they must learn to detect Oil of Anise. This is one of my rules as you will learn later. It can be purchased at any food store in the spice or baking section and it has the odor of licorice "There is another BIG reason I like to use oil of anise, Robert. We can discuss it later when the time is right." I said.

"Robert, I noticed Emil had a big tattoo on his chest." I said as I looked back down towards the bayou. "It said something like 'Legio Patria Nostra.' I don't read or speak French or Italian, but I do remember what it said."

Robert looked at me and said "It is Latin, Charlie. It means 'The Legion is our home,' from the old Roman Legions' motto. Emil was in the French Legion for six years prior to working for French Customs. In fact, they separated him from the 13th Demi-Brigade two years early to be a Customs Agent since he speaks several languages."

"Why wasn't I briefed on all this when we signed him on?" I said a little short with Robert.

"I was going to, but you told me you trusted my decisions and you really never asked about his full history. I think it was put off when you had Steve fly you back to Texas for some personal family business, around Christmas. Is there something wrong?' Robert asked.

"No, no, no. You did right, I .....er, ah…just forgot," I chuckled.

About that time Patricia and Emil were walking up the hill towards the Big House, as the old restored mansion was being called. Emil was walking in slow but very long strides up the hill without effort, with Patricia taking two steps for his one. I saw the Legionnaire in him now. He had seen the Legion Headquarters in French Morocco back in the 1950's, before the revolt. I was stationed there temporarily at Port Leyote, French Morocco. We were flying support for the French when the Mau Maus were burning Leopoldville and killing all Europeans.

The Legion marches at 60 steps per minute, but there strides are 36 inches long, compared to the U.S. Army who marches at 110 paces a minute with 30 inch steps The reason the Legion marches at the slow pace is a custom from the old days in the dessert, where the motto was and still is "March or Die," but they will march the average soldier into the ground. The United States should come up with a standing Army like that, very professional and make sure that politicos can touch them. Not official, but the Legionaries still go by the rules of "rape and pillage" during a battle. It may not be nice, but they win. They are feared and there are no "rules of war" for them as long as they obey their officers. Same thing happened in Dessert Storm, the Iraqis would not even stand and fight them. According to tradition, all men are killed and all women raped. Those are their rules of war. Ask the citizens of Chad what happened in the early 1980's when Colonel Kadafi tried to invade an old French Province of Chad from Tripoli. The 13th Demi-Brigade Parachuted in and well, that's history. We can talk about that later.

When Pat and Emil walked up, I asked Emil. "You were in the Legion?"

"Oui, mon Capitan". Emil said in French as he drew himself up straight, saluted and returned his right hand to his side by slapping it with such force, it could have left

a bruise. The Bass Pro Shop baseball cap he was wearing turned into a *Kepi Blanc* for a second...as he stood there.

We smiled and said something about when I was in Port Leyote. Emil said "I am afraid that was before I was even born Charlie." We laughed.

Something Emil did tell us about something about hand slapping the right side that I found interesting. They used to put a small paperback book in the side pocket to give a louder ring when they slapped there side, and also to protect the leg. If a Legionnaire saw an Officer of the Legion, no matter the distance, no matter if were day or night, they were to stand, face the officer and salute until either they were out of sight or the salute was returned. They were NOT required to salute or obey any other officer, French or otherwise. This is what makes them so loyal and such good soldiers. As long as they were in uniform, they could not be arrested or detained except by their own officers or NCO's.

If a Legionnaire did not salute properly and with vigor, the officer would report him and he and his unit would be required to stand in full battle gear and salute the officer's *Kepi Blanc* a hundred times, or until the offended officer was satisfied. Of course this did not make the offending Legionnaire very popular with his partners. Oftentimes it led to an industrial strength ass whupping, but the Legion takes care of it own for that loyalty. They do not pledge allegiance to France, only to the French Foreign Legion.

Amber, Sassy and Sammie came back from running a track with the Bloodhounds. Sassy's hair, which normally was up in a braid, was hanging down and was wet. Amber was what I called a "neat freak" about her clothes, but she was wet and muddy and Sammie was not much better. They had been in the swamp.

They were laughing and having a good time about Amber being pulled along by a big 100 pound Bloodhound named "Jake" after he picked up Sammie's track. It was a race. Amber had used a "tracking belt" to tie off onto "Jake" so if she fell during the track, the dog would not get away from her. The leash was a nylon strap about 15 feet long attached to a Ray Allen TH-1 leather harness. When Jake picked up the scent of Sammie, he started pulling and Amber fell several times, pulled along by the belt. Sassy, who was acting as coach, had to grab the leash to allow Amber to get up. Sammie, to my surprise, went into the swamp in knee deep water and waded about 200 yards off into the swamp thinking that Amber, Sassy and Jake would not, or could not, follow her. Wrong! Wrong! Wrong! Jake did not know he could not track in water and besides, the scent off the human would catch on the bark of the trees, the blades of grass and does not count the dead skin that come off and float in the water. The dogs can track in water.

Sammie was so surprised that a dog could track her in that water and also that she was "visual tracked" too by Sassy. Sassy pointed out to her how fresh "high water" marks on the tree trunks and water reeds gave her away. Not counting the "green goopy slim" that had been parted and did not look the same any more, using the technical terms.

I thought Sammie would be a titty baby about 'gators and swamps. Since she was a "city girl," but she was not. She would drive on to the best of them. Sassy was tough from jump, no problem. I did have a few problems with her taking foolish chances. Fool hardy I would say, and with "tombstone courage."

Since Amber has M.S. I thought I would have to nurse her along, but we did not. I guess I am the only one that knows about this terrible disease she has. Except the medical folks that did the exams when the team members signed their formal contract and the insurance company. Each team member had a one million dollar policy through Lloyds of London if they were killed or disabled in the line of duty.

The Big House was almost ready. We had twenty rooms in the old house now, fourteen bedrooms. A whole new wing had been added on each end. Each bedroom had a private shower, a bath, and a "sitting room." Each one of the team members were allowed to decorate and furnish the rooms as they wanted. Everyone had private phone lines in and cable TV, but we had not moved in yet.

The ladies had a ball furnishing the house. Amber and Sammie decorated it like an Old Southern Plantation in the formal area of the house. In fact Amber, Sammie and Sassy flew to New York to buy furniture at a "trade show" as Amber kept calling it. Since Sassy had connections in New York with wholesale furniture dealers. That was the route they took.

When they bought the furniture, they ganged up on me, the girls did, that is. I was held hostage and…well, that is not all true, but here is how it did go.

Ever afternoon after a hard days work, we gathered out in the front of the kennels for a "Miller Time Conference" as we called it. It was during this time, after training that Amber, Sassy and Sammie ganged up on me.

"Charlie?" one of them said. "Yes, dear." I answered.

"Didn't you say we could buy any type of furniture we wanted?" Amber said as she came over and sat on the corner of the big yard chair I was in.

"Yes, Darling, that is what I told you." as if she was my daughter.

"Charlie?" Sassy said as she sat on the other arm of the chair placing her arm on my shoulder.

I looked from side to side. I was trapped. I kept quiet, too late. They had "that look" on their faces as Sammie tried to curl the hair on my forehead with her finger, but could not. There was not much left there. They were playing me like a cat does with a mouse.

"Yes, Baby"

"Do we HAVE to buy at Sears or Wal-Mart? I mean, this is our home now. We sorta thought that you liked to have nice stuff in the house?"

This was the first time Sassy had said anything about making the move, coming to work here, or anything. I paid close attention to this.

"We haven't moved in and you haven't said you wanted to be with us. Have you?" I asked.

"Well, not yet anyway, but I will" she purred. Oooooops, conned again.

"You girls can buy what you want where ever you want." I said.

"You promise Charlie? Word of honor?" they all chimed in as Robert and Emil who were setting on the newly sod lawn howling with glee and spilling their beer.

"You two assholes know about this con job?" I asked.

That really brought the howls of laughter. At that time Stella and Maria rode up in a golf cart and just sat there and watched the fun.

"You going to make it right with Shirley if we spend a little bitsy more money than she thinks is right?"

"Yes, I am still in charge around here. Ain't I?" Going along with the joke.

"Of course you are" they all said in one manner or another. You will always be in charge." "So why the big Flim Flam job?

"We are going to New York, to a Trade market for furniture. We are going to fly too, Charlie. Amber, Sammie and I, and Maria and Stella too," Sassy said. "And you promised, Charlie, you gave your word. We could go 'anywhere' to buy the furniture. You just made the decision and gave your word." they said.

"You have been 'had' Charlie." Emil roared with laughter. "Okay. I see. I have been beat down" I said as I stood up.

I then saw something I thought I would never see. Maria got out of the golf cart, raised her right leg up under her, raised her right fist in the air and exclaimed "Yes!" She then looked around and regained her composure. That made us all laugh.

About that time I heard the "flap flap flap" of a helicopter.

The Bell Executive II circled the house a few times and then landed on the newly built helo pad with a large white "H" in a circle between the kennels and the house. As the pilot allowed the RPM on the rotors bleed off and waiting for the TPT (Tail Pipe Tempature) to go down, we wandered over to the edge of the pad to see who we had as visitors. We had not invited anyone, that I knew of.

The pilot killed the engine and the large right hand door opened and out stepped Steve Johnson, the Atlantic Airlines pilot. We shook hands and walked over to the shade near the kennel where we had been setting and drinking beer before. Of course I had orange juice. You would have thought I was a Mormon.

"Step into our conference room Steve," I said as I motioned to the lawn chairs setting around the base of the tree. The hot Louisiana afternoon sun was beating down, but the large trees were always shady with the moss hanging off.

"Nice place you got, Charlie" as Steve looked around. "Just how big is the house?"

"I dunno for sure. Robert cut the deal on restoring, maybe a couple of bedrooms more." I tried to be modest. "Come on in and look around, ain't nothing in it, no furniture. Whitey and his crew will be through sometimes by the end of the month. He had a lot more to do than we thought. We did get the kennel finished, have been training the dogs for about three months steady and have someone in the Trainers Apartment upstairs, over the kennel. She has two daughters who should be getting off the bus about now." I said looking at my watch.

I looked around and seen that Patricia was down at the bus stop we had built by the road with a John Deere "Mule" to give the girls a ride back. Funny thing, they still had not talked to me, but they will shake their head when

I ask a question that only requires a "yes" or "no". I guess that was progress. They talked to Stella and Robert though. I had seen that.

We walked through the house with Maria doing most of the explaining about this and that. Amber, Sassy, Sammie and Stella were also inspecting the day's progress as we walked. Emil and Robert just wandered around, looking and touching the paint to see if it was dry. There must have been fifteen or twenty people still on the job this afternoon. I guess being Friday, Whitey had paid his "subs" off and they left to cash their checks.

"What brings you out this way, Steve?" as we walked back out the front door towards the big tree.

"Oh, it's about the trip," he said as I raised an eyebrow in trying to remember a trip we had planned or talked about.

"What trip?" I asked.

"The one to New York to buy furniture." Steve said as Emil and Robert turned around started walking quickly towards the kennel, trying to stifle laughs and snickers.

"We promised to help, Patricia…hee hee…feed this afternoon," Robert said as he and Emil started running towards the kennel.

I looked at the little "Angels" standing there in a row, smiling like "What, me?"

"What a bunch of brats I thought. Yeah, that is what I will call them, BRATS!" I thought to myself.

"Steve, when are 'we' going to New York?" I asked as I stood with my arms crossed over my chest with my hands stuck under the arm pits to hold them up as I stood looking at the Brats.

"Monday is what I had laid on." He took a 3 x 5 card out of his pocket. "Depart from Executive Terminal again...0800...Arrive La Guardia Executive terminal." "Oh, yes. The limo is arraigned and hotel rooms for six at the..." as Steve was interrupted by Stella.

"Oh, Stevey, Charlie is not interested in the little ol' details of the trip. Are you Charlie?" Stella said.

"Okay! Okay! I know when I been had by a bunch of Brats, but ladies and gentlemen here is the big 'BUT' and I'm serious as a heart attack...." I gave a long pause, "...are we mission ready as we have planned?"

I looked at each one and waited for Emil and Robert to come out of the kennel. "Robert?"
"Yes" "Amber?"
"Dogs, yes, weapons and individual training, no, but we have discussed this. I have a man that has a range capable of automatic weapons training. He sent us a VCR tape of the

facilities and Emil, Robert and I think we can make it work. This man that has the automatic weapons, a collector by the name of…just a minute, I have the name…right here." She searched through a small tablet she had in the side pocket of her BDU's.

"Never mind, you cut the deal and I will go for it." I said as I held up my hand like a traffic cop again.

"Sassy? I know you have a not signed a contract, but you have come out a lot and have trained." I said.

"She is ready, Charlie, I will vouch for the two Shepherds we imported, and she can handle them. I had a guy come over from Lafayette and test her. She is ready." Robert said. He was designated at "head canine trainer."

"I asked Sassy, Robert"

"I'm ready, dogs are ready, where do I sign?" she beamed up at me. I reached out and gave her a little hug and she responded in kind.

"Welcome aboard". I said.

They all went over and gave her a hug, a "group hug" I think is it called. Sassy, Sammie and Amber I think had tears in their eyes. Patricia came out and just stood watching, not understanding what she was seeing. Maria stood by me beaming. Emil and Robert joined in.

"Well, if we are through with the Mongolian Gang Bang, we can get some serious work done."

"Sammie?"

"Yes, I have Jake ready and two more getting close. Yes, I can meet the mission statement." Sammie said.

"Emil?"

"Yes, explosives and dogs too," he said in almost a formal report as if he was still a Legionnaire.

"Sassy, you can move your dogs over here. We have plenty of room." I said. "Charlie, I sold all my dogs except Prince last week. The labs will be with hunting families."

"You mean last week you knew? I said.

Everyone laughed including Steve who had caught on to the game by now. "I'll bring him out here before we go to New York."

"What about your house, Sassy?" asked Amber.

"I put a 'For Sale' sign out last week. I think Stan Hines Senior wants to buy it. He has first choice." Stella said as she walked up.

"What about Stanley Hines?" she asked.

"He is buying my house. Almost a done deal."

"What about Rebecca?" Stella asked. "Is she coming to live here too?"

"She is more than welcome if she wants to. We have room and can put her on the payroll too, if she wants." I said.

"No, she wants to move in with her father in the downtown area so she can continue college." Sassy answered.

"Well, the offer is always open, Sassy. Tell her that for me." I said. "Thanks, Charlie, will do." Sassy said.

Just a Steve was leaving in the chopper, Bart Duffy rode up on an eight wheeled ATV. He had a Labrador Retriever with him in the four placed model bath tub shaped vehicle. Bart had been out test driving the ATV to see if we could use it for future operations. The lab stayed in the vehicle when Bart drove up and shut off the engine.

"How did it go?" I asked.

"Well, it works. You can cross the swamps, floats good. Would not want to use it in a flood or fast running water, good for crossing soggy fields or down muddy roads, but I only had me and the pup in here." Bart said. "I think the four wheeled ATV is better, but you can't carry a dog."

The vehicle that Bart was driving was a one piece molded bathtub-looking vehicle with four small tires on each side. It had lever controls like a bulldozer which released the drive to the wheels when a lever was pulled. This allowed the other wheels to continue under power, thus controlling the direction of travel. It could carry four people and a little freight.

"Well, do we buy some or not?' I asked.

"I would say get two and try them out, field test them." Bart said as he got out and started towards the kennel with the dog.

"Okay." I said, "Handle it."

Bart raised a little wave of the hand as he walked away.

It was getting late and everyone was getting ready to head back to the motel. Whitey the contractor said he could get a crew to start on the horse's stable Monday morning and we discussed a few minor changes he recommended.

It was Friday and everyone was getting ready to shut down. I was ready to go to the Motel. I was always a little worried about Patricia and the girls out here alone, but she said she would be okay.

"Charlie, this is the safest place the girls and I have lived in. Even at my home…" Patricia faded off.

I couldn't argue with that.

Things were coming along pretty well. Now we were ready for whatever would come along. We needed to get the classrooms built. We had to talk to the Team and see what they recommend for a training area. Inside the gym-sized training building had the slab poured for it last week. They were ready to start the building up next week.

Chapter 16

"Charlie? Steve Ford here"

"Yo Stevey Boy, when did you get back?"

"I ain't Charlie, I am about 50 miles East of where you seen me last time."

"But you sound so clear. I thought you were in ConUs (Continental U.S.) from the way you sound. But how?" I said.

"Charlie, this is not a secure line, but have you heard of Tel Star?"

"Sure Steve. It's that Sputnik thing they shoot up with a rocket a couple of years ago, ain't it", I said.

"Yup, that's it. Look, I am lucky I caught you in the office. But look, I need you and your friends. We are getting our ass waxed real regular and....well, can you meet us in Hawaii tomorrow?" Steve said.

"Sure, do you want me to bring my friends with me? You know they can't get a "passport clearance" for Hawaii." I reminded Steve that dogs could not come into Hawaii without going through quarantine for 180 days. Hawaii is one of the few places with no rabies, and they want to keep it that way too.

Charlie was trying to tell me he was still "in country" at Ben Tuey, south of Saigon in the Delta country. I did not know what he wanted but I knew it took a lot for a SEAL Team Chief to call a non-SEAL like this.

"Steve?" Can you still hear me?" I asked as the service began to sound like he was in a barrel.

"Yeah..." he sounded like Donald Duck.

"Send me an EFTO with all the details and I will see what I can do." I said about the Encoded Fleet Tactical Operation message, and the line went dead.

In about four hours, Comm. Center called and said, "Chief Gray, you have an EFTO. You will need to sign for it."

"Okay, Sparky, be right there." I said. All Navy Radiomen are called "Sparky".

I walked down the block to NAS North Island Communication Center, showed them my ID card which they checked against their records and handed me a clipboard to sign. Like everything else involved with bureaucratic paperwork, you sign. I could have been signing for the National debt for all I knew, but they handed me a sealed five-page message from Steve Ford, SEAL Team Seven, RVN.

The message said they had swimmers blowing boats, ships, and barges and getting into places they should not have been in and they were getting tired of it. He was asking if the dogs could help them find the hidey-holes like we did a few months before. The Cong were good at building and using their hidey-holes.

I sat down and answered his message. I said I thought I could help but, I had several questions for him to answer first: (and he sent his answers early the next morning) Now, you have got to remember during this time period, getting a message from Saigon to San Diego in 4 hours is like talking on a computer today. It was amazing that they could move traffic that fast, but by today's communications standards, this would be considered unacceptable.

A. Are they using breathing equipment? Yes.

B. What type French made, of course. Good stuff

C. Is this the new "re-breathing" type that has no bubbles coming to the surface?

Yes, there are sometime bubbles. That is how we found out what they were doing it when we see bubbles we dump frags(fragmentation grenades) in the water…So far so good I thought…but we think they have caves along the bank of the river leading to the Port of Saigon.

D. Is there anything different about the air in the air tanks the divers are using?

Yes, in ours, it is cleaned and filtered. I think the little people use dirty air from a bicycle type pump.

Message to Steve Ford: "Steve, I think I can help. Can you pick me and three team members with their friends at TSN (Ton Son Nhut Air Base, Saigon) day after tomorrow or would you rather meet at AFG (Anderson Field, Guam. A very large Air Force Base on Guam)"

Steve's reply. : "Need you here Pri-999"...if I can get ComNavV (Commander Naval Forces Viet Nam) to approve...Can do. Will advise ETA(Estimated Time Arrival)."

All the above messages took 24 hours to send and receive. Not like today when you have "flash traffic" there and back in just a few seconds.

Priority 999 is the highest travel orders you can get. You can bump anyone, and I mean anyone, Admirals and Generals included. Everything else except for U.S. First Class mail can be bumped under Priority 999.

Since ComNavAirPac had a "war room," they knew the flight schedule of everything moving in the Pacific area of operations.

A C-141 was leaving Miramar Naval Air Station in a couple of hours. Miramar is located about an hour's drive from where we were located. So we grabbed the "bone hoisters"

and our pre-packed deployment bags and away we went. We flew from Miramar San Diego to BPH (Barber's Point Hawaii) in 8 eight hours elapsed time. What a difference that was. In the "old days" when we flew P5M-2's, which are very large seaplanes, from Alameda, California to Hawaii and it took 16 hours. We did not have the navigation gear like they do now. We were not worried about getting to any particular island in the Hawaiian chain. We just tried to hit Hawaii, any island would do.

If you ever look closely at old movies or old prop planes, you will see that there is a little glass bubble on top of the aircraft just behind the pilot's seat, just big enough for the average man to squeeze his head and shoulders in to look out, about 10 inches above the main frame of the aircraft. This is where the Navigator used a sextant to "shoot the stars." If we were within 50 miles of the Ford Island, Oahu we were elated. Today's modern Navigation gear can take you within 50 feet of the approach end of the runway, but in those were days of adventure, a 14 hour flight with 16 hours of fuel, you had better pay attention.

The shipping crates we used in those days were made of metal, the G.I. issue kind. They weighed about 80 pounds empty, but they were crush proof and had the ability to hold some of the real bad boys that D.O.D. Dog Center turned out. Nothing like the plastic kennels we use today. The old crates were about the size of the P-700 kennels.

We used a ton and half stake side truck to move the four dogs to Miramar while we were transported in a van. When we got to Miramar, we contacted Base Ops and presented our orders. The Air Force Major in command of the C-141 was not going to let us on the plane until we pointed out our Priority-999.

"But we don't have a passenger module. We only have the canvas folding troop seats." he complained to the "Air Boss" at Miramar.

As if we cared. We did not have a plush seat to ride in, they were not comfortable seats. They were a lot like the canvas folding chairs you buy for the beach, but we said we had to get there. So we got the gear on board and away we went.

The aircraft was loaded with jet engines going to a major Air Force repair depot in Guam, we found out after being airborne.

"Good, we will go all the way to Anderson with you and see what happens there." I said. At least Guam was half way to our destination.

We stopped at Hickam Field, Hawaii. The USAF Flight line supervisor was excited about the dogs and being quarantined.

"No, problem Lt. We will just be here for a couple of hours while the aircraft refuels and we will be on our way." I explained.

He was right, the dogs were supposed to be quarantined upon arrival in Hawaii, but one thing he did not know was that way down, at the bottom of the State of Hawaii Department of Agriculture regulations, is one paragraph that says that "military working dogs and law enforcement dogs are exempt if they are under the care and control of an official of the military or in case of law enforcement dogs a Hawaiian D.O.A. official"

Even after all the hub bub, we made it to Guam. We stayed a couple of hours in Guam and moved on to Sangley Point Naval Air Station, Republic of Philippines aboard a USAF C-130. The C-130 was refueled and loaded with a load of baby chickens. I don't know how many, but many crates of baby chicks to win the "hearts and minds of the people" in Viet Nam. While there, I sent a message to Steve Ford that we would arrive in Saigon that night. Finally, we made it.

Steve's Team met us at TSN and gave us a ride their compound.

"Keep that evil bitch away from me." He told Howie Muhler pointing at Cup Cake, a very bad-tempered German Shepherd. Steve liked Cup Cake, but Cup Cake did not like Steve.

The USAF at TSN's kennels was a real help. Our dogs had to live in the crates if we were not with them. The Air Force handler brought us several buckets G.I. issue dog food called Maximum Stress Diet "or M.S.D. Food, Dog, Concentrated" made by Hills Company. Good stuff, in a pellet form about one third the size of a small Tootsie Roll Candy bar. They were highly concentrated, a canine version of C-Rations, but in the bush we fed them what we ate.

German Shepherds are noted as being finicky eaters anyway and always having loose stools when traveling. I have always felt since seeing the dogs "in country" that the reason for this was because they were not allowed to build up the bacteria in their digestive systems. However, we have people breeding dogs for confirmation as opposed to ability.

Once we met with Steve, we saw a simple solution to the problem. We did not know if it could be done or not. The Viet Cong swimmers were entering the water close to their intended targets was our best guess. "How?" we asked while in a secure briefing room. Q: Are they swimming from a nearby shore?

A. Don't think so...too many "eyes" watching
Q   Are they being brought up river in a "bum boat" (a small river flat bottomed boat used by locals as transportation.)
A: Possible, but the river is supposed to be secured from water traffic at night and the river has USN / ARVN Patrol Boats on the river.

Comment: "We feel we have enough good A-1 Intelligence to think that they are swimming from underwater caves near the scene of the incidents. HumIntelNet (Human Intelligence Network, or "spies" if you will, have reported seeing devices that are described as being similar to the tanks that UDT Teams use.

"Interesting..." I thought.

At that time frame in 1971, we did not know that a dog could, under the right conditions, detect a human body or swimmer, alive or dead underwater. This little experiment confirmed what we had been thinking for years. Dogs can track on water under the right conditions and could detect drowning victims underwater:

A. The bare bodied swimmer gives off a unique odor, the same as if on land, and the odor would rise to the top of the water and float on the surface until such time as it was dissipated and drifted down river (in this case).

B. The swimmer with a "wet suit" on also left an odor, but the wet suit had a unique odor that could be detected by humans while we were on dry land.

C. The air bubbles coming from the swimmer's breathing equipment also gave off a unique odor, and

D. Dogs could be taught to work, standing in a boat and "track' a scent on the water.

So how were we going to prove any of this? Oil of Anise. We could place the scent of the oil on an object and sink it in the water. If the dog would "alert" on the anise, then we proved our theory.

One thing we did learn is that some dogs "barked" for an alert, something that we did not want for obvious reasons. We did not want to (a) draw attention and (b) we did not want to alert the bad guys.

Now, to prove what we thought we could do.

The dugout canoes used on the rivers in Southeast Asia were all about the same. We needed to procure a canoe and have several divers to assist us while we trained. Steve Ford's bunch was able to handle all the above.

The next question was where to do the training? Steve knew we could use several islands off the coast that had the type of terrain we needed. The "bum boat" was easy.

We went to one of the islands and put a swimmer underwater with just a wet suit and SCUBA equipment.

We could not use Cup Cake at all. She would stand in the boat and "shake," but Bo and Jesse Long's dog "Sam" loved the boats.

The dugouts we were using were made of long tree trunks split in half and "dug out" with an axe. Often they had outriggers to act as stabilizers. We used the type with stabilizers since we did not know how well the dogs would behave in the dugouts. As it turned out, the dogs did well and we could use small outriggers or none at all and feel safe.

We got anise oil from the cooks and bakers' for the project. We poured a small amount on a 4 x 4 battle dressing and then with a piece of parachute cord, tied it to a swimmer's weight. We dropped it in the water and left it there for a short while. Again, we did not know how scent worked underwater, but we had an idea. Since we were using "oil" it would float on top of the water like gasoline. As it turned out, the dogs loved the game and would alert by scratching the bottom of the boat.

Next we smeared a small amount of anise on the wet suit of a diver. The diver would just sit on the bottom of the lagoon we were working until we banged on a piece of metal we had in the boat. For example if we banged twice, the diver would come to the surface. If we banged one time, the diver would swim away towards a second predetermined designated point.

At one point we had the diver come to the surface and grab the dog as he popped out of the water. After a few times of this, there was no doubt in your mind, the dog would tell you and "alert" that a diver was down there.

A few more days of training, three altogether I think, and we would not use the anise anymore. We would "patrol" the lagoon until we found the divers. All went well, but would the dogs "alert" on divers they did not know? The divers we were using were from Steve's Team. Steve made arrangements with his counterpart in the Vietnamese Special Forces to go to another nearby island and play "bad guy". The next day the ARVN divers were in place at another island. It was about a one hour run in a PBR (Patrol Boat River) to the other island. The Navy did not want to send two boats as it would weaken their patrol net. They wanted to bring the ARVN divers over to their island and then come pick us up. It was a little hard to explain to a "non-dog" person that the scent of the ARVN (Army, Rep. of Viet Nam) divers would still be in the boat and be a "pre-scent" or "clue" to the dogs.

But they did send a PBR to us and another boat took the ARVN divers. At a predetermined time we boarded the PBR and took the dugout in tow. When we reached our "patrol area" we left "Sam" and Jesse Long on the PBR and "Bo" and I went in the canoe.

In a very short time, we found and alerted on the "bad guys" who were underwater next to a sunken hulk about 200 yards off the beach. A second one was near a pier jetting out into the water. We were happy as a pig in poo poo, as they say.

The next few days we put the theory to work, and it worked. A Lykes Brother Steamer came into Port of Saigon and was tied up at the U.S. Navy Pier. After dark we put a small canoe in the water with two paddlers and "Bo" and I. After an hour or so "Bo" got bored and laid down in the bottom of the boat as best he could with his muzzle over the side.

The ships are lit up when in port to allow enough light to work. In this case, a beam of light went out about fifty feet from the ship's hull and reflected on the water. We stayed out of the light because this meant a diver underwater who was looking up at the light could see us. We slowly drifted with the current and then paddled back up stream.

About midnight we changed dogs. Jesse and "Sam" with two new SEAL Team paddlers took over.

We were all on the pier about 0300 just snoozing, when we heard a loud "whump" and another "whump" which sounded like a mortar round going off underwater. It was Jesse Long, "Sam" and the other two people he was with him. We jumped to the edge of the pier just in time to see the second geyser of water coming down. The alerted PBR's were making their way to the pier and the Marine Reaction Forces were poring out of their bunkers so we had plenty of help.

"Sam" was barking and someone in the boat, and I don't know who yelled, "I bet that mother fucker won't do that anymore".

A body was floating on the surface. The dark skinned diver didn't have a tank on, but a mouthpiece and a small amount of hose was still attached to him. He wore a knife and no belts. The diver was already bloated from the water and air entering his body under a tremendous pressure. A second diver broached the surface a short distance away, but was never found. It appeared as though he was trying to go down river.

"Well, we thought at least we have a direction of travel to start a search." Steve Ford said. After it had settled down and sunrise came, I had Jesse come over and debrief the rest of us. We ALWAYS debriefed after an operation or incident to insure all facts were fresh in our mind. I do it even today.

Jesse said that "Sam" had done the same as "Bo". After a short period of time, he got bored and hung his muzzle over the side. The reason he hung his muzzle over the side is that the bottom of the dugout canoe had water in it and at times the water sloshed forward and got on his face. And as anyone knows about a GSD, they do not like water around the muzzle.

Jesse explained "that they were bored, dog was bored and they had drifted down stream a short ways just whispering about anything."Sam" stood up and bristled looking up stream towards the ship, which was about 150 feet away. We had been sitting still and holding on to some reeds along the shore. We got quiet and started to ease back up stream. When they were close to the edge of the light glowing around the ship, "Sam" stood up in the bow of the boat and was looking straight down. About that time one of the SEAL Team members paddling the boat noticed a line of bubbles coming up from the water off to one side of the canoe. He motioned to his partner and they started paddling backwards. When they had backed down about

20 feet, they tossed a frag in the spot where the bubbles were coming up and after a short period, tossed the second. This is when they all saw the second swimmer breech the surface for a split second at the edge of the light, heading down stream.

When Jesse tried to assist in recovering the bad guy's body, Sam would have nothing to do with that.

"Ain't no dude looking like that getting in the boat with me." said Sam the dog.

A week went by and we had no more "bites" while we "were fishing" as we called it. In the mean time Steve got permission to write an "OpOrder (Operational Order) to search the river banks on both sides of the river to open water for caves and "to search for and destroy such enemy fortifications with the most effective means."

"Charlie, can we do it?" Steve said.

"We can try, Steve. We can try". I answered with no conviction in my voice.

Early the next morning, SEAL Team 7 and the K-9 Teams set out on the river with a couple of "bum boats" and three PBR's in the area to back our play. Steve had also been working the MACV Intelligence folks to see if they had any "sniffs" as to what was going on. A Marine Captain at MACV said they had heard of caves along the river for years, but nothing like we were proposing. Still, he would keep his ears open for us.

As Steve was walking away, a young corporal stopped him and said he had just received an HumInTel report about several men carrying "butane tanks" to a fish farm located along the river, near the place where we had fragged the divers in the water. The corporal stated he was a sports diver "back in the world" and that this had caught his attention.

Steve thanked the Corporal and asked that if he heard any more whispers coming in on divers, to get in touch with him at his office.

After the Operations Order became official, we kept "fishing" in the river. We would float along the edge of the river looking for anything that could be used as a cave entrance. But we found nothing and thought maybe we were wrong. We looked step by step every reed bed was searched by no signs of divers.

One afternoon we decided to put the dogs on the bank and walk alongside looking for divers. The boat teams would paddle. We were getting sore from kneeling in the bow of dugouts for eight to ten hours a day. The shore party would be made up of two dog teams and several "shooters" from the SEALS. The canine and handler would go first with a "shooter" following about twenty paces back, then a dog team and another "shooter." The party of four would be spread out far enough where it would not be tempting for the bad guys to try and get us all at once.

We would try and move at the same speed as the paddlers in the water below us. We could not see them all the time, but when we caught a glimpse, we would adjust our speed to match theirs. Sometimes we got ahead of the boats, other times we had to catch up.

The handlers were doing the searching and the "shooters" were watching inshore. "Dutch-Boy this is Box Top. You have several people moving across a paddy coming from the bush moving towards the river. They are about 300 meters in front of you and 200 meters inshore from the river" crackled one the PBR's, who were moving along the river with us.

We rounded the curve in the river to our right, arrived at the apex in the curve, and did not see any movement. That bothered me. Seeing a potential bad guy is one thing because you can take whatever action is required, but when you cannot see them, you worry.

"Box Top ...say again location of target........we have not made contact yet..." One of the "shooters" said in the PRC-25 radio.

After a few minutes of waiting, "Box Top do you have a visual on us?" we asked. "Roger a visual Dutch Boy...wait one...out." the PBR answered back.

A quarter of an hour passed. We were squatted down along a trail in the open sun. The dogs were hot and we should have tried and get them to better shade, but we dared not move until we found the bad guys.

"Dutch Boy - Box Top.......negative contact....the...er, ah...disappeared." Ooooops, now we needed to look closer. This may be the answer.

Once you get in a "safe spot" in a situation like this, it is hard to move out again at the same pace you had when you "went to ground." We needed to get out of the open and into some shade. We moved forward about a hundred yards and found a few trees along the bank that offered some shade from the hot tropical sun. Also, the spot made a good extraction point if we needed to "di di mau," an asian version of "Get Out of Dodge."

We could see a PBR easing back and forth a few hundred yards down river from us, looking.

The canoe paddlers had reached the spot just below us and whispered that they were going further downstream to see if they could find anything. We were advised to "stay put" until the mystery could be solved.

After an hour elapsed, we saw nothing, but the boat teams had found a irrigation canal. It was the type that worked by raising up a set of the boards that allowed for water to flow into the rice fields.

The irrigation canal was about eight feet wide and was dry on the land side, as if someone wanted to keep the water OUT of the rice paddy. This did not look right to the SEAL Team, so they got curious. These guys were good at "reading" signs and the habits of the local indigenous personnel.

By then the rest of us had decided to move back on top of the dike and walk further east, towards the location where the boats were concentrating their search.

We had walked approximately fifty feet when "Sam" stopped. Froze while still looking off to the left, towards the area where the mystery people had disappeared and slowly went "down-stay."

Jesse eased up behind his dog and lay beside him. There was a grove of mango trees just ahead. It was a small one, the trees were in poor looking condition for being so close to the water like this. They looked "different" from the others.

"Click click" was heard in our earpiece. It was Jesse. We all stopped, the other teams stopped too since we were all on the same frequency. The river patrol boats eased just a little closer. You could see the crew on the guns and launchers waiting.

Jesse had been looking ahead with his dog and pointed his finger at his "dog," then his own "nose," and then pointed "ahead," towards the mango trees where "Sam" was still starring. "The dog smells something ahead" was the message.

There was a small rise about ten yards ahead of Jesse. It might have been two feet higher than where we were, but to us right then, it could have been the Great Wall of China, blocking our vision.

Jesse patted himself on the head meaning "me" or "I" and pointed forward down the trail. "I am going to have a look." I had seen this gesture many times before.

Jesse and "Sam" low crawled ahead, neither of them rising but a few inches off the ground until they reached the top of the rise. I could only see part of what was happening after they reached the small rise due to the brush on the trail, but I saw "Sam" tense up as if he was going to spring up and run but Jesse had his hand on his withers.

I saw Jesse roll over on his left side and ease the .45 caliber ACP out of the holster. I thought "O.K Boys and Girls, its 'Howdy Doody Time." Do not ask me where we got started with that saying. I do not remember and do not want to remember.

Something was going to happen.

Everyone was quite. No one moved. Jesse was by the ridge and could see what was ahead while we could not see shit.

In the ear piece I heard in a soft whisper, "Bee Bop and Willie......ease up." I could not tell who it was, but I knew they were near us because of the signal strength and how clear the message was. I still could see Jesse Long and "Sam." I saw Jesse replace his weapon and start easing forward again, crawling with "Sam." Jesse looked over his shoulder and motioned with his right hand to "come" and a "down" motion, meaning "come on but stay low."

Since there was a SEAL Team member ahead of me on the trail, I had to wait for him to clear the rise before I could start forward. I made sure that the man behind me knew what was happening before I started forward, as he was facing backwards down the trail, watching the rear.

We all made it over the rise and I saw that Jesse was walking forward in a crouch with "Sam" on alert looking ahead. Again, we heard "Click! Click!" and we went to ground. I saw the mango trees ahead and knew that was our target.

All of a sudden I heard a Claymore mine go off, followed by two grenades and a lot of automatic weapon fire. The PBRs cranked up and presented a broad side to the river bank so all their guns could be brought to bear and aimed at the bank. However, they did not fire since they did not know where the good guys were. Good discipline on the PBR crew's part, everyone was shooting but them and they were standing on deck in the open. It takes guts to do that.

In three minutes it was over and here is what I was told what happened as I could not see. It makes you wonder sometimes...

The PBR's did NOT see the bad guys again after they started across the open rice field because they dropped into a "hidey hole" and walked underground towards the river in a tunnel. The bad guys had a "smoke hole" or vent at the base of the mango trees and that was why the trees looked different. The smoke hole or air vent was made in such a manner that the smoke would travel up the trunks of the trees and dissipate into the atmosphere through the branches without being seen.

The bad guys had an "out hole" well hidden in the dried up irrigation canal near the water gate that the SEALs noticed. The SEALs followed it to the base of the mangos without being seen. The SEALS operational radios were on a different frequency from our canine teams but when "Sam" went on a "Down alert" they started looking closer and found the "hidey hole" opening.

The VC, in this case, not the NVA (North Vietnamese Army), had beat us to the trail we were on and were going to ambush us. Sam's alert stopped that, and the truth in the matter is that "Sam" was not trained as a "patrol dog." Somehow he figured it all out on his on and what we were trying to do.

The VC had a Claymore mine, which were easy for them to get, but the SEALS "Bee Bop" and "Willie" had found the mine, but "Bee Bop" and "Willie" did not know where the VC were located, they only knew the general location was in the mango trees. In the process they could almost "feel" a small motor running and the vibrations it made while they were laying in the water. It turned out that a Dutch made generator running on butane was being used, because it did not give off "smoke" like a gas or diesel motor.

The VC had been watching us for a long time, we later found out. They had a "spy hole" in a mango tree. It was the "different" tree, the tree trunk had been hollowed out and they had us under observation. They could see us all the way down the trail we were on up to the small rise we were worried about, but as long as were prone on the ground, we were not a clear shot for them.

The VC did not know the SEALS were in the dugout. They only knew about us on the shore. While we unknowingly kept their attention, the SEALs slammed them from the opposite side. When the SEALs triggered the Claymore it surprised the VC since they had the "clicker" (detonator) with them. The VC moved, gave away their location, and had two frags and a lot of ammo expended on them.

After the SEALS called in a full platoon, the tunnels were examined and found to be a major communications bunker for reporting river traffic and a central location for NVA sapper teams. This was by far not the "biggest" bunker system found by SEALS, but after this discovery, the ships in port were rarely hit anymore, all because of a team of canines…

…and then I woke up. It was all as clear to me as if it had happened yesterday.

Chapter 17

Major construction on the house, kennels, stables and guest cottages had been completed. Hard-topped surface roadways between the barns, garages and house had been installed for the ATV's, Golf Carts and "Mules" to run on. They were not designed for big trucks. Gravel roads had been installed where big trucks were required to deliver feed and hay.

The first look at the house and grounds when you arrive is very pleasant. When you turn off the road you drive through a wide, double electric gate onto a paved boulevard with natural trees and grass along the center. It is a quarter mile from the road to the house itself. The driveway comes up to a park, which is as big a football field, and you turn right to go around it. There is a large band stand, and park benches with arbors scattered throughout the park. Inside the park are paved sidewalks and small hidden buildings that blend in with the scenery. These are used as restrooms, the garden house, and utility buildings to serve food and beverages to our guests.

There was lighting outside where you could play baseball, or soft casual lighting along the paths and buildings for more interment affairs.

"Bart, look at that park...have you ever seen anything like it?" Those Brats conned me again." I said. "All I was going to have was a couple of lawn chairs and a drinking fountain out there, maybe a string of light in the trees if we wanted to stay out late, and look what we ended up with?"

"It started with a band stand, just makes it look good, the Brats said...Bah....then we had to have paved sidewalks, and then lights around the edge of the sidewalk...." I walked off pretending to be angry.

It was a nice, warm Friday and all the work had been finished early. We were setting around the pool, even I had a bathing suit on. The Brats all looked fabulous in their swim suits, along with Robert and Emil. Bart and I had threatened to buy a "Speedo," but the Brats bought ours for us, they were afraid that we were serious.

"Didn't want you to scar't the dogs" Patricia said as they all laughed.

Stella was almost wearing a bathing suit...but on her petite frame it looked good. Even Maria looked good in her swimsuit, Bart and I looked like sad sacks. We tried to act like we were indignant, but it did not work.

Paticia's two girls, I can never keep them straight, came running over to me while we were sitting by the pool. They had started calling me "Big Papa" for some reason. Jody and Jenny had very pronounced Cajun accents that were cute to listen to. Patricia had a Cajun accent too, but not like the girls. Among themselves they spoke French, but not in front of others.

It was a Friday afternoon and nothing was going on this weekend. Sammie and Emil had left in Sammie's Suburban. Both of them had packed their bags and did not say where they were going. Robert said Sammie was giving him a ride to the airport, since he did not have a driver's license yet, and that he was flying to see some friends in Washington, D.C. We did not think Sammie was going with him, however Sammie is very secretive about her after-hours life.

Sassy was sitting around the pool getting a tan and was also "on call". I wanted one of the principals of the company to be available "just in case." So the weekly duties ran from Monday to Monday in a rotation manner. The only restrictions were to be available and sober to conduct business if something arose.

Robert and Stella were planning a trip to Memphis for an Elvis meeting of some type. Stella was a big fan of "The King," as she called him, so they were going early in the morning. They had become very open about their romance.

Maria was always here. I could not get her to take a day off. She enjoyed her job as Staff Manager, I think that was what her official title was. She supervised the 23 staff members she had hired for the house like a Drill Sergeant. Gardeners, maids and cooks all shivered when she was present. I did not know any of the "staff," as she called them, but I do know things happened when she was around.

We had built quarters for "our hands" as I called them, to one side of the property. Nice apartments, like the ones you see in town, I would live in them. They had a separate driveway after you entered through the big gates. Each one had a separate mail box down by the road, next to the kids' bus stop. I have always been a firm believer of treating the staff well and will always continue to do so.

Patricia had felt left out when the dogs were purchased and she said that she wanted to learn how to be a handler. So she was given a large male German Shepherd to have as "her dog." When the dog was tested for courage, he had failed. He was "gun shy" and would not "come out." This dog was given to Patricia. I was somewhat worried about having the dog around the children, but Sassy felt that there would not be a problem and I felt comfortable with her decision.

Amber had asked to leave early that morning after she received a call on her cell phone. She did not offer to share with me what it was about and I did not ask. She looked upset and tried to cover it up when I asked her about it, but it is her life. She left about ten that morning and she did not come back. However, I knew that she did not take any clothes out of the side portico when she left.

"Sassy, if you have somewhere to go, I can take the duty for you…take off and I will hold the fort down." I said.

"Thanks, Charley…but that is okay," she said after a long pause. I could not tell if she was asleep or not. She had a large pair of sunglasses on that covered her eyes. She looked at her watch and then jumped up, put on her robe and started back to the house at a fast pace. Like Amber, she left without ever saying a word.

Maria came out of the side door with one of the maids. She walked over to the beverage area and unlocked the doors with a key from a large ring she carried on a snap. The "beverage area" was actual a fully equipped bar with a large stereo and tables. During the winter months, the sliding doors could be slid shut to enclose it, but on nice summer days, it was left open.

Maria came over to the table and sat down with me… we were on the shady side now and the afternoon sun was going down in the bayou. The dogs in the kennel were quiet. Patricia had feed them and allowed them out in the training field to "clean out".

We had two kennel-men who took care of the kennels and the horses. Maria said she did not know who they were and that they were not her *Primos,* but they showed up and asked for a job. She hired them for three weeks to mow and cut around the place. We had promised Patricia some hands to help with kennels and stables, so these two were hired.

We had a kitchen area that we could seat twenty people at three long tables, so the hands, or "staff" as Maria kept reminding me, could eat in their own apartments or eat with us. Meal time was set and announced. So if you signed up for a meal, you had better be there or the "*bruja*" would cast a bad spell on you. I cannot recall what she was saying since she spoke Spanish so fast, but I did understand what was said back to Maria, "*Si, Senora...Si, Senora,*" as she stood in the middle of the kitchen. All meals were served buffet style and there was always plenty to eat.

During the week, those that were "home" ate in the big dinning room. Usually, four or five times a week we ate together and enjoyed each other's company. Sometimes we even had guests from the local neighborhood visit us. Maria would sit at the head of the table nearest the kitchen door. She would taste the food and maybe take a sip of wine, but she did not eat much. It took me a long time to figure out she had a button under her foot and when she pressed that button with her foot, a serving maid would come in and talk to her. It took me a while before I figured this out.

While Maria and I were sitting at the table, Patricia and the girls came out to the poolside bar. Rex, her dog, followed along with Patricia and lied down on the cement pool deck while the kids went swimming. Maria kept going to the bar to "check on something" and a few of the hands came up to the pool to swim. Since the bar was open, they went in and either had the young lady who was working there fix them a drink, or they did it themselves.

They acted very much like a family members would do if they were over at your house.

I only had one rule: "you will conduct yourself as ladies and gentlemen or leave."

Patricia noticed me watching Rex lying beside her. "What's with him?" I asked as she looked towards the bar where the two new hands were sitting at an outside table.

"Nothing" she said and reached over and patted Rex's head. "Tell me" I almost said as an order.

"Well, I dunno. Those two new guys Maria hired to work in the kennel, they scare me. The way they look at me and all and they are drinking sometimes. I won't let the girls go down to the stables or kennel at all anymore," Patricia said as the girls were sliding down the water slide yelling "Watch me, Big Papa! Watch this!"

"Have they said or done anything? I quizzed. "No, just they way they look....."

I called over Juan "Johnny" Gonazales, my *"Segundo,"* or Foreman, and asked him about the two new guys.

"Un dos hombres es hombres muy malo, Jefe. Es pelegro para La Senora y los ninas. Tome cervesa quien trabajo. Yo no tengo nada para un dos pendejos. Nada." Johnny said as he sat there and drank his beer.

"Gracias, Juan."

"Denada, Jefe." He walked back over to where his wife and brother-in-law were sitting in the bar.

Patricia looked at me after Johnny walked away. "What was all of that?" she asked. "Oh, Johnny will talk to them… don't worry."

Maria brought me a portable phone, "Sharlie, its par jew…jew want to take it?" Maria said as she brought me the phone. She had been standing to the side, talking to Juan and his wife.

"Sure Maria. Who is it?" I asked.

She set her orange juice down and walked away from the noise a little and inquired who it was. While she had her back to me I took a taste of her "orange juice." It almost took my head off. "Don Pedro Brandy" I said, and put it down.

Don Pedro Brandy is good, some of the best in the world, and she was drinking it almost straight. No wonder she was talking the way she was. The old lady was ripped. "Hee heeeee…" I chuckled.

"He says his name is Paul something….*a gringo*" and she flopped into a chair and shoved the phone towards me.

"Charlie Gray here…..!" I said.

It was Paul Pierce, the Assistant Warden of Angola Prison in Louisiana.

Paul was an old friend of mine and a "dog man" too. We had talked several times in the last few weeks.

"Your man will be there in the morning to shoe the horse if you don't mind, Charlie...." "Thanks, Paul. I have been looking good hot shoe'r for a while. He can have all the work he wants with these three dozen flea bags we got." I laughed.

"He will do you a good job...and thanks, Charlie. I will tell you sometimes about him sometimes, if he don't. He is a good man. No one knows he has been paroled except you." Paul said after a few minutes of conversation.

"Say, Paul. We are going to have a house warming in a couple of weeks. Can you come down? We got the room."... pause..."sure thing then. I will send you an e-mail. Yup, getting where I can do more than turn it on...good talking to you too...and I will." I hung up.

I turned the phone off and looked over at Maria. I was going to discuss a house warming party we had planned, but she had fallen asleep. I reached over, shook her and she woke up and looked around. "I guess you had better turn in," I said as the sun was going down.

I motioned for the duty bar maid to help me take her up to her apartment in the Big House where she had her own suite.

"I will have fun teasing her about this tomorrow," I chuckled as we helped her up the steps.

The next morning was a cool breezy day. Fall was coming on in the Bayou Country. No place like it in the world, moss hanging off the trees. I walked through the kitchen and grabbed a cup of coffee.

"Donde es La Senora?" I asked the cook, who just giggled and shook her head."Hmmmm…I wonder if my Spanish is getting to be that bad?" I asked myself.

I went to the very large back porch and was gazing over the land, sipping the coffee and thinking life is good. I watched the horses easing up to the stables to be fed and listened as one dog was frantic in his barking at something. Sounded like a Shepherd. "Oh, they always bark at anything" I thought.

There is a strange van down at the stables. A forge and anvil were sitting on the ground. Must be the new horse shoe'r Paul called me about. Good, glad to see he likes to start early, a good sign.

A short time before, down at the stables, Patricia was passing through the long center aisle between the stalls to check on a new mare we had bought a few days before and had shipped in. She was wearing her normal working attire: a pair of too big rubber boots, a T-shirt and jogging shorts.

As she was walking by a stall, she noticed it was open. She reached to close it and noticed there were beer bottles and several liquor bottles scattered around on the saw dust floor. She looked inside and saw one of the two stable helpers laying on a fresh pile of hay.

"You guys are going to get in trouble. You know Charley don't allow no drinking in the stables or kennels."

"Puta." the shorter of the two said as she looked in.

"Where is your friend?" Patricia was saying when the second of the two walked behind her and shoved into the stall so hard she fell down. At that time, "Rex" her German Shepherd, came in the stables looking for Patricia and saw the one man push Patricia into the stall.

A deep throated growl came from Rex as his hackles rose up. He charged the man who turned and saw the dog coming, but slammed the stall door just in time to keep Rex out. When the door closed, it was a solid wall.

Patricia was trying to get up when the first man who was in the stall, moved like a cat and grabbed her from behind putting his arms under hers and across her chest. He was holding her, ripping at her bra. Rex barked frantically, trying to get in the stall, but couldn't because the solid door was closed. After they were sure the dog could not get in, they both turned their attention to Patricia.

Patricia was kicking and screaming as hard as she could, the dog was barking, but these two wanted revenge for her "snitching to the boss."

As one held her from behind, the other grabbed her boots and pulled them off. After the boots were thrown aside, her shorts were pulled off. Patricia was only wearing panties and a T-shirt. With wild laughs of glee, they were trying to pull her panties down, but she was fighting and kicking so hard, they just decided to rip them off. They did not expect that the elastic string would turn out to be as tough as it was though. In the mean time, Rex ran out of the stables, around to the opposite side of the stables while Patricia was still struggling with her attackers. They had finally succeeded in ripping her panties down, but in the process had scratched her thighs and stomach area. One of the men had unbuckled his pants and had allowed them to drop to his ankles while telling his friend to hold her on the ground for him.

He was attempting to pry her legs open when he became angry and slapped Patricia across the face several times. She was stunned, but still fighting. She did manage to raise a leg up and kick her attacker in the stomach, causing him to fall backwards since he was drunk and his pants were down.

When this happened, the second man attempted roll over on top of her and was trying to unbuckle his pants when Patricia managed to get both feet in his chest and shoved with all her might tossing him over to one side. They were both so drunk and laughing so hard, that they did not see Rex jump through the open window into the stall. As Rex came through the window, his rear legs propelled him forward onto the man Patricia had just tossed off her. The man with his pants down was trying to get up, but Patricia was much faster now. She was up, and she grabbed a pitch fork as Rex had his victim by the collar bone, which had snapped on the first bite. The man was screaming in pain as Rex shook him like a rag doll.

Patricia jabbed the man with his pants down in the crotch. Four tines of the forks found meat: one through the now flaccid penis, one in the pubic hairs, and two in the soft inside part of the thigh. Patricia pulled the pitch fork out and was going to thrust for the head and heart area with all her strength, which was high at this time, when the pitch fork handle acted as if it was frozen at the top of the stroke.

"It ain't wurf' it lady." said a big voice deep voice. "They ain't wurf it'." she heard, as the biggest black man she had ever seen held the pitch fork motionless.

The dog was still shaking the screaming man while the other was holding his crotch area and looking at the flowing blood.

"Get you dawg, Lady" he said.

Patricia called Rex and he came "out" like he was suppose to have done in training. He went over to Patricia and started licking her hand.

Patricia was looking around for her clothes when the black man in a horse shoer's apron handed her a slicker coat to cover herself with.

She put on the large slicker coat, that was far too large for her, and then wondered what to do. She turned and called Rex as she backed out of the stall. The large black man was grabbing the two culprits by their shirts. He banged them together like a cymbal player and tossed them in the corner. He did not have to tell them in any language to stay put.

"What the hell is going on her?" Bart Duffy said, as he ran over to the stables. He had recently driven up in an ATV and had heard the commotion. "...and who are you?" he said looking at the black man.

"I'm the horse shoer you hired, Cap'en. The one Mr. Paul called you about last night." he said.

"I don't know what the hell you are talking about." Bart said. "Patricia Darling, are you alright? What happened?"

As she kneeled down to pet her dog, Patricia explained in a calm voice what had happened and how Rex came to help her. Rex was being held back by Patricia, he was ready for round two and whoever the black man was..."Where did he go?" Patricia asked as she looked around as Charley and Maria came running up.

Patricia explained what had happened again to Charlie and Maria. Maria asked Patricia. "Did they.,.er, ah, er, did they...?"
"No Maria. Rex and a man helped me out...."

The two men over in the corner were screaming and moaning in pain, one with a broken collar bone, and the other with puncture wounds.

Bart said "There is a black dude outside, starting to shoe horses. Said we hired him."

I went over to the man and asked what his name was. He said his name was Sam Rose and "Mr. Paul said I got a job her shoing horses. To see the Cap'an here." he said.

Sam Rose stopped shaking the horse shoes in the hot coals for a minute and looked at me in the eye, with the coldest look I have ever seen.

"Want me to take care of 'em, Cap'in?" Sam Rose said.

I looked at him for a full minute. "No, Sam Rose. We better call the law…"

There was a cellular phone handy as always and Bart called 911. In less than five minutes a Parish Police Unit drove into the front gate. One of the hands waved them over.

Two very well dressed Parish Officers got out of the car, a male and female officer and they were briefed on what had happened. We told them about the two men in the stall.

They went over and looked at them. One of them took out a hand held radio and called for EMTs.

In the mean time the Sheriff of the Parish drove up and we all introduced ourselves. The Sheriff asked the deputies if they had called a Trauma Team and was told no, the victim did not want all the fuss, but they would still call if she wanted them to.

"Sheriff, may I make a suggestion. Let's take all this business up to the house and talk about it. What you say?" I looked at the others standing around.

"Of course Mr. Gray, but we may need to get photos of...of...of..." he was looking for Patricia.

"Cox, Patricia Cox, Sheriff and call me Charlie please. I promise to vote for you now." as we walked towards the house.

Patricia, Maria and the Deputy June something or another, walked up stairs to the kennel apartment where Patricia lived. The two girls had walked down to the apartment complex to play with the other children. They were not aware of anything that had happened.

After a few more minutes, an EMT Unit rolled up and looked after the two men that some of the hands were standing watch over. A couple of machetes had appeared and if the law had not been here, an "incident may have occurred." All of the staff were very close, like a family, especially to Patricia. She treated everyone with respect. I have no doubt that between the hands, Sam Rose, and the gators in the swamp something would have happened. We would have saved the state a lot of money if I had let them.

The EMTs fixed the prisoners up to be transported and another set of deputies followed the ambulance as they rolled towards the hospital.

Photos had been taken of the scratch marks and statements written by the Deputies . Maria had doctored the bruises and scratches, which were not deep and would heal. Patricia's lip was swollen and she would have a bruise on her cheek and maybe a black eye, but she was in pretty good shape considering what had happened. She and Rex had won the fight.

It was only 10:00 AM when all the excitement was over. I wonder what the rest of the day would bring...

The Sheriff was a very nice man, a retired Louisiana State Trooper. This was his home Parish and where he was assigned as a Trooper.

Sam Rose had to be interviewed. The Sheriff knew Sam Rose and took his statement. "You know his background don't you?" the Sheriff asked.

"No, but Paul said Sam Rose may tell me one day." I said.

"Well, two crack heads broke in his house, raped and killed his wife. Sam has always been a horse shoer, went to church, never into anything, good citizen. Well, he went down to one of the juke joints on South Main here looking for the two culprits. Someone had told him who did it, seen them coming out of the house. When Sam went through the front door and up to the roof where they were standing, the bar owner called 911. We arrived and seen Sam up on the roof, beating the crap out of them. 'Sam! Sam! Don't do that! Let me have 'em! I will handle them!" I said.

"You want'em Sheriff? Here they are." Sam Rose said to me, and he tossed them off the third floor to me. They were dead before he tossed them over the side." the Sheriff stated.

I shook hands with the Sheriff and they all left.

Chapter 18

The horses we used for our program were all bought from working cattle ranches in South Texas. Their ages were an average of eight to ten years old. Horses of that caliber were not spooked by anything. They were very stable and very sure-footed. Prior to buying them, all the horses had been working cattle for three to four years.

Since we wanted the dogs to work with the horses, we had to teach them a different "heel." The "heel" we used for the horses was meant to be the same as the original command: "heel to the rear of the horse."

When the dogs were taken around the horses the first few times, the dogs had a tendency to run up and nip at the horses' heels. There were two ways to attempt to break the dogs from nipping the heels of the horses. One was to put a shock collar on the dog, or when they nipped the heels, the rider would tell the pony "roll them" with a sharp kick. One kick would break them from coming up onto the horse, but the rider also needed to be ready in case there was a "rodeo."

The dogs and the horses enjoyed the little runs the handlers had for them, but the dogs had to be under complete control by voice commands before the horse phases were ever introduced. Most handlers carried a bull whip to "pop" and correct the dog if they did not "out," or respond when given a command, or when they would not go to "heel."

If the dog was running a track, it was up to the mounted rider to keep up with the dog. We had extra horses for the local law enforcement to ride in case we were involved in a felony tracking. You always want a local law enforcement officer with you. If we came to a fence, we would cut it with the fencing pliers we carried on the saddle. This action falls under the "hot pursuit" rule used by law enforcement, but if you cut a fence, you are responsible for getting it repaired. The law is not broken when you cut a fence in hot pursuit, but let the local law enforcement officer is the one to make the decision.

The old saying about training a horse of "four and forty" is true. That means ride forty miles in four hours over open terrain. It is an old Mexican vaqueros saying and it works. You build up to it and when you reach that goal, you have a pony that will have a lot of "depth" or stamina, but you cannot train one that stands the stall.

Another issue to consider is loading the horses into trailers. If done properly, they should walk in with no fear and wait to be secured in the trailer.

Bart Duffy, Amber Ames, Stella Dunn, Pat Cox and Emil Dupree were out on one of the dirt roads coming in from the main road learning to back a thirty-four foot Goose Neck Horse Trailer. They were using a series of cones that Bart had so they could learn how to drive the 4-door Ford 350-Diesel towing the trailer. They were all surprised at how well they were doing, and after they understood what was going on behind them, they felt confident.

Next, Bart taught them how to backup to a ramp using only the mirrors. They had been training for a few days in the afternoon during break times. Sassy could back the trailer up and park it on a dime with no problem. Stella had the most problems because she did not always get to come to practice since she had to be in the office a lot.

If you are going to say you have a horse team, then you had better do it right and do not just put a few signs on a truck. All of our Special Ops Teams people could ride well and the ponies were kept in shape by taking regular rides, not by letting them sit in the stalls.

The "Equestrian Teams" that I had seen around the country so far, especially the "Search and Rescue Teams," had all been a joke. Out of all of the ten or twelve teams I have seen, none of them worked. What a joke.

Robert Perez taught them all to ride motorcycles over rough country as well, as safely as on the streets. Any of the countries we might have to visit would likely use motorcycles as the main mode of transportation. Again, we all learned. I got a few bruises on my old carcass, but Robert taught us well.

Next up was boat training. Everyone learned to safely handle Zodiacs in the Gulf and in the Bayous here in Louisiana. We had plans to do rough water training on the Tygert River in Grafton, West Virginia or in Phillipi, the next town over. Grafton has a beautiful river flowing near it, and we thought that it will make a good training area.

It was my weekend to be on duty, so Maria and I were alone by the pool. It was going to be a long weekend and most of the hands had left to visit family.

Amber left right after supper. She said she had to meet a friend who was coming from Atlanta area to meet her at some place called Powder Springs. She said she would see us Monday night.

Sassy was dressed up. I mean, she was a doll when she put on her "girl stuff" as she called it. She had asked to use the Towncar and of course "Ole Charlie Tuna" got conned by the baby green eyes. She did not have to give me the keys to her truck since all the vehicles were keyed alike by brand name. For example, all Chevys and all Fords used the same keys.

Robert, Stella, Emil and Pat were still in the house getting ready. They had some concert they were going to attend in New Orleans. Patricia's two girls were spending the night at one of the hands' houses, which they did regularly.

"If we get any more kids around here, Maria, we're going to have to add on to the school bus stop." I said as she sat down on the bench in the park across from me without commenting.

It was quiet in the park across from the house. Birds were chasing bugs and the owls hooted in the bayou nearby. It was the end of a perfect day when I felt the tingle of my pager vibrating on my left side.

The pager scared me since I never received many calls. I looked at the phone number that was on the voicemail we all used in the "War Room." We called it the "Bat Phone," it was our operational emergency phone.

I got Maria's keys and opened up one of the small buildings we had in the park where a phone was located and called the number. It was Red Baxter according to the recorded message. "Red Baxter? Red Baxter?...Oh yeah," then I remembered him, he was a retiree from the ATF or something...

I walked across the street to the office with Maria and called the number while she went to the coffee bar and put on a pot of good Colombian coffee. She looked in the refrigerator for a bottle of Baileys Cream for the coffee which she found in there.

I called the number Red had left and when he answered, we talked a few minutes about some old friends.

"Charlie, the reason I called you is, well... I understand you have people that can find things....Is that right?" he asked.

"Red, I don't know....I would have to know what you 'lost'?" I responded. "Its a person, Charlie....South America... in Peru..." Red hesitated.

"You got to share with me, Red, before we can help..."

"Well, several days ago one the executives that we have on contract with our Executive Protection Service was kidnapped on the outskirts of Lima coming home from work. The driver was not harmed, and the kidnappers left with Jack in the back seat. That is all we knew until a couple of hours ago. The bodyguard was sprayed with pepper spray and pistol whipped. Someone just called from Lima and said they had Jack. They gave us some information that only Jack would know, so we believe they are on the square, but they would not let us talk to Jack. They gave a price in U.S. Dollars, but we don't pay ransom. Jack knew that we have a "no pay" policy when he went down there, but we will spend all we have to get our clients back, and the perpetrators..."

"So, what is the game plan now?"

"We have assets there to assist. They are good. Locals who have a good network, but the local citizens are afraid of this bad guy bunch, Shining Path, and the locals have a "know- nothing-hear-nothing-see-nothing" attitude. We did find out one thing. They did drive out the *Calle de Sur,* a main highway and then walked into the jungle. Down one of the many paths leading into the jungle, but we are talking about a hundred paths in a ten mile area. Our local assets even attempted to place an electronic listening device on the car that was involved, just in case he went back to the area. They got it on the vehicle, but they seemed to have changed vehicles because the "black car" came back to where they started. Our assets said they know the car and driver, but did not approach him. He was not a "volunteer" in this matter..."

"Again...what is next?" I asked.

"Well, that is why I called you, Charlie...on recommendation from a couple of folks that know you in State," meaning the U.S. Department of State.

"Red...State has some good security folks. Let them run with..." I advised.

"They won't touch it. Oh, they will make inquiries and all, at the nightly cocktail party, but this is a Peruvian Company that hired Jack Thompson. Even if he is a U.S. citizen, there has not been any report of the grab. The local folks in Lima will want to be the lead on this deal." Red added.

"How much time can they spend on it? I mean, with them being in a local political rumble, military wanting to take over and all?" I asked.

"Well, if we put some money down in the right places... but all the locals are afraid to move." Red said. "There is a big political shake up in the wind, and who knows who is going to win?" Red said.

"Look Charlie, we got to do something. How do you charge? You know, I mean to go down there and help us?" Red asked.

"Red, it will cost you nothing, but what we spend out of our pocket, and we do like to spend money...." as I mentioned an estimated figure for expenses.
"Wow, that is a chunk of change, but....go for it. I will get it cleared by the front office." "Red, there is one more thing. You go with us, we 'help' people, we don't 'do' for them." I stated and waited for an answer.

After a ten count pause he said, "Okay, but jeez Charlie, I been polishing a chair for a couple of years...and you know..." Red stated.

"Yeah, I know. You got a fat ass like me from not working out for too many years," we chuckled, "but that is the deal, when can you be here?" I asked.

"Well, today's Friday and Mondays a holiday and I guess I could.... Red said.

There is a Delta flight from Atlanta to New Orleans that will get in here tomorrow morning at 0730, be on it. I will have someone pick you up. They will be wearing a baseball hat with "Purina Pro Plan" on it and a khaki shirt." I said.

"Say, now wait a minute. I am the Chief of Security for..." Red blustered.

"Red your ass is in a crack. You were caught flat footed and you need me...or rather us. You have a half-assed incompetent group in Peru that wouldn't or couldn't catch clap in a whorehouse. You need me....do we understand each other?" I said to Red.

"Okay, Charlie...you are right. We need to..." he tried to laugh it off.

"Good. Now that we understand each other here is what I want your folks in Lima to do within the next 48 hours, because it is not a holiday in Peru some poor asshole is scared stiff because you dropped the ball and we shall be in Lima by Tuesday latest." I advised Red.

After I explained to Red what we needed done I hung up the phone.

"Maria? You know how to make all these buttons work? So we can get people back her pronto?" as I tried to remember what Stella told me to do.

"No...not my "yob" she teased.

"Well, I will just have to page each one in turn." I started trying to get the auto-dialer to work. There was supposed to be a button you pushed and it paged everyone… After a few minutes, I managed to use it to page all the folks.

In less than ten minutes I contacted with all of the team members except Emil. Amber said she had dropped him off at the airport and had not seen him since. She was waiting for her "friend's" flight from Atlanta to land.

"I really need to see him, Charlie. I will be there as soon as I can." Amber said. I hung up the phone very puzzled.

"I advised Amber she had better make it a "quickie" and cut it short. We had a job." I told Maria.

Maria looked at me over the top of her glasses and told me to not to be so crude. "Stella just called in on the other phone and she said they had turned around and were heading back." Maria said as she hung up the phone.

"Okay…" I said as I was digging around in Stella's desk trying to find Steve with Atlantic Airlines, "need to talk to him." I mumbled.

Oh, well. I went to my desk and found a bill on the desk from Atlantic Airline. I was supposed to send to Shirley, the C.P.A.. I dialed the number and I got a recording, a long series of "If you wish to stick your finger in my ass… please press three…and if you want me to put my finger in your ass…" I hated those things, but finally I got a "person" and asked for Steve, but was advised that he was off for the weekend.

"Look young lady, I want Steve. You get him, or someone who is the ramrod in that God dammed lash up. My name is Charlie Gray. You have to have a list of customers that do a large amount business with you. Find it, and here is my number…" which she copied down. "I know it ain't your fault and you are doing what you are supposed to do, but this is an emergency. Capeche?" I finished.

"Charlie, you sure are a grouch these last few days, is there something wrong?" as Maria brought a wonderful cup of 100% Colombian coffee over.

"Yeah. I am going to start my period, and I feel…" I teased. "Charlie, stop. That is not nice…" she said.

The phone rang in my office. I knew there was a way to "pick up" a call. "Let's see…is it 'pound star 1?'" It turned out to be right and I answered. It was Steve from Atlantic Air. I explained that I wanted a plane to take us to Lima Peru, ASAP. Could he find us one, what did he have?

"Charlie, this is a big football weekend. Every plane is leased out….pretty tough to find something and I know we don't have anything, but I do know someone in Belize City that has a stretched Merlin. Seats about 10 passengers and can carry some freight if need be. You interested?"

"Who is this guy? He ain't a dope smuggler is he?" I inquired.

"No. No. No. He is a nice young man, a British citizen, he was born there when it was British Honduras. Married

282

a local girl, a black, and she was not happy here in Atlanta so he saved his bucks and bought this plane. He flew as my co-pilot for several years. Nice kid. He has a charter service now, but Charlie...I suspect you may have to advance him some money...for fuel and all. You know just getting started and all...." Steve said in a small voice.

"Okay...on your say so. Tell him to call me. Can you find him?" I asked.

"Yeah, I have a pager number on him someplace, but I can find him." Steve said.

After he hung up, I never thought of Belize City, British Honduras having phones, much less a pager system, but that was 50 years ago when we were down there. They are known as Belize now. Oh well, they are getting modern.

"Yo." said Bart Duffy as he walked into the room.

"Where you been?" I asked. Hmmm...he looked strange, he had the "cat that ate the canary" look on his face.

"He has been up to something..." I thought.

"I thought you were going gambling?" I smiled.

"Oh, I changed my mind...I can do that can't I?" he chuckled.

"Sure can…just wondering." I said, "Bart, what the hell you doing wearing a suit and all? You going 'sparking' or something," I teased. I knew he had been having a hard time since the death of his wife last year. I had not said a word to him. We must all grieve in our own way.

"You would not believe me if I told you." he snickered.

"Okay, where you been?" I asked, waiting for the joke I knew was coming. "Church" he said "Church?" I stopped dead. "Church." he repeated. "Funeral?"
"Nope"

"What then?" I sat down across from him after he got a cup of coffee. "I meet this woman…" he started.
"I KNEW IT! I KNEW IT!" I shouted and slapped the counter top.

"No, No, it's the truth…real nice widow woman. Works at the Ace Hardware Store in…" he was saying, "we went to a church social deal for 'Singles'."

The phone rang.

"Goeff Albright here, Mr. Gray," as he pronounced "Geoff" like "Jeff."

"I understand from our mutual friend Steve you are in need of an aircraft?" the voice said on the phone.

"That's correct, when can you be here?" I asked.

"I can be there in the morning...oh, let's say...after I clear U.S. Customs, 0730, is that okay?"

"Fits the schedule just right, we will have a car there to meet you. We want you here for the briefings and all. Go to the Executive Air Terminal please, have them completely service the aircraft, hanger it too. Do a 120 hour check on the plane and have anything done that needs to be done... including wax and polish." I said.

"Well, Mr. Gray...er, ah...Well, you see..." He mumbled.

"Geoff, don't worry, my treat. You can take it off the tab," I said. "What do you normally haul?"

"Tourist is my main business. We have some wonderful beaches here, lots of tourists from Houston and New Orleans." he said. "I keep the plane in tip top shape. Oh, where will we be going and how long will we be gone?" Goeff asked.

"We will make this trip worth your time. You can start the clock when you get here and you will be briefed. Ever been to Peru?" I inquired.

"No, no, I can't say that I have..." Goeff almost became inaudible. "Mr. Gray, look here..." he was searching for words.

"Charlie. Everyone calls me Charlie, and don't worry Geoff, you won't be carrying nothing that you would not tell your mother about." I chuckled.

"Well, that is a relief. I thought maybe you were gong to try and sneak in and out of places. Like in the cinemas, you know...eh, what?" he laughed real loud.

"Naw. Nothing like that, just regular tourist stuff. I will see you in the morning. Okay?" I hung up.

Chapter 19

The next morning, the *Segundo*, John Ramirez, went to the airport and picked up Red Baxter, the security consultant and Goeff Baxter, the pilot from Belize City at New Orleans International Airport. It was a Saturday morning, and the traffic was light going to and coming from the airport.

Johnny had picked up Emil Dupree as well. Emil had called Friday night while I was trying to get all the folks together and said that he was on the plane when the pager went off. He had to stay on the plane until it turned around and flew back from Washington National. Emil was the type of man who would have walked back in he had to meet his obligations. He said that he would have called on the "airphone," located on the aircraft, but he felt that it was not secure. Instead, he called from Washington National airport, and was picked up when he arrived in New Orleans.

So, our Operational Team was made up of the following:

Bart Duffy: Bart was taking a Labrador Retriever that was trained for "Scent ID." This is where the scent of the subject, in this case Jack Thompson in Peru, could be identified. If the kidnappers gave us an object and said it came from Jack, the dog would tell us if Jack's scent was on the article. We did not know what Jack had been wearing, so we relied on the dog. Bart would also carry a 9 mm S&W in a shoulder holster just in case.

Amber Ames: Our Operational Team Leader. Being a former Marine Captain, she knew tactics and she knew her weapons. If you looked at Amber, you would never even guess that she was as strong and capable as she was. She could play the West Virginia hillbilly girl act to the hilt. She could play it so well, that you would never know that she was a U.S. Naval Academy graduate with a degree in Marine Engineering. Her M.S. was under control and she had no symptoms affecting her, yet.

Samantha Joann McGee: She looked and talked as if she stepped out of a role from *Gone with the Wind*. A college professor and chemist for Dow Chemical, she was the explosives expert for us. She had to work twice as hard to qualify since she had no experience in any of this type of weaponry. She was initially afraid of using a .22 rifle when Amber started working with her, but went to the heavier weapons in a heartbeat. She was a crack shot with a 7.62 rifle and could drive nails with a Walthar. She handled a 9 mm Uzi as well as anyone, and had built up her body strength with lots of hard work.

Cassandra (Sassy) Malloy Phillips: Oklahoma cowgirl, agile as a deer. She could handle her weapons as well as anyone else. She always had on a "secret smile" when she talked to you and became very interested in explosives while working with Samantha. Sassy claimed she had never been or would be a "Suzie Homemaker,"

but she made Filet Mignon in a wine sauce for us one night when Maria was away, and I did not even know what to call the chocolate dessert she made. The way she pronounced it in French made it sound exotic. Sassy was taking with her the German shepherd "Prince," a great tracking dog, the best and most reliable in the kennel, and a 9 mm Starr. She could "eyeball" an M-79 Launcher well enough to drop rounds in a bucket. She also liked using the bow and arrow too, and had the upper body strength to handle it well.

Robert Perez: He was our Heavy Weapons guy, as strong as a bull moose and could carry a FLN and many belts of ammo. Still, each team member would carry two belts of 7.62 ammo for Robert. He was also bilingual, which was another plus for us.

Emil Dupree: Former French Foreign Legion. He looked the part. Emil could be the lead man in any movie.

He was going to carry an M-79 Grenade Launcher with 20 rounds in a vest-like pouch. Emil was also a master at making booby traps. He taught Samantha and Sassy how to make traps, and they picked it up so well that they could make traps on their own.

And of course there is "Ol' Charlie," me: I liked using a Remington 870, 12 gage shotgun with a folding stock and extended magazine. You do not have to be a good shot with it, you just need to shoot first. The weapon was a little heavy, but it was a good one for "close order drill" and it could clear any room with one round.

Each person would also have a sidearm of choice. Most carried a 9mm so that the extra Uzi ammo could be used if needed.

We asked for four "shooters" when we arrived to Peru. I did not know a soul there, and I hoped that it would better than what I had heard about. That is why I wanted Red Baxter with us. If he fucked up and hired shitheads, he would be with us, it was that simple.

Speaking of Red Baxter, I had found out that he was a "ribbon clerk." A front office puke with the ATF, and I believed it after seeing him. His pot belly was bigger than mine, and when I shook hands with him, his hands were as soft as a whore's. He was a lawyer in the Seizure Section. There was nothing wrong with that, but he was not what I expected.

We had all gathered in the War Room when Red and I walked in. This included Patricia Cox and Johnny Ramirez, my *Segundo*. As long we were going to be a team, everyone would be involved.

When we entered the room, everyone was either stoned-faced or had their "game face" on. They acknowledged Red, but that was all. We had never discussed doing this, but it showed me how they felt about outsiders, and that they were unified. It was frightening to see their hard looks, not a smile in the crowd. If you took a photograph of them, it would have been called "Stone Cold Killers." It was very unreal and it sent a visible chill down Red Baxter's spine. Normally, Red would be the center of attention, but not today and I did not think that he wanted to be it either.

Amber had been doing some background work through her friends in Washington D.C. on Red Baxter and his Security Company called R.I.O, Inc., pronounced "Rio," Spanish for river. I noticed she had a folder lying in front of her and knowing Amber, she was loaded for bear.

"Red. What kind of cases does your Security Company handle?" I asked. "Oh, just some 'special cases.' Why?" Red looked at me.

"Does 'Red's Information Office' mean anything? Electronic listening post in Lima? A "Company Store?" I asked in a very low and soft tone.

"I don't know what you talking about, Gray. Who the hell have you been talking to. That is so fucked up, you don't even get a laugh for it." he stuttered.

"And the business office is on the 23rd floor of a building called…called, uh…" I was trying to remember.

"*El International*" Amber answered in a quiet voice from the far end of the table.

I said.

"Red, I don't know if we want this job. I smell a rat, and you are holding the bag,"

"I don't know what you are talking about, Charlie. We just have a security consultant firm." Red tried to explain.

"Why did you select us? There are many more and better qualified people than us. We have no Central Intelligence Agency connections; no one even knows we exist." I said after a looking out the window blinds and saw a van drive by the front gate, real slow. I made eye contact with Johnny Ramirez, he got up and left the room without a second glance.

Red started fumbling in his brief case. He brought out a large manila folder. Untied the string at the top, and removed a stack of 8 x 10 color photos and passed them around. No one in the room had said a word or made a sound since Red entered. Everyone looked at each photo as it was passed around the large table.

One showed "The Shadows" from the road and another from the air. One showed Maria and I in the Winn-Dixie store with two of her grandchildren children. Another showed Samantha at the airport meeting an unknown Caucasian male who appeared to be getting off the plane. One showed Sassy by a pool at a very large motel talking to several admirers. Several photos were of Emil, Patricia, Robert and Stella at a movie, a rock concert and walking in a mall somewhere. One showed Emil carrying one of Patricia's girls on his shoulders. It looked like they were on the beach somewhere. One picture was of Bart Duffy standing in front of a hardware store talking to a very attractive lady. There were several others of the hands and their family members too. John and Lucy before Lucy had the baby. That meant these photos were made six months ago.

When all of the pictures made the rounds and came back there was a silence, dead silence. Electricity was in the air.

After the photos were put away, Goeff Albright came to the room and stopped at the door.

"Sorry," Goeff said, "Didn't mean to interrupt anything." and he started back out the door.

"Come on in Goeff. No problem," as I stood to greet him, shook his hand and introduced him to everyone in the room. They all nodded slightly in turn, but never changed from what I started calling "the look."

A few minutes of chit chat and Geoff was offered coffee from the side bar and asked if he was hungry.

"Well, actually…yes. I had not had a chance to eat." he said.

As if rehearsed, the side door from the living quarters opened,and a house staff member entered the room and went directly to Maria and spoke softly in Spanish.

"Geoff, would you mind eating in here with us? We are briefing and there are a few points you may want to have your input on and some of the information that is being developed may affect our…er, uh…future plans. You have not met Red Baxter." Being very British and very proper, Geoff walked over and introduced himself to Red. I half expected Geoff to say "tennis anyone" like in the old movies.

"As a matter of fact I have met Mr. Baxter before. In Atlanta, I believe, a year or so ago." Goeff said.

Geoff could have set off an atomic bomb and got the same reaction from Red Baxter.

"Red, you are the most fucked up "spy" I ever met. Oh…ah, er, ah…Sorry Ladies." and laughed out loud real hard.

For the first time, the others in the room almost smiled, but their eyes gave them away to me.

"Did I miss something here, what?" Goeff looked puzzled.

About that time Johnny Ramirez walked back in and sat down. He did not say a word. There was only a slight "nod" of the head when I looked at him.

"Well, good," I said, "we have all had a little laugh, so why don't we take a break. My kidneys are screaming." as I walked out the door.

Outside on the main road, a siren went by at high speed, and then another. Strange, I thought, the road past our house was a dead end into the swamp. Well, if you have a four wheel drive you can get by on the levy, but otherwise, it goes nowhere.

As I was walking by Stella's office, the phone rang and she answered. "Charlie, where is Johnny. Miguel says it is *muy importante*," Stella said. Still giggling about Red Baxter and Goeff.

"Yo, Johnny! Telephone in here" I yelled across the hall.

Johnny came in and answered the phone. After a short conversation in Spanish he hung up.

"Charlie, there has been an accident. Miguel reports that Pepe was driving the tractor on the main road and hit a van. The van went in the bayou. It had three men in the van. No one was hurt, just got real wet, but they are pretty angry. Local S.O. is there now and wants to put Pepe in jail. You want me to handle it or what?" Johnny said with a straight face.

"Yeah, go ahead and handle it, Johnny. Better call the Sheriff on his private line and ask him to look into it, Stella has the number. We can handle any damages and better call Max the Mouth Piece too. Make sure we get a full ID on the passengers too. Have the hospital check them out and get back to us. Advise Doc Lindsay, he can make sure they get a good check-up." and I turned and walked back into the War Room.

After we got back, Stella walked in and around the table to my side and handed me a plain manila folder. I opened the folder and read the single page typed note, "he has a transmitter on his person, I think it is the brief case. We found the frequency and jammed it. Nothing got out of the room. I detected it when he entered the building and put ECM (Electronic Countermeasures) to work. No signal got out. –Sassy."

I closed the folder and passed it around to the others as Sassy walked in the room as cool as can be. She looked at me with a "smile" and said nothing. She looked like the cat that ate the canary. I would have never thought of that. Checking the folks as they walked in the main entrance, smart girl, but she was a big input on making an "electronic warfare room" right under the War Room.

The ECM room, as we called it, was not much more than a closet. It was just a room for checking phones for taps and also to check for bugs. It was originally going to be used to monitor all incoming and outgoing calls, but we never got around to using it, until now.

During this time, one of the kitchen staff brought a large covered food cart with fresh pastries into the room, mainly for Goeff's breakfast.

After we had all settled down with coffee and scones, the phone rang in the conference room. Samantha picked it up, listened for a moment and started writing. She never said a word, but the yellow tablet page was full and she slid it over to me.

The hand written note said: "The S.O. just left, all have been identified, no charges against Pepe, passengers refused medical help, vehicle leased at airport this morning, Johnny said he saw electronic equipment inside the van, van was on its side, all equipment looked wet, along with passengers, all talked like Yankees, tow truck on the way, don't know how they are going to get to town."

I wrote on the bottom. "Have Johnny give them a ride, play "dumb Mexican," see what he can find out." and slid it back to her.

Samantha excused herself and left the room.

Billy L. Smith Sr.

While we were talking about a flight plans with Goeff, load limits and fuel stops, Samantha came back in a slid me a note that said: "Pepe is taking them to town, using ranch's Suburban. Johnny told him what to do, he said 'no speak English' bit…"

All this time Red had been very quiet and did not say much. Had he figured out that we knew what we are doing? To keep him busy, I asked him to check with Peru's Embassy about bringing dogs. I also asked him to make sure that his people were ready for us and for the latest updates on whether there had been any demands by kidnappers.

"Red, use my office so you can have a privacy, if you like. Just dial straight out, any number on the phone is okay." I said as Sassy went to the door acting like she was reading something in a folder. I knew she was going to the ECM room to monitor his calls.

"Oh, let me just use this phone," Red said taking a small cell phone from his brief case. "No need in spending your money, I'll just step out in the hall if you don't mind."

"No problem, Red, whatever you like best." I said and went to my office.

A short time later Red came to the office and said his phone would not work this far out in the woods. "I wonder if Sassy is up to her mischief again?" I thought to myself.

We offered him the phone in my office, as Sassy walked by the open office door, she paused a second and just smiled. She could say more with a slight smile than any human being I know.

Goeff wanted to use a vehicle to go back to the airport and check on the aircraft to make sure that it was ready for a long flight. Stella gave him a number to call her for billing instructions to get fuel and service.

The staff was drifting away from the meeting rooms and office. Everyone had their own chores to do if we were going to pull this off, but no one was talking to Red. They did not act impolite; they just did not pay any attention to him.

Around noon, Pepe came back from taking the three passengers to the Marriott Hotel near the airport, and told Johnny the three passengers did not say much on the way back. They just stared out the window and mumbled something about "getting eat'n by a 'gator was not part of the job description." Pepe tried to find out if they were staying or leaving by offering to wait and take them to the airport, but they told him not to wait, so he left. Pepe is a good man.

I told Patricia I needed to talk to her when she got a chance. She looked at me in a curious way and nodded her head "okay" and walked away. She was acting strange, but whatever it was, we could talk about it.

We were taking a little break while Red made phone calls in my office, so Patricia and I sat down at Emil's desk in the corner cubicle for a talk.

What I wanted to discuss with he was her schooling. She had received her G.E.D. last year and had recently started college. I told her that I would pay all college expenses as long as she passed all her courses. She could use one of the vehicles anytime she needed it, since we had several pickups and the two Suburbans. The old car she had rolled up in was parked in back, and we were now using it to train dogs. Of course, I had bought the car from her and made sure she had a good replacement, nothing fancy, but good. Arrangements were made to have a copy of her grades come to my office since the Bowl Weevil Foundation was paying for the school.

Patricia's grades from the college had come in several days before. In yesterday's mail in fact and I had not had a chance to open it until then. I opened the printout and looked and the grades. "Just as I thought."

Patricia came into the cubicle and sat in the small chair next to the desk. She was shaking and almost in tears. "What is wrong, Patricia?" I asked as I scooted the roller chair at Emil's desk closer so I could reach her hand. She started sobbing.

Maria came into the small cubicle and then went to the next office to get a small chair and sit down beside Patricia. Maria put her arm around her. Patricia leaned on Maria and sobbed in her breast, like a child. Maria just let her cry. I

300

looked at Maria and raised an eyebrow in question, "What is wrong?" Maria made a motion to be quiet for a moment, so I did. I left and came back with a box of tissues from the bathroom and a glass of orange juice from the refrigerator located behind the bar in the War Room. While I was doing all of this I looked at the rest of the crew. They looked at me like I had a tail, with faces saying "you mean old man, you made sweet little Patricia cry."

"Whaaaaat?" I wanted to say, but just let it lie and kept walking. Even Stella looked at me like I had my pants unzipped. "What in the hell did I do?" I said to myself.

When I got back from getting the orange juice and tissues, I noticed the room was empty except for Red, who was now in my office with the door closed and all the others were back in the War Room.

I entered the small office, sat down and placed hands on the desk with my fingers in a position as if I were praying. I sat there a full five minutes waiting for the sniffles and nose blowing to be over with.

Again I looked at Maria with an unspoken question.

"It is a thing of the heart, Charlie Gray and you don't help it a bit." Maria chastised me in words and looks.

"Maria, if Patricia has medical needs, it will be covered by medical insurance and…" I said.

"She is in love, *pendejo.*" Maria said sharply.

"Great, but why am I to blame? She is not in love with me is she?" I said, trying to break the tension.

"No, it is Emil, and in some ways, you too, but not the same." Maria said softly, and the tears started again.

After a few more sobs the tears stopped, and Patricia began to speak.

"Charlie, when I showed up here last year, I had nothing. I was broke and hungry, willing to do almost anything to get food for my babies, and I was going to do anything... you know, with men, for money. I thought that was all I was good for, but...but...."she said between sniffles.

"Well, Honey, you know." I started to say.

Maria looked at me like a mother looking at a rude child that spoke when they should have been listening. I shut up.

"Charlie, you encouraged me to go back to school, and I did every night, and the rest of the folk here, Samantha, Amber and Sassy," she sniffled, "helped with the school work, and looked after the girls while I was at night school. And then Emil came and helped. I got my G.E.D., a regular high school diploma and everything. I had a graduation ceremony. Bart came, and the rest of the people here, but you didn't..." Patricia said and started crying again.

"I didn't know anything about this, Patricia. I knew you were going back to high school, but I don't recall ever being asked to a graduation ceremony. Help me out on this Stella, I didn't know." I pleaded.

"You had to go back to *Tejas,* court dates," Maria said. "You didn't even buy your *mija* a present, but don't worry, we did and you with all your money." she said.

"*Mija?* Maria, she is not my daughter," and the tears started big time, "well, you know what I mean. She is like a daughter and the kids, well…" I faded away.

"Excuse me. I have to go to the potty" Patricia said and left the office.

Maria just looked at me. I stood up and looked over the top of the wall as Patricia went into the restroom and walked out into the main part of the room. I noticed "The Brats" just looking, arms folded across their chest or in some other form of displeasure.

"Charlie, I have backed you on everything, some of the little things you did, but this. Well this is a hard pill to swallow." Samantha said with Amber and Sassy nodding.

"What? Dammit! What did I do? So I screwed up and missed the graduation. When was it? Where was I, Stella, you are in the know. Where was I?" I let my voice rise a little too loud and anger was showing.

"You were in North Dakota, looking at some dogs," Stella replied. "Oh, well…er, ah, ah…Why wasn't I told about this?" I demanded. "You were Charlie, I told you." the pixie red head said.

Patricia came back in the room and as she went by each Brat, she got a hug and a word of encouragement.

"Charlie, about my grades in college, I tried Charlie, I studied. Ask Amber and Samantha, and Sassy too, they helped me. I did try, Charlie, but the stuff they wanted me to read in English, *Red Badge of Courage*, I knew what he was going through. I did it too, but I just don't think I put it on paper right, the English teacher…well, she makes fun of the way I talk and always correcting me in class in front of the others. So I have a hard time talking to anyone." she said as she looked around at the others.

They were all facing me when Emil walked into the back of the room and stood listening, not saying a word.

"Well, that ain't all of it Charlie…I mean isn't all," she giggled a little, the others smiled approvingly.

Patricia looked at the other women in the room. Information was exchanged between them faster than an IBM computer and yet, not a sound was made, not a word was uttered.

"I don't want Emil to go wherever you are going. I mean, I know where Lima, Peru is. I looked it up, but Charlie, he….er, ah, I…" she stammered. One of the girls got

her a new tissue," Emil is the only man I ever knew that…
well, never tried anything or you know…He never even has
tried to kiss me. Well…and the girls adore him, he is so kind
to them, takes us everywhere and…" she stood there with
tears running down her checks looking at me.

There was a long silence, no one even moved. All eyes
were diverted to somewhere.

"Patricia," I said slowly, measuring each word to make
sure I did it right. "The college grades could not be better,
I am proud of you, proud for you," I went back to Emil's
office and got the envelope from the college, removed the
grade sheet and passed to the others.

"Your grade average for the semester was 3.8 in Math
101, 3.4 in English 101 and 3.9 History 101. " I said with
real pride as she reached for the score sheet in almost shock.

"I can't believe it. I passed. I passed! I really did do good
didn't I?" as she asked at the other girls.

Emil had not moved from where he was standing beside
the copy machine. Sassy turned around and saw him, but
did not acknowledge him to the others and turned back
around and learned on a desk.

"Charlie, does Emil HAVE to go. I mean…what if
he…" Patricia said just holding her hand out to me, which
I took.

"Why don't you want him to go? You think he is afraid, or a coward, not enough man to go with us?" I asked.

"Oh, no Charlie, nothing like that. He is a real man. A man I have read about in books, the ones I get from the library." she pleaded with me "You tell me to leave him here, and I will. You tell me this would not hurt a man's pride and dignity. You tell me that he will not hate you for it, your choice." I said.

"No, no, no, I love him Charlie." she gasped, surprised that she had said anything like that. She put her hand up to her mouth as if she had said naughty word. "Well, I do love him." as she looked at the other women and to Maria, who now turned and saw Emil across the large room. "I don't want to have anything happen to him." she said and spun around, seeing Emil in the room for the first time.

Patricia started to run from the room out the only door. Tiny Patricia could not get by a large man like Emil who scooped her up in his arms as she ran by like a small child and kissed her.

"I was always afraid to say anything to you, about my feelings." Emil whispered, as Patricia kissed him, her small frame pressed against his large square body.

Emil looked around at the rest of us and said. "I hoped we would kiss one day like this, but not in front of the whole family." he smiled.

For some reason, we all applauded and Patricia blushed and I didn't know what to do. I walked out on the Widow's Walk at the end of the hall. It was a little stuffy in there anyway. Maria must have thought it was stuffy too. She walked out and stood facing the opposite direction, we did not speak for a full five minutes.

"Charlie?" Maria said

"Yes, Ma'am?" I answered.

"Charlie..." she said, just looking at me, "Charlie, sometimes you piss me off." and slammed the door going back inside to the meeting.

I stood there, not knowing what to say, "Sometimes I think I should have stayed in bed," I thought as I went back to the War Room.

Chapter 20

"This will be our final Operations Briefing," I said after everyone was back in the room, "we should be packed except for the dogs, all the equipment is in the van, all baggage in the van. So, let's go down the check list."

"Bart?"

"I have sent all our equipment ahead by Airborne Freight, sent our uniforms and associated equipment. It should be at Jorge Chavez Airport in Lima about…2 hours from now." Bart said, looking at his watch.

"Amber?"

"I have received a scrambled e-mail from Red's people in Lima saying they have the required amount of ammo and weapons in a safe house for us. Transportation has been arraigned. We are going in as tourist, rich Texas investors and also we are there to buy *Paso Fino* horses, have several breeding farms lined out to visit."

"Samantha?"

"I have all the chemical loaded in a make-up case. They are disguised as perfume bottles, hair spray and the like. The bigger the bottle the bigger the bang, all the bottles are operational, and by that I mean if a customs agent get curious we can squirt him with perfume and tease with him. However, when the tops are twisted 180 degrees counter-clockwise, you have 15 and 30 seconds delay, depending on how many times you twist the top. Each bottle is RDX or HBX as a primary charge, about twice that of a regular hand grenade. We can also use them with a trip wire if needed," Samantha said in a very professional tone like a college professor would do. "But they are excellent as time delays".

"Sassy?"

"All communications equipment has been checked. I also have a direct satellite phone available if we get into a clear spot to transmit. Personal body mikes are in my case disguised as hair dryers and curlers, have 8 of them."

"Emil?"

"I have all documents we will need to evade if needed, good stuff. Also, each person will be issued a money belt with $5,000.00 in U.S. Funds, 12 Canadian Maple Leafs and "a get out of jail card in plastic," Emil stated.

The "get out of jail free" plastic card was a water proof card that said "if the person with this card is returned to the American Embassy without delay, a $10,000.00 reward will be paid by the Bowl Weevil Foundation of Houston, Texas."

I had noticed Emil was sitting very straight and still, with his hands clasped in front of him on the table. There was tension in his throat, his voice trembled. "Oh, shit!" I thought, "Don't let me find out I have one that freezes up on me in a clinch." I rolled my chair backwards to go to the coffee bar. "That's all I need," I thought

"Robert?" I asked.

"I have all the plane tickets to return to different countries and by different routes in case we need them. The names on the tickets match the names on the passports. Also, our international Visa ATM cards have been activated with unlimited funds, American Express cards are activated and also I have left a list of code words and phrases with Johnny, Stella and Maria." Robert stated.

While I was getting to my coffee, I turned around to watch Robert make his report and I noticed that Patricia was sitting to Emil's left at the far end of the table. She was looking at Emil with the end of a pencil eraser in her mouth, just looking at him. I also noticed a big decorative mirror on the wall behind her. It showed that Patricia had slipped her tennis shoe off and was rubbing her foot on the inside of Emil's knees while sitting at the table. "That little vixen" I chuckled to myself, "Ain't nothing wrong with Emil that... oh well, that can be solved later." I thought.

Patricia noticed I was looking at her and she moved her foot, but she didn't know I could see under the table. I shook my head ever so slightly and closed my eyes. She knew I was saying "no." I could see her blush all the way across the room. Robert, who was setting to her left, almost laughed out loud. Instead, he just snickered and made a very small cough. As for Emil, he hadn't moved a muscle. "Ain't nothing wrong with him."

"Geoff?"

"I have the aircraft ready. I will file a flight plan: New Orleans-Houston-Cancun- Belize City I.F.R. We will go to Belize, refuel, pick up my co-pilot and wait for a "go" for Lima from you. I will also file a flight plan from Belize direct Lima I.F.R. with an open return. I have indicated I will drop my passengers and depart after refueling. However, while on the ground I will discover a leaking oil line and then request a "Transit Status" while the parts are located and the line is replaced. I have spare parts with me, however, that will give me a reason to be on the ground for as long as I need. I may 'have to get parts from Bristol, England,' the Rolls-Royce turbo-props used on a Stretched Merlin. As soon as I get word, I will ensure the aircraft is ready, will have the engines turning at the exact ETA you give me. I also have charts for other airports in the area. I will have a cell phone from Lima, to be given to me by a...ah, yes. Mr. Brown of the R.I.O. Corporation, that is connected to someone I don't know, will always ask for a Mr. Crow or some other bird name to know that the call is authentic. Checking with some of my fellow pilots, air control is pretty lax except for the major airlines. Small aircraft, meaning non-commercial intra-transit are not paid too much attention. At this time of year it is so foggy, most of the time the control tower can not see the end of the runway. We could 'piggy back' off with another aircraft and they would not miss us. Upon departure from Lima, we will go direct Belize City where a second aircraft will be pre-positioned to meet us. I don't know who, that was your call. I believe it covers everything." as Goeff closed his notebook.

"Stella?"

"I will stand by here in the War Room. Handle all communications by phone from the team. I have a list of duress code words from each of you, unknown to the others, in case of duress. In case duress is detected, I shall report this to Johnny."

"Johnny?" I said to my *Segundo,* or Ranch Foreman. "I am to stay here with Mr. Baxter."
"What the fu..." Red almost jumped up.

"To insure we have constant communications with all parties concerned and that a minimum amount of bad things happen. In the event I do not get the correct series of code words from Stella each time a team member calls. Well, don't worry *Jefe*, I understand."

Red Baxter was clearly unhappy. "You have a problem with helping Johnny with "communications, Red?" I asked.

Red did not say a word. "And what happens if I decide to leave? Now, or while you are gone?" he said in a quiet voice.

No one said a word. Patricia's eyes were wide and she was frozen as if a picture. No one moved or said a word.

"I understand." Red said after a moment.

"Thank you, Red. Routine procedures, you understand. I learned it from your operations manual several years ago."

"Yeah," he said.

"Red, is there anything we need to know before we leave?" I asked. "Because if anything goes wrong, well, we don't need to stress ourselves out on a minor problem. Right, Red?" I said.

"No, no. Everything is on the square. Nothing is up. We just want Jack back safe and sound." Red said.

'We will do our best, Red. However, let there be no doubt." I was saying as Red raised his hands up off the table in a surrender fashion.

"I know, Charlie. I know the game too." Red said to everyone in the room.

Stella walked in the room with another one of her famous folders and set it in front of me. I opened it and read that a "Mr. Brown, Mr. Smith and a Mr. Jones have been calling the answering service, wanting to speak to Mr. Baxter. Answering service said they finally left a message. The number is the Airport Marriott Hotel in New Orleans."

"Red, Mr. Brown, Mr. Smith and a Mr. Jones need to talk to you at the Marriott." as Sassy got up and left the room. "Use my office, and Red…Don't mess up, okay?"

"I know Charlie, I know."

"Okay Gang. We are on a short time alert. I have made room reservations at the Sheraton Hotel-Casino in the Miraflores section of Lima, about 20 minutes from the airport. We have several suites on the same floor. If we have to stay there a few days, go to the casino and gamble with your "girl." Go shopping, play the "bimbo" roles. Now, as for today, this afternoon, stay close to the house. Once we ring the bell, be ready to move out in fifteen minutes. Get some rest and I don't foresee anything for at least a couple of hours, but don't get lost. We have the *quinceanera* tonight so let's have a good time." I said as we all stood up.

"What is a queensea…er, ura…Whatever that word?" Emil asked.

"When a young Mexican girl turns 15, it is her "coming out party." It is part religious and part traditional introduction to society. You will have fun. Bart Duffy is the *patrona* for a young lady, since she does not have a father here. Robert and I will be in the ceremony too. You will like it." Johnny said. "There will be two bands and some adult beverages and also, it is black tie".

I thought for a minute. It seems a tuxedo was how all of this got started.

"Stella, do we have a second aircraft on "standby" for Belize City once we get a 'go'?" I asked.

"All done, Charlie, don't worry. I have it wired up, a cargo plane that flies flowers in from Argentina. Old DC-6, Bolivian registry, no problem." she said.

"Where did you get the information on this plane, Stella? If it was from Red Baxter, I don't think." I said.

"Robert, he still has connections you know." Stella replied.

"Thanks, that was a good idea on a Bolivian plane." I said as she walked back to her office across the hall.

"Hey, wait a minute!" I said to myself. "I have seen those aircraft. They are even considered dangerous in Bolivia."

So, now we were ready, just waiting for a call.

I went downstairs to walk outside and go down to the barn and kennels just to look around. I had been cooped up in the house since late last night when all this mess started and there were a couple of hours before the *Quinceanera* started.

I walked out the side portico and was going across the drive to the park to just take a walk when I noticed twenty vehicles sitting in the driveway.

"What the…? Maria, what the hell is going on here? Who are all of these people here?" I said as she walked by going back towards the house with several house staff following her like puppies. "Maria, hold up a minute. Hey! You! Come here, what's your name anyway. I have never seen you before." I shouted at one of the many people running around.

"Quien? Yo?" One of the men said.

"Yeah, you." I said in my best "I'm the Boss" voice.

"Vian se con tu trabajo, Miguel. Yo palabra con el jefe". Maria said.

"Charlie, you can be the boss again tomorrow I promise, but right now I have to get ready for a party. A *quinceanera*, but I cannot do it with you in the way. Shooo, shoo, shoo. Go away." Maria said in a very firm voice.

"Charlie, you said for me to do this. You said make it a good party, didn't you? Make sure we have plenty of food and all, right? and *musica y mariachi, verda?"*

"Well, yes Maria. I did, but who are all of these people? Here look, there is everything here but a circus clown and elephant act."

"Don't worry Charlie, they will be here. They called, said they got lost, but I sent someone to meet them at the store." as she turned and gave orders like a drill instructor. "Charlie, I am sorry, but we have work to do and it is only four hours away." and she turned and walked over to the park.

Now in case you have forgotten, this was a lit park, about five square acres, with an open area in the center about like a football field. I only wanted this to be a dog training area, but "The Brats" turned it into a garden where I had to hire two full time gardeners. There were lit sidewalks, buildings for a bar and recreational area, park benches...

And now look at it. The band stand, which we never used before, was decorated with white carnations. There were red, green and white ribbons, and banners over everything. And look at those carpenters! They looked like they are building a dance floor over the tennis court, all of it, and that was another thing. "The Brats" wanted a little recreational area, but this was a full sports complex. Kid swings, a soccer field and the original dog training confidence course got moved to the other side of the barn one weekend while I was gone.

I walked by a big truck. "Crecent City Sound Systems" was on the side and about that time there was a terrible "squeal" from feedback in the biggest group of speakers I ever did see. In fact, there were some speakers on all sides of the place and on top of one of the buildings.

"Hey, Charlie, you sure got everything looking good? Looks like it will be a great party," Emil said as all the team jogged by. I noticed Patricia was running with them, her little short legs had to pump hard to keep up, but she did.

"I can hardly wait, Charlie…for the fireworks and all." Samantha shouted as she jogged backwards.

I waved my hand and acknowledged their good natured ribbing. They knew who had brought this together.

Fireworks? No one mentioned fireworks…

I walked to the barns. I couldn't take my electric golf cart like I normally would. I couldn't get it out of the shed. Cars were parked all over the place.

As I approached the barn, I noticed Pepe and a couple of the hands were bathing the horse. They had the manes and tailed plaited. Peroxide had been used on my Palomino guiding. Several of the younger boys were saddle soaping and cleaning the bridles.

"Pepe, que es aqui…con los caballos. Porque?" I said.

"Por la fiesta, Patron. La Jefa dije mi." Pepe was saying as he sprayed the horse he was bathing.

"Okay, Pepe, yo se. La Senora." meaning Maria.

"Si, si, patrón, Tia Maria." He almost stopped what he was doing, but recovered his composure.

"Aunt Maria said?" I thought as I walked on by. "Hmmm. Well nothing to it."

I walked around the barns and looked around. I was impressed by the fact that Johnny kept the hands moving and the place clean. Everything was always neat and tidy. Stalls were areas raked every morning, no hay scattered around, I was impressed.

"Fire!" I said aloud. I smelled smoke. Which way is the wind coming from? I ran to the corner of the barn and saw smoke coming from the park. It was just a BBQ pit being used for the party tonight.

I had finished my inspection when I walked past the kennels. Two of the older girls were feeding and cleaning the kennels. Patricia said that she wanted these two young women as part time help, daughters of one of the hands. In fact, it was the Garza twins, Linda and Lucy. Patricia said the boys always got jobs in the summer, but the girls never did and I said it was okay with me, as if it made a difference.

"Those Brats think they are running things around here. Well, they ain't....I am." I thought to myself and smiled, "let them think they are running something."

The sun was starting to go down. As I walked back to the house I noticed all the cars were gone from the front of the house. A few were parked in grass on the otherside of a stand of trees. Still, many people were running back and forth, but I guess they had run out of things to do.

I had to admit, the place sure looked pretty. The sidewalk border lights were on. Some of the hands were checking the lights to make sure they worked.

I guess I had better get up to the house and put on the monkey suit. I hate those things. "Charlie?" it was Goeff, the pilot. "Look, I didn't know this would be formal and I only have jeans to wear. I hope…"

"No problem, Goeff. The only people that wear monkey suits are the people in the ceremony. No problem, you will be more than welcome." I said as I walked with him up the steps to the house.

I was up in my room trying to get the tie on right. I couldn't ever remember if the big tips go up or down Then there was a soft knock on the door. "Come in," I yelled and the door opened.

"Yo, Charlie. I come to give you some help." It was Stella. She was dressed and looked beautiful and Robert was with her. Dressed in his tux, his Latin completion complimented the white shirt of the tuxedo. "I know you have a problem with this, and Charlie, your cummerbund is on upside down."

I finally passed Stella's inspection and was informed I was need downstairs at the main entrance.

"Why am I needed at the "main entrance"? Why not call it the front room?" I asked? "Charlie, I don't know. Maria said for me..." She said.

"Say no more. That woman is going to drive me to drink." I said as I walked to the stairs leading downstairs.

One of the things I insisted on when we remodeled the house was a big staircase with a banister. I always saw big staircases in the movies with kids sliding down them and I always wanted to do that.

"In fact I believe I will." I got on the banister and started to slide. "Charlie! Don't do that." Stella said in a stage whisper.

"Why not? Am I not the *Jefe* around here?" I said as I heard Robert laugh.

I slide down the banister and said "whee" like a little kid. I had wanted to do that for over a year and I felt better for doing it. I got off the banister and dusted myself off and straightened my cummerbund. I had a feeling someone was watching. I turned around, there must have been fifty people in the Main Hall, all looking at me.

I stood there. What could I do?

Stella walked down the stairs with as much dignity as could be mustered, Robert behind her, smiling and making a gesture as if to say "I tried to tell you."

From the crowd came a single pair of hands applauding. It was Bart Duffy, smiling and thinking it was a great achievement, then two, then three, four and finally all of them cheering and applauding.

I bowed slightly to Stella. Robert came over and shook my hand and held up one hand like the winner at a boxing match. It was a funny joke, everyone was laughing except one, Maria.

Maria was dressed in a beautiful ball gown, its color was some sort of green. Off her shoulders with a delicate Spanish shawl and her hair piled high on her head, with a little doo-dad in her hair for a veil to hang from. I don't know how to describe ladies dresses, but I do know how to appreciate them.

Maria glared at me. "I guess that was a foolish thing to do, wasn't it?" I tried to say to Maria.

She snapped her fan open and held in front of her face.

"We must greet the guest, Senor Gray" she said from behind her fan. "Sometimes, sometimes, sometimes...I could just box your ears." she said between her clenched teeth.

I was directed to the front entrance where a red carpet had been rolled out. As I reached the bottom step, I noticed several pairs of headlights coming up the drive. Two limousines pulled up to the front steps.

One of the hands dressed in a suit opened the rear door vehicle. Out stepped one of the Garza twins and then the other twin, Linda and Lucy, with their escorts in full tux. I didn't know the two young men with them, but the twins looked gorgeous. The escorts took their arms and guided them up the steps towards me. As they reached me, the girls in turn curtsied, very deep, I didn't know what to do.

Maria nudged me in the ribs. I stepped forward and said, "Welcome to my home Miss Garza," and took her hand to assist her in arising from the curtsey, "and to you, Sir." I said to the young man who looked like a high school senior, maybe college.

"My pleasure, Mr. Gray. Thank you for your hospitality." Whichever this one was, Lucy or Linda. I did the same with the other twin and received the same formal reply.

I gestured them forward and they walked up the steps into the main room. I watched them walk, their dresses did not move. The girls looked as if the were standing on wheels and just rolled up the steps. These were the same two young ladies I seen cleaning kennels just a few hours ago. They are no longer children, now they were to be considered women.

The second vehicle arrived and they same ceremony was repeated for the other two couples.

After the guests had entered the main room, I offered my arm to Maria and she surprised me by taking my arm as we walked up the steps into the main room.

The first thing I noticed upon entering the main room was the smell of candle wax. There were many candles lining the room. To the right of the staircase was an altar. Father Don stepped forward, turned to the crowd and began saying the Mass, placing the responsibility of womanhood on the young ladies. It was a beautiful ceremony and it lasted about twenty minutes.

Upon the completion of the rituals, a mariachi band across in the park started to play as if on cue. The couples filed across the street into a scene that could have been a plaza in any Mexican village. The Fiesta was about to begin.

The couples danced and the *Abuelas*, Grandmothers lined the dance floors in chairs to watch. The younger parents danced and all had a good time. After a short recess a *Tejano Country Band* took over and the pace was picking up.

As usual, the men gathered outside the lights and had a few "tastes." Bart and I were over with the *viejos*, or old ones, having a few drinks. The bar in the recreation room was running full bore. We noticed that Patricia had Emil on the dance floor trying to teach him to Cajun Dance, which are very similar to *Tejano* dancing. Robert and Stella were dancing. Robert had shown Stella the traditional Mexican dances and Stella was good at it, a natural. Samantha and Amber were the Belles of the Ball. Some of the young bucks stood in line to dance with them. Sassy had a dozen young men standing around her as she sat on a high stool near the dance floor, shaking her long mane like a pony named "Flossy" I had as a child. All the girls looked so pretty, each in their own way.

Like I said, I don't know how to describe ladies clothes, but I do know how to enjoy them.

After the first set of the Country Western band, the slight pop of the sound system let you know a microphone had be actuated. In the soft lights at the far end of the park, about a hundred yards away, a group of horsemen were riding slowly. Soft strings of a guitar were heard and several voices in Spanish began to sing, just like in a movie. They sang as they rode.

It was Pepe and Johnny dressed in the traditional *Charro* costumes. Embroidered jackets with large sombreros and a prancing horse, it was quite a sight to see.

The *Charros* rode up to the young ladies and sang several songs to each of them, mounted and "rode off into the sunset." The lights of the park were dimmed in the open area as they rode away. Now I know why the Crescent City Sound System was present, they did the lighting too. This was great.

The band started again. The ties were getting loosened, the girls' high heel shoes were being placed on the side and then…

My pager went off. I almost jumped off the stool and I knew it was coming. As if on command, every person involved in the operation walked towards the house. It was strange, the music stopped. They all knew something was up, but like a family, they did not say a word and Pepe got things going again. The four young ladies that were being celebrated, looked around and wanted to know what was going on. They looked frightened, concerned.

"Nada, Mijas. Solomente trabado por la jefe." One of the mothers said and the band fired up and the youngsters were back on the floor. There must have been two hundred people at the party.

When we had all gathered in the War Room, I had finished answering the page with Red Baxter on an extension phone. We talked softly to the voice on the other end.

I hung up the phone and turned to the gathered team. "Show Time."

Chapter 21

"We will move out in thirty minutes. Meet behind the house, I had the cars moved there before dark. The only thing we need to do is "walk the dogs" and go. We can do it again at the airport just prior to loading them on the plane. We will walk out together, drive out the side entrance to the main road, one at a time, and then ease by the front gate with the lights off. Make sure whoever is driving disables the tail lights with the switch we had installed so the brake lights do not come on when you step on the brakes. When we get close to the store, we will turn on the lights. Goeff, your driver and vehicle are ready now, whenever you are. Pepe's oldest son will drive you in his car. In case our designated drivers do not show up, we will leave the vehicles at the Executive Air Terminal Parking Lot. Johnny can pick up later." I said in the steadiest tone I could muster.

"Questions or comments?" I asked after a pause.

"How long are we going to be in Belize City?" Sassy asked.

"We won't know until we get a 'show time' from Red's people in Lima. Just play it by ear. I will keep you all up to speed as I get information." I said.

"We just wear casual clothes then tonight?" Samantha asked.

"Yeah, we can get our "clowning" clothes on when we get there." I said.

"I can make sure of motel rooms now if you like. It is small and not the Hilton, but very nice and clean, near the airport and 'secure.'" Goeff volunteered.

"Yeah, and ground transportation too. Can you handle that too, please?" Robert asked. "Think there will be problems with Belize Customs on my French passport?" Emil asked while Patricia held his arm with her tiny hand.

"Like here. I too have 'kinfolk's' in Belize." Goeff smiled, as did all in the room.

"You ladies just put your gowns on your beds. I will see they are taken care of by Dulce and Carlotta." Maria said.

"And one last thing, you ladies look lovely. You made the roses blush with envy when you walked by, but you hairy legged dudes, can't say much for you." I said.

The ladies all smiled. I looked at Maria, I had received a friendlier smile from a Marine Drill Sergeant, except the eyes, they were smiling. I looked at Patricia it was hard to believe she had two children as old as they were. She looked like one of the girls celebrating their *quinceanera.* Amber and Samantha were regal, taller than I was in high heels. Sassy with the most daring low cut dress, defying engineers in keeping it up, it would make a new baby cry for milk.

In the room was some of the finest men and women the United States could offer up and I was leading them into "Harm's Way," "Into the Valley of the Shadow of Death," "Into a Shit Storm." Bart Duffy and I discussed this many hours across the street in the park last year. Did we have this right? Except for Emil, Bart and I, none of these men and women have seen the "elephant" as they said in a book I once read. Seen death caused by…caused by…whatever method.

Their contracts would be up shortly after we got back. Maybe I will just close this down. Bart and I don't mind getting a little bark knocked off us. Emil, well it his "profession" as they say.

If I close it down, where will all the hands go? Amber will need help in a few years with her M.S., I guess she can go back to her family.

Sassy is a survivor. She can always get a position with a major hotel or even go back to Lakeside Polo Club. Her daughter Becky is almost out of college. I know that Stanley Hines has called her several times, according to Stella, and she has been known to go back to the Polo Club since she has a Lifetime Membership, as we all do.

As to Samantha, she said she is ready to settle down. Whatever that is after this adventure, but will she be able to? She has saved and invested almost all her salary.

Stella and Robert, I have to mention them as one person now for obvious reasons. U.S. Customs wants him back. He has been cleared to return to work at an Intelligence job in El Paso somewhere. He is now 42 and Stella…let's see, she is 49, good age difference. She can raise him like she wants to.

Patricia? She is our "daughter," she will always be with us, but if Bart and I…well, ain't here, what will happen to her? Bart and I have made arrangements for her, she doesn't know it, but she and the children will be taken care of. Shirley, my CPA and Max the Mouth Piece's wife, said I was "so sweet to do that." Humphhhh! I don't know about that…

Maria also has been taken care of. Her family property is in real danger of being seized by a bank for non-payment, farm land right on the Rio Grande near Mission, Texas. I found out about it through Johnny Ramerez, my *Segundo* one night while we were having a "man's" meeting across the street across the street in the Recreational Area Bar. It had been set up like a sidewalk Cantina and someone wrote a hand written sign and nailed to a tree. "No girls allowed," it was done as a joke. Since I was "Bratted out" as I said to the hands, we spent most of the night trying to translate "Brat" into Spanish. Also because these "Brats" were so beautiful and intelligent it did not make sense to them, "Are you not the *Jefe y Patron* they wanted to know?"

"Yeah. Sometimes, when they let me." I answered as we laughed.

*"Eee haa…*Sometimes I think Maria is your *esposa,"* Flacko said one night at a meeting,
"pero, solemente tu novea."

"No No No, Flacko, she is not my Sweetheart. My friend, *mi amiga, solemente.*" and we all laughed.

Meanwhile the Brats were in Patricia's apartment over the kennels. We could see the lights on in all the rooms. One of the bitches was having puppies and, well they all gathered there for the big event. We could see one of them walk down the center stairs to the Whelping Room and check on the momma dog, and then back upstairs. We couldn't "see" them but we could see the inside light come one.

These were the things I was thinking as I stood before them. In the War Room all of them were still dressed in ball gowns and tuxedos. An unreal picture, because in a few hours we were going to try and rescue a man from a group of foreign terrorist. We did know that our government "would have no knowledge of the activities of these citizens, the United States deeply regrets…" I could hear them say as the paper shredders went full tilt.

And then the government would want to seize this place, The Shadows, as we call it now, but let them. We have photos and recordings of the white van. "Mr. Smith,

Mr. Brown and Mr. Green" fingerprints and drivers licenses and the reason why we were so quiet in the War Room, because Sassy was recording everything being said and photographing with a video camera. All of Mr. Red Baxter's conversations and telephone calls. I wasn't told about all the recording until later. Sassy said if I knew, I would not talk natural to Red. Sneaky little girl wasn't she, but smart as a whip.

Goeff walked back in with his small bag and "Well, Cheerio. See you in a bit at the airport, eh what?" and left.

"Thirty minutes out back" I said, as they left the War Room for their apartments to change.

Patricia left to get the two dogs, "Prince," Sassy's male German Shepherd and "Duke," Bart Duffy's big male Labrador Retriever. Patricia could walk in the kennel without the dogs "firing off" or barking, take them out through the back entrance and let the "clean out" prior to putting them in shipping crates in a van behind the house.

We could hear the party going full blast as we walked out the back entrance. Patricia was there with the dogs already loaded. We got in and started to leave, two vans, two Suburbans and the Towncar were there and running. A couple of the hands were driving the cars back.

"I am going to the airport with you," Maria said as she got into the back seat of the Towncar with me, "and so is Patricia and Stella." as Stella got in the Suburban with

Robert, with Luis driving, "to make sure you don't slide down any more banisters or mess something up." she said as she looked out the window of the big car. Amber jumped in front with Jose. Sassy was in the van. Bart was with the baggage in one of the Surburbans, and who was the lady setting beside him? I saw her at the party and was going to ask her name. "Hey, that is the lady in the photo that Red Baxter had, in front of the hardware store." I said to Amber and Maria. They both nodded. "Her name is Emily, her husband owned the Ace Hardware Store. Her daughter runs it now." Amber said.

"And you should have introduced yourself Charlie Gray instead of being over there drinking *pulke* with all the *viejos y pendajos*" Maria retorted.

"Maria, it was not '*pulke*,' which is illegal in this country and the 'foolish old men,' as you call them, are my friends." as the vehicles started rolling out. "What is wrong with you these last two days, Maria. You been on my case over...over...I don't know what." as Maria reached over and touched my hand and squeezed very gently, never taking her eyes off whatever she was looking at out the window into the dark.

As we eased past the front gate on the main road, the fireworks started. I wished I could stay to see them, but we were going to make our own fireworks in a few hours. Still, I looked at all the pretty burst of colors...

We drove the mile to the main road and met up at the blinking light at the highway, turned left and started to the New Orleans International Airport for an immediate departure for Belize City. We would have to clear U.S. Customs and the only part I would feel uncomfortable about was "Reason for Travel" on the form. I just checked "Tourist".

Maria kept her hand on mine most of the one hour trip to the airport. When we arrived at the Executive Air Terminal she removed it when we started driving under the lights of the airport entrance.

Goeff was waiting out front, a bad sign.

"Charlie, I got some good news and some bad news." Goeff started out.

"What is the bad news, Goeff" I said quickly as I felt my blood pressure surge. "The plane got a 'strike.' A vehicle rolled into the plane, hit a prop."
"Okay, what is the good news?" I asked.

"It was a Southeast Airlines vehicle that hit my aircraft. They are going to repair it okay, but is will take several days and Steve Johnson was the driver of the vehicle. Forgot to set the brake and well, it rolled." he was explaining.

"Steve Johnson? I know Steve. In fact he recommended you. He also flew a charter for us to West Virginia not long ago and I know you use to co-pilot for him, that Steve Johnson?"

"The very same, Sir." Goeff said.

"Where is Stevey Boy now?" I said as I got out of the car.

"He is on the ramp loading some Senator's party for departure" Goeff said.

"Amber, grab the camera from your brief case. Start taking pictures when I tell you." I said as I started through the terminal to the flight line.

"Steven. How you doing? Say, I understand that you "dinged" Goeff's bird there. I am so sorry that it happened. Say, isn't that Senator….?" I said.

"Yes, Yes it is Charlie…er, ah, Mr. Gray." he stammered.

"Hey, Amber. Get a picture of the Senator there. He may be out next President of these United States." I shouted to Amber as she started shooting photos.

The flash made the Senator and his party turn and face us as Amber let the film snap six or eight pictures in quick order.

"Stevey Boy. The young lady with the Senator, that ain't Mrs. …?" I asked quietly.

"No Charlie. That is his executive assistant." Steve Johnson was trying to stand in front of Amber as the camera flashed.

"Oh ho, ho, ho, Stevey Boy. Is that what they call them now days?" as I gigged him on the ribs.

By this time, all the others were out of the vehicles which had driven through the security gates onto the ramp and parked beside Goeffs aircraft. They quickly picked up flim flam and started shouting "Hello, Senator" and calling his first name with the little political sing song for President…

Of course the Senator had to wave to the 25 or thirty people shouting at him and the people from the terminal started coming out to see what all the noise was about at midnight on the ramp, mechanics, ramp personnel, all of them. The crowd was growing.

The little blonde was directed into the aircraft by another person standing with the Senator, but alas, it was too late. The "camera never blinks."

"Who is the lady with the Senator?" someone from the crowd shouted. I think it was Sassy.

"Okay, Charlie. What's the deal?" Steve Johnson said.

"Stevey, we need a plane. You know some of the deal, so we need an aircraft now." I said.

"Look Charlie. I will fly the Senator and his party back to his hometown and I will be right back, and I will fly you myself." Steve was trying to cut a deal.

"Nope. Why don't you encourage the Senator to…say, consider waiting for a few hours while your nice airplane company flies him in a new plane?" I said gesturing to Amber who was holding the camera up beside her face. Smiling and looking like she was getting ready to shot an ad for a girly calendar.

"I will have my personal Towncar, Surburban and van take him and his staff to the Marriott here by the airport. They do look tired. My treat, and of course we will give him this camera." I said. "Why not at least consult with him?"

Steve walked to the airplane as we leaned on the cars waiting for an answer. In a few minutes the front cargo door of the French made ATR opened and baggage carts were brought up. We down loaded the Towncar and had the driver roll up to the fold out steps and wait. Soon the Senator, his "Executive Assistant" and two other males, got off the plane and departed in the Towncar. All the baggage they had was put on a baggage cart and rolled toward the hanger.

One of the hands standing with us said in Spanish, "Poor girl, she must not have had enough money to buy all of the front of that dress."

Another answered in just a dry tone. "Or the bottom either."

One of the girls turned around and walked away, snickering. "She understands Spanish?" I thought.

Within the hour, Steven had filed a flight plan for Belize City, and was waiting for U.S. Customs to clear us.

One of the assistance to the Senator came back and asked Steve about the camera. "When we get ready to taxi, you get the camera. Now don't bug me about it." I told the wimp. He looked like the type that had to soak his socks in coal oil to keep the ants from crawling up his leg and eat his candy ass.

All the freight was loaded, the people and the dogs were on board and we were ready. The Immigration and Naturalization Service cleared all of us and made a call concerning the dogs, showed them rabies certificates and all health documents. He had to make a call to USDA Agents concerning traveling back in. We were good "tourist" and we made sure the dogs were okay to bring back into the U.S.

Just as the engines were turning, the Senator's "boy" came on board for the camera. "Where is the camera. That was the deal" he demanded.

Amber handed him the camera from her purse as the starboard engine started spinning. He looked at the camera and walked off the plane. The stairs were pulled up and the door was secured. The "boy" was over by the hanger trying to figure how to open the camera.

"Amber?" who was seated across the aisle.

"Yes, Sir", she answered with a coy smile. A smile that would melt a banker's heart. "The camera you gave to that man. Was there any film in it?"
"No, Sir", she answered.

"Was there ever any film in it?" I asked.

"No, Sir", as she reached up and turned her overhead light off, reclined the chair and turned her head away.

"Wait till he figures out how to open the camera." I thought to myself as the pilot applied flight power and the plane surged forward pressing me against the seat. I chuckled. I should tell Steve, maybe later.

Since we were only a portion of the weight limit, the plane climbed almost straight up out of New Orleans International Airport With a ground speed of 300 miles per hour we would be there in short order.

The Gulf of Mexico was reflecting like a mirror on that clear night passing under the starboard wing. Lights from the oil rigs were shinning like small candles as we passed through the clouds. Wait a minute, if the Gulf is on our right side...that means we are heading east not west towards

Houston as we planned. Well, maybe he is following New Orleans Control.

The Intercommunications System loudspeaker in the passenger cabin clicked. "Charlie, can you step up to the cockpit a minute, we have a little change in plan." and the ICS went quiet. Now what?

I went forward to the Flight Deck and knocked on the door. It opened almost as soon as I knocked. I recognized most of the gadgets glowing in the dark, but today's airplanes are very sophisticated.

Steve pulled back the right ear piece of the small light weight ear phones and motioned to Goeff "you got it" and pulled the chair handle and slide three feet to the rear and spun the chair around. Steve motioned me to take the "jump seat" behind the pilot's chair.

"Charlie" I had to make a couple of quick decisions and here's what I did. There is a storm in the Western Gulf, near the Bay of Campeche, off the Coast of Mexico and I am flying around it since I could not fly over it, and while I was filing a flight plan our Chief Pilot contacted me on the company frequency. Since we are flying over water, we have to have a Navigator, so we are stopping in Miami and picking one up. The navigator is on a Delta Flight now going to Miami. Also, we need a Cabin Attendant. The Cabin Attendant is also on that flight with the Navigator. I have no idea who it is, but I do know the Navigator and I think you would approve. We are dealing with International

Law now, so I think we have to go for it with a minimal amount of talk. This is according to the Warsaw Pact…" as I nodded my head. I agreed that we needed those things.

"We will fly to Belize City from Miami. It may cost us another hour, but not much more and you will be way ahead of the Merlin Aircraft Goeff had scheduled. The good Senator called our Board of Directors Chairman. Said he was going to raise hell in the Senate about our next scheduled annual FAA Inspection. Our Chairman told him to fuck off since he didn't like him anyway, so we are clear to go."

Steve said and said something to Goeff in the microphone attached to his head set. "Charlie, you know anything about a roll of film or something? I didn't get that straight."

Steve asked.

"Well, you seen as much as I did, Stevey." I answered.

"Okay, I hoped all this met with your approval, Charlie." Steve said.

"Yeah, Steve, do what you have to do. You are driving." I continued to look at the instruments like a billy-goat looking at a wrist watch.

Steve nodded and turned around and slide the seat back into position and started looking over the airway charts to Miami. I patted him on the shoulder "good bye." He acknowledged with a thumbs up and I went back to the passenger cabin.

Bart was napping with his hat pulled over his eyes. Robert had his seat back and a blanket over his head. Emil was just looking out the window, but gave a slight smile as I walked by.

Sassy and Samantha were talking by the galley as I went by, looking in the ice box for goodies. I don't know how they kept such trim figures and eat as much as they did. Yeah I do, you shake hands with them and you can feel the strength in the hands and they are hard hands. Hard from work, and power lifting.

Amber was asleep by now. I got a blanket out of the overhead compartment and draped it over her. She sorta moved as I tucked it under her chin and curled up in the seat. She has the face of an angel, a fine woman.

I sat back down in my seat, turned off the overhead light and looked out the window at nothing except the reflections of the aircraft running light reflecting on the clouds. "Have I thought of everything? What else do we need?" I thought.

Sometimes during that chain of thoughts I went to sleep. I did not become aware of things again until the flaps started down and the wheels came out of the wheel wells, getting ready to land.

After we landed, we taxied to the General Aviation Transit Terminal, a very nice terminal, shut down the turbo-props and waited to see what happened next.

Steve Johnson walked out of the cockpit and spoke to a ground crewman who lowered the built in steps.

"Charlie I am going to send the plane over to our maintenance folks to have a look at a couple of things. You can wait in the Lounge if you like. They have coffee, a restaurant and rest rooms." Steve said. "I don't feel this going to be much more than an hour or so check out. The day shift is coming on, so we are number one in getting attention." said.

"Okay Steve." I nodded. "This trip has been snake bit from jump."

"Yeah, well Goeff was able to raise his office when we were at 30,000 feet. They will have transportation for us when we get there this afternoon. Sorry, but we need to have this bird flying with all its feathers. Considering where we are going and why we are going.

As we were standing by the aircraft, a woman carrying a large brief case came walking towards the plane. She was wearing the wings of a pilot, a company uniform and a regulation pilot's hat. In her other hand she was pulling a small suitcase with wheels and several smaller bags strapped on top.

"Ah, this must be our stewardess." I said.

"Here, Ma'am, let me help you with those heavy bags." Robert said as he was coming down the steps of the aircraft.

"No thank you. I can manage" the young lady said in a very professional sounding voice.

I noticed for the first time she was wearing three gold stripes of a co-pilot and the wings were gold with a star on the top of the eagle the company used as a logo. She was a qualified Command Pilot. I guess she was ready and just waiting for a Captain's Position to open up. Wonder why she was flying as a Stewardess or Cabin Attendant as they called them now.

"Hi, Steve," she said and offered her hand, which he took. "Hey, Rita" Steve said.
"Rita, this is Charlie Gray and he will insist you call him Charlie. So we may as well get that straight now" Steve said with a slight lilt in his voice.

"Hi, Charlie, I'm Rita Ponce. Glad to meet you." she offered her hand.

Emil and Robert were standing about ten feet away and looked at Rita like she was from outer space.

Bart and Sassy walked off the plane with the two dogs to give them an "airing" over on the grass beside the Terminal Building.

"Rita, we had a little hot TPT showing on taxing, so I am sending it to the barn for a quick look-see. Also, we are going to do a Hundred Twenty Hour Check while we are here. Goeff Albright is in the cockpit. He is going to stay with the aircraft. Wanna come in the terminal and talk to us a minute?" He guided her by the arm towards the lighted terminal.

Robert and Emil followed. They had not said a word, but followed, totally taken by the young lady.

Rita was a very nice looking young lady. Dark hair and in what is called "French " something or another. Where it is plaited like a horses main up the back.

I detected a slight Spanish accent when she said her name. She did not "look" Spanish, but that could be her married name. She was not wearing any rings, but she may not have wanted to wear them while she was on the job.

"Oh, just a minute, I need the flight plan out of my case." and Rita spun around to go back to the aircraft. She ran up the steps like a deer and in a few seconds was back at the door. She started down the steps when someone called her from inside the aircraft and she turned around. It was Samantha.

.

"Rita? Margarita Rita?" Samantha was saying.

"Sam? I can't believe it. Is that you?" Rita shouted.

The two women hugged each other for a few seconds and made small talk. Rita was about 5 foot six and Samantha was a head taller.

"Charlie, you are not going to believe this. This is Rita Ponce, a college classmate and sorority sister of mine from college days. Rita, this is Charlie Gray." Samantha said.

"We have met," Rita said. "Another Brat," I mumbled.
"What?" Steve asked as he looked at me.
"Oh, nothing Stevey. It is a long story." I said and just turned and walked in the terminal. Rita and Samantha walked arm in arm into the Terminal and entered a door that said "Pilots Only," each talking over each other.

"Charlie, let me ask you something. Several years ago when I first met you, I heard you use the term "Brat" when I landed the chopper to pick up the girls for a shopping trip to New York. And then that time we flew to a funeral in West Virginia. Why do you call them 'Brats'?" Steve said as we got a cup of coffee.

"Stevey, a Brat is a title that can not be awarded, it has to be earned. It stands for "Brave- Reliable-Adaptable-Trustworthy." I said. "Hey, that sounds good if I must say so myself since I just made it up." I thought to myself.

I did not want to tell him I thought it stood for "Be-Right-All-Time."

"Steve, if you had four or five "knock out" girls around you all time, that are beautiful and very intelligent, do you think they could run a game on this old man?" I said and laughed.

He didn't say anything but just walked over and sat down at one of the tables in the lounge.

"They are like my daughters. I know I spoil them rotten and I let them think they "game" and "clown" me, but I don't fall for any of that. But it keeps them happy." I said to Steve.

About that time Bart and Sassy came in the terminal with "Prince" and "Duke." They walked over to a corner table and put each dog on a down stay with hand signals. Both dogs went to a "down" and stayed there without a word as Sassy went to the ladies room.

Bart got a cup of coffee and came over to our table.

"Who was that with Samantha?" Bart asked as he stirred his coffee. "Another Brat, Bart, another Brat I am afraid." I said.

Bart stopped in mid-stir of his coffee. "How? Impossible, I thought we had all of them already." he said and continued to stir his coffee.

"Nope, I think we just picked up another one." I shook my head. "Who was the girl pulling the baggage cart?" Bart asked.

"That is Rita Ponce, our navigator, and a college sorority sister of Samantha." I smiled at Bart and Steve.

"What do you know about her, Stevey? I don't need a female-type who was given a "social promotion" to keep down Equal Rights law suits" I asked.

"Why did you guys leave me? Why didn't you wake me up?" It was Amber. "Amber, I am so sorry. What happened?"
"The first thing I know is I was in a hanger with guys banging around and two people in the cabin cleaning up. I had to bum a ride with a Ramp Rat back over here. I didn't even know where I was or where to ask them where to take me. Goeff was still there going over some electronics type stuff. Was I relieved. Where is the 'ladies'?" she finally stopped and looked around.

I gestured over my shoulder and she walked away and laughed. I felt bad, but I just forgot her.

"Now, about this Rita. What do you know about her?" I asked Steve.

"Well, she has been with us about two years. She had flying experience when she came to us. She was flying helos for..." Steve was interrupted by a loud squeal and babbling.

"Rita?"

"Amber ?" Rita said with a breathy voice.

"…for the Marines during Dessert Storm." Steve continued.

I had my back to the excitement but I saw Bart just push his coffee cup aside and put his head on the table and laugh like he had lost his mind.

"Charlie Gray. Mister Charlie Gray, please pick up a white courtesy phone for a message." an announcer said.

I walked over to the far side of the room and picked up the phone. After a few moments the same voice answered and I identified myself. "This is Charlie Gray."

"Hold for a call, please…go ahead".

"Charlie?" It was Maria, we exchanged code words and she acknowledged correctly. "Charlie, Red Baxter needs to talk to you." Maria said.

"Charlie? Red Baxter here. I got a call from our friend, Mr. Crow. Nothing really new, but they said you should come to the party…er, ah, errr…their friends have been in contact with them and have made an offer and want to meet you at a horse farm outside of Lima. They said the party would be at the Sheraton. They made reservation for you at the Sheraton as you wanted. Also, all of the items you requested will be available to you when you arrive. They are at the *El International* building. You can pick them up there. Also, the research assistants are standing by to meet you when you land. You have anything else we need to order?" he finally ended.

"Yeah, we need ground transportation for about a dozen people when we arrive. Did you get anything lined out?" I asked.

"Yup, got a tourist bus thingy that will work, lots of room for your folks and the baggage." Red said.

"Okay, let me talk to Maria, please, and thanks Red." I concluded. "Yes?" Maria was on the line.
"Maria, you know the vehicle that Paco was driving the other day when he got it stuck?" I asked.

"Yes, and he said he was sorry. Juanito talked to…" she was saying.

"No, No, No. I want you to think of the type of vehicle. Don't say it, and when we hang up, tell Red we need two of them ready when we go looking for the horse farm. Okay?" I said.

"Yes, I think…yes. I do." she said. "Okay. Everything cool there?" I asked.

"Yes, everything is okay and *Viejo? Vaya con los manos de los dios.*" Maria said in a sincere voice.

"Thanks, Sweetheart. I will." I answered, and hung up.

I noticed it was full daylight now. The sun was bright and the people outside were all wearing shorts and trying to be very "Florida."

I know I was about to run out of gas. In fact, I was hungry. I tried and see if anyone wanted to eat.

I looked at Bart and he started laughing again. Steve smiled, I think he understands. I walked over to the girls and I said "Girl." I didn't mean a thing about it, but I walked over to them and they were just still just jabbering like school girls.

"I gotta go pee. I am about to wet my pants" she did a stage whisper and all three headed for the Lady's Room, still giggling like school girls. They didn't say a word to me. I don't think they saw me, and I was standing right there.

I went back and asked Bart and Steve if they wanted breakfast. They had had a nice diner in the building, we were told, and Steve had been there several times, said it was good food.

Emil, Robert and Sassy were seated at a corner table in the Transit Lounge. I asked them if they wanted to go eat breakfast.

"What do you guys think of our new Navigator?" I asked Emil and Robert. "What navigator?" Robert said as he and Sassy stepped into the morning sun. "Didn't notice," said Emil as we walked down the sidewalk in the muggy heat.

We walked to the door of the diner and paused just before I opened the door. "You two are bigger liars than I am. And besides, you know "The Brats" would snitch you off." as I opened the door for Sassy to go first.

As Sassy entered the door she turned and looked at Emil, Robert and then me, and did her "smile." It said to all of us: "Yep, we sure would."

After breakfast we were standing around the lounge being bored when we noticed a tow tractor towing an aircraft that looked like ours across the ramp and position it near the front door. Geoff exited it and started walking towards the building. Steve had filed a flight plan for Belize City and received a weather briefing from the same office. Rita had been with him. When they came back, Steve said we were ready to roll. Bart and Sassy had taken care of the dog's and loaded them on the plane.

I was worried. Steve and Goeff had been up over 24 hours and their eyes were red and bloodshot, but, he was Pilot-in-Command and I let him figure it out.

Steve said "We should be in Belize City by 1600 hours this afternoon. It is 1300 miles to Mexico City and another two hours south from there. Maybe a tail wind….yup, be there for a nice warm bath and a very nice meal. Goeff has made all the arrangements."

When we got back on the aircraft, the new meals had been loaded on the aircraft and it smelled "clean." Goeff had gone to the rear of the plane and had stretched out across the rear seats in the main cabin. I looked in the cockpit, Steve was in the right seat and Rita was in the left seat. Normally, the pilot in command would be in the left seat. Well, I guess that was good sense, since Steve had been up for so long.

Bart and Sassy were bringing the two dogs up the stairs and putting them in there P-500
Vari Kennels, when I noticed a white ramp service vehicle come driving towards our plane with a checkered flag fluttering the rear.

Rita looked out the window and saw the vehicle. She said something to Steve and got out of her seat and headed back towards the exit door.

"Well, here is our Cabin Attendant we are required to have." Rita said in a very unpleasant tone.

A very well built young lady got out of the pick up and started up the steps with her baggage. I reached down and took the bags and placed them next to the other baggage in the forward freight section right behind the pilot's cockpit. In this type of aircraft there was not a "belly compartment." Freight is carried in the main cabin. The passengers normally load and unload through the rear drop down stairs.

"Oh. Hi Rita. Sorry I am late, but I had to get my hair done before we left. Danny, er, er, ah…Capt. Holman said that it would be okay since you guys had a broke down airplane." The dizzy blonde said.

"That's okay, Eunice. We were just getting ready to "Start Engines" now anyway. Come on in and do your Pre-Flight". Rita said. Rita looked at me with a quick glance and rolled her eyes back, I didn't like that. Eunice was taller than I was, wearing high heels too. I had never seen a female stewardess, or whatever they are called, wear high heels on a plane. They make it hard to walk in rough weather.

Eunice went about checking the galley, counting passengers and filling out some paperwork. I kept noticing that she was opening and closing doors in a strange manner. Then I noticed that she did not want to damage her nails. I didn't say a word, she had to have the right training or she would not be assigned a flight. We did not need her anyway, just to meet some standards that the airline folks had.

After a few minutes, a ground crewman came on board and took some of the papers Eunice had, gave her a receipt, and left the plane. The starboard engine started, the door closed, and the port engine started.

Lights went from bright to dim as ground power was removed, and then they came back on, bright. A tone sounded that went "bing bong," and Eunice got out the life vest and air mask to do a passenger brief prior to take off.

Everyone stopped what they were doing and watched. She was trying to talk in the microphone and demonstrate the equipment, it was pathetic.

After about three or four minutes of fumbling, we had taxied to the end of the runway and were ready for the "numbers" as they say. That means they were ready to move on the active runway where the numbers were painted on the end.

Rita came on the intercom and said, "Sit down Eunice. We are rolling." and at about that time you could hear the propellers go from "Ground Taxi" to "Flight" as Rita went to full throttle on the power levers. The plane surged forward and Eunice was dumped on her pretty little ass, right in the middle of the freight compartment.

I jumped up and went over to help her up. By the time I got her on her feet, I wanted to help "dust her off," but thought better of the idea. The plane had become airborne and the flaps were coming up.

Another "bing bong" on the intercom and Eunice asked me. "I wonder what that is for? The little bell thingies." she said.

I shook my head in a negative manner and said I did not know. It was almost impossible to hear because we were standing right at the propeller arc, the loudest part of the aircraft.

I shouted in her ear. "Why don't you get on that little telephone and ask the Captain? She may know."

"Good idea. I will." Eunice said.

After we were airborne about thirty minutes, Steve came out of the cockpit and went and told Samantha and Amber that Rita wanted them in the cockpit. The two girls went forward and closed the door to the cockpit

"This could be dangerous, having three Brats in the cockpit at one time." I thought to myself.

Steve went to the rear of the aircraft and found two seat and got a blanket and went to sleep. Eunice kept walking back and forth asking Robert, Emil and myself if we wanted any "Coffee, Tea or drinks, they are free on this flight, you know." she said.

"No thank you, Eunice." We are just trying to get a few a few winks.

"Oh, where are we going? I know my Flight Pack said we were going to Belief, or something like that." As we reached cruise altitude and the propellers' pitch were adjusted for maximum cruise range.

"I think it is called Belize. It is just south of Mexico, on the Gulf of Honduras, north of Guatemala." I explained to her.

Eunice nodded her head I swear I could hear it rattle as I walked away.

I could not stand it, I had to go look in the cockpit. Those Brats are probably up there painting each other toe nails and doing there make up.

I knocked on the door and it came open. Rita, was in the left seat of course. Samantha was in the right seat with headsets on and Amber was in the Navigator's position behind the co-pilot. It was very quiet in the cockpit.

Amber was looking at a chart and handed it to Rita for her to see. They were talking on the intercom and I could not hear them. Rita nodded and said something back. Samantha was adjusting radio frequencies and dialing in new numbers on something.

Rita turned around and smiled a "hello," but she was busy, so I left.

I went back to my seat, sat down and was asleep almost as soon as I hit the seat. After what seemed like a few minutes later, I awoke when the plane was making turns and starting to lose altitude. My ears were popping a little. I noticed that Steve and Geoeff were not in their seats, but Amber and Samantha were sitting together talking. Sassy was reading a book of some type and Bart was just looking out the window.

Eunice was in the galley doing whatever Flight Attendants do prior to landing. I heard a faint "ding ding" and saw Eunice pick up the telephone handset in the galley. She then went to a drawer and took out a folder and brought them to me. "Will you pass these out for me to the others? I am afraid to go to the back of the plane anymore. Those two back their patted my behind when I bent over just a while ago." She pointed to Emil and Robert, who had very angelic looks on their faces.

The documents were Government of Belize Customs Forms, standard stuff. I passed them out. We scrounged enough ball point pens to get the job done and passed them back to Eunice who put them in a folder and sealed them.

After a routine landing we were directed to a large hanger where an official in a khaki uniform came to the aircraft after we shut down and waited for the stairs to be lowered from the aircraft.

After a few minutes, Eunice figured out how to open the door, lower the ramp, and allow the official on the aircraft.

When the Belize Customs Official opened the packet, he counted the papers. Then, he was counting heads, you could tell. When he was satisfied, he turned to the cabin as the ground power was plugged in. The air conditioner came on and it helped stifle the heat a little, but it was hot.

"Hey, Goeff, good to see you. Marlene and the kids are over in the office waiting for you. Man, have those kids grown since last year." the official said.

Goeff greeted the Customs Official and introduced Steve. Everyone shook hands while they were talking. The Custom Official was signing papers and then said to everyone over the intercom. "Welcome to Belize and you may now deplane. Please proceed inside the terminal office to clear Belize Customs. Have your passports available for me to stamp when you reach the terminal.

"Hey, Albert. Can we get the doggies off for a minute, it has been a long flight. We don't want a mess you know, Ol'Boy." Goeff said.

"Sure. Folks please don't wander off. We are very informal here in Belize, but…" the official said.

"Sir, we will be right over there by the hanger and then be right inside. May we bring the dogs inside out of the heat, please?" I asked.

"Sure, no problem" he said. "Goeff, you got any chaps to help with the bags and freight for Customs inspection?" the Customs Official asked.

"Yeah, Willie is bringing the pick up now. We will be right in, just a few passengers. Tell Marlene I will be right in." Goeff said.

In a few minutes, a very beautiful woman walked out of the office near the plane with two grade school age children, a boy and a girl. She was what is called a Creole in some parts of the world. A mixture of African and European blood and she had the best of both. She looked like the model Naomi, and the two children were coffee colored with blonde hair like their father. They broke away and ran up the steps like any nine and ten year olds.

Up the stairs the children ran, turned left into the cockpit yelling "Daddy! Daddy!"

"Children," in a very stern British father figure tone."Is that the manners you are supposed to use when greeting guest?" Goeff said, as they hugged his neck.

For the first time, they noticed the dogs and squatted down before the kennels, sticking their finger through the bars. Any other dogs I would have been very concerned, but not these two.

Sassy came forward with a leather leash and squatted down beside the children and asked if they would like to pet the dog in a motherly manner, and of course they did. She explained she had to get them out and let them go potty and then they could pet them.

The children were elated and allowed the dogs to be taken off the plane. The girl, Victoria, went with Sassy and was asking a million questions. Phillip, the boy, went with his father.

"What beautiful children you have, Goeff. Be proud of them", I said.

"Thanks, Charlie, I am. Oh, this is my wife, Marlene." Goeff said as he was leaving the co-pilots seat.

"Hello, Charlie. I was told on the radio while you were taxing in that I am to call you 'Charlie.'" she said in a very cultured British accent. "Hi, Steve, good to see you again too." she said.

"Hi Marlene, good to see you too." Steve said as he hugged her. "Evelyn said to tell you thanks for the present you sent her for her birthday." Steve replied.

I nodded and shook the offered hand as Bart came by with "Duke" on his way out the door.

"Welcome to Belize everybody." Marlene waved to everyone on the plane.

Chapter 22

After routine clearance of customs, two Dodge Vans and a truck drove to the aircraft and loaded the baggage and dogs for the short ride to the hotel where we were to stay. Not knowing what type of motel it was, I was curious, but for some reason I trusted Geoff Albright's judgment.

Geoff had said his in-laws owned the hotel, but I was not prepared for what we saw upon arrival. Belize was once a British Crown Colony until 1975 when it gained independence from England. The British influence was seen everywhere we went. The hotel looked like it was from the movies about British imperial days at the turn of the century. I expected Gunga Din to come running out to meet us. It was very beautiful, with well-manicured lawns and high porticos for an entrance.

It had been the Governor's Mansion. I understood that Marlene Albright's family bought the old Mansion and turned it into the present hotel.

The clientele were old British Colonials, Europeans and Americans who liked the old world ambiance. Manicured lawns for bowling and cricket, large open verandas where "tea time" was stilled observed at 5:00 PM each afternoon.

It was midafternoon when we arrived and we did make "an entrance" with all the baggage: two dogs and a group of eight to ten people. We were going to get the baggage out of the vans and trucks that brought us to the hotel, but was almost run over by staff members doing it for us. We did not even have to check in, we were shown to our very modern rooms straight away.

"Geoff, we need to make arraignments for billing." I said. "You know. Give you a credit card or something?"

"Don't worry, Charlie, I will make sure I send you a bill, a BIG bill at that." Geoff said and laughed as he walked away.

"Marlene, did you advise all the ladies they have been invited to the Independence Day Celebration tonight?" Geoff said as he turned to me. "We will have cocktails at 8:00 and then dine at 9:00 or so. Will that be alright with you?"

"Sure...sure, anything you say, Geoff." I said. "Why so late?"

"Well, we must be civilized you know? Eh what? Dine at nine or so." Geoff laughed mimicking a thick British accent and pretending to have a monocle.

Billy L. Smith Sr.

Geoff turned to Marlene as she said "Yes, I did advise the ladies we were dining formal tonight, and we are going into town for a few hours, to pick up a few items. We will see you gentlemen when we get back in the Club Room." as she kissed Geoff lightly on the check. "Ramon will drive us to town in the van and mother is looking after the children."

As if on cue, "The Brats" in jeans and sneakers, Rita, who had changed into a slack suit, and Eunice, in a sun dress with sandals, came down the stairs and walked to the front door where a driver and van were waiting. I got a smile from Sassy and a little finger tip waves from the rest as they walked to the door.

I looked at my watch and thought. "Well, they have four hours or so, they can't do too much damage before diner." I felt like these were my children, my daughters going to town shopping.

The dogs had been placed in a kennel on the property and Geoff assured us they would guarded well cared for. I went upstairs for a short "power nap" before we had to get dressed. Since we were all going to Lima, Peru, to play the role as big time Texas ranchers, we had tuxedos for the occasion.

I stopped by the desk and asked the young lady on duty to make sure I woke up at 7:00
PM so I would have time to dress for diner.

"I will have someone come round and knock you up, Sir." she said, which is a British way of saying they will awaken you by knocking on the door.

I stood there looking at her and then she blushed and said "Oh, I forgot. You are an American and do not use that term in the same manner as we do."

"Not so you would know it," I said, "but it does sound like a good idea to me."

At 7:00 PM I was properly "knocked up" by a smiling young man who brought my tuxedo into the room that he had been taken to a press and iron. The tuxedo was placed on the closet door and the shirt was hung beside it, along with the tie, cummerbund and suspenders. The shoes were placed on the small bench at the end of the bed.

As the concierge left the room, I could hear a voice from Bart Duffy's room through the slated windows as he was getting up.

"Hey, Bart! You ready to get the monkey suit on and go down stairs to the 'Club Room'
or whatever they call it?"

"Yeah, give me a few minutes to figure out this rig they are making me wear and I will be right with you." He yelled through a partially opened door.

I wondered where Steve, Robert and Emil were. They had rooms at the opposite end of the long veranda, but I had not seen them once we were settled in. I asked the bellman if he had seen the two young "Sahibs." I wanted to use the word "Sahib" but didn't of course. That was how I felt here, as if we were in East Africa or India, not a few miles from the Southeast Mexican border.

The staff member stated that the two men who came with me were down at the stables with Geoff looking at the horses. I was surprised that Geoff had a string of polo ponies and jumpers. He did not seem the type, but of course, what is the type?

I walked down the large curving stair case and for a minute had this feeling I wanted to slide down the banister again, but considering what happened the last time, I thought better.

Upon entering the Game Room, where cocktails were to be served, I noticed or "felt" a special feeling you can't explain, maybe "grandeur." To this day I can not explain the pleasant feeling, but I do know it was a feeling we should all have sometime in our life.

Bart came in a few minutes later in his tuxedo looking very handsome. He was met by Geoff at the door and greeted. Everything was very "proper," British style, it was something everyone should experience.

After a few minutes of chatting with some of the Club members, the large double doors from the main room were opened and Marlene Albright made an entrance. She was wearing an elegant but simple black gown and she looked as if she were floating, as regal as any queen could ever hope to be.

Marlene greeted the guests like a proper hostess while making sure everything was exactly as it should be. She whispered a few instructions to the staff while smiling at all the guests.

In a few moments after Marlene entered, the entrance way was filled with a group of the most beautiful women you would ever want to see. Each dressed in a long gown, their hair piled on their heads, earrings and necklaces of tiny white pearls.

Sassy had a gown that was off the shoulders and her long hair cascaded down her back to the waist.

Amber, who had shorter hair and was tallest of the women, wore a slinky type dress that went to the floor, but had a slit up the right side to the thigh. When she walked, it showed her graceful legs.

Samantha had a black evening gown that was full from the shoulders that showed off her very white skin and blonde curls.

Rita had a white gown on that caused her olive skin to shine and her black hair was swept up with a small "crown" on top of her hair that made her appear much taller from a distance.

Eunice was dressed and looked like a movie star. She reminded me of the films I have seen where Marilyn Monroe sang "Happy Birthday" to JFK in the White House. She did not come in with the other women, but came in last, maybe by design because the rest did not want to associate with her. I did not know, but she stood there a little longer than the rest as the music stopped and all looked at her. A young Belize National Guard Captain offered Eunice his arm in a gallant manner, which she took and directed her towards the group of young officers standing near the bar.

The British have always impressed me with their ability to not be phased by anything. Like the old British war movie where the Captain of the HMS something or another, standing on the bridge of his ship that has just taken a direct hit from a German Battle Cruiser and in a typical British manner says: "Steady there, Number One. We do not want panic the crew do we?" but in this case the crowd stopped and gawked at the "guest." As most of the club members were in their later years when they saw these young men and beautiful women, who made them remember their younger years, it became very quiet as they stood in the door with the lights from the Main Room shining behind them. Steven, Robert and Emil walked towards the ladies and escorted them to the receiving line where Geoff and Marlene kissed each on the check and shook the hands of Robert, Steve and Emil.

After a few seconds, the music started again and the new guest were absorbed by crowd who still turned heads and stared at them. There were a bevy of beauties.

The Governor General arrived with his official party and was received in an official manner with the playing of "God Save the Queen" and the Belize National Anthem by the orchestra.

As toasts were raised to the "Brats" by the Governor General, who was not aware of whom they were or why they were there. If he had known, I am sure he would have cringed. These young ladies and gentlemen were warriors in the highest degree, but he was a gracious gentleman and they responded accordingly.

Bart and I went through the receiving line and then wandered over to the bar area to chat with a couple of the "old guard" from Britain's finest hour. They had names like "Brigadier Sir James Bridgestone-Smyth, formerly of His Majesties African Rifles, OD, CBE" and all the other titles. Bart and I were also told that no matter how many gin and tonics we drank with the old gentlemen, they should be addressed by their titles, such as "Sir James," not "Jimmy" or "Bobby" in the case of the Governor General Sir Robert Dillingham. Funny, they did not seem to mind they called us Charlie and Bart. They acted like they were having a great time, but we were guests.

During the Cocktail Hour, several more guests arrived and were introduced around. Of course "The Brats" were the main attractions. I had never seen cultured gentlemen kiss the hands and bow in a courtly manner. It was great to see it and the Brats were enjoying it to.

I watched Sir Arthur someone…liked to have dropped his monocle down the front of Samantha's dress when she came over to say something to Bart. The dress had a little part cut out real low in the front …and….and…oh, never mind, I can't explain it. I just enjoyed looking at it, but if a crook ran in with a gun and said "Stick 'em up'" and she did, they would.

It was hard to believe the same beautiful hands that were being kissed were very capable of cutting your throat or pulling the trigger in an Uzi without flinching.

Just like in the movies, the dining room doors were opened and a butler announced "Diner is served"

Samantha had two Knights and a Duke offer their arms to escort her to the dinning room. Bart and I stood there like two lumps of coal and just watched. I walked over to Lady Elizabeth and offered my arm, which she took as the other ladies were escorted to the dinning room by the Belize's Officer Corp that was present.

The ladies were seated at a long table with Geoff at one end and Marlene at the other. The meal was grand, fish and meats prepared as if we were in the finest restaurant in London or New York, several wines and of course liquor.

One thing almost blew me away. After dessert was served and cleared away, a servant came to Marlene's side and whispered "Doctor, you have a call, from the hospital. Said it was an emergency, they insisted they talk to you."

Marlene rose and said, "Ladies and Gentlemen, please excuse me, duty calls. Please keep your seats, Gentlemen." but of course we all rose to our feet.

"Doctor?" I accidentally said aloud, as I looked around.

Lady Elizabeth, who was seated to my left looked at me and said "Why yes, Mr. Gray, I thought you knew. Dr. Albright is Director of the Queens Hospital here, which is a pediatric hospital."

I know I sat there and stared at Lady Elizabeth with my mouth open.

I later learned that Geoff and Marlene had met here in the days when Belize was known as British Honduras. Geoff's farther had been a Colonial Foreign Service official and Marlene's parents were merchants and farmers in Belize. They had attended pre-school and grade school together as children. Geoff had not seen Marlene until they were both attending the University of Glasgow in Scotland. Geoff was studying anthropology or something and Marlene was in medical school. After Dessert Storm and while Geoff was still in the hospital in London, he met with Marlene again who was now a full-fledged doctor. Marlene stated she was going to Atlanta, Georgia, to study at the Center for Disease Control and do pediatric work at County General Hospital.

After a whirlwind romance, they were married in a civil ceremony in London. Upon completion of her internship and residency in London, Marlene received a United Nation's World Health Organization Scholarship to study in Atlanta at the CDC for Tropical Disease, and do pediatric work at the local county hospital.

During the time they were in Atlanta, Phillip and Victoria were born. Geoff had his U.S. pilots license squared away and did a little flying for an aircraft delivery service and taught a few flying lessons. However, after flying high performance aircraft in the RAF, Cessna 210's were mild.

As luck would have it, Geoff met Steve Johnson when he gave Evelyn, his wife, flying lessons. Geoff and Steve hit it off and Geoff went to do co-pilot work with Southeast Airlines as a charter pilot.

As it happened Evelyn was a nurse at the same hospital as Marlene was working and well, the rest is history as they say.

After the dinner was completed and a few after dinner speeches were made, the ladies retired to the Drawing Room for coffee and the men went to the Billiard Room, where ladies were not invited. There had never been a lady in the

Billiard's Room since it was built in 1847 or something. "It is not cricket for the ladies to be in a Men's Billiard's Room," I was advised by one of the old timers, "there has to be one sacred place left in this world for men of quality. This is not a pub where trollops come in and out, with all these "rights" and all that balder dash, man. It was unheard of in my time in the Punjab." As the gentleman took three or four puffs off his Cuban Cigar and the other men nodded. "Disgraceful, women driving cars alone, and showing their bosoms." This is the same man that looked down the front of Samantha's dress.

One of the others chimed in, "Did you see that beautiful young Spanish girl? I bet she just finished some fancy convent school where she was waited on hand and foot. Bet she doesn't even have a driver's license, disgraceful." As another looked at me for a response, "That young lady is with your party isn't she Mr. Gray?" Sir James said to me.

"Yeah, she is Jimmy, she is the pilot that flew us here." I said with a smile. "Ain't married either, but she did say she wanted to have a baby though, but she wants one from a test tube. What do they call it?" as I walked over to a pool table without looking at any of them. I picked up a cue from the rack. "Pool anyone?" I asked.

I broke the rack and looked around and they were all gone except a gentleman who was introduced as the local newspaper editor. "You ever been to England, Mr. Gray?"

"Been there several times." I said. "I have family in Scotland and Northumberland. I seen them a few years back, very nice folks. Been on the same place since William the Conqueror landed there in 1066 AD." as I shot a combination into the side pocket I could never do again in twenty years. "Shows too, they look a little inbred." as I missed an easy one.

The newspaper man laughed, picked up a cue and shot all the rest and called for an attendant to rack them again.

"What do you think of the rest of England, Mr. Gray, the people and all?" he continued. "Well, Sir, I have a little problem with some of the mothers in England. I don't mean anything bad about that, wonderful women, but they have no imagination when it comes to naming their young'uns." I said as I made another shot to the side pocket. "Just look in this room here, how many men her are named "Earl," "Duke," and "Baron," why didn't the mothers call them Joe, Sam or Ralph?" I stood up to look for his reaction.

The fine English gentleman looked at me for a full ten seconds and then burst out into laughter that brought the others over for a "jolly good laugh." After he explained the "joke" to them, they all laughed lavishly. Slapped me on the back and said "Jolly good one, eh what?"

At that time a house staff came to Geoff and spoke to him. Geoff looked around and spotted me at the pool tables and directed the staff member to me. The staff member came to me and said that I had a phone call and I could take in the private sitting room. I would have called it a large telephone booth.

It was Amber. "Charlie? Can you come up to my room? I need to…ah…to talk to you." "You bet, Baby, be right there." I said as I huffed up the steps. "Naaaaw, that ain't it, it has to be something else, slow down before you have another heart attack," I thought as I knocked on the door.

Amber came to the door and I could see Sassy in the background reflection of the dresser mirror. "Damn, I knew it was too good to be true." I went in the room.

"Charlie, we have had a call from Red Baxter back home. He said he needs to talk to you. Sassy is setting up the direct satellite phone dish, but we can't get a signal at this time of night from this side of the house. Can we use your room?" Amber said.

"Of course, let's go." We went down the hall to my room, which faced the opposite direction. When we got there, we went to the veranda and sat the suitcase looking device on the table. Sassy unfolded the receiver dish and pointed it in the general direction of south, while listening in a small ear piece for the squeal of the satellite transmission.

After a few seconds, Sassy seemed satisfied with her handy work and dialed in a number.

After a few seconds of dialing and other identification numbers she had memorized, she said "Stella? Hold on for

Charlie." She handed me the telephone receiver, "darndest thing I ever seen, what will they think up next?"

Stella and I exchanged greetings and code words so I knew there was no duress over there. "Red Baxter is on the extension, Charlie. How is...you know. So how is everything going..." Stella said.

"Robert is fine, Stella. I will tell him you still love him when I see him, right now he is downstairs at a party dancing with some of the local beauties. Official business and all you know." I smiled to myself.

"You are a real asshole, Charles Gray" Sassy said with a frown and a smile. I still don't know how she does it. "Let me talk to her when you get through, and you had better hurry, you only have ten minutes worth of battery."

"Charlie? Red Baxter here. Mr. Crow wants you there Wednesday morning at 0800 at Jorge Chavez Airport in Lima, can you do it? He was real firm on the time. Something has happened and he will not share it with me or the other office in Lima by phone. Go to the transit air terminal on the east side by the Shell Dutch Aviation sign and wait for customs. You got that?

"Okay, Red, I have it. So we need to leave here at about 2200 hours, will do. Red, did our equipment get there?" I asked.

"Yes, more equipment than you ordered and your associates are top of the line too. A guy we have in Lima named Vinnie Rideout said he knew you, has everything lined out. He has been there for the last three days and for you not to be a 'fucking squid.' You know this guy? The guys in Atlanta said he was very crude. They were afraid to say anything. He is a big, mean son of a bitch and we have used before. Said he threatened to take their heads off one by one if they screwed the deal up down in Lima and insisted he go himself, and not send one of his operatives. You know him?"

I chuckled. "Yeah, I know him, and my suggestion to any of your people is don't mess with him, he will take you apart. Anything else, Red?"

We got off the phone and Stella and Sassy talked for a minute as we went back to Amber's room. I had to go to the bathroom and I asked Amber if I could use hers. A woman's bathroom always has a special odor, a good odor. I looked at all the girl stuff lying on the dressing table while I was using the bathroom. "Charlie, you are a freak in your old age" I said to myself.

When I came back to the room, Sassy had stored the satellite phone in the carrying case, unplugged the tape recorder we always used on phone calls, and placed it back in its special little case.

They both stood there and looked at me in my elegant tuxedo for a long time. "Whut?" I asked.

"Your pants are unzipped, Charlie." Amber said as Sassy laughed. I looked down and… "They are not" I declared.

"Gotcha!" As they walked out of the room, I could hear them giggling as they walked around the corner.

"BRATS!" I called after them as they stepped into the old elevator.

It was near midnight when I got back down stairs. The main room had been set up to look like a ballroom with the rotating glass ball turning and a local band had fired up with the latest popular songs. The BRATS were dancing with the young men. I watched Amber dance. I didn't think it was possible to make those moves to a Latin Beat with a tight dress on, but I was wrong.

Steve and Rita made the next slow dance, and I cut in "Meet me outside when this dance is over," I whispered to Steve so that Rita could here me.

Rita and I made about ten steps when the noise stopped. They called it music, but I didn't. "Whatever happened to Lawrence Welk, Tommy Dorsey and all the good bands, Rita?" I said as we started for the veranda door.

"Who are they, Charlie?" Rita said as a staff member opened the door for us.

"Never mind, darling." as I escorted the beautiful lady out for a "breathe of fresh air." Steve was standing on the steps looking out over the formal garden which smelled beautiful in the tropical night. "Let's stroll down the path and smell the roses," I said to Steve and Rita as I looked around and saw Sassy smooching with a young Guards Officer in the shadow of the arbor arch.

"I talked to Red Baxter on the phone a few minutes ago. Mr. Crow wants us in Lima at 0800 Wednesday morning. Do you see any problems guys?" I asked them both. Rita said "Steve is the Pilot in Command, his call."

"We can do it, Charlie, but we have fog to deal with and to ask us to be there at 0800 is tough. We cannot control what the Lima Tower or Ground Control Approach will do. There must be a reason for being there at that time. We will give it our best shot." Steve said.

Steve escorted Rita back to the ballroom and as they entered another side door, several of the Ol' Guard gentlemen men were about half "plastered," but still very much gentlemen, stopped them and said, "Young Lady, are you the aviator for that air machine that brought you here?" As they waited for her response, and from such a tiny little frail lady at that.

"You mean Lil' O' me? Fly one of those big ol' airplanes? Gentlemen, I have a hard time just riding in my Daddy's limousine without becoming ill." Rita said in her best Scarlet O' Hara voice, as they turned and nodded to each other.

"That Yank, he is balmy you know, thinking a female could fly one of those contraptions. Back in my day when I was with Sir Jeffery in Malta…" he was saying as Rita and Steve walked away. I just rolled my eyes and kept going too.

I found Steve, Robert and Emil "chatting up" the bar maid and told them to pass the word that we would brief at the kennels tomorrow at 0900 hours. They immediately went to find the others.

Steve went straight to the gazebo and found Sassy and her "friend" in the gazebo "talking."

She did come into the Ball Room and made her good byes. I would have bet a month's pay she would. She was as reliable as a clock when duty calls.

All the ladies went to Geoff, Marlene and the Governor. Steve, Bart, Robert, Emil and I did the same. I even bowed graciously to Lady Elizabeth in my best manners, saying a good bye to her and her court.

Bart went over to Baroness Gwendolyn of Castle Downs and tried to say something nice, as they had been dancing most of the night. She was a very pleasant woman, a widow, who took a shine to Ol' Bart as they say in Texas, but I think he screwed it up when he said, "You don't sweat much at all for a fat lady."

I took Bart's arm and lead him to the door and asked one of the staff members to see Mr. Duffy to the lift as they called the elevator.

Chapter 23

The next morning was Tuesday. At 0900 we all met at the kennels for an informal briefing. Sassy and Bart had "Prince" and "Duke" and were outside, exercising them. After a few minutes, they were put in the kennel and we went to sit under a large tree on the white park benches that were there. What a pleasant place to discuss business, Geoff, Steve, Rita and Eunice were there of course. Eunice had no idea what was going on, she had not been briefed, but I decided that if she was going on the trip she should know what is going on. Robert and Emil did most of the talking, the Brats added facts as required.

No details were left out, but to our surprise, or least mine, Eunice did not bat an eye. She just looked back and forth to each of us as we spoke.

Eunice spoke very quietly, in a steady tone, voice firm and steady. "I was raised in the South Side of Philly, Philadelphia, Pennsylvania." Eunice said while sitting cross legged on the manicured lawn. She looked at her own shoes all the time she spoke.

"One of the few whites girls in our school, and I knew I wanted "out" and the only thing I had going were my looks. But to survive in the streets, I had to…well…do things and see things I will not put in my autobiography. Every pimp in South Philly wanted me to work for them, a white girl with big tits. They thought I would be a whore, never did, they tried to make me, tried to rape me a couple of times until they discovered this white girl carried a knife and would and did use it. Kept my game together, smoked a little dope, but never any heavy stuff. Had to, just to be able to walk down the street, so you would not be called a "snitch." So the "Bimbo" act is just that, developed it and used it as a way to cover up being scared." Eunice said as tears came to her eyes. No one said a word or made a sound as Eunice spoke.

"So, if you are trying to scare me it won't work. I been there, seen death on the streets, in the tenement hallways from heroin overdose. I got a scholarship to a small college near Atlanta and had to work three jobs just too be able to live and I had to screw the Professors when I did not turn in research papers to get an extension or a passing grade. I received an MBA in Business from a small but prestigious religious college where rich girls' daddy's sent them to be educated and get a degree in "MRS." In other words to be "Mrs. John Jones" or something. It was tough being a poor kid in a rich kids' school, but no one would hire me, would not take me serious because I was a "Bimbo" or acted like one. One told me up front, a woman, that if I would put on thirty pounds and wear my hair unbleached I could have had the job, but it was a family orientated company and the wives would have me out on my ass before the weekend…

and just for your information, I am a real blonde and I will prove it to anyone here and now, that don't believe." She raised her eyes up for the first time to meet each and every one of ours.

"Not required here, Honey, you may start a trend we could not all pass." Samantha said. There was a nervous laugh from a few in the crowd and it was quiet for a long time.

"You will not be required to go with us to attempt the rescue, Eunice." I said "By the way, what is your last name?"

"Pamela Eunice Powers, but my mother's name was Pam, so I got stuck with Eunice. Pepper is my nickname because my initials were P.E.P." she said. "Well, what do you want us to call you?" I asked.

She thought a moment. "Eunice, Pepper brings back too many bad memories from Philly," she said slowly, "so Eunice is best" "Okay. Eunice it is." Amber said after a moment.

"Eunice?" Amber said. Eunice looked up at her with the sun shining in her eyes. "I for one, am sorry we snubbed you last night, but….well…"

"I know, you thought I was a "bimbo" and Chief Pilot Dan Holman's main squeeze. Well, if Rita and Steve ain't told you, I will. Well, we are sleeping together on the side and I get a few easy charter flights a month, why?" she paused "Well I made a mistake. Thought that was the only way I could get a job and when word got out, none of the other crews and command pilots would hire me on as a regular crewmember. No matter what the Union Rep says, they didn't want the company "chip" flying with them. They think I will run back and tell "The Boss" what they are doing while THEY are on turn around. Well I got news for you, I don't. When Dan does come over, it ain't my information he is after. 'Wham-Bam-Thank-You-Ma'am' at noon time if he has time." Eunice said as she stood up and brushed her bottom off. I think Emil wanted to help, but Robert grabbed his arm.

"Well, no more, not after this trip. I was treated like a real lady for the first time in my life last night. Just the same as you girls were and I did not have to put up with groping and crude jokes about the size of my breast. Oh, the old goats did look, I caught them at it." As she said that, the other BRATS smiled. "I have seen how it was supposed to be and I want to thank you ladies for that, and you Charlie" as I looked up at her.

"Me? Thank me for what?" I said.

"For the beautiful dress and shoes the string of pearls with matching ear rings, and the hair stylist"
Eunice said as she walked over and gave me a little peck on the top of my bald head. Robert, Emil and Steve had been sitting on the grass and started rolling around on the ground in stitches, laughing. The Brats were just giggling more at Steve, Robert and Emil, acting like the little angels they were supposed to be.

"Your very welcome, Eunice, my pleasure." I said, knowing I had been "had" again.

Steve was screaming and laughing and Rita was just dumb founded. She had no idea what was going on. Steve remembered the flight to New York last year to buy furniture for the mansion.

"Ever time you sit under a tree, Charlie," he had to stop laughing to talk, "the Brats help you spend money."

"What is with the BRATS thing? I have heard that several times and I don't understand." Rita said.

They explained to Rita what a BRAT stood for and that it had started as a joke by me. Still, Rita and Eunice were more confused now, but accepted what they heard "The bottom line, Rita, every time they go to town, it cost me money, but I don't care what these young ladies do, they help me spend money, but…" I paused and looked proudly at each of them, "they are worth it."

"Charlie, are you really a rich Texas oil man?" Eunice asked as she shaded her eyes from the morning sun, holding her hand over her eyebrows.

"No, Eunice, just a lucky guy, who got lucky." I reached out and tousled each of the Brats' hair that was near me. They tried to look indignant while I "messed" their hair. "I wish I could be a BRAT someday, however it is done." She lamented.

"Okay, let's get down to business at hand. How is the bird, Stevey?" I asked. "When we put it to bed last night it was great." Steve said.

"I have had a guard on it 24 hours a day, Charlie." Geoff chimed in.

"I have charts in my room and will start a flight plan as soon as we get through here." Rita stated. "I don't know how good the meteorologist info is here at the airport Flight Services, do you know Geoff?"

"They are the same as you get in Atlanta and Miami, Rita. In fact, a direct satellite feed." Geoff answered.

"What about In Flight Services when we leave, do they have any here?" I asked no one in particular.

"That is the least of our problems. I will get the kitchen staff to get something together. Eunice, please get in contact with Chris, the chef on duty this morning, and see what he can do for food. Stock up a little, we may be going places where food will not be available. Something easy to fix, you know?" Geoff said.

"You bet, can do," Eunice said with a lot of enthusiasm I had not heard before, "and I guess I had better check and make sure we have plenty of water. I will use the water we have in the water canisters on the plane for coffee since it is Miami water and get bottled water to take with us. We'll need space in the cargo compartment if that is all right with you, Steve." Eunice said looking at Steve.

After we had done the brief, Bart, Eunice and I walked down to the stables to look at the horses. Bart had "Duke" walking along side at heel when Eunice said, "It feels good to be with you guys. I don't feel I have to perform like a trained seal when I am around men. You guys accept me as I am." she said wistfully.

"Well, how come you were afraid to go to the rear of the plane before we landed yesterday?" I teased her.

Eunice laughed aloud, "I wish I had known them yesterday as well as I feel I do today. Robert and Emil I mean..." after a pause, "Are either of them married or anything?"

No one answered. "Oh, I get it, they are spoken for. I see, it figures" she said as we reached the horse paddocks.

"Eunice, they are not married, but they have...oh, how can I say, special friends. We use to call them girlfriends, I don't know how they are referred to now days, but yes and they are sorta spoken for, and they are part of the BRAT Pack. The quickest way to break up a good team is to have the folks become involved in each others love life like that. It will tear up a group, an organization or family, even a whole nation as history has shown us." as Eunice leaned on the fence and stroked the muzzle of an Arab mare.

"I would not even think of that, not me I have been the "other woman" too many times and it is not my style any more, I hope." Eunice said softly.

"Charlie?" Eunice paused. "How can I get on with your company? How can I get a job like this?" she stood up and asked me.

"I dunno Eunice, let's wait and see what happens when we get back, then we can talk, I promise. You can come to Louisiana for a visit as our guest, how is that? You may not want to work for us at all after this trip." I said as we walked back to the hotel.

Bart asked "What time do we go to the airport, Charlie?"

"I dunno, Bart. I will check with Steve and Rita, their call." I said to no one in particular. "I would like to go check the aircraft after I make arrangements for food, Charlie. Can I get a ride to the airport you think? Get it cleaned up and all, that is my job and for the first time in my life, I want to be part of the team. Even if it a fancy waitress." Eunice stated.

"I think that is a good idea, Eunice, but the operation of the aircraft is up to Steve. I only lease it and the crew to run it, but I will bet you a big ice cream cone that Steve say "go for it," and even go with you. Besides, you will need a key to get the stairs to come down. You have a key?" I asked.

"Nope, but I will get in touch with Steve right now." as Eunice quickened her step to get to the hotel while Bart and I stopped at the kennel to put "Duke" in the kennel.

The young security guard, who was responsible for the dogs while at the kennel, was standing there waiting for us and smiled as I said hello.

"Sir, do you know when the young lady will return with "Prince?" he asked.

"No, it won't be long, she is just down at the stables." I said as I pointed towards the stables.

"I know, Sir, but have had reports of rebels traveling this way and well, it is something to be concerned about." he said.

I looked at the paddocks and I saw Sassy riding the Arab mare bareback around the paddock, just a halter and a lead rope, with "Prince" running beside her. She is a wonderful rider I thought.

"I will tell her not to leave the main area. Will that be okay then?" I asked.

"Yes, Sir. If she stays near and sight." he said and resumed his post near the kennel safety gate.

"Sir?" the young guard stated, "May I send someone for her and say that you need to see her?"

Billy L. Smith Sr.

"All right. Are you that worried?" I questioned.

"Sir, she does have a lot of spirit, she may decide to ride off." the guard stated as he watched her.

The guard waved over a youngster grooming the bushes and sent him to get Sassy. When she rode near the gate, the youngster waved her over and gestured towards us. She patted the mare and got off, climbed over the fence and handed the young man the lead rope. The youngster was to walk the mare and cool her off.

Sassy came over to the kennel and put "Prince" in the kennel.

"Darling, I wish you would stay close to the house. Kevin here said there are bandits and rebels reported in the area. Please, we have a job to do." I said in a fatherly manner.

"Okay" she smiled and went to the hotel backdoor and went in the kitchen. That was too easy. She was probably ready to come in the house anyway.

That night, we said our good byes to Marelene and her immediate family at an informal supper. During the day we had all tried to take a little nap, but I am sure the rest of the crew was as "wired up" as I was with anticipation of the coming events. We had been in touch the home office. Each had a chance to talk to someone special on the scramble- phone. It was connected to a 110 volt converter power source so the battery was not a problem. We tried to

390

be out of the immediate area when someone was talking, but you knew each person was trying to reassure the ones on the home front that all was okay. Robert spoke to Stella. Emil spoke with Patricia and the children who were in the office when the call came in. I spoke to Maria who said all was well and to be careful. Sassy and Amber of course just spoke to the home office crew and Samantha made a separate phone call to someone in Atlanta. It only lasted about two minutes and she did not say anything that would even hint that she was in Belize preparing to go try and rescue a hostage in the Andes Mountains of Peru. Whoever it was, it could have been her brother if anyone was listening to the conversation.

The aircraft flight crew, Steve, Rita and Eunice, were dressed in uniform. Geoff, who did not work for Southeast Airways was dressed in his own uniform of Air Belize Charter Service, had departed approximately one hour prior to our departure to get the aircraft ready for flight and file a flight plan to Lima.

Geoff had laid out the flight schedule and had faxed it to International Flight Services in Mexico City earlier in the afternoon since he knew the routine. If someone was watching, he did not appear to be doing anything unusual.

The Flight Plan would take us out of Belize City over the Caribbean Sea, turn on a southwest course to Tegucigalpa, Honduras, then to Managua, Nicaragua and San Jose, Costa Rico, where would fuel about 9:00 am Wednesday morning. We would not get the dogs off the aircraft. The dogs would be okay since we would let them "air out" real good before the trip and we would not get off the aircraft. If Costa Rican officials boarded the aircraft we would pretend to be asleep and let the flight crew do all the talking. Costa Rico is a very friendly country. "The Switzerland of the Americas" someone once told me.

The flight plan went according to schedule. When we arrived at the San Jose, Costa Rico Airport, and we were directed to the Transit Flight Line for fuel. The fuel was paid with an international credit card as was routine, and away we go for Lima, Peru.

We headed out over the Atlantic and headed south. When we got in range of Colon, Panama we were able to get a weather briefing while in flight. It seemed it would be a routine flight with a 0800 arrival in Lima and no fog was predicted for Jorge Chavez Airport in Lima for once. Our luck was holding.

Upon arrival in Lima, Peru, we were met by several persons from the R.I.O Corporation in Mercedes-Benzes and a Chevrolet flatbed truck. The R.I.O. company officials must have cleared the way since Peruvian Customs was swift and the bags were marked with chalk as they came off the aircraft. The dogs were allowed to be "walked" by Sassy and Bart in a small grassy area near the edge of the tarmac and then loaded in their crates on the back of the flat bed truck for the trip to the Sheraton Inn in Lima.

As the limos pulled up beside the aircraft, a person from my past life got out of the vehicle, Vinnie Rideout. We looked at each other but made no recognition or acknowledgement. Vinnie was like me, a lot grayer around the temples and thirty pounds too heavy, but there was no doubt that this was Master Gunnery Sergeant Leonard Rideout, USMC (retired). It was good to see him.

All the drivers were "locals" and there was a group in several other vehicles that were bodyguards. We got in the limousines and headed for Lima, but no one said much. Our bunch did not know Vinnie, and our contact man from R.I.O. Corporation was named Roger Byrd, who gave everyone the "glad hand" when he met us. Everyone was on guard until we could find out who was what.

I never thought I would say this, but I was glad to see Vinnie Rideout again.

The Sheraton Inn in Lima was lavish to say the least. If appeared we had rented the whole twelfth floor for our team. The two rooms the dogs were in had small balconies attached where they were allowed to take care of business. We would just have to clean up the mess when it was made, but the dogs were being fed a low volume, high protein food, ProPlan. Each dog had a trunk with dog food, equipment and other "froo froo" toys in it, as if they were pampered pets. In most cases they were pampered.

I noticed on arrival that the elevator was met by "Security Staff" from R.I.O. They all had on RayBan–type sun glasses and tried to immolate all the other security forces in the world. There were bulges under the shirts they were wearing, very professional looking staff Vinnie had put together, if in fact he did.

When we arrived and got settled in, I sent a fax back to our "office" in Houston. It was routine "gobbeldy gook" that went to Houston and was automatically switched and forwarded to Stella in Louisiana. The information just let them know we had arrived and all was well. I also made several land line calls to Houston and other places just to cover for our operation. I thought, "Ain't call forwarding wonderful, you can set up dummy offices and numbers all over the world and the calls will still all end up at one number."

We had all the "smoke and mirrors" in place just in case we drew any interest from the Peruvian intelligence officials in Peru or any place else. We had bank account numbers, credit checks and office buildings that could be checked on, and all done by my lawyer, Max Gurrera.

We had a meeting scheduled at R.I.O. Offices in the "El International" building at 1:00 PM that afternoon.

Steve, Rita, Eunice and Geoff were not needed and we wanted them near by with the aircraft "just in case." They were issued cell-phones and were asked to carry them with them 24 hours a day. We did not plan to stay longer than a minimal amount of time on this operation. The longer we stayed, the greater the chance the operation would be compromised.

At approximately 12:30, Robert, Emil, Bart, Amber, Samantha, Sassy and I were picked up in two stretched limos and taken to meeting at the R.I.O. Offices. The "front" for this office was that "R.I.O." stood for Riverside Investment Organization, Limited, of Atlanta, Georgia. The idea was to attract foreign investment, American money to be precise, to Peru's tin and copper mines. This gave the "R.I.O. Organization" a good reason to have so many strangers come to their offices.

Since we did not know who was on the team, we said very little in the rooms, cars or anywhere. The electronic surveillance equipment available was very exotic, one had to be careful.

When we arrived at the RIO offices, we were escorted to the 23rd top floor suites. When we walked in, you had to be impressed with the front office and the entrance areas. However, when we entered the back offices, we could see a whole array of electronic devices that I assumed were used for surveillance, but that was not what we were there for.

I had to laugh at the BRATS. To play the roll, they had to dress the part of a mistress. They had to be overdressed, Sassy said she did not like to wear a dress and until she took up with us she did not own a dress. With the outfit she had on, she said she looked like a "potted plant or a hooker having a bad hair day." I had to chuckle as that, it seemed to be the most she had said since I had known her, but the BRATS played their parts well. Amber, in a moment of playfulness, acted like she was chewing gum and swinging a purse around. We kept snickering at Samantha too, she had the act going where she was "adjusting her boobs." All of this was happening as we were going down the outside elevator to the waiting limos.

When we arrived at the meeting of the RIO Company, Vinnie Rideout was there and met us. I did not know what to expect, but he was all business. We shook hands and asked about each other's kids and families, but he was very professional. I knew he could be of course, I had known him since we had been "in country" back in the '60's.

Vinnie stated we had all the weapons we asked for and then some. We would use a tour bus to move around since they did not draw much attention. The windows had been tinted and the bus could hold about twenty people. That was more than enough room.

Vinnie said when the bus picked us up in the morning, it would be loaded, it would have the uniforms, boots and all equipment we requested. We could change in the bus as needed.

The kidnappers had made demands for money, two million American dollars. Vinnie had been able to stall them off saying we could not get that much U.S. currency in Peru on such short notices, and with the U.S. government's laws on moving large amounts of cash around, that it would take time. They went for it.

Of course Vinnie himself had not talked directly to the kidnappers, but through contacts, and the bad guys did not know that all of their calls had been electronically monitored. Both from this building and satellites which were being monitored in Langley, Virginia, they could not turn any of their phones on without a tape recorder being automatically turned on. All phone calls, by cell phones and landlines were being monitored in "real time" 24 hours a day.

Now this operation did not just start when Jack Thompson was snatched off the streets of Lima last week. The station had been electronically listening to some numbers for a long time. Every time they changed phones, which was often, the computers would "fingerprint" their voices. When they came back on line, even with a new phone, the computers would recognize the voice "fingerprints" and make a note. I was just amazed at how far electronics had come in the last twenty years.

The "briefing room" was actually the hallway with no windows. Any electronic listening devices directed at the building from outside would be defeated in most cases. Constant sweeps for bugs were conducted at each shift change. The electronic sensors had detected microwave transducers directed toward the building from the Japanese, French, and Chinese Embassies. It was a case of "we know, they know, that we know" what is going on. They were doing the same thing.

The "briefing room" hallway contained a dozen folding chairs and heavy wooden tables. There were video players, electronic oscilloscopes and other gadgets needed by the R.I.O. company employees.

"How secure is this building, Eddie?" I asked.

Eddie was the "On Duty Shift Leader" for the day. "It is as secure as we can make it. Anything behind the "green door" from the front office is secure, we think…we hope." He smiled at us.

"Who are the ladies in the front office, are they cleared for this?" I inquired.

"Yeah, they are okay. They are all wives, girlfriends and relatives. In fact, they are doing actual data processing for us. Their computers are connected only to our data base here in the back. If we have a surprise visitor such as house cleaning staff, they just switch programs when they walk in, keep typing 'reports.' That is not often since we lease the whole floor. We have our own cleaning company and everything."

We went to the briefing room and sat at the table with a cup of good South American coffee, nothing formal. Some sat on the heavy tables and others in chairs. A very informal group to be so highly technical in what they were about to do.

"So, Eddie, what is going on?" I asked. "You know where these guys are calling from? Any ideas?

"There is a horse farm about a hundred kilometers east, towards the Andes. A town named Huangayo. We feel their calls are coming from that *estanzia*. Only logical place, and we have landline interceptions that may match one of the voices from a cell phone. Langley says it is a definite 'maybe.'" He raised his hands palm up in a guessing gesture.

"Big Bird, one of the satellites in geosync, has looked at this place this morning after sunrise, but there is so much snow shinning off the mountains, that the pictures are not too clear…but we have "real time" feed from them and if anything comes in we will advise you before we go."

"What kind of road comes into the farm, Eddie?" Bart wanted to know.

About that time, one of the tech folks came in from the back room and said they had a live feed of the farm. He asked if we wanted it switched into our room.

"Please do," Eddie said. After a few minutes the monitor hanging on the wall brightened up and an image came on…

I walked closer to the monitor. I could see the house, buildings and people walking. It looked as if we were in an airplane, maybe, a thousand feet high. Amazed I just stood there. This was the first time I had seen a live shot from a satellite. The operator pulled the image out a little and we could see a main road coming in from the tracks where trucks or cars had passed. We could see railroad tracks and secondary roads. I realized that we were to go in there we could be trapped trying to get out.

"How far do you think it is from the main road to the house there, Eddie? I just can't judge the distance. I am still amazed at this whole thing." I said.

"15,359 feet from the edge of the main road to the front door of the house," said a voice came from the other room over a speaker. "and from the smaller road to the main house is…1,009 feet." the voice said again.

"Three hundred yards, okay, no problem, I wonder if there are any little bridges or obstacles that could give us problems when we try to clear out?" I asked the "speaker box."

"I cannot detect anything like that. I think the road is all gravel too, not showing any warm spots." the voice said.

"You mean you can take the temperature of the ground?" Samantha asked, being a scientist-type, this interested her.

"Yes, we can and do a lot more that is classified." Eddie said.

We watched for a long time and even got a few printouts to use as maps, with compass directions and exact distances in feet.

Satisfied at what we saw and how it worked, we departed and went back to the Hotel. We had plans to be picked up at 0800 the next morning for a visit to the horse farm in Huangayo. Since we were "tourists" we were expected to do "tourist things."

The next morning, Thursday, we were picked up in a very fancy "bus." It was a Benz Bus with all the amenities you would expect on a First Class Cruise on the Queen Mary. I never even knew they made tourist facilities like that.

Inside the bus was a microwave that was powered by an auxiliary diesel generator somewhere in the rear of the bus. Instead of regular plush airline seats, there were lounge chairs, one on each side of the bus and ten down each side. Also, each seat had its own TV Monitor for the cameras that were mounted on the outside of the bus. There was also a young lady that was dressed in a flight attendant-esque uniform. She brought us coffee, warm hot clothes to wipe our hands, and anything else we needed. "The only way to travel" came to mind.

Vinnie was sitting inside the bus facin toward the rear in what first looked like a cabinet, but it was an array of electronic equipment. It included a monitor for "live feeds" from a satellite, several telephone receivers and an array of other black boxes. Beside him were two of the technical folks we saw at the R.I.O. offices.

We were dressed in western fashion to go along with the roles we were playing. The Brats looked good in western styled skirts and blouse with fringed deer skin jackets. I wondered what all this was costing me. A funny thought went through my mind: "will the IRS go for it?" Oh, well, that will be "Yogi" Berra's problem won't it?

We drove slowly through Lima looking at the sights, with three other vehicles nearby, a Suburban, a van and an older Mercedes. We could hear Vinnie and his Communication Team in the back make calls on the phones and on the radio.

"Charlie, we have some good news" Vinnie said as he sat down between Bart and me. "Langley just confirmed that some of the background noise we picked up on a previous call from a phone we know to be at the Horse Farm was Jackson's voice. They also have "fingerprints" from several voices they had recorded previously. We got them "laid down," we think at the farm, our 'shooters' are in the vehicles following us. Good men, mercenaries of the highest order. Guarantee them because they do not get one red cent unless we get Jack out and your folks out safely. That is why I am here. They don't do things for fun and games, all business."

How do you want to handle it?" Vinnie finished and waited for an answer.

"Vinnie, we just don't have enough intelligence to make a strike right now. We won't get a second chance. Once they discover we have a team trying to make a snatch they will kill him and shut down the whole operation. We got to get them on our ground, someplace where we have a chance, where they are right now. There is one road in and one road out that we know of. They, on the other hand may know of other roads. There is a light snow covering the roads according to Big Bird. We got to make them move, we can snatch the victim on the road or at the new place, but right now I don't feel comfortable where he is. It is their game and we don't have the resources or manpower to make a frontal assault. Let's give it some more thought. Okay?" I said.

Vinnie shook his head and walked to the back of the bus.

Chapter 24

We went back to the hotel and changed into something we could wear to the dining room at the hotel. We had to "play the role" of high rollers with a couple of bimbos. Robert and Emil would escort the Brats to the gaming tables. I told them that this was to include Eunice as well.

"And keep an eye on them. My money and Brats don't mix at well." I teased. I knew my money was as safe as if was stored in Bank of America, but they did need to play the role and I knew they would enjoy it too.

After dinner, Vinnie, Eddie, Bart and I with the four local "shooters" changed clothes and walked outside. The shooters had several rooms on the floor too. We dressed as casually as we could, so we would not draw attention. Still, we could be "made" as *touristas* by Ray Charles in the next block. But tat is what we wanted to look like.

We were afraid to talk in the hotel rooms, dining rooms or bar. We had no information that anyone knew we were in town, or cared, but we had to have a safe place. So what is the safest place…in a crowd.

The local folks we had hired need to be in on the game plan, Vinnie said they were "his" boys. He felt comfortable with most of the operational plans, but the intelligence stuff would have to be screened. Eddie, the Technical Expert, was hanging his head way out to be chopped off by The Company if he gave out too much.

The four shooters, Bart, Eddie, Vinnie and I went to a local sidewalk cafe one of the shooters with us had recommended. Typical downtown Lima sidewalk bar, lots of noise and lights, with about twenty tables sitting on the side walk. We sat down at one of the larger tables away from the big crowd so we could see who was coming and going.

I asked the "shooters", or bodyguards, Vinnie had hired if they spoke English. Two of them said they had attended the "School of the Americas" in Ft. Bragg. The other two looked at me as if the did not comprehend anything I said.

"Well, this may be tough." I said to the two who said they spoke English. "What about the other two?" as I gestured to the other two body guards.

"We will keep them informed, Senor." The oldest of the four stated with a steady gaze. "Yeah, we need to make sure we are all on the same sheet of music, Bubba" I said. "*Que?* Sorry what, Sir?" the other questioned.

"Great. Well, we will just have to make do. You two will translate for those two over there, keep them informed of what is going on, briefed." I said.

"Oh, yes Sir, we will do that. Remember Senor, we have to be there too." he said, laying his finger alongside his nose, an international gesture of being "in the know."

Made sense, I thought. "Okay, we will get started with this little discussion, but I would feel better if those two acted as lookouts and sat on the other side, over there." I gestured to a couple of tables nearer the street. In that way, if anyone decides to do something stupid, we will have a little help not sitting at this table. Maybe give us a little warning too."

He turned to the other two and spoke for a few minutes. Their eyes never went off the speaker. When he finished, they moved out and went to the best places for them. It looked like they may know their business, I was impressed.

"Gentlemen, what we have here is a legal term often used in the International Court of Law at The Hague, Netherlands: it is called a Cluster Fuck. We come down here, in a hurry, no intelligence and with limited manpower against an opposing force of …well, we don't know how many. We don't know the enemy or anything else. So I am open to suggestions." I said as I looked at each one of them.

This was a professional group and everyone should have been there, but we were too big to be seen in public. That would draw too much attention. Robert and Emil should have been here, and the Brats, but they were not.

We sat there for a while and just looked at nothing, each within our own thoughts. "We gotta get them out of that house" Bart said. "Why not just cut the power off. It would get cold and they would have to move out, and the phone…"

"They may move, but they would leave Jack Thompson up there to suffer." Vinnie injected.

"Maybe they have a fireplace." I said smugly.

"Nope." Eddie the R.I.O. Tech Rep stated and smiled.

"Eddie, you holding out on us? You know more than you are saying. We need you on this one, peoples' lives at stake, all we want is to get the man out and us out of Dodge as quickly and quietly as possible," I said. "You know they don't have a fireplace in the house?"

"Charlie, I can't share a lot with you. I have stuck my neck out ten yards on this." Eddie said. "I am doing it because Jack is a friend of mine and I was supposed to have been in that car, not Jack, but I will not let you get in trouble. I know what you are trying to do, and I will help. This ain't my first rodeo as they say in Wyoming, but I cannot give you a lot of information. Especially working with information we have. It is "No For Nat" (no foreign nationals) information." He said gesturing with his eyes to the local shooters, who I felt were not following all of the conversation.

"I can accept that Ed." Bart said. "But let's play a game of "what if" and you start it off." Bart continued.

"Ah, come on Bart. You know where I am coming from, but I will do what I can." "Do we know who owns the place?" I asked.

"The estate is owned by a German Industrialist who has never seen it." Vinnie said. "Okay, back to square one. How do we get them to move out?" I said again.

"Why not tell them you are ready to pay off and set up a meeting place." said one of the shooters in broken English. "You will have the money in 24 hours, but you have to see the man first, talk to him or something. That way you can get an idea where he may be. Just a suggestion." he said shyly.

"Okay. Anyone else have a better idea?" I asked.

"Vinnie, do we have a way to contact them? Or do you wait for them to call you?" Bart asked with raised eyebrows.

"They have to call us. We know their numbers, but...." Vinnie was interrupted by Eddie, The R.I.O. Company Tech.

"Vinnie!!!" It was almost like a father talking to a son who had spoken up among adults. "We have to control the meeting place. We can get away with it by saying we don't know the area, but we do know such and such a place is located and logical place where they would not suspect anything, like a land mark, public area, a park…a tourist place. Yeah, that is it, a tourist place, where a Tour Bus would not be out of place." I became alert at that.

"Senor Gray?" One of the shooters said, "I know of such a place. It is up in the mountains, not too far from the *finca* where the person you say is named Thompson" he finished.

"Carlos, how far is that place. I mean in miles?" I asked.

He and the other man spoke among themselves for a few minutes and said they thought it was a 100 kilometers from the farm, about 70 miles I guessed. Through some rough mountain terrain at about 6,000 feet of altitude.

Carlos went on to say after consulting with his friend, "It is a construction place where they make road…*como se dice*…big…wider. Yes, wider. Make four ways to go," he gestured. Eddie spoke to him a minute and decided it was a road construction site going into a long valley in the base of the Andes Mountains. That would put the bad guys about 35 miles away according to the map from their horse farm. On our way back, we would be going downhill into a city with several assholes on our tail not wanting to chat and consider the time of day. It was worth some thought.

"Eddie, can we get a map of this area, see what it is like?" Bart asked.

"I don't know. I do have MAPS, but if they are current or accurate, I don't know, but we can try." he said.

"Why not take the plane? We have it don't we? Make a tourist flight and see what we can see?" I said.

They all looked and shrugged their shoulders saying "why not" in gestures rather than in words.

We all sat there a moment more and just drank our wine and watched the people.

After a few minutes, Eddie jumped as if he been goosed like a high school kid and looked at his pager. He checked the read out and reached for his cellphone, dialed a number, and spoke a single word, "Boomerang."

After a few minutes Eddie hung up and smiled. "We have some good news for a change. Jack is in the house, he is well and they are willing to wait as long as needed to get one million American dollars."

"Great, let's get hold of Steve and Geoff. Have the plane ready for a 0600 take off the morning" I said to Eddie. He had the phone and knew who to call, I did not.

The next morning, we had our tour bus waiting for us and we departed for the airport to meet up with the aircraft and crew.

Upon arrival, we boarded the plane and made a routine departure for a "local flight over the mountains and return." The Control Tower acknowledged as we rolled for a takeoff.

After we had leveled off at 12,000 feet and made a slow turn to the east, the ground started rising up to meet the plane. Since we were holding steady, the ground appeared to be rising.

When we got near the horse farm where Jack Thompson was being held as a captive, I photographed it from several angels without being obvious. We continued to follow the highway and railroad east. After a few moments we entered a valley. The mountain pass was beautiful and from this altitude the snow was ivory white, but as we crossed the Andes into this jungle valley, it was like entering a whole different world as we lost altitude.

The road ran east to west and the valley was north to south. It looked about two miles wide and 10 miles long. I could not tell what altitude it dropped down to, but, we were over a jungle. I think it was more that a hundred kilometers too. Our ground speed was 300 miles per hour and we flew for over a hundred and fifty miles. The four lane highway looked like an unbroken freshly ironed white ribbon. Some of road on the eastern side of the valley was paved, but most of the road was black pavement or old oil topped road, straight and flat.

When we circled the valley a few times and noticed construction workers and equipment working on the new road, on the eastern side of the valley. There were dump trucks, graders and the rollers associated with building a road, and a small compound of some sort was near the jungle's edge where it appeared that the equipment was stored at night. This would be a good spot to set up a switch with the kidnappers.

We took a lot of video and still shots of the area for future reference, but today was Friday and we had been on the road a week now. Well, almost a week, and we still had done nothing but spend money.

Steve had been flying left seat, the Pilot in Command's seat, and Rita was flying right seat as co-pilot. Geoff had been watching the instruments and keeping a look out as there were lots of planes coming and going through the pass. He was in the jump seat behind Steve most of the time.

The door to the cockpit was open and we could see out of the wind screen if we leaned out into the aisle.

We were all just looking out the windows trying to see any roads we could note or houses in the area, anything that would make our job easier. Each of us trying to get the "lay of the land" if we needed to.

After a few passes over the area, we departed and continued on south, doing "the tourist thing." Eddie had been with us and he was very interested as what was going on here. He also had a camera and was taking pictures. I thought we had all the info we needed. Geoff had been making scratch marks on a flight chart and notes for future references.

After we gained altitude and had leveled out, Eddie suggested we make passes over the normal sights before going home. Although we were in a valley, Peruvian Air Traffic Control, or ATC, was located on the mountain and we were being "painted" by the radar so we had to make it good. I watched Rita as she switched dials and turned knobs for radio traffic. I bet the Peruvian Controllers were very interested in hearing a very soft and sexy female voice speaking Spanish and flying an aircraft, especially a big aircraft like this. Rita had a very pleasant voice when she wanted to "turn it on" and I bet she was cranking it out. I could not hear what she was saying, but I could see Steve laugh a few times as she talked to Air Traffic Control. She would have been a potential BRAT if she wanted to, a real little imp, but smart as a whip.

I am still amazed at the way she could handle the aircraft. The landings were much gentler than Geoff or Steve's. Her turns were very coordinated and smooth. I am from the "old school" where girls only played with dolls and grew up to "bake cookies and have babies" June Cleaver type on "Leave It To Beaver." I guess I am wrong on that one, big time, and I am glad.

After we gained altitude again and leveled out, Rita got out of the right seat and Geoff got in. Rita walked back to the main cabin, went into the potty and came out to sit beside Eunice. She and Eunice kept looking out of the window and pointing, then they settled back to discuss something as we flew back over the construction area. They were sitting in the very front seats and Rita motioned me up front from where I was about midway back. I didn't like the front seats in this model aircraft as they seemed to be noisier than the other seats. Besides, when the wheels were lowered for landing, it was real noisy.

"Eunice has come with a very good observation and idea. Wanna hear it?" Rita asked. "Sure, but do we need to talk about it right now? I can't hear too well and my ears are popping." I replied.

"We can wait, but I think what she said was worth hearing" Rita said.

"Of course, but can we do it on the ground." I smiled and looked at Eunice.

Eunice's face was like a little girl's in some ways. It was perfect, smooth and clear, not a wrinkle. She had something she wanted to share and it showed, shinning like a new penny.

About that time the aircraft power levers were pulled back, or the pitch was changed on the propellers and the noise was reduced, I acknowledged the ladies and knelt down between them to listen. I then gestured "okay go ahead."

One of the first things I noticed was Eunice's tone of voice, not the little mousy squeaky voice like when she was trying to imitate Marilyn Monroe, but a very adult voice two octaves lower, loud and clear.

"Charlie, you guys considering using that construction place down there?" she asked. "Yeah, just looking at it, we are going to discuss it when we get back. Why?" I replied. "Well, you could use the place, there is a place to park cars and a few houses up the road in the jungle. When you get the guy rescued, why not land the plane right there on the highway pick them up and fly out? Steve and Rita can do it. It is wide enough. I was watching a big truck and cars down there and it looks as wide as the runways we have been using." She finished and watched my face for a reaction.

"Something to consider, Sugar and a damn good thought. We will need to talk about it of course. I didn't see the houses off in the bush. What did they look like?" I asked.

"Big houses, like maybe rich people live in them, some barns and stuff. We only went over it one time and it was on my side. I got to look down and see the houses. Well, some of them were barns." she said.

"You have a tablet or note paper?" I asked and she nodded affirmative. "Well, draw the house and barns for us. Do it now while it is fresh in your mind. Get with Amber and Emil, tell them exactly what you saw. Go do it now." Eunice got up to go to the galley area.

"YO!" I yelled over the aircraft noises and raised my index finger, making a small circle movement while pointing straight up and then pointing to the ground. This was the standard hand signal for "assemble here." I nodded at Amber and Emil. "Get with Eunice, she has an idea. She is drawing a few houses she saw. This may be useful later." I yelled.

They both nodded and said okay and walked forward.

After we landed back at the Lima airport, we stayed in the aircraft and waited for the Peruvian Mercenaries, or "shooters" as I call them, to board the aircraft. It was a good a place as any to have a quick meeting.

When we were all assembled, I stood at the front of the aircraft's main cabin where the Flight Attendant normally stands to do the Pre-Flight briefing for the passengers. Everyone else was as close as possible so I did not have to shout in case there was someone there that didn't need to know about our little game.

"Carlos," I said to the one shooter that seemed to be the leader, "Can you put two of your folks outside to make sure that we are not interrupted, please? I said.

Carlos nodded and tapped two of the Shooters on the shoulder and they followed him off the aircraft. The suburban and the vans had been pulled up to the aircraft and the drivers were still behind the wheel. After a few seconds, Carlos came back on board and nodded, indicating all was secure.

Eddie was on the phone talking to someone and then hung up.

Eddie said, "Charlie, tomorrow is Saturday, a holiday in Peru. No work at the site we were looking at. It would appear to be a good place. If you like, I can get my people to set up a meet for…say, 12:00 o'clock noon. The sun will be highest and there will be less shadows to deal with if we have to go in the jungle. The sun will be at its highest."

I sat and thought for a moment and asked Amber. "Can we get our people in there tonight to cover us when we come in tomorrow?

Amber answered quickly, "Sure, we will need transpiration and a head start, like now. We have all our gear in that van and tour bus…Yeah, give us an hour and we can move out."

"Transportation is out there, do you feel you have enough here with our people and the local Shooters?" I asked.

"I think so. What do you think, Emil?" she turned to Emil for an answer.

"If we get too big we will be noticed. I know our team is good and I have been talking to the local shooters here. I feel confident with Carlos and his bunch." Emil said acknowledging the local Peruvian Shooter.

Carlos acknowledged with a slight nod and a smile indicating acknowledgement of the complement.

"Vinnie, you and Eddie can go with me. We will drive over there early in the morning. I feel we will be followed by the bad guys if they have any idea we are in town. Plus the two mile ride across the straight flat valley will give us away unless we drive past the location and come from the opposite direction. Come from the East as they are watching the West. Any comments?"

"No problem, and if you don't mind I will have a few extra folks and vehicles with us too. We may need the help if things turn to shit." Vinnie said as a matter of fact.

"Up to you, Vinnie, Eddie, you have any comment?"

"I am not allowed to go with you, but I may be there in a different vehicle. I know it is my man, but there are many things that affect my decision." he said sheepishly.

"I know, Ed. You have got to protect the 'big picture.' No problems, but can we be in radio contact with you all the way so we can get a 'heads up' if things turn to shit?" I asked.

"That is no problem. You will have radios and cell phones that will keep us in instant real time communications." Eddie said. "Vinnie will have all that, and also have radios for your teams going over a little early."

"Okay. One more thing, Steve, Rita and Geoff, can you land this thing on the road near the construction site and get it off again?" I asked.

Both Rita and Goeff looked at Steve since he was the Pilot in Command.

Steve thought for a few seconds and said it could be done. "You mean do a 'hot extraction,' Charlie?" Steve asked.

"Yup, unless you feel you can not do it. I know you have the balls to do it, but you are also obligated to keep lumps off your company's equipment. It is called responsibility and if we break it, I will buy it. Or we could try and land a couple of helicopters for a pickup, if we can find them. What you think Eddie?" I said.

"All the Huey-type helicopters belong to the government. I don't feel comfortable asking around about that at this late in the game." Eddie said. "If you land out at the site, make a pick up. Would you come back to Lima?"

"I don't think that would be too wise. We may need to get out of Dodge as they say, keep going back to Belize City. We will not have enough fuel so, stop in San Jose again for fuel and then keep going. Eddie, we may need your help with Peruvian Customs and ATC, square things with them to keep shit from happening. We will file for a routine departure from Lima to San Jose. We will just make one stop before leaving there airspace." Steve Johnson said.

Vinnie and Eddie both shook their heads and said word to the effect that that would be easy and would get done if needed.

"I will tell you all," said Eddie, "we do not want this in the morning papers. The kidnappers are not going to complain, so I feel we can get the plane and teams out of the country with little problems. If that is what you want to do."

I thought a minute. "Okay, Eddie, make it happen. Get your people to set it up. We will meet at 12:00 noon at the construction site on International Highway East. Can you do it?" I asked.

"I can try, Charlie." Eddie said as he and Vinnie went outside the aircraft to talk on his cell phone.

We chatted a few moments with the crew. Amber wanted to make sure all the radio frequencies had been checked and put new batteries in the radios, both the handheld and the boom mic's. She wanted to get to the weapons located in the Tour Bus. Hidden under the seats to make sure they were in proper working order. These weapons had not been seen by the crew, but Vinnie said he had cleaned and packed them himself. Still, we wanted to test them ourselves, but we had to have faith in Vinnie. It is going to have to be that way because of Peruvian gun laws.

Also, since this was short fuzed, minimum time, everyone stood around looking at the VCR tapes through the small eye piece at the lay of the land. They must have run that two minute tape ten times each to make sure they knew the area. They looked at the trail to a house off the road, behind construction compound, and saw the road that Eunice had noticed.

"We don't know who lives there or if they will cause problems. But, we need to be careful. They may have dogs that will give us up and we will have dogs with us which may attract them." Emil warned.

"We need to have the Security people at the hotel get the dogs down the back steps and get them here so we can leave. How can we do that?" Sassy asked.

About that time Eddie and Vinnie came back in the plane. "Okay, they went for it, 12:00 tomorrow at the construction site. We can bring two cars, no more. Told them we had a Suburban and a Sedan. We are to stop at the edge of the rode, stay in the car and they will come to us. I told them we needed to see jack Thompson, make sure he is okay before we give them any money. No Jack, no money, they agreed" Vinnie said.

"Vinnie, we need the dawgs here ASAP. Can you handle?" I asked.

"No problem" Vinnie said and whipped out the cell phone and made a call. In a few minutes he came back and said, "They are on the way. They will be here in twenty minutes unless they hit bad traffic."

"Okay, let's start getting ready. Amber, you are now in charge of the operation." I said, turning to Carlos. "You have any problem with her being in charge? I want you to make sure your two friends understand that she was a Captain the U.S. Marine, ain't an amateur. Make sure they understand." As I waited for him to translate, one of the three said something in slang and they chuckled.

"We understand, *Senor. La Senora es la jefa.*" Carlos said. "What was funny?" Amber asked.

"He said it was better to follow *La Senora* than me, she is prettier anyway." Carlos said. We all chuckled, except Amber, she did not change her expression.

"Any questions?" I asked and waited. There was none. "Good luck and God help us all," I said. "Let's go."

Chapter 25

I watched the vans and trucks leave the airport as Vinnie and I stood beside the aircraft. They went to the road leading to the main highway and turned left, Amber, Samantha, Sassy, Emil, Robert and Bart, along with the four Shooters and two dogs, their drivers and a few extras Shooters I did not get a chance to meet. Fifteen souls altogether, who were following me because they believed in me, and what we were doing. But we were going up against an unknown force where the words "mercy," "fair play," and "rules" were for others, getting killed or wounded so far from home and medical aid, worse still if the girls were captured. I hated to even think of that, but everything was in motion.

I looked a Vinnie, who looked like he had a quiver in his chin suddenly looked around and said "Fuck you Squid" and turned to go inside the aircraft to "check on something."

Eddie came over and shook hands, said for me to take a new cell phone. A number was on the carrying case in one of the plastic labels you print.

"Here. Keep this plugged in, and take this pager. If it goes off, turn the phone on means I have a message for you. The number on the case is my pager. If you call that number, I will call you right back. I have your number programmed in this phone. I will keep you up to speed on anything I can give you and just for your information, there are a lot of big people looking at this operation in Washington." Eddie said.

Eddie shook my hand and Vinnie's hand, got in his car and drove off. He waved as he left, a small wave, and we waved back.

Vinnie and I called the drivers over from the Suburban and van. I was surprised Carlos was in the Suburban. I thought he had left with the rest of the Shooters with Amber's team. He knew I looked surprised and said in a quiet voice, "You Americanos may get lost. I thought I would stay with you."

I nodded my head in thanks and turned to go back to the aircraft.

Steve, Geoff, Rita and Eunice were still inside the aircraft when Vinnie and I walked up towards the Galley area. They offered Vinnie and I cup of "airline coffee" and we took it.

I noticed the dogs crates had been put on the aircraft. "We need to go back to the hotel. Get all the baggage and bring it to the aircraft. I hope everyone has packed everything, and wiped the room down from top to bottom for finger prints. We don't need to leave any hints." I said.

"Carlos, can we get another van to load all the baggage in and bring to the aircraft?" I asked.

"No problem. We will have a truck there by the time we arrive." Carlos said, as he pulled out his own cell phone and made a call.

"*Listo, Jefe?*" (you ready, Boss?) Carlos said. "Yeah... Lets go." I said.

It took about one hour, round trip, to get the bags on the plane. Steve, Rita, Geoff and Eunice went through all the motions of getting ready for a departure. Steve filed a flight plan with Flight Services for a direct flight from Lima, Peru, to San Jose, Costa Rica. The aircraft had been topped off and pre-flighted. Steve called for a tow tractor to tow the aircraft inside a hanger he had rented and Eunice had made arraignments for twenty meals to be delivered to the aircraft at 8:00 AM the next morning. A local aircraft cleaning crew had come and cleaned up the inside of the aircraft, vacuuming and dusting. The little paper headrest had been replaced with Peruvian Airlines logos and they looked real spiffy. Everything looked like the cover was going well, a crew had been called over to wash down the aircraft and now it sparkled.

All that needed to be done was "kick the tires and light the fires," as they say in aviation slang.

Vinnie and I loaded ourselves into the Suburban and van with our group and started towards the meeting place. It was a five hour drive normally, but we wanted to be there early, just in case.

Steve and the flight crew would take an airport shuttle bus to their hotel, which was what flight crews normally did when in a transit status. They would pack and be ready to come back to the aircraft at 0700 for a pre-flight. We wanted everything in place. I wanted them airborne no later than 1045 hours, heading over to the area. Then they would try to stay in the area where we could get them in a short time if need be. Steve and the flight crew had the proper frequencies for the handheld radios on the ground and could monitor all traffic.

It had been decided that the Shooters could get away on there own after we had left the area. They knew the back roads and could blend in with the locals. I had a problem with this at first, but Carlos said it was the best way. "Besides, if we go with you, how will we get back into this country from where ever you go?" Carlos said.

"Good point, *Mi Amigo,* but I just don't want to you to think we are bailing out on you and your men." I said.

"Don't worry. As you said, this isn't our first *rodeo* either," we both chuckled.

We pulled out into the traffic and started out, toward the main highway heading East, as we had done a few days before. Time had run together these last few days. Had it only been a week ago when we were in the park across from the house, celebrating a couple of fifteen year old girls being introduced to society? Where does time go when you are having fun?

Vinnie and I laid our heads back and snoozed a little as our two drivers navigated through the traffic in Lima, Peru, and then to the countryside where the landscape started rising before us. Just before dark, we came into a small village and the driver asked if it was alright if we stopped to get something to eat.

We went into a small café and the woman in the kitchen came out and hugged Jesus's neck and made a big to do. Between the small amount of Spanish I spoke, and the small amount of English "Chewy"(a nickname for Jesus) spoke, we were introduced. It was an Aunt Julia. I later found out that this was his home town and that was why he felt safe stopping there.

At Chewy's command, a couple young teenagers went outside and sat on the hood of the Surburban and another went to the front Dodge van. This is a common custom, to have a "car attendant." Funny thing is, the locals respect a "car attendants" presence, and they won't try to steal anything.

We got back in the vehicles and started east again and we slept. We had been running on nerves these last few days and it was starting to show on me. The BRATS, Emil and

Robert were in excellent physical shape and I guess it did make a difference.

About midnight the pager went off and I turned on the phone. The phone rang and it was Eddie from R.I.O. Office.

"Charlie, your people have arrived. They are making their way to the meeting point now as we speak. They appear to be about one half mile East of where they want to be. In a couple of hours they will have a nice moon to work with. I hope they are in place soon, that moon will shine for the bad guys too." Eddie said.

"Thanks Eddie. Anything else?" I asked.

"Yeah, the bad guys are on the move with Jack Thompson. We do not have a position on them, but they are not at the horse farm. I suspect they are either on the way or in place nearby. If I hear anything I will advise you." Eddie said.

"Thanks, man. I am worried about those kids." I said.

"From what I have seen and what Vinnie has told me, they can take care of themselves" he reassured me.

I woke up as we pulled off the main road and went North on a dirt road. The driver had turned the lights off, but it was just like Eddie had told us, the moon was bright and you could see the white sand and rocks in the moonlight.

We drove for about five hundred yards and came to a clearing that overlooked the valley. The driver stopped and we all got out. We could see a few very small lights and a few headlights on the road down into the valley. A perimeter was set up for security and we were set to just watch for a while.

Vinnie produced two devices that I call "Starlight Scopes," but that name was from the "old days." They were called Night Vision Scopes and they were much better than we ever had in The 'Nam. "Wow!" I thought. These things lit up the valley as if it were high noon.

We focused our attention to the far side of the valley, about two miles away. There was absolutely no problem seeing due to the Night Vision Scopes (they were awesome). We could see the dump trucks parked inside the compound, the paving equipment, and someone walking around with a flashlight.

"Vinnie." I said in a small voice.

"I see 'em. Looks like a night watchman or something. He came out of that shack. He may have heard something. Looks like a dog may be with him." Vinnie said slowly, as if describing a baseball game."

After a few minutes, the light went out and the person walking around went back inside. When the man opened the door to the shack, the oil lamp light almost blinded us, due to how sensitive our gear was.

Several times during the night, Vinnie, myself, and the Shooters we had with us, took turns on the night scopes. The "Watchman," as we started calling him, came out and made his rounds, but we did not see the dog. I hoped that the dog didn't try to approach Bart and Sassy since they had dogs with them. If the local dog raised an alarm by barking, it would be bad for all of us, so the shooters would be forced to "neutralize the threat without prejudice" as the training manual states.

My pager went off again. I turned on the phone and Eddie called immediately. "Charlie, your people are in place, well concealed. They had to take out the little dog.

Too bad, but business is business." he said. "Where are you, Eddie? You near us?" I asked.

"No, I am in the office right now and before you say anything,…don't ask." Eddie quickly added.

"Okay, I will take your word."

"Charlie, there is movement from behind the team…" Eddie paused for a minute. "…They are coming from the house, and walking down the road. One of them almost stepped on one of the good guys near a ditch." Eddie continued.

I waited for a few minutes and listened to Eddie talk. I could hear him on the background speaking very low and quietly as if he were on the radio. I could not understand what he was saying, but I later learned what they were doing.

"Charlie, your team is aware of the approach of the bad guys. They have all acknowledged. I am a little concerned about one of your people…a little too close to the bad guys, but they have not seemed to have noticed." Eddie said. I just listened, not saying a word.

"Eddie, we are only about thirty minutes from sunrise. The sun will be up over the mountain in a few minutes, but the valley will be dark for a half hour more. Anything special we should know about?" I asked.

"How many vehicles do you have with you?" he asked. "Two…Why?" I responded.

"You need another one. I have a sedan nearby, they will come to you, I will guide them in. It is a white Mercedes, guy's name is Tito, one of my men. He will honk one time when he leaves the road and his password for identity is "Pepsi." The countersign will be "Please." Use Tito and the car for your "drive up" car and the Suburban as your 'body guard's' vehicle. At the right time, have the van drive by with your "Shooters" and we will try and spring the trap. How does that sound?" Eddie asked.

"Complicated. What if the shooters ain't there and the trap goes down? " I asked. "It could happen. You got a better plan?" Eddie asked.

"No, just thinking out loud." I said.

"Eddie, I thought you said your guys would blow the horn when they come off the paved road. A car just pulled off, coming this way. I can see the lights." I said as I dropped behind a tree.

"It ain't my guys, they are still ten miles away. Those may be bad guys." Eddie said quickly.

I alerted the others that someone was coming and I made a loud stage whisper to the outpost near the road to let them in. We would stop them when they got to where we were.

It was light enough by now to see the car coming without lights. They drove around a curve and skidded to a stop. They were surprised to see our vehicles ahead of them. They hesitated a moment and then tried to put the vehicle in reverse. When they did, a slight sound like a knock on the door sounded.

"Tap! Tap! Tap!" and the doors flew open and then several more "Tap! Tap!... Tap! Tap!...Tap! Tap! Tap!" as the silencers on the 9mm Glocks did their deed.

All the shooting was done by the local mercenaries. Vinnie and I had our weapons out but did not fire them because they were not muffled or silenced and we did not have a target. The shooting was done by the Peruvian folks and the driver and two passengers were extremely dead, clean head shots on all three. In dim light too…good shooting, but now what?

Carlos went over to the bodies and looked in the vehicle to make sure that was all there was. All of this was done in a very professional manner, right out of the text book. The trunk was opened and inspected, but nothing was found.

"You know them Carlos?" I asked. After a few minutes, a car horn made a single blast from the direction of the road. All of us went back to the ditches and trees.

This was supposed to be Eddie's guys in a white Mercedes coming in. The white Mercedes appeared from around the bend. I stepped out of the jungle and let them see me. It was full daylight now. One of the Mercenaries hollered a single word or name and stepped out of the jungle too. The doors eased open and a four people got out. You could see the adrenaline go down in all concerned. The Shooters slung their arms and holstered pistols as they approached the white Mercedes. I just stood still until I knew that everyone concerned had seen me and knew that I was not a threat. I did not know it, but Vinnie was just to my rear and off to one side.

"Shit, is there anyone else in town coming to this picnic?" Vinnie said. "I dunno, but it is getting crowded." I said.

I walked over to where Carlos and all the others were talking. They were going through their pockets and taking the contents and dividing it up among themselves. One took a gold lighter and a watch, another some bills and credit cards and put them in their pockets. Carlos looked at me for a full five count "Carlos, I have no problems with this." I said, "It is the way of the world."

Carlos smiled and went back to work. I asked Carlos if he knew any of them. He seemed to ignore me, but I knew the adrenaline was still running high. He spoke to the others and they conversed a while.

"This one over here, the driver, we called "Weeso"(bones). Knew him as a kid, no *cajones* (balls). I am surprised that they let him even around the gang. The others are the same." Carlos said as they dragged the three bodies over to the jungle and pushed them down the side of a cliff.

One of the shooters started the car and backed it out of the way, hiding it in the jungle. There was a little blood on one of the seats, but they wiped it off very quickly before it dried.

Eddie called again and we briefed him what happened. He did not seem to worry, so I wasn't going to worry.

Eddie said we had a perfect setup now. The white Mercedes could be used, the Surburban, the Dodge Van, and the Volvo. Since the Volvo that the three bad guys came in was known, we could roll up on the bad guys and be right on top of them before they knew we were in their car. Hmmm…good thinking.

"Okay, it is about time to go and try and get our man." I said. "Let's saddle up and get turned around. We can send the van first, be just ahead of us. Drive past the place and try to find a place to hide so you can come in like the Calvary since you have the automatic weapons and all. The Mercedes and the Suburban will come with me to make the contact and pick up, but we don't do anything until we see Jack Thompson and we are able to determine he is alive and well, period. Then we rip them a new asshole. We have a box with funny money in it and they can have it. As soon as it gets over one hundred and fifty feet from me, a timer will start and it will blow. The Volvo can just ease in when you see things start to happen. Any questions?" I asked.

Carlos translated for the rest. There were a few questions that were answered, but it seemed all was well.

We sat in place for several more hours. It was near high noon when we decided it was time to get ready. The van moved out and turned left back on the main road. Every radio had been checked and double checked. I don't know if Amber's team could hear us or not.

I was on the phone to Eddie again and told him what the deal was. He acknowledged it and said we had better get moving. Eddie acknowledged that the plane was off the ground and in the air.

I know how Henry Fonda felt in the movie "High Noon." It was getting time… We watched the van move the two short miles over the flat valley floor, past the construction site and then we eased out the Mercedes and the Surburban. We went to the road, turned left, drove for about 500 yards and came to the crest of the ridge and pulled over. The traffic was light. Only a few cars were on the road since this was a Peruvian National Holiday.

The driver of the van with the Shooters radioed back and said he could not see a thing when they passed the construction site, not a soul. They acknowledged that they had pulled over on the side of the road and pretended to be working on the van. They had turned around and were headed back downhill. The Shooters had pulled off at a wide spot left by the construction crew when they were building the highway and now they were waiting. They knew that things were going to happen soon.

The two Shooters in the Volvo were going to wait ten minutes and then start down the hill unless they heard the "bust" signal over the radio. If they heard "BINGO" on the radio, they were to come in shooting.

All of our people were in black BDU's, the same as the Peruvians. The bad guys were dressed in all sorts of clothing, but no uniforms. Everyone had been given a photo of Jack Thompson, taken about two months ago at an office party. So all of us would know what he looked like. The van had a pair of big bolt cutters in it as well, just in case he was handcuffed or shackled in any way or form.

If the Volvo started down the hill and did not hear the "go" signal, then they were to pull off the road about one mile West of the Construction Site and wait. They were to do anything to prevent themselves from getting there too soon. The bad guys would recognize the Volvo and think it was their people coming to help. The Volvo would be able to get in among the bad guys before they know what was happening.

Both of Mickey's hands were straight up in the air... I guess it was show time.

Chapter 26

As we approached the construction are, we noticed no other vehicle was in sight. As planned, the Suburban with the Shooters stayed away from us, about fifty feet back and next to the road.

We drove the white Mercedes to the construction site storage compound and waited. I knew we were being watched. The windows on the Mercedes were darkened down so you could not see inside. We strained our necks to look around, everything looked quiet.

From our left, towards the houses we could not see from the road, came three vehicles, but Eddie and "Big Bird" had advised us about these vehicles. They were driving slow, the lead vehicle was a beat up van and the second vehicle was a new Toyota Land Cruiser. The van stopped just after it came in view and the cruiser pulled around it. The third sedan pulled over where they could face our Suburban. They were a hundred feet away and we sat there, waiting to see who did what first I was on the phone with Eddie as we drove up, explaining what we were seeing. He confirmed that there were only three vehicles and that our van up the road knew we had arrived. Eddie also confirmed that one of the vehicles was transmitting something on a radio but it was "scrambled" and would take a while to decode. We decided that they were doing the same thing as we were. Due to the sun being at its apex, "Big Bird" was not as effective with heat imaging as it was at night, but we took whatever info we could get.

I was sure that Vinne and I had the same pulse rate and blood pressure, but we were trying to maintain our composure as much as possible. Still no movement, but after a little less than five minutes, the doors to the Toyota opened and a very large, well dressed individual got out and started walking towards us. I told Vinnie to be cool and I would get out also. I walked towards the Toyota, we met around the halfway point. The man was not as big as I thought he was, his size may have been proportional to my fear.

"You speak English?" I asked. "*Tu habla espanol?*" he returned.

"No, I do not speak Spanish, but if English is a problem, I will go get one of my associates. He may be able to speak *chongo* (monkey) and you two can have a meaningful conversation." I retorted.

"I speak English… Do you have the money?" he asked.

"Well, I won't talk to you about it. I wanna talk to the "Organ Grinder," not to the monkey. When the *Jefe* shows up, tell him I will be in that car, come get me." and I spun around and started walking back towards the car. I couldn't let these assholes run a bluff on me, but they did. Things were not going as advertised and I was getting worried. I was not handling it well at all.

"Wait…" he said, "I will get *El Supremo.*" and with that the other rear door opened and another person got out and walked towards us.

The man came up to us, he was a slimmer and taller than the first. "Who are you?" he asked in a snotty manner.

"Gene Autry." I answered in the same manner.

"Look, I came here to get a man I do not know or give a fuck about. I run a delivery service. I pay for the goods and then deliver, but in this case I have been instructed to see the man, whatever his name is. Compare this photo, ask him his name and a few questions. If he gives the right answers, I pay you and drive off. I have been paid and I don't care either way. Now, do we understand each other?" I said and looked at him in a steady gaze.

He dropped the cigar he had been smoking on the road and ground it out with his foot. "Okay, we are in the same business I see." he smiled. I did not trust the smile or his manner, but at least we had come to a mutual respect for each other, no matter what that means.

"Where is Thompson?" I asked.

"He is safe. I too have my orders. I am supposed to see the money. Bring it to my employer and then after it has been counted, we bring you the man." he smiled.

I chuckled, "You don't really expect me to go for that shit do you, Sport?"

Sport, as I had dubbed him in my mind, threw his head back and gave a good honest laugh. "I tried to tell them that, but we are dealing with, how you say? ... Amateurs?"

"Well, that makes it tough on both of us." as I tried to smile too. "So we are down to the point that 'you show me yours and I will show you mine.'"

He thought about that a minute and smiled again. "I have not heard that in years. You see, I spent my youth in Miami. That is in Florida, USA..."

"I have heard that." I said.

"...and my father was deported back to Cuba, and we decided to go with him. So I remember a lot of the expressions." Sport said.

Sport reached in his coat breast pocket and then stopped when he realized that doing so might be a problem. He opened his coat to show he did not have a weapon, but was reaching for a cigar in his shirt pocket. My heart did a five hundred beat increase over that. I could just see the safeties going off with the teams laying in the bush and in the van.

Sport lit the cigar, took a few puffs and said, "I'll tell you what. You get your money out so I can at least say I seen it. Place it on the ground right here and I will take you or one of your people to the house to see the man. Funny, I don't even know his name either. When all is satisfied, we make the trade. Okay?"

I waited a few seconds to make him feel I was considering "all the options" as we stood there. Hell, I didn't have any better ideas.

"Well, I have to stay with the money, but my friend in the car will be more than happy to go with you. You see, I have to stay with the money." I said. "Confidentially, I don't trust some of these people." I gestured towards the van.

Sport laughed again and said. "Neither do I."

I walked to the back of the Mercedes and stood there. That was a signal to the Shooters to bring the very large "steamer trunk" over to me. I gestured for them to bring it to the meeting place between the cars where "Sport" and his gorilla was standing. They placed the trunk on the ground and retreated back to the van. When I heard the van door slide closed, I bent over and unsnapped the latches and raised the lid. I watched the expression on Sport's face, he was greedy.

I let him feel the money and pick up a few bundles of hundreds and twenties to see that it was real. I then took a small, slim set of wires from under one side of the money bundles. It had a small four-pronged plug, sticking up like the plugs you would use to connect trailer lights to the car, except smaller. I pulled the plug and put one half of into my pocket.

"This is an explosive device safety switch if I get more than 100 feet away from this trunk, (I lied about the distance) there is a two pound block of Thermite that will ignite and make this money into ashes. There will be no way to stop it. If anything funny happens, I will ignite it with a switch I have under my clothing. There will be no second chances, there will be no mistakes. Do we all understand each other, Gentlemen?" I said in a voice that was an octave lower than I normally speak and a hundred decibels softer.

Sport and his gorilla never took their eyes off the money, even as I closed the lid. "Now, may we see the subject of this conversation?"

"Sure, we will have to go back to the small house in the jungle here. Come with me, please."

Sport indicated towards the car. "I will advise my friends what the game plan is so there will be no mistakes." I said as I walked back to the Mercedes and got in.

"Vinnie, I actuated the safety switch like you said. I am putting it in the seat pocket here, just in case. Now you need to go with Sport there and…" I said.

"Wait a minute, we did not turn the transmitter on. It is on the small box you have under your clothes." as Vinnie started trying to untuck my shirt from my pants. We looked mighty strange to the driver who was watching all this through the rear view mirror. We got my shirt up. The transmitter turned on and I was trying to rearrange my clothes. I think the driver was considering bailing out if these two *jotos* (homosexuals) in the back seat before they tried anything funny with him, especially while we were all wired up.

"And what do you mean 'I' have to go with them?" Vinnie finally realizing what I had said. "Why don't YOU go? Oh, yeah, you got the transmitter on."

"Okay, what do I do?" Vinnie asked.
I explained what the deal was and he thought a few minutes and said. "Okay, let's do it." "If anything looks bad or I hear anything, I am giving the "Bingo" signal and we will come in like Gang Busters. And Vinnie, be careful… you still owe me a Martini," I said.

Without a word, Vinnie exited the car and walked over to where Sport and his gorilla were standing. Their eyes had never left the trunk.

"Gentlemen, my associate will accompany you to see the subject." They walked away. Sport and Vinnie got in the car. Vinnie had a hard time getting in because he was so big and tall, but they slowly drove off down a small cart trail into the jungle.

After about fifteen minutes, Vinnie came back.

"I saw him. He answered the right questions. They have him hand cuffed with a standard set of cuffs and a waist chain. There are leg irons in the corner that they may put on him at night" Vinnie said. "There are four or five in and around the house I seen, but there are a lot of vehicles there, so there is a good chance they have some in the bush." he continued.

"Okay…what do they want us to do?" I asked.

"They want us to come to the house, bring the money and make the trade there. Just this car and nothing else." he said.

"Sound like bull shit. They need to bring him out here in the open." I said half to myself.

"Yeah, I tried to convince them of that, but…" Vinnie said as my pager went off. "Yeah Eddie, what you got?"I said.

Eddie said words to the effect that several people went out the back door. "Three are walking together, as if one was on each side of a person in the middle. They are headed out the back to a small barn. Hold on, they are in a jeep and heading into the jungle. That is about all I can see. I get a glimpse of them every now and then, but being the time of day and the jungle cover…Switch to thermal, Eddie said to someone in the background. "…Yup, they have pulled down the hill. I don't know where they could be going. There are no known roads back that way, but we may not see small cart trails either, and there are millions of them in this country that only horse drawn cart use," Eddie said.

"You still see them Eddie?"

"No. They may be under a stand of trees…Okay, we see them. They have stopped just down the trail about a half a mile away from the building. Thermal sensors show heat staying one spot. Looks like the image of a vehicle's motor. Yup, they have stopped," Eddie said.

"Okay, Eddie, here is the deal. Vinnie and I are going to the house. We will each have several grenades in our coats. As soon as we get to the house and get out, will you be able to see us?"

"Yes"

"Good. Then, when we get out, give the "Bingo" signal. That will give use about thirty seconds to get in the house and secure it. Have the Shooters in the Suburban come to the house and help us secure it. Now, here is the ace in the hole, have the Shooters in the Volvo, come in, go around the house to the back and down the trail. Try and get the bad guys pinned down if possible. The Volvo should be able to get close in since they will still think the Volvo has some of their friends in it. As the van starts in, have them hold short until Amber and her Team neutralizes those in the bush with her team, that is the bad guys, and then come to the house. Where the van Shooters will pick up Amber and her team, put them in the van and got down the trail also and get Jack Thompson. Come back out the same way. We will cover their retreat as far as the house. When we get Jack Thompson, have the aircraft land on the highway and hold short at the far end until we call for him, don't want the plane to get hit by a stray bullet. Then the plane is to come to the construction site area and pick us up....Got that?" I said.

"Got it..." Eddie said, "...and good luck".

We drove up to the house and existed the vehicle as casual as could be expected. The driver stayed with the car. Vinnie and I went in. We had straightened out the safety pins in the grenades prior to approaching the house. As we went through the door, we took the safety pins out and rushed into the room where they were holding Jack Thompson...it was empty.

About that time we heard automatic weapons fire closing in. We dove to the floor and crawled over to the still open door to look. We knew it was not Amber's team as they all had silenced weapons, but soon the firing stopped.

I looked down the drive way and the van with the Shooters was rolling in. They slid the side door open and Amber, Samantha, Bart and Sassy and the dogs jumped in the van as the Volvo went around them at a high rate of speed. At the same time, Robert and Emil came out of the jungle and ran towards the van. I could not hear what Amber said, but Robert and Emil acknowledged with a slight wave.

Vinnie and I finished searching the house and found no one on the first floor. We did not bother with the second floor at that time.

In turn, we heard automatic fire again down the trail.

Our driver in the Mercedes had bailed out of the car and was on the ground near the car in a prone position facing down the road where Emil and Robert were coming from.

"What the hell is going on now?" I asked.

"I dunno!" yelled Vinnie from the other side of the house. As he saw Emil and Robert jump in the Mercedes, the driver jumped in as they backed away from the house and…

"Vinnie, I still have the transmitter safety device on for the trunk. Emil and Robert are in the car with one of the Shooters!" I tried to rip my shirt off to get to the black box.

Vinnie ran across the room, grabbed my shirt, pulled it up and turned off the small black transmitter taped to the middle of my back.

"Let's go." Vinnie said as we ran out a side door of the house, the Mercedes screamed away and went down the trail. The firing had become sporadic, but we knew we could hear our team and their suppressed weapons. Piff, piff, piff...piff, piff...

As Vinnie and I ran out the side door, we noticed very large Isuzu dump trunk next to a barn. Vinnie and I got in with Vinnie in the driver's seat. The keys were in the truck and the big diesel came to life with a black puff of smoke. The trail was only wide enough for a single car at a time to travel, but after Vinnie ran down that trail in the big dump truck, it was somewhat wider.

We only had to go only a short distance until we ran up on the Mercedes with the windshield blown out. We then saw the van and Volvos sitting side by side. The Suburban was off in the jungle and on fire. Two of the Shooters' bodies were hanging out the door. The area showed all the signs of an ambush.

Vinnie and I got to the Mercedes at about the same time and grabbed our radios so we would at least know what was going on. We switched the knob to "ALL" so we could here and transmit on all channels in the radio.

The first thing I heard was Amber. "They have the subject and have moved down that trail to your right, Bart...but it splits a half dozen places on down the trail. I have no idea which way they went." She said in a whisper.

"I have a scent and we are working it. You want me to try and follow?" Bart's voice said very steady and even.

"Yeah, but let some of use catch up and..." Amber answered as several muffled shots went off very near us.

"Okay people, let's slow this down and get organized a minute...Checkmate." Amber said.

"Bart." "Sassy."" "Emil." "Robert."
"Charlie." I answered. "Vinnie."
"Where is Samantha...Samantha...Checkmate... Samantha....Samantha where are you?" A very weak signal came over the air, Samantha's voice, "No, No...get away... No." and two muffled shots, then silence.

"Sassy....where was the last place you saw Samantha?" Amber said.

"About fifty to seventy five yards further down the wide trail the bad guys took with the captive." Sassy said into her boom mike. You could tell she was running.

"Okay, we are on the way." Amber said.

At that time we heard a man yell. As we ran through the bush towards the sound, two pistol shots were fired and a dog yelped.

Automatic weapon fire could be heard just ahead of Vinnie and I. We could hear the lead cutting the tree leaves and limbs above our head, but we kept going…silence.

Then, after few seconds, Sassy's voice came over the radio. "I am with Samantha. She is wounded…minor, they shot Prince (her dog)."

About that time a strange voice came from the brush. "Hey! Hey! Over here! I'm Jack Thompson!" he ran towards us with hand cuffs on.

Vinnie grabbed him as he came by and used a standard cuff key to remove the cuffs. "Sassy, where are you?" Emil's voice yelled out.

"Over here." Sassy said very quietly in her head set. "They shot Prince."

Emil and Robert ran to Sassy. Emil grabbed "Prince" up and put him in a fireman's carry and started back down the trail. Any other dog would have tried to bite, but Prince allowed Emil to carry him.

Sassy carried Emil's weapon and Robert helped. She had a "John Wayne" wound in the leg.

As I went by the area, I noticed seven dead where Samantha was laying. One had a wound to his side from the knife that Samantha carried. He was alive, but we solved his medical problem with a single shot. No witnesses allowed.

Jack Thompson said he had never seen anything like that before. "The dog came in and took out that guy that was going to try and kill that lady who was wounded, but took the bullets for her. Flew through the air like a bird, but the guy shot the dog instead and that girl took out the bad guy…"

During this time, the hired Shooters were intermingling with the Team and had made a good accounting for themselves.

Amber gave the order to fall back in an orderly fashion, which meant one fire team covered the other as you made a withdrawal. The Shooters might not have understood English, but they understood common tactics used all over the world.

Our casualties were light so far. Samantha had a leg wound in the upper thigh, painful but not life threatening. Two shooters wounded and four were dead. Prince of course was shot through the chest with a .38 at close range.

We assembled back at the vehicles. The only one we could get to that would run was the Isuzu Dump truck, a very large grain hauling model. Just a big general purpose truck you see all over the world.

We assembled at the dump truck and set a perimeter security team out. We did not know what was going on or how many bad guys were left and we were about a mile from our pick up point.

The dog handlers had complete medical kits with them, so Sassy went to work on Prince. She bandaged his wounds and gave him morphine. That made him quiet, but he was still bleeding. That little Oklahoma country girl should have been a veterinarian, she was good.

As Robert was bandaging Samantha's wound, she started leaning over and puking, gagging and making dry heaves. As she heaved, Robert continued to apply bandages to her bloody thighs.

"Don't be afraid, Samantha..." Robert said cheerfully. "...I am the best physician in 200 hundred yards. Ol' Doc Perez ain't never lost a patient yet. Just call on me anytime."

"Thanks, Doc..." Samantha said through clenched teeth as he applied a dash or two of powder to the wound. "I may call upon you in a bout six months or so..."

"Oh, yeah? Why six months?"

"I pregnant...I am going to have a baby," she said. Robert froze. He looked at her in a daze.

"What did you say?" we all stopped to listen. "I know I was not sure of what we heard." "I am going to have a baby...you know, when a girl and a guy..."

Billy L. Smith Sr.

"I know! I know about that…" I said. "But why? How? When?... Oh shit! Who?" was all I could say as Robert gave Samantha a syringe of morphine.

"Charlie, right now is not the time to discuss the birds and the bees. We need to move out!" Bart said as he gathered up "Duke' to start for the road.

A voice came over the radio I was holding. "Charlie?" It was Eddie.

"Yo, go ahead Eddie. We have a few casualties, but we are bringing out our dead and wounded." Vince said as the shooters loaded their dead friends into the big steel bed of the truck.

"Charlie, you got company coming…From the house area…Many, unknown number. This is fifteen minute old information since Big Bird has 'smoke in his eyes,'" meaning cloud cover and they can not see well.

The bad guys sure do want that money. Too bad, all of it was counterfeit. They had not noticed that it was only printed on one side. The counterfeiters were busted before they could print the second side.

Chapter 27

"Charlie? …It looks like they are hunkered down about halfway between you and the house. We would like to help you more…Standby for a 10-21 (standard police code for a phone call). This station will be 10-6." Eddie said, wherever he was.

"Don't use the radios any more if you can help it. They have counterintelligence folks on line with them running 800 megahertz. The bad guys can hear every word you say. Rain is moving your way and you may be getting wet soon. I told the aircraft to go back to Lima and refuel. I have it lined out where no questions will be asked. Anyway, they will be in a transit status and Steve is telling them he has engine trouble. He told the locals the reason he came back to Lima was their maintenance facilities were so much better than any where else in the area…Right…"

"Okay Eddie. I will keep you advised. On when and what we plan on doing. Are any Calvary in the area?" I asked.

"Nary a soul, Pal, just you and *Tonto*. How is Samantha?" Eddie asked. Tonto was a Spanish word for "stupid" or "foolish."

"She is fine, morphine is holding. Hope it don't hurt the baby" I said. "What baby, Charlie? You got a baby with you?" Eddie quizzed.

"Nope, Samantha is going to be a mommy, she told us all tonight." I said.

There was a long silence. "Well, we can talk about that later." Eddie went on to say that we had about three hours of daylight left and then the rain would hit around dark. "Big Bird can help you on and off…but not too reliable when he gets tears in his eyes (rain)."

"What are you thinking?"

"Loading up the big Isuzu truck and hauling ass. Everything else is in bad shape I think. This big truck will run over anything they want to try and stop us with." I said.

"Eddie, if they start moving, let us know ASAP. I'm going to have the troops gather everything laying around and load it in the truck. I ain't leaving nothing. The bed on the truck must be equal to a big semi-trailer. Never seen any like this before…" I said.

"Good idea, leave nothing…Okay, will call you if I see anything, but you cannot depend on me right now, I am blind." Eddie said sadly.

"Okay, will do." I shut the phone off to save batteries. I decided to see if the charger cable was still in the Mercedes, the Suburban was still smoldering.

I briefed the troops on what I found out. Carlos, the Shooter who seemed to be in charge of the local Peruvians, translated each sentence. There were a few comments back and forth, but the bottom line was to gather all weapons and bring any water you find to the area. We would make our C.P. (Command Post) over near the area between a couple of large boulders and bring Samantha over there and Prince.

Robert helped Sassy bring Prince over to the new C.P., but Prince did not look well at all. His gums were not pink as they should have been. Prince has lost too much blood. On the other hand, Samantha was doing well. We bundled her up in a few pieces of clothing we found and a large tarpaulin that was taken from the back of the truck. The truck had several tarps that looked like they were used to cover grain loads with. I could smell grain and the "damp" smell it has when it was in a silo.

The troops all gathered weapons, ammo and food from wherever they could find it, good guys' and bad guys' equipment. The bad guys did not have too much with them, except their weapons as they lived in the house. The Suburban had a lot of spare ammo, but it had "cooked off"

457

the ammo in the fire. The van had GI (Government Issue) M.R.E.'s (Meals Ready to Eat) by the case, so we would not go hungry tonight. Still, water was going to be a problem. All of us had A.L.I.C.E. (Army Light Infantry Combat Equipment) web gear on with two canteens. Prince and Duke would need a share of the water also. The handlers would share with them. All dog handlers understand this when they take the job, but Prince, the noble German Shepherd, would die unless we could get him some help.

Jack Thompson had settled down. His nerves had calmed, but after a week in captivity where he was told ever day he was going to be killed, he was doing well. He was a little hungry and wolfed down two MRE main courses.

After we had gathered all the gear, noted the land, and placed outpost out, we had a briefing on what our options were.

I told them we could drive out using the big truck, but we would go through an ambush. That was a done deal and fact. Plus, where would we go? The plane was back in Lima being refueled and could not land at night. These were the facts. I asked Carlos, "You know this land?"

"Yes, I know it, but I am not leaving you." he said quietly. "I will stay here and go out with dignity, not slip away like *un perro* (a dog). I will take my brother's body home to his mother."

That is when I learned that Jesus (Chewey) was dead. The same guy who stopped at his Aunt's restaurant last night and had shown us such great hospitality, was in the back of the dump truck.

Carlos turned away and went outside the perimeter. I could not say a word.

Vinnie and Bart had the Night Vision Scopes out and placed them on a couple of high places so we could peer into the jungle. It was still daylight and they were of no use until it got dark.

One of the Peruvian Mercenaries gave a small alarm. Someone was in the bush, coming this way. A Shooter with a muffled Uzi came forward and listened. I heard it too and I was hard of hearing. Bart slipped off into the jungle with Vinnie on his heels. It was almost comical since Bart was about five foot seven and Vinnie was six foot six. Still, for a big man, Vinnie could move through the bush like a cat. They soon came back.

"It was a big dog sniffing around where some of the dead guys are laying." Bart said. "Big dogs?" Sassy said with glee. "Will they come to you, you think?"

"I guess so." Bart said. "It seemed friendly. Hey look, there is one now."

"What you want that ol' scrounge dog for, Lady. He has fleas as big as turtles." Vinnie said.

"I'll go get him." Sassy said and walked into the jungle, with Robert and Emil going with her.

In a few minutes they came back with a big dog. It appeared to be a hound of some type with a belt around his neck and Sassy with her leash on him. The dog was a little afraid, but Sassy calmed him down and gave him part of her MRE.

"Hey don't give that to that dog, you wanna kill him?" Robert teased. "Nope, want him alive, he can give Prince blood." Sassy said.

"How do you know they are the same blood type?" Vinnie asked.

"All dogs are the same. One dog can give to another" Sassy said as she coaxed the dog into a "down" position. She gently took his front paw and inserted a needle in it and taped it while Robert and Emil feed the dog tidbits from the MRE packages. The needle was connected to a long tube that went to Prince. With each beat of the heart, Prince got life giving blood. The pup lay still and thought he was getting the best of the deal, not knowing he was donating blood to another canine friend. The wounds in Prince were bleeding again, so Sassy stopped the transfusion. She did not want to use all the blood that was available, but she would if would save her dog. Amber came to me and made a suggestion.

"Charlie, I am going to do a reconnoitering. See what the bad guys are doing. It is almost dark. We cannot stay here forever and besides, we need to know what is going on. I will take Vinnie and Carlos." they prepared to move out.

Just like Eddie had said it would, it began to rain. It was a cold rain. We told everyone to keep alert and get in the available vehicles or under them. Amber, Vinnie and Carlos had already left the security perimeter and were going to be cold and wet when they got back, but no fires would be made. Sassy was sitting under a rock ledge with a tarp around her with Prince on her lap, rocking the dog like a baby. Every once in a while she would try and spoon feed him water using the plastic spoon from the MRE's.

About 0100 the patrol returned. They had discovered most of the bad guys were asleep. They had walked through the camp and only saw five, who were all asleep. They disarmed a couple of Claymore–type mines they found and turned three around to face the bad guys. That way, when the bad guys set them off, it would be directed towards them. They were the Argentinean FMK-1 and MAPG mines and at less than $6.00 dollars a copy, they were cheap weapons, but the bad guys were not real professionals.

It was starting to clear up and we had to do something. We decided to move, each team member had been able to get about 2 hours sleep. We changed out the watch whenever we could. Sassy had not slept at all. She and Robert gave the stray dog and Prince all their water and were using the tarpaulins to catch more for themselves and the team. Team members had brought their canteens to them and refilled them during the night. Samantha was asleep in the cab of the big Isuzu truck since she had another syringe of morphine, but she did not want any more because of the baby. While she was out and nearly half asleep, Robert and Emil took a needle and thread they had in the Medic Kit and sewed the flesh back together on the inside of her thigh. Samantha could feel the pain and sweat popped out on her forehead, but she told them to keep going. Emil told me later he was afraid the shock and pain would make her abort, but it didn't.

I called Eddie, who answered the phone on the first ring and I told him that we were going to move out when the rain stopped. Eddie advised us that the rain would be passing within the hour and clear skies were expected with an extremely bright moon. He also told us that the plane was fueled. The crew was on the plane and could be off the ground in short order.

"Amber, how long would it take you and a couple of troops to get up near the bad guys and distract them while we started the truck and made a run for it? Get them to think they are being attacked from the rear and if these are green troops, you may even get them to run. Make lots of noise and chunk a few grenades, think it would work?" I asked.

"Yup, we could do it, but where would we get picked up?" she asked. It was still dark, but I knew she was looking at me, even if the rain stopped and the moon had yet to come out from behind the mountains to the east...

"You are going to have to tell me. I have not been in the bush and do not know the lay of the land" I said.

"Well, one of the trails from the ambush site appears to run up to the house. We could take that and meet you on the east side of the house where this truck was parked." Amber indicated the large Isuzu truck. "Can you do that?" she asked.

"We will be there. What do you think of moving out and us giving you time to get in place. When you hear the truck start, you get ready. It will take us about three minutes to get up that hill with the rain and slick mud. Maybe even a little longer to get to the point where the turds are trying to ambush us. We should be rolling when we get to that point. So, to have minimum exposure to hostile fire, as they say, it is about fifty yards further to where we can pick you up by the house. I have a feeling that the leaders of the group are inside where they are nice and warm. When we go by we will rake the house and chunk some grenades in the windows." I said.

"Give us about thirty minutes to get in place since we only have to go about a quarter mile." she said as she stood up and stretched.

In a few minutes, we were loaded and we checked our watches. "Okay, be careful and we will move out on the hour at 0400. Who you take'n with you?" I asked.

"Vinnie, Carlos and myself, we have been there and seen the land." "Okay, anytime you are ready, we are." Bart said.

463

Bart was going to drive and one of the Shooters would be in the cab with him. The rest of us would be in the back, two in front and thirteen in back. "Lucky Thirteen," I thought, plus the deceased who were wrapped in the tarpaulins.

As luck would have it, we had found the bad guys had two U.S. made M-60 7.62

Machine guns with Pendleton mounts. The guns had been in the jeep that originally left with Jack Thompson. The Pendleton mounts fitted on the bottom of the machine guns and could be mounted on a swivel. The dump truck had mounts already installed. The kidnappers must have been using this truck as a "gun truck" to run dope. We mounted the guns in a makeshift lash up on the two front corners of the dump truck bed. The rest of the troops had stuffed clips and magazines into all there pockets for the weapons they were shooting, and they were ready. One of the Shooters had taken "Duke," Bart's dog, and put him in the back with him since Bart was driving.

At 0400, Bart was tapped on the shoulder and the big Isuzu Industrial diesel engine roared into life. While standing in the back, it sounded like a Boeing 747. In just a few seconds, Bart slipped it into gear and started up the trail towards the house. Fortunately, the four big tires in the back were moving us out with no skidding or slipping. First gear, second gear, we heard shooting and Claymores going off, along with more automatic fire. Third gear, we were rolling. These Isuzus were giants. We were getting close to the fire fight and could see muzzles flashing. A figure could be seen running out into the trail. He turned and looked just as the big truck ran over him. Bart turned on the lights. They did not make any difference now, everyone knew we were coming. As we passed through the ambush, everyone was firing into the bush. I was thinking of Amber and her crew, hoping they would not be hit by friendly fire. Another 200 yards and we made the left turn in the trail towards the house. We could see flashlights inside. Everyone concentrated all their fire toward the house. As we passed it, several people tossed grenades at the windows. Some must have went inside because we heard screams of pain and a fire started. Someone had thrown a "Willie Peter," a white phosphorous grenade, a nasty device. Whatever it hit, it stuck to it.

Bart stopped the truck and waited for Amber and her team. Vince ran out of the bush with Carlos and tossed their weapons up to waiting hands as they climbed the ladder leading to the back of the truck. The house was ablaze. Automatic weapons fire was pouring from inside and we were pouring it back in. Someone had moved the two M-60s to the rear of the truck and had mounted them in the corner sockets, which provided for the mounts. Sassy was pouring in automatic fire from the M-60. Emil and Robert were playing a fine tune on the second M-60. I was trying to keep Sassy supplied with belted ammo and feed the ammo for her too. M-60's were not bad about jamming, so long as you kept the belt straight going in.

About that time we saw Amber running, you could recognize her easy, graceful strides as she moved to the truck. She threw her weapon up to waiting hands and was about to be hauled up by two of the Peruvian Mercenaries, when three men came from behind a barn and fired.

"Amber's hit! Stop the truck! Stop Bart, we gotta get Amber!" Bart slammed on the pedal and the air brakes responded, skidding the truck to a halt.

Emil and Robert went over the sides. They grabbed Amber's web gear and almost through her up into the truck, but she was caught by two Peruvian Shooters. Her limp body was unceremoniously dropped on the floor next to me. I could not stop to help her and I could not see because of the darkness, but by the light of the burning house, she did not look good.

During all of this, I heard Sassy scream. "GET SOME! GET SOME MOTHER FUCKER! GET SOME! HERE! HERE IS SOME FOR YOU TOO, MOTHER FUCKER!" she steadily mowed down the bad guys. The three that shot Amber were hem stitched, top to bottom, with three and four round bursts, and in the "ten ring" on all three of them. Sassy swiveled the M-60 around and started raking the second floor. After she threw a few rounds in the window with the muzzle flashes flickering, they lost interest in the fire fight, or they were hit.

In the meantime Bart had started the big truck rolling. As he went by, he smashed a few of the cars sitting in the driveway. They did not even slow the truck down. Bart got to the road by the construction site and right where we had shown the bad guys the money, he turned back towards the mountains on the far side of the valley. By then, we were rolling with no lights coming out of the road to give chase.

We reached the other side of the valley and pulled to a stop. We did not leave the road, but we could see behind us. We stopped for a few minutes .and I noticed the sun had come up. I could see Amber lying in the bottom of the truck like a rag doll.

I looked closely at Amber, using a flashlight that I carried on the ALICE gear. She blinked her eyes, she was alive, but her chin was gone. There was no mouth left, her tongue just rolled out of the space that was supposed to be her mouth. She had also been shot through the back and arms. This thing in front of me did not look human.

I straightened her out, took my knife and ripped the laces from her boots. I removed the boots and socks. I noticed her toe nails were painted red under the glare of the red lens flashlight. I could not see all the blood because of the red lens, but I could smell it and I could feel it under my knees as I knelt beside her.

"Duke," the Labrador Retriever was laying on her right side, restrained by one of the Shooters. He was licking Amber's right hand. Sassy was cradling her head in her lap as I began a futile attempt to give first aid. I undid her belt buckle, unzipped her BDU trousers and ran a sharp knife down the legs to take the trousers away from the wounded area. I noticed she was wearing *Haynes* underwear.

Amber was wearing men's underwear? I almost laughed till I noticed the words "lady's underwear" on the delicate lace waist band, they were a soft gray.

I knew it was hopeless. Tears ran down my cheeks as I looked at the gaping wounds in her abdomen and chest. She was leaking blood from everywhere. I took her left hand.

While I was holding her hand, she used her index finger on my palm. She was sending me a Morse Code message. We had learned Morse Code during training for fun, on cold days when we could not go outside.

She was pressing, faintly, on the palm of my hand. "Yes, Honey… I hear your transmission…" She sent the code for "C.Q. …C.Q., C.Q." (Code of "any station"). That was when she answered me. "A-1 to C-1" (Amber to Charlie)… "R" (over).

"Go ahead Alpha One" I said. She continued to lightly press here index finger in my palm. In code she tapped out, "Tell Tommy I love him…end of message" and her hand relaxed. She shuddered and was still.

Sassy softly sobbed. So did I, along with Emil and Robert. Samantha and Bart were in the front of the cab, they did not know what was going on here. We did not know what was happening up front, but Bart had been hit.

After a few minutes, the sun was fully up. Most of the shooters had turned away, not wanting to see the remains of a face that only a few minutes before had been a goddess, and was now it was gone…a blob.

Sassy held the head of her friend, our friend, a few minutes longer and then looked up at me. She tried to rise and that was when we noticed half her knee was gone. Her knee cap had been shot away. Her face was contorted with pain and the beautiful green eyes were red from crying, loss of sleep, and everything else that had happened.

We moved Amber over, tore a portion of a tarpaulin off, and wrapped Amber's body in the tarpaulin. The bottom of the truck was flowing with blood. "Prince" was lying down, still watching Sassy with big sad eyes. The Lab was whining, nudging the bag that Amber was wrapped in, not understanding why Amber did not want to play with him anymore. Unbeknownst to any of us, the "Scrounge Dog" as he was later known by, was in the truck too.

"I had to bring him." Sassy said. "He helped us out and I was not going to leave him…so I brought him along." That was so like Sassy.

In order to get her out of the blood and mess at the rear, we gently moved Sassy to the front of the long bed of the truck. We moved all the dogs to her as well, gave her a syringe of morphine and just waited. We had no idea why we just stood and looked at the bodies, we were still in shock.

I heard Samantha's voice, calling me. I looked over the side and could see Bart slumped over the wheel with blood on his shirt.

I got Robert's attention as he helped Emil dress Sassy's wound. "Robert. Robert…Robert, Bart needs help" I yelled.

Robert's eyes fluttered a few times and he came out of his trance. "Bart has been hit…can you help him? I asked.

Immediately, he was over the side of the truck, down the ladder and into the cab with Bart.

Samantha was trying to help, but her leg was so swollen from her wound. It had turned nasty shade of red. The only thing she could do was try and move out of the way so Bart could get over to the passenger side.

Bart had a broken left arm and maybe a bullet in the chest. We could not tell, but one of the Mercenaries was splinting his arm. When they finished doing all that could be done, one of the Shooters said in the Spanish equivalent: "We got company coming."

Chapter 28

The trucks pulled out of the construction compound and lined up near the roads. Some haphazardly faced one way and then the other. It was over a mile across the valley, but big enough to see big trucks moving. Meanwhile, someone had produced several sets of binoculars from the gear we picked up and put in back of the big Isuzu truck.

We focused on the trucks and on the smoke coming up from the burning house, but the fire was a long way from the construction compound.

"Why are they moving the trucks? It must be a couple of hundred yards to the house. Unless they're getting ready to come after us…" I said.

"Something is getting them excited." Emil noted as he scanned the area.

We could see the black smoke coming up from out of the trees were the house was on fire. Every once in a while we could see flames lick up into the air. Suddenly, there was a bright flash of light and a loud "whoooomp" sound a second later. A small mushroom cloud rose above the trees, there had been a big explosion. My first thought was that butane or a gas tank blew, but it was too big for that. The fire had subsided in a short time and only white smoke remained, signs of a chemical based fire.

I had Eddie on the radio. He had advised us that it was okay to use the radios again since the counterintelligence equipment had been in the house and it was no more We were now free to use the hand held radios.

"Eddie, did Big Bird see that fire?" I asked.

"Yup" he said. "My associates are trying to get a read out on it. They say it is a meth based gas, from the heat and pressure it created and ...Yup, the world's biggest methamphetamine lab left the world's biggest hole in the ground, about five hundred feet long. Used to be a tunnel and the house and foundation are in the next county. What a mess..."

'Hello Eddie. Hello Charlie." it was Rita. "We watched the fires and the explosion. We are about 10,000 feet above you. Are you ready for us to pick you up?" Rita said coolly, as if she was asking for a drink of water.

"Yeah, Rita, thanks. We do need a ride. We will go down the hill and meet you on the west side of the valley." I said.

"Okay, Charlie. We will be there in a bout fifteen minutes. We will do a hot turn around while the bad guys are busy. We need you to check the road and make sure that no sign post or obstructions are sticking up along the side of the road that would damage a wing." Rita said.

"Okay. Will check, but I don't see any from here," I answered, "but I will move out and advise."

I asked Carlos if he could have one of his troops check the cluster of small trees alongside the road for anything the plane that might hit when they landed. "Use the truck."

Carlos told two of the Shooters take the truck. They were to go down the road about one and a half kilometers and run down anything that might be in the way.

The two Peruvian Mercenaries got in the truck and after few minutes of grinding gears, got the truck turned around and started down the hill. We watched them with binoculars till they had gone the required distance. They turned around and started back when a civilian car came up from behind us and stopped. One of the Mercenaries approached the car. The driver asked what was going on. He had seen the explosion and was coming to help. The quick thinking Peruvian told the driver he could be a big help he would go to the other side of the valley and stop all vehicles for one hour.

The driver willingly agreed to help and left for the other side. We did not need any vehicles coming if Steve was going to land the big ATR 46 on the road.

After a few minutes, the big plane made a slow left turn and lined up with the highway for a landing. As it eased onto the highway, the plane immediately reversed props to stop the aircraft's forward movement and then slowly taxied in our direction. During this time, we had kept as many eyes as possible on the construction compound.

Watching for any movement coming our way, we saw nothing.

We climbed in the truck when it came back. Once again we saw Amber's body wrapped in a tarpaulin and the two Mercenaries as well, along with dogs, Prince, Duke and Scrounge Hound.

The plane turned around and prepared for a takeoff. Dust blew up as the big Rolls Royce turbo props screamed. The pilot shut down the left engine and the stairs came down. Eunice was at the top of the stairs looking out, when she suddenly pointed straight out of the aircraft to the north. We jerked around and looked and noticed dust at the far end of the valley. It looked like several motorcycles and four wheel vehicles coming across the open area, about three or four miles away. I could not be sure, but they were headed our way, and fast. That meant we had about five minutes to get away.

We pulled up to the aircraft, unloaded the three dogs and Amber's wrapped body. All the weapons and equipment, plus the two wrapped bodies of their dead, were left for the mercenaries. We helped Bart and Samantha from the cab. Emil carried Sassy to the cargo door behind the cockpit door. On this model of plane, the freight was usually carried where first class passengers normally are, up front since there was no cargo compartment in the belly. Emil handed Sassy to Geoff and Steve, who picked her up like a baby and carried her to the first row of seats in the main cabin. Jack Thompson was in a fog, easy to understand. He was told to sit in that seat there and "don't move."

Goeff took the dogs and put Duke in one of the kennels already secured on board. The Scrounge Hound was put in the other kennel. Prince was placed at Sassy's feet so she could care for him. The big truck backed away from the plane as Robert helped Bart board the aircraft from the rear stairs. The cargo door was slammed shut as the Pilot started the left engine in preparation for takeoff. Robert and Emil were on board and Emil helped Samantha up the rear stairs as the aircraft started moving. The rear stairs were in staring their rising motion as the pilot placed the Power Levers in the "Flight" position. The big propellers started grabbing air and we were moving.

"ABORT! ABORT! ABORT!" yelled Steve into the microphone by the rear steps as they were coming up. "EUNICE IS STILL ON THE GROUND!" The power levers were reversed and the plane stopped as if it had hit a wall. The steps were starting back down when I turned and squatted low, only to see Eunice knelt down beside one of the Shooters who had fallen off the truck as they were trying to get away. Automatic weapon fire could be heard coming from the Isuzu truck as they looked towards the dust rising from the valley floor. They were close enough now where you could see the motorcycle riders.

Eunice had her arm around the Mercenary as she started towards the rear ramp stairs of the plane. She was about fifty feet away when she fell in a heap. She had been hit by one of the "Golden B.B.'s" you always hear about, a lucky shot.

Emil, Robert, Steve and I were down the stairs in record time. Emil and Robert grabbed the Shooter. Steve and I grabbed Eunice and started running towards the plane. We could see dust rising as bullets were hitting the ground around us on the edge of the road, but due to the noise we could not see who was shooting. However, if we had to stop and vote on the issue, we would not have cared to know who was shooting at us, just that someone was.

Robert and Emil dragged their man up the stairs as if he was a rag doll, but Eunice was a big girl and she was trying to help us. We stumbled and fell trying to get her up the stairs, but Steve went up first and dragged her up the stairs by her two outstretched arms. I slipped and fell on the stairs and was trying to recover when the plane started moving again, fast. I was clinging to the rear stairs. I managed to get a foot hold on the bottom two or three steps and was holding the railings. The plane started gaining speed and my thoughts were that that was "A Hell Of A Way To

Run An Airline." The forward momentum of the plane was keeping me from pulling myself up the steps. I felt the stairs rising under me and tucking into the tail. The tail dipped down as the nose was raised to gain flight attitude. The stairs closed in place and I was almost upside down, but safely in the plane as I felt it rise into the air.

Eunice was laying in the aisle, laughing at me as I was hauled down from my perch in what was now known as the "tunnel" when the steps were in place. I noticed the blue Flight Attendant pants she was wearing were stained with blood, and she was laughing at me?

When I got down and crawled over to Eunice, Rita was pulling back on the stick and the plane was "climbing like a homesick angel" as I heard in an old World War Two movie.

"What the hell are you laughing at? I almost got my ass killed." I yelled.

"Charlie, you should have seen…OH SHIT!…your face. Heee heee. It is starting to hurt…Shit!" Eunice said between laughs as she lay on the floor of the climbing aircraft.

"Eunice, you been shot!" I yelled at her.

"I know, right in the ass!" she yelled back at me as the plane's turbo props came back to the cruise settings and she rolled on her left side like a swimmer doing the side stroke.

All of this had happened in less than a minute, but it felt like an hour. "Here let me help you." I said.

I looked at her and saw a gash going across the right buttock. Not too deep, but bleeding. I grabbed a blanket from the overhead luggage rack and placed it over her.

"Eunice, I gotta look and clean this wound." I said as I tried to pull the bloodied pants she was wearing down just enough to see the wound. "Here, I will put this blanket over you so…"

"Oh, hell Charlie, I have had lots of men try to get my panties off, but you have the most unique approach." she gritted her teeth as the cloth from the panties pulled away from the wound. "Go ahead. I will tell my …Ouch! Shit! …grandchildren how I had this Dirty Old Man tried to take my panties off on an airplane over a jungle in South America." I thought. "This lady has a sense of humor, I like her."

That was when I noticed Vinnie Rideout. He was sitting in the last seat. He had a strange look on his face and was groping the back of the seat. I noticed a slight head wound on his scalp and a great big lump.

"Vinnie?…Vinnie?" I had not even noticed the big man get on the plane. "Vinnie?" I said.

"Charlie! I can't see man, I am blind, I can't see!" he almost cried. "Charlie, help me!" "How did this happen, when were you wounded?" I asked.

"When we were driving out by the house, I just thought it was a scalp wound. It knocked me out. I didn't come to until the plane started landing. I have a pounding headache. I didn't say anything. All the others being hurt and everything, but I lost vision when I walked up the rear steps to get on the plane. One of the Merc's helped me on the plane. I walked up here and sat down. Charlie? Can you see a wound? I got a hell of a head ache." he said.

"Vinnie, hang tough. Let me look after these folks and then Robert or Emil will be with you." I said. I didn't know what to do or tell him.

Emil came back with a Medic's bag and looked at Eunice's wound. He poured surgical betadine solution on it straight from the bottle, applied a gel and bandaged the wound. "That will hold her till we can get better medical care. She won't die from it but keep her warm. She may go into shock." Emil said.

"Leave her on the floor. Get her a pillow and she will be okay. I don't have enough morphine left to give her a shot, but there is some brandy in the galley. Give her that or whatever booze she wants. Sassy, Carlos and Samantha need the morphine but I only have six left."

I went forward to the galley and got bottles of booze and handed them out to the wounded. I knew Sassy was in pain but she did not want to have morphine because she would go to sleep and she wanted to be awake for Prince. The dog seemed to be getting weaker. He did not move much as before and he was bleeding again after the bouncing from transferring him from the truck to the plane.

Sassy was in the first row of seats on the right side, next to the bulkhead that separated the passenger cabin from the freight compartment. Prince was lying at her feet with several blankets over him and his head on a pillow. Sassy left the seat and lay on the floor next to him. I knew she was in pain, so I offered her a small bottle of rum or scotch. She refused a first, but when I came back by, she said she would take one. Sassy opened the bottle and drank the contents in one pull and returned me the bottle.

I left six small bottles with Vinnie. He was a big man and would have a big thirst. You are probably not supposed to give a man with a head wound booze, but I did. He needed some kind of painkiller.

I got Eunice to take several swallows of Crown Royal. She drank it and gagged a few times. I found out she was not a drinker of alcohol, she would have some wine or a beer now and then, but no hard booze.

"Eunice, this is like medicine, drink it. It will put a stop to a lot of the pain," I advised her like a father. "and besides, it is good booze."

"I ain't never drank hard booze. Not even in college." she said.

"You ain't never been shot in the ass either have you?" I asked. "No"

"Then drink it." I said.

Robert and Emil were still working on Carlos. He had a "sucking" chest wound, but they had him bound up tight and the wound was not "sucking" as bad. They took an empty plastic ice bag that they found in the galley and placed it over the wound and bound it tight, it held.

Carlos was still out and was not in pain. So he did not get a morphine syringe. We had to save them. It was going to be a long flight.

After an hour into the flight, Steve called me to the front of the plane for a conference. "Charlie, if we stop in San Jose, Costa Rico, we will be on the ground for an hour. If the local National Guard troops get a glimpse inside this flying hospital, we may have an international incident on our hands. We have five wounded and one body bag, not your routine flight would you say?" he said.

"Okay, Stevey, what do you suggest?" I asked.

"We may have enough fuel to fly all the way to Belize City." he said.

"You said we may? And what if we don't? You get out and find a gas station?" I said. "No, we stop in Tegucigalpa, Honduras." he added.

"Man…that sucks. They are having a little light running revolution as we speak, those boys play rough." I said.

"Well, Managua, Nicaragua, next best…" he said.

"How about Howard Air Force Base in Panama, better and more secure." I said. "Charlie, it may have slipped by you, but we ain't an Air Force plane. Plus, we have wounded and a Peruvian national with no papers or ID, a dead body and whatever else. Plus, I think Big Bird may have snitched us off too. I have an aircraft that people in Atlanta would be very upset if we got it impounded by some third world Banana Republic, See what I mean?" Steve said.

"You got radio contact with Eddie still? "No."

"Will you try?"

"Okay…what can he do?" Steve asked.

"Look, we have the 'U' 'S' of 'A' backing this play. They do not want questions asked by a foreign government either…Bad politics, and Sunday papers will be out in a few hours. So, get me in touch with Eddie and I will explain it in terms he can understand." I started to get angry.

In a few minutes, Stevey motioned me to the cockpit and handed me a set of head phones and a microphone.

"Eddie, did Steve explain the problem? We need to get into Howard Air Force Base in Panama or has the Georgia Peanut Picker gave that away too? We have a problem and we need an answer suddenly." I looked over at the cathode ray tube plotter between the pilot and co-pilot. It showed that we were coming up on the coast of Panama.

"Eddie, you have thirty minutes and then we make an approach towards Panama and do a 'May Day' squawk to Balboa Airport and declare an emergency. That will have all the fire trucks and nice folks out to this plane suddenly. We have six wounded and a dead body. We also have rescued one of their fine employees from the bad guys...Eddie, let the boys at Langley work on that Monday morning, out" I threw the phones down on the empty co-pilot seat.

Rita never turned around. Never acknowledged I was in the cockpit.

I walked out of the cockpit and went to the main cabin. Sassy and Robert had Scrounge Hound out and were giving more blood to Prince. The smell of the wounds and the blood was starting to come through, but we were in trouble and we needed some help. Bullshit and real life don't mix. We went down a few days ago on an "adventure." Now we had our nose bloodied, but we did what we said we would, that counts. Now we needed help and now... Now the U.S. Government was bailing out on us. "Bull-Shit. Let's make some noise." I said.

"Charlie, I can't get the Airline involved in this. We, or rather I, lied to them about this trip, a straight charter. Shit is going to hit the fan when we get back. I ain't going to jeopardize my career with…with this operation." Steve said.

"Steve, you will do as I tell you. It ain't gonna be multiple choice. Understand that?" I said very firmly.

"That's a violation of the International Air Piracy Act, Charlie, you know that?" Steve said in a high voice.

"Steve, you had better reconsider your options, you are in charge of this aircraft. You do what you think is best." I stated simply.

We stood there looking eye to eye. He was trying to decide what to do. I knew what I would do and that was protect my team, period.

While we were standing there, the Flight Attendant's call button went off. Rita had turned it on from the cockpit. All Steve had to do was open the cockpit door. When he did, Rita held up the extra head set indicating for Steve to take it.

Steve put on the head set and grabbed the Microphone as he stood behind the empty co- pilot's seat.

I could see him talking but I could not hear what he was saying over the noise of the aircraft.

"We have been cleared for landing at Howard Air Force Base." Steve said as he put the headset back.

Chapter 29

The sun was setting as Steve made the approach from the west to Howard Air Force Base, Panama. After a routine landing, we were directed by the tower to taxi to the main terminal and Base Operation. A yellow "follow me" truck, with large checkered flags, pulled onto the taxiway ahead of us and turned his yellow lights on, indicating for us to follow. We did, but were not taken to the Main Terminal.

We were directed to a large hanger, where a ramp director using red wands directed gave the "cut engine" sign. He stood by after he raised his wands over his head in a "X" to indicated "hold" or "apply the brakes," while chocks were placed under the main wheels. After thirty seconds or so, the engines stopped spinning and it was quiet.

I went to the exit door and attempted to open it. I began following the instructions written on the door but Geoff came over, opened the door with one move and actuated a button that made the front stairs go down.

Emil had figured out the rear exit stairs and they were lowered also. A smell of fresh air came in the plane as both doors opened. A slight bumping noise was heard and felt as a tow bar was attached to the front strut and a tow tractor was hooked to the aircraft. We were pulled into the hanger in front of us and the doors closed behind us.

The hanger was completely empty of other aircraft and other vehicles, except for several ambulances and small buses, similar to the ones used to transport passengers at the airport from the car parking lots to the terminal. It was quiet in the hanger, and it was large enough to hold a Boeing 747.

In a few seconds, the air conditioner on the aircraft came back on when Ground Power cables were plugged in. We felt the tow bar being removed from the aircraft and heard the tow tractor move away. Everyone in the aircraft was quiet. Still, you could feel the stress leave every person on that aircraft. We were safe at last.

When the steps completely deployed, a young Air Force Captain came bounding up the steps and held out his hand for me to shake. "Welcome to Howard Air Force Base, on behalf of the Base Commander I would like to wel…" he stopped talking as he looked around. "Holy shit."

Sassy was on the floor trying to feed Prince a few spoonful of water. Jack Thompson was across the aisle in a trance. The young Captain looked down the aisle and saw Eunice on the floor with a bloody bandage. Bart Duffy was slumped in a seat about halfway down. At the Captain's feet was Carlos, with Robert beside him, trying to comfort him.

Vinnie in the very back with his eyes wrapped, blind, and the rest of us were covered with someone's blood.

"We had word you needed medical assistance, but... but..." the Captain trailed off.

At that time, a very small and petite officer in a white coat came up the stairs and said, "I am Dr. Cash, what do you have here?"

Emil came up and with a very pronounced French accent, started to explain. He pointed to Amber's body wrapped in the tarpaulin, "One dead, one with sucking chest wound." he pointed to Carlos. While walking her down the aisle to Bart she yelled out "Give me two stretcher teams here, use the back door."

When she reached Bart he was awake, but in pain and with blood on his shirt. His arm was in a splint made from one of the magazines located in the rear seat pockets.

I felt the plane shake and noticed two more people coming on board. One was in civilian clothes and the other was a one star General. The Captain saluted and moved to one side.

Dr. Cash did not acknowledge the general's presence, but started having people moved off the aircraft.

In three minutes, Eunice was on a stretcher and in the ambulance. Vinnie was led off by two medics and Bart was loaded onto a stretcher and man handled out the rear exit. Sassy did not want to be moved until she was sure that Prince would be taken care of.

The General turned to the Captain and said "I want the Provost Marshall and the Kennel Supervisor here NOW, Captain." He turned to Sassy, "Miss, we have a Veterinarian on the base and a Kennel Master is on the way to look after you dogs. How about these two?" he pointed to "Duke" and "Scrounge Hound."

"No, they are fine. The mixed breed hound may be a little dehydrated because she was a blood donor several times during the flight." Sassy answered as Dr. Cash moved the General and the man in civilian clothes out of the way.

"General, with all due respect, Sir…I have wounded to care for and you are in the way…Sir." she stood there and looked at them.

"Yes, Doctor, sure…er…" the General said as he and the other man moved back forward to the freight area, almost stepping on Amber.

The scream of sirens was heard as several Air Police sedans rolled up. A Chief Master Sergeant came over to the General, saluted, and waited for the General to acknowledge. "General?"

"Evening, John, see that these animals are looked after. Get the Veterinarian out and lets make things happen." the General said.

The Master Sgt. saluted and got on his radio. Several Air Police in utility uniforms came to the aircraft and down loaded the dogs. Prince was placed on a stretcher with no resistance. He was so weak from losing blood, he looked bad. Prince was placed in the Patrol Unit and taken out of the area, sirens and lights going off as they drove away. Duke and Scrounge Hound were kept in their kennels and placed in the back of the "Follow Me" pick up and drove away.

Sassy was placed in one of the several ambulances and everyone was taken to the hospital.

Emil, Robert, Geoff, Steve, Rita and myself, walked down the steps and just stood there. We turned and looked at the plane. It was dirty and there were several bullet holes in the outer skin. The tail section had a few "dings" in the engine nacelle.

The General came over to Steve after he asked who the Plane Commander was.

"I have been instructed by the highest authority to offer you and your crew any assistance I can. How may I help." he said quietly.

"We have a body on board, in the tarpaulin. Can you get her prepared? She has been dead about 12 hours and, well…" I said.

"Of course, anything else?" He turned and just looked at the Captain, who was on the radio calling for a mortician. "I guess the aircraft is okay, looks like a little bark was knocked off." Steve said as he poked his finger in a hole on the fuselage.

"Get the Line Maintenance Chief over here now, Captain." the General said. "We will go over it top to bottom. Captain, I want this hanger posted, only authorized personnel shall have access. If anyone has any problem with this, have them call me. Understood?" the General said.

A forklift was pulling up to the cargo door. It raised the door to the level required to take the baggage off and three people started removing the baggage. All of us took our baggage and set it to one side and advised the ground crew on which bags belonged to the people in the hospital. We took Amber's luggage with us, we would take care of it.

"Ladies and Gentlemen, we have a bus here to take you to the Visiting Officers Quarters when you are ready." the General said, gesturing towards the small door at the end of the hanger. We just stood there, looking at the men taking Amber's body off the plane, placing it on the pallet that the forklift was using. They did it with respect, but it was still "our" Amber. They took the rolled tarpaulin over to the waiting ambulance, placed it on a stretcher, shut the doors and left.

I advised the Flight Line Captain that there were several weapons in the aircraft and that he might need to secure them. A young Tech Sergeant went and found Carlo's sidearm and the Uzi he had been carrying when Eunice went off the plane to get him. The bolt was still open but the safety was on. The 9mm Starr Pistol had a full clip in the weapon and the hammer was back, safety was off. Several Israeli grenades were in Carlos'

pockets and one of us had removed them from his BDU (Battle Dress Uniform) pants when they were trying to treat him.

Our luggage was loaded on the bus and we went to the Visiting Officer Quarters. We agreed to meet in the lobby in about an hour to get to supper. We had not eaten for twenty four hours. After we cleaned up, we also asked if we could go to the hospital.

It was almost 8:00 PM when we met in the lobby. Several vans were outside with drivers and armed escorts in Air Police vehicles when we walked out. The Chief Master Sergeant was there, the one who had taken Prince to the Veterinarian. Robert asked about the dog and was told that he was in surgery when he left about ten minutes ago, but the Vet Techs felt he would be fine. The other two dogs were thirsty and were a little dehydrated, but nothing a little water and rest would not cure. The Sergeant advised us that he would keep us informed. In fact, he said that he had just come back from the hospital and spoke to Miss Phillips about her dog. She would not let them operate or repair her knee until she was sure Prince had been cared for, that sounded like Sassy.

I gestured to the Chief Master Sergeant asking what all the "escort" was about. I was advised that due to the unusual "top brass" interested in our arrival, he had been directed to "escort our honored guests wherever they went."

"You ain't to let us out of your sight is that the bottom line 'Top'?" "Top" is an old Army term for the "Top Sergeant" or First Sgt.

"Something like that, Sir." he smiled.

"Okay, we will help you, we understand." I said to the Air Policeman. "Thanks, that helps us…Marine?" He asked.
"Nope, Navy…Inshore Warfare Group, Pacific." I answered.

"Yeah, I heard about them, long time ago when I first came in. You guys caused trouble everywhere you went I heard and the Viet Cong had problems with you too." He smiled and shook his head.

"Is there a 'Top Three' on base?" I asked. "A Top Three" stands for pay grades E-7, 8 &
9, the "Top Three Enlisted Pay" grades.

"Yeah, a good one, but you guys can only go to the Officer Club. Orders you know." he said.

"Okay, no problem. Just let us know the "do's and don'ts." I told him. "Thanks, Mr. er…" He stumbled.

"Charlie Gray. Call me Charlie, Texas." I answered. "Swede Soderholm, Minnesota." we shook hands.

We arrived at the hospital and were met by Dr. Cash, the same one that met on the aircraft. She was a very nice lady, she took us in a side room and explained things to us like we were all family.

Dr. Cash had several other people with her. I don't know if they were doctors or nurses, but they made us feel at ease with them.

We sat down at a large round table and drank coffee from paper cups as she went over the charts.

"Let's see…Miss Eunice Bennett will have a sore butt and nice scar to tell her husband about. She has been patched up and in her room, asleep. We have given them a little something." she mumbled.

"Mr. Vincent Rideout has a big bump. He is in surgery now. We feel we can relieve the pressure off the brain and he will be okay. However, with a wound like this, nothing is sure. We have two of the Army's best combat surgeons here on staff. They are working on him. We'll do an MRI in the morning when the Technician gets here." she changed charts.

"Mr. Bart Duffy, a dislocated shoulder, broken left wrist and a bullet wound to the upper chest. Entered and exited, hit nothing of importance, he will be sore…Oh, broke a rib, nothing dramatic, he has been cleaned up and is in Recovery. At least he was ten minutes ago, going to take a few more x-rays just to be sure." Dr. Cash said.

"Miss Samantha McGee has a very nasty wound in the right inside thigh area. Infection may have set in, will be fine we think. Will have a very nasty scar, could have been worse, the stitches did help keep down muscle damage. She may not want to wear a bikini for a few months." We all laughed. It was more of a stress reliever. The good doctor did not know she was pregnant and Samantha would not want to wear a bikini anyway. She looked at the charts, "Did I miss something funny? Whoever the doctor was did a good job considering the battle field conditions he or she had to work under…" we did not tell her it was Emil's handy work.

"Miss Cassandra Phillips, left knee cap, we can fix that easy, seen worse wounds on basketball players and soccer players. She wanted to watch the surgeon do the job. Wanted a mirror so she could watch, quiet a girl. She is still in surgery. She did not want to have anything done until she checked on one of your co-workers. An Air Policeman came up and talked to her privately, then she said she was ready." Dr. Cash completed.

"And, last but not least, Major Carlos Frios, Operational Especial de Peru, has a very bad wound. It is touch and go with him right now, but we do have a great trauma team here. I know if I was anywhere in the world with a wound like that, I would want to be right here, in Howard Air Force Base. They are good" she said.

Well, that was comforting.

"Ah, yes, one more. Mr. Jack Thompson, he is in deep shock. We knocked him out. I feel that 'sleep therapy' will help him. He was in deep shock, trauma type shock, but not wounded. Had a few scrapes around the wrist area and his ankles were swollen, but other than that, his physical condition was good."

"Now, how about you guys? Anything wrong with you?" Dr. Cash questioned us. "Nothing that a good meal and couple of double Martinis won't cure, Doc." I tried to chuckle, but I didn't do too well.

"I will give you a little something to help you sleep if you like?" she sounded very concerned.

"No, thanks, We will need to have our wits about us. We need to fly out in the morning." Steve said as Rita and Geoff nodded. "We are the flight crew," they pointed to each other.

"Nope, you guys are grounded. I am a flight surgeon and you are on a U.S. base. I have that authority. Besides, I

got word from 'upstairs' to hold you guys on ice for a while."
she said coyly.

"What do you mean 'On ice?'" we all asked at once.

"I don't know who or why, honest, but I would have
done it anyway. You guys are zombies. When was the last
time you had a good night sleep?" she asked.

We looked at each other and looked sheepish. "Okay,
see what I mean?" Dr. Cash said as she rose to answer a
page. She walked over to the phone, dialed a number and
then hung up.

"I'm sorry, but we need identification on the…deceased
you brought in on your aircraft, for a death certificate and
all." Dr. Cash said.

"That won't be required Doctor." It was the man in
civilian clothes who boarded the aircraft when we arrived a
couple of hours ago.

He showed Dr. Cash a set of identification credentials
which she looked at and then back at him. "Very well, but
what shall I tell the Morgue crew? They are the ones who
make out the death certificates."

"I will discuss it with the Morgue Detail, Dr. Cash."
The mystery man said as he turned and went out the door.

"Doctor, may we use that phone? We would like to call home, we have been gone for a…"

"Of course." she nodded her head to the other medical staff in the conference room. "Let me know when you are finished and I will need to check you out too. Routine 'after action' stuff." She walked out the swinging doors.

Swede Soderholm, the Air Police Supervisor walked in just as the medical staff was walking out and heard the part about the phone calls. He looked at me with a "well, I don't know" look.

"Don't worry, Swede. These guys know about security, believe me. They don't want this story out any more than you do."

"Mr. Gray…er, Charlie, I should at least be in the room and I will tell you all phone calls back to ConUS (Continental U.S. lower 48 states) are often monitored, so help me out on this, please?" Swede asked.

"No problem. All this is a 'sugar report' anyway. Okay?" I said.

Stella answered the phone on the second ring. "Oh Charlie, where you been! We have been worried sick. The last report we had was from a guy named 'Eddie.' Said you were on your way out and was stopping in…oh, I forgot. Is everyone okay? How is…"

I paused and thought about it. "We are bringing everyone home with us that left with us." "Maria! Maria! Call Patricia!" I could here Stella shouting over a covered mouth piece.

Several phone extensions picked up. You could tell by the extra background noise by the sound of the voices.

"Charlie, is Robert there?" Stella asked.

"Yes, he is here, we only have a few minutes." I lied. "Here, talk to Stella." Robert looked at me and he understood what I had said.

"Hey, Red." he said happily. "We will be home in a couple of days, just need to get the airplane fixed a little…Yes…Yes, I'm fine…Okay…I love you too…Yes… get Patricia…okay, you too" as he handed the phone to Emil.

Emil and Patricia had about the same conversation and he handed me the phone. "Hello. Charlie?" It was Maria.

"Glad you are okay and bringing *mi ninos* (my children) home. Where are the girls?" she asked.

"Oh, they are all in bed, Maria." I lied again. "Look, we have to go. I will advise you on the Bat Phone when to pick us up." and I hung up.

We all stood there trying not to look at anything, thinking about how we were going to tell them. It was going to be rough.

We stayed at Howard Air Force base a total of three days.

Geoff called Marlene and said he would stop in on the way through. Marline said someone had brought their plane back to Belize City and that she had talked to Albert about it. Tito, her brother and Goeff's flying business partner, had been flying charters the last two days from Mexico City to Belize City for fishing trips. They had to make payments after all. Then a funny thing had happened, Evelyn Johnson, Steve's wife, was flying in for a short visit and would grab a ride back when we came through. We told her that it would be no problem.

We felt rested, bored in fact. We went to the hospital every few hours for something to do, but they kept us on a short leash. We were not to be going anywhere except to the hospital, dining facilities at the Officer's Club, and then back to our room. Some of us got the feeling that they wanted us to leave, but we told them we would only do so when all of our original team was able to travel. We did not want to leave anyone. Carlos Frios would not go with us of course, but whenever the rest of our group could travel, we would leave.

"Dr. Cash, We appreciate all you have done for us. You have not asked any questions or imposed on us, but we want to leave and we want to take our team with us. When will that be?" I asked.

Dr. Cash was a tiny woman, 5'2" tall and 110 lbs., maybe 45 years old. She gave me a long hard look, like she was thinking hard. "If it were in a hospital plane, with a stretcher, I would say no problem. They are young and tough, except for Bart Duffy, but he is tough, but..." Dr. Cash began thinking out loud.

"Look Doc, we could take a litter with us. Like the ones you use to roll them up and down the halls here. We can return it or we can buy it. You seen the large cargo compartment. Or we could put it across the top of the seats and strap it down, anything." Steve and Rita said.

Again, another pause from Dr. Cash, as if she was seriously considering the idea.

"Okay, we can do it, and I believe the United States Air Force can afford a regulation in- flight litter." She said with a pixie grin and a twinkle in her eye. "When will you be ready to travel?" she asked.

Steve answered "Within the hour if our bird is ready."

"Swede, can you make a call for us?" I asked the Chief Master Sergeant.

"Sure thing" he said as he went to the phone, picked it up and dialed. In a few minutes the phone rang again, He answered it in a strict military fashion, then he turned to me he asked, "When you want to leave?"

Steve answered, "In about an hour. Have it pulled out and fueled, if they can please." Swede Soderholm spoke in the phone, received an answer and hung up.

"Okay, it will be ready in about an hour.

"Okay, Doc. We need the Morgue's number...for our friend." I said quietly. "She goes with us."

"I will make sure she is there too." Dr. Cash said.

She came over and hugged each one of us. "I don't know why you have drawn all the interest, but you must have done something real good."

"Thank you, maybe one of these days." I said, "But it is nothing that would make two days news on Dallas Morning News."

We went to the hanger. The plane was still in the hanger, but turned around the opposite direction, ready to start engines and taxi out when the doors were opened. It sparkled like it had just come out of the factory.

Steve was escorted to the Flight Operation Building to file a flight plan from "Howard Air Force Base to Belize City, Belize." The reason for the flight blocks were already marked "Training."

We went to load the baggage and I dreaded walking on the aircraft because I knew the smell of the wounded would still be on the aircraft, that "sick room smell." The odor of Amber laying there in a wrapped tarpaulin, but we had to do it. I walked into the aircraft.

The odor I had been dreading was not there. The inside was clean and with no odor. The spots on the floor where Eunice had "leaked blood," were not there either. Neither was the seat that Samantha bled on, nothing, not even Sassy's seat or the floor where Prince had bled. In fact, the soft blue interior carpet and seat covers all looked brand new. Amazing, I have to give the U.S. Air Force credit.

An Air Force Sergeant met Geoff and Rita when they walked up to the aircraft. He introduced himself and briefed them on the aircraft. He showed them a long list of items that had been repaired or checked. All the radios had been calibrated and "bench checked." In fact, all the avionics (aviation electronics) had been checked along with the navigation equipment.

"We didn't know the last time the aircraft had been in for a Major Check, so we performed a 250 hour Maintenance Check. Replaced a few items, here, and your APS 180 radar was off a little. I tweaked it up but did not see a need to pull it down. Looks like it may have been jarred by a rough landing or something." the Sergeant stated. "The under carriage had a lot of sand blasting like you had landed on a dirt strip, or not a very clean runway. We repaired and painted that and of course the holes in the skin. Sir, we did not have a chance to Test Flight. Do you want to do that before you go? Normally we would insist on a Test Flight, but due to the circumstances of you being here…"

"No, thank you, Sergeant, we will do a test during our training flight. Looks like your department did a jam up job on this aircraft." Steve Johnson stated.

When the baggage was loaded, the dogs showed up. "Duke" and "Scrounge Hound" were wiggling and twisting, they were ready to go. They liked to have knocked Robert and Emil down when t hey went to help get them on the aircraft. They got a nice long "potty break" and were then loaded on. Prince came in a separate vehicle. He was eased down from the back of the truck and he walked under his own power. The young Airman, First Class that brought Prince, named Nancy something-or-another, said he had eaten that day and had a good stool. She recommended a "no-soybean diet" for about another week, but said that he was in good shape and healthy. He was raised into the aircraft by a fork lift and he went over to the place where he had been with Sassy.

Several large Medical Busses drove up. Big "Blue Bird" busses according to the name plate on the side of the bus. They eased into the hanger and drove near the aircraft. Sassy was taken off first in a wheel chair and lifted into the aircraft by the fork lift. There must have been four or five young Air Force Medics trying to help her and get her baggage loaded. The "baby green eyes are working overtime" I thought to myself and smiled. She was feeling okay, even flirting. As soon as she got on the aircraft and Prince saw her, his tail started wagging, "thump" "thump" "thump" on the new blue carpet. Sassy leaned down and gave him a big hug and patted him on the shoulders.

Eunice got off the bus with help as she walked down the ramp leading from the side door of the bus to the ground. She walked up the rear steps, one step at a time. Two young medics were in attendance. When she finally made it, she sat in one of the seats. She had several pillows and blankets placed on the bottom for padding. Eunice said they had gave her a "little something" for the pain and that she would be okay, she looked stoned.

Samantha came off the bus next and was taken to the aircraft. Her leg was straight out in front of her on a leg rest, but they moved her across the aisle from Sassy. She sat sideways in the seat and raised the center arm rest so they could get her leg straightened out.

Bart Duffy was on a standard "In Flight" stretcher and looked good. He wanted to get off and walk on the aircraft but Dr. Cash told him, "Sgt. Duffy, you promised me."

"Lady, I ain't a sergeant. I was a Master Chief Petty Officer in the Navy, and I don't need no midget Saw Bones telling me." Bart was saying as they brought him up the steps in the rear. They laid him on the top of the seat backs and used the seat belts to hold his stretcher in place.

When they got him in place, Dr. Cash came to me and said, "I hope I never have another patient like that again." as she looked at Bart.

Bart was strapped in. Steve was back and went to the cockpit with Rita as Geoff did the "walk around" with the Flight Line Airman to check the plane.

Bart called Dr. Cash over and said quietly. "Lucy, thanks for everything and when you get leave, come to Louisiana and we will do New Orleans as it needs to be done. Believe me, we have room and would love to have you. Ain't that right, Charlie?"

"So it's Lucy and Bart now?" I teased. "And yes, Dr. Cash, please come by. We have a small place on the Bayou, nothing fancy." I said.

"I figured something like that." she said. "Tried to tell me you guys had a twenty three room mansion with servants, almost had me believing it for a minute. Bart Duffy, you are the biggest liar in town." Lucy Cash laughed. I handed her one of my cards. She took it and looked at the picture of The Shadows on the card.

"Call us when you get to New Orleans Airport, you may be pleasantly surprised." I said to Dr. Cash as she walked off the aircraft.

Vinnie Rideout was brought on the plane on a stretcher and placed on the opposite side of the plane from Bart.

"Hey, you fucking squid, is that you?"

"Yep Vinnie, we are all here." I said as I heard the fork lift next to the plane. I saw Emil and Robert's heads slowly rising into sight by the cargo hatch. Then I saw the gray metal box come into sight. We were all very quiet and just watched as Amber's casket was scooted across the floor and strapped in place by Robert and Emil.

Hands were shaken, hugs were given, and much gratitude was shown as the door of the aircraft shut.

The engines were started and we taxied out. We made a standard takeoff on Runway 21
Left and turned north out over the Gulf of Mexico for a trip to Belize City.

It was midafternoon when we arrived in Belize City. Albert from Belize Customs met us on the plane. When he looked inside he was startled, but did not say a word. We processed the paperwork and down loaded just like last time.

Marlene Albright, Geoff's wife, wanted all of us to come to the hotel. She said she could have a staff there to help with the wounded and less questions would be asked.

Evelyn Johnson was also there, and she helped Marlene get the wounded down loaded. They did not have the fancy buses the Air Force had, but the vans and pick ups were just as effective for the short ride.

Evelyn kissed her husband and was still looking around as we drove to the hotel. She was no rookie at working in an Emergency Room, but she was still stunned. She had no idea what her husband was involved in.

"Steve…What in the world happened?" she asked as we rode to the hotel. Steve just shook his head as Evelyn Johnson just held his hand.

Marlene changed bandages and cleaned wounds along with Evelyn and one the nurses from Queen Elizabeth Hospital in Belize City. Evelyn though she came to Belize to meet her husband and have a long weekend at company expense, she never expected anything like this.

The next morning, the aircraft was reloaded and we were cleared for New Orleans, where we had left seven days before.

Chapter 30

After we landed at New Orleans International Airport, we were directed to taxi to the Executive Air Terminal. As always we were to be met there by U.S. Customs and Immigration and Naturalization Officers for a routine entrance clearance.

The door opened and the warmth of the New Orleans afternoon came in. We noticed a crowd was there to meet us with yellow ribbons on the cars.

We had called this morning from the hotel in Belize City and advised them of the estimated time of arrival. I had called Red Baxter, the man at the house who "hired" us. I made a few other arraignments too. Arraignments and decisions that I had never thought I would ever need to make when this all started. I wish I had told everyone this morning when I called. I was too chicken shit to tell them what they should expect. I should have had enough guts, but I didn't.

After border clearance and the correct papers were turned over to the government, I noticed the Mystery

Man was standing at the foot of the ladder talking to the Immigration Inspectors, they shook hands. Technically, since Amber was coming in as a returning citizen, her passport was stamped as if she was alive. Everything was cleared and we could deplane.

I motioned Emil and Robert off first. Patricia and the girls ran towards the aircraft and hugs were exchanged. I noticed that Emil held all three of them a little longer than I would have expected since we had only been gone eight days.

Stella walked up to Robert and gave a cheery hello and a kiss, a pleasant welcome.

I slowly walked off the plane. I hated to say it, but I wish I did not have to come home. Patricia gave me a peck on the check, a quick hug and went back to Emil's side. The two girls would not leave Emil, they hung onto him and were jabbering, each one wanting his attention. Emil knelt down, still hugging the two little girls.

Robert went back to the aircraft. Stella came over and looked at me. "Charlie. What's wrong? Charlie?" She looked around. Several ambulances drove up, along with a hearse.

Stella's hand went up to mouth but she did not say a word as she stood and watched. The rear steps were let down and Bart was taken off. It was then that the lady I had seen at the hardware store in town appeared out of the crowd and walked over to Bart. I didn't know her, but she looked at

Bart on the stretcher, took the hand he extended. She let out a small cry and said "My God. What has happened here?" She got into the large "cracker box" ambulance with him.

Stella looked at me. Patricia stood back in disbelief as they took Vinnie off the plane on a stretcher too. His head was bandaged, but they did not know him or know about him.

Maria walked up to me and squeezed my hand as she stood next to me. A question was on her face. I tried to look at her, but tears were in my eyes.

Sassy and Samantha were carried down the steps in a small "chair" looking device where the patients sat up right, to waiting wheelchairs. The crowd got quiet. They realized that things were not right. Several of the hands were motioned over to the cargo compartment as Eunice limped out the back of the aircraft and was assisted to a waiting wheelchair. Emil went back to the aircraft.

Robert and Emil unstrapped the casket and slid it over to the aircraft cargo door edge. The hands were instructed to help take it down. They gently eased the casket to the ground and were told quietly that it was Amber's body. As if in unison and on command, they all removed their hats and crossed themselves.

The black Cadillac hearse from the funeral home we contacted backed up to the aircraft and the casket was loaded. You could hear weeping as the crowd moved over to the aircraft.

Maria knew who it was even though she had not been told. There was no one getting off the plane.

"Oh, God in Heaven, why?" she began to cry. I did too and so did the rest. I could not help it. Maria had to be helped over to the van.

Patricia led the girls away towards the vehicles, trying not to cry as her daughters began to cry. "Mommy? Mommy? What is wrong? Why are you crying? Emil, why is Mommy crying?" They looked back towards the aircraft for Emil.

I looked at Maria as I walked over to where Juan Torres had the Lincoln Towncar parked. Johnny Rameriz, my strong right hand, the foreman, left the casket and walked over. "Johnny, have everyone meet at the house. Bring their families, we will talk there and explain what happened." I said.

Johnny nodded and put his new western hat back on after he had walked away from Amber's casket. He directed several hands to load baggage in one of the big Dodge Diesel pickups.

After we arrived at the house, I went upstairs to my apartment and just stood in the bathroom and sobbed.

"What have I done? What did I do? People were killed, wounded and hurt...for what? Some asshole we didn't even

511

know. I should have known better. I took women, young beautiful women, who now have battle scars…marked for life, inside and outside. One is dead and I have to tell her father and her family that I took their daughter and got her killed and brought her home in such a condition that they can not even see her for the last time. Do I tell them she has no beautiful face left anymore? It is scattered inside a dump trunk at some God forsaken Andes Mountain valley in Peru. How do I justify that?" I sobbed as I sat on a small stool.

After about ten minutes, I washed my face and walked downstairs. All the hands were there. The ambulances were pulling up with Samantha, Sassy, Bart, Vinnie and Eunice. One of the pickups went to the side entrance where baggage was being unloaded while another went to the kennels. I noticed that Patricia's truck was parked at the kennels and the dogs were barking. I knew she would take care of business.

Coffee was made and placed in the dining room, along with a few pastries and doughnuts. As everyone started drifting in, the bar was opened. The men had a tacit invitation to have a drink.

We were like family. I was raised in the Spanish, no, Mexican tradition of "family first," and "family business is not for outsiders," and "La Raza." Yet, I had caused one of them to be lost, would they hate me too much?

Maria walked in and never looked at me. She just made sure that our guests were served and looked after. Her face

512

was swollen from crying. I wished she would come over and just stand by me. I needed a little morale support too, but she didn't. It was not her place to comfort me. I caused all this anyway, I was looking at the fifty or so adult faces and they were all looking at me, waiting.

Sassy and Samantha were wheeled in by Robert and one of the hands. Bart and Vinnie were on gurney carts and wheeled into the room. Vinnie had to stay flat of his back because of the head wound and operation. Eunice was wheeled in by one of the ambulance attendants.

I had Red Baxter make arraignments for private nurses to be on duty and a doctor on call. We would set up anything they needed right here, no one was critical but they needed help, whatever it took.

Bart wanted a "light" bourbon and water, but he had been taking medication for pain, so he got orange juice. The lady from the hardware store got it for him. "Wish I knew her name," I thought.

Samantha wanted a glass of whole milk, no alcohol, "the baby you know. Sassy and Eunice had a glass of wine and Sassy was smoking a cigarette. Humph! I didn't even know she smoked. Vinnie got a glass of orange juice and a straw. Carlota de la Cruz helped him drink. See what I mean? This woman did not even know Vinnie, but helped him without even being asked. This was a family.

Billy L. Smith Sr.

Johnny Ramirez drove up in one of the Suburbans with Steve, Goeff and Rita and a stranger. A tall athletic man, well-tanned and in a business suit, right behind them was another vehicle I did not know. As I stood looking out the large front windows in the Grand Hall, I thought, "Wonder who that is?"

It was Stanley Hines, still in polo riding gear. Stella went over to him and led him up behind Sassy, who was sipping her glass of wine and talking to a young mother with a baby. Stanley Hines knelt down beside the wheel chair on the opposite side of where she was talking to the woman and baby. When Sassy turned to him and she said "Hi." No sound came from her mouth, but a million word best seller come from her green eyes.

Stanley asked a million questions with his expressions when looked around the room after a few minutes. He looked at the others on stretchers and wheelchairs. He was holding her hand and asking, "What happened?"

"A hunting accident, I will tell you later." Sassy said.

In the meantime, the Stranger came in, looked around and acted if he was lost. I went over to him, introduced him and asked if I could help him.

"Yes, I'm looking for my wife, Samantha McGee. I'm Bruce McGee." he said as he continued to look around me.

I turned and looked around too. As Maria walked by I told her, "Maria, this is Samantha's husband, Bruce. Have you seen Samantha?" I asked.

"I think she went to the Lady's Room." she said politely to Bruce. She never looked at me as she walked on to help the next guest.

I knew that Samantha had called and talked to someone last night. She asked if it was okay for someone to meet the aircraft in New Orleans. Of course it was, but when she said "husband," that surprised me. For some reason I thought she was divorced or something, but there was a baby on the way.

About that time Samantha was wheeled back in the room and Bruce went over to her, kissed her, and knelt down beside her wheelchair. He had a million questions but got no answers.

I looked up to see Eunice, just sitting there, sipping on something in a glass and be admired by several young bucks in the crowd. She looked around and asked one of them if they would hand her a soft pillow that was lying on the couch. Five pairs of heavy duty cowboy boots thumped across the living room to get her a "softer pillow." The crowd turned around and looked to see what all the noise was from and two took her arm for support and she tucked it under her. Eunice was still wearing a hospital gown, the kind that looked like it was on backwards and tied in the back. Due to the nature and location of the injury, she had wanted to wear oversized jogging shorts like Samantha and Sassy, but could not stand the pressure when she sat down. She smiled a "thank you" and the temperature in the room went up ten degrees.

Emil, Patricia and the girls came in the room. The girls were clinging to Emil and would not let him put them down. They had been through so much in their young lives before meeting Emil. He was their protector, a real life knight on a white horse to the girls, and Patricia too I bet.

I stood up. Everyone got quiet. A few babies were whimpering and were nursing. I had to say something. Johnny was standing over to one side and would translate for the few that needed a little help with English.

I stood there. I had never been at a loss for words before, but what could I say? I looked at each face in the room and could not think of the proper thing to say.

"Most of you knew we were going to try and 'find a missing person' when we left here a couple of days ago. Well, we found them and in the process…we got hurt…One killed, and I am responsible, no one else." I said.

From the end of the room came a croaking voice, like an old bull frog. It was Bart Duffy. "Wait a minute Charlie, you are wrong. I have backed your play on everything, never said a word against you, but now I have to" Bart said as someone helped raise the end of the gurney cart he was on so he could speak in a setting up position.

"I never heard anyone in this crowd say 'No, I don't want this' or anyone of these people say anything except lets go do it. Samantha and Sassy, you got a little bark knocked off your tree. You got a squawk?" The crowd turned and looked at them. The lady from the hardware store was beside him, holding his good hand.

Both shook their heads in a negative manner. "No, except for Amber…" Samantha said. "Yeah…I think it was worth it, Charlie. I would do a few things different, but as you always say, 'You are either part of the problem or part of the solution.'" Sassy looked back down at her feet.

Stanley Hines just knelt there, his mouth open. Looking at Sassy and then at me and back to Sassy.

"What has happened? What is…" Stanley said.

"Oh, be quiet, Stanley. I will tell you what you need to know when I am ready to tell you and not until then." Sassy said in a calm voice as she looked directly at Stanley.

"Oh, of course Dear, whatever you say, I was just…."

"Shut up." She said in a final tone as he attempted to adjust the light blanket around her legs.

Now this was a big man around New Orleans circles, over six feet three inches who managed a financial empire, brought down to a parade rest by a five foot, two inch giant with piercing green eyes.

"Amber is dead. I can't change that. I wish to God I could. Amber did not want to die, but she had M.S." It took Johnny a few minutes to translate and explain what M.S. does to the body and the hands started shaking their heads like they understood.

"Anyway, she was a Marine, a warrior, a friend to us all." I could not say anything else. I walked away, a coward. I could not face the crowd.

The crowd started to talk among themselves and drifted out. The meeting was over.

I went up to the Conference or War Room as we so glibly called it. It was empty. I turned on the lights, went over to the bar, and looked in the refrigerator…only juice. I got one, opened it and sat down at the large table, alone.

In a few minutes, people started walking in or being wheeled in. Bart was brought up the wide stairs where I had slide down in a playful manner a few days before. Sassy and Samantha were wheeled in, Sassy by Stanley and Samantha by her husband, Bruce.

I noticed Vinnie was not there, but was told he was asleep. He had taken a pain pill about the time we got to the house so they took him to one of the apartments. One of the ladies was with him to help him out if he woke up, even though the still did not know who he was.

Maria came in with a household staff member carrying coffee and light sandwiches. I asked to get a bottle of vodka for a few martinis and whatever else people wanted. It had been a long day. I looked at Maria and transmitted by telepathy, "Don't start with me, woman, I ain't in the mood." and she understood.

Steve, Rita and Geoff came in also, but they had come in a separate vehicle since they had to put the plane to "bed."

Emil and Patricia were there, Robert and Stella, Eunice too, but no Amber. Patricia said the Gomez twins were helping them feed the dogs.

The mobile bar was rolled in and the young lady who had been trained as the "bartender" was there and served drinks along with Maria, who still had not talked to me. By now, I didn't care anymore, I had an attitude.

After we had been seated a few minutes and the numbness of the booze had set in, I asked Stella to get me Amber's file. I had to make phone calls.

Stella got the file and I opened it up. There was an envelope in the file. Sealed and addressed to her father. I looked at Stella and she explained she had put that in there about a month ago. I then noticed a small "While you were out" note attached to the inside cover of the file. I opened it up and it said "Tommy" and gave a phone number.

I called the number and a man answered.

"Tommy, my name is Charlie Gray...ah thank you, too." I said to a very pleasant sounding man.

"Tommy are you where you can talk?" I asked.

"I don't know of any way to tell you. Amber is dead... Yes...if you like ...You know where we are located?...Yes..... please,...we will wait for you..." and I hung up.

"Now for the hard one," I said to all assembled. I went to a side office and called Amber's home number from her file. I had the speaker phone on the table so everyone could hear. Patricia was crying softly. I could hear Bart explain things to his "lady friend," who was almost in shock.

The phone rang a few times and a recording came on stating that the number was no longer in service. Now what? I dialed again and there was a clicking noise and a person answered. It was a cousin of Amber's we had met before, when we went to West Virginia to attend Amber's mother's funeral. She remembered me and started in on small talk when I had to interrupt her.

"Gloria, Amber is dead, an accident. She fell from a cliff she was climbing...rock climbing....Her safety gear malfunctioned and she fell... No... It happened in Peru..." I said as I lied to her cousin.

"Gloria, where his Frank?" (her husband) I asked.

"He is over in Grafton, visiting Uncle Herman since Aunt Libby died. He moved into a Senior Citizens condominium in Grafton. The next town over and… and… .".she started crying "Gloria, when Frank gets back have him call this number." I gave her the number to the Bat Phone. "It is a toll free number. So you just call and we can talk all you want. We will be in tomorrow to bring Amber home." I looked at Steve who nodded in agreement.

"I am too Gloria…I will see you tomorrow."

"Steve, where is Marlene and Evelyn? I didn't see them." I asked. "They are here. They went to the rooms here someplace." Steve said.

"I know where they are, I will get them." Geoff said.

I went over to Bart, shook his hand and thanked him for trying to make me feel better. I introduced myself to Bart's lady friend. "I'm Charlie Gray, Ma'am. I sorry but I don't know your name."

"I'm Emily Masters, Mr. Gray. I don't think we have met formally, but I have seen you in the store before." She said.

"Well, Emily call me Charlie. We ain't too formal around here, and you are welcome here. We have plenty of room." I said.

"Charlie, I will stay in Bart's apartment. My gosh, I never thought I would be saying that. Saying I was going to stay in a man's apartment." She blushed.

"Emily, don't worry about it in the condition he is in. He will be harmless." I teased. "Well, I hope this doesn't get back to the ladies in the church. It would be hard to explain." she said.

We all got a giggle out of the conversation when Marlene and Evelyn came in. "Look, we are going to be busy here for a few days. Please, please, make yourself at home, we are family here. We don't know how the folks in the Big City run a house like this, but we don't put on the dog. We have plenty of help. If you need to make phone calls to family and stuff, there are phones in the apartments, so help yourselves, okay?" I asked and they all agreed. They said they did not know what to do and felt like they were in the way, but thanked us all for the hospitality.

"After what you did for us? Marlene, we can NEVER repay you and Geoff with money, and Evelyn....if I remember right, you stayed up all last night with this bunch of crybabies." I said gestured to the Team, who smiled at her with genuine affection. "So, I don't want to hear that again, okay? Both of you."

"Okay, we got it. Thank you." Evelyn said.

The phone rang, Stella answered and gestured towards me slightly with the hand set. I knew it was Amber's family.

It was Frank, Gloria's husband. I explained what we were going to do and that we had contacted a funeral home in Phillipi who had been there over a hundred years. I had arranged for all the expenses to be paid. I lied again and said Amber had insurance with the company that paid for everything, told the family not to worry and that it will be handled.

Frank hung up and we sat there in silence. I did not know how tired and exhausted I was until I sat back down.

"Steve, you getting another plane to go to Phillipi?" I asked.

He informed me that there were two more company pilots available who were on the "extra board," and would fly Amber and whomever else to West Virginia. He said that they were going to use the runway over by the college this time, a little better surface, and asked what time we wanted to leave in the morning.

"Let me work on it. Just put them on standby. We will get with them as soon as we have a firm time for all of this." I said.

Chapter 31

Amber's body was taken home to the family the next morning. The local funeral home came to the airport over by the college and picked up the body. There are some nice folks in Philippi, West Virginia, and I hated to be the one that had to bring one of their daughters home like this.

In a separate suitcase were Amber's Marine uniform, medals and her officer's sword from the U.S. Naval Academy, Annapolis. A Wilkerson sword with her name and the "Class of 1988" inscribed in the blade, a beautiful piece of craftsmanship.

The funeral home director insured me she would be completely dressed in her uniform, with medals, her cover (a hat to a Marine), sword on her side and at attention. Still, the casket would need to be closed, but we knew that.

It was decided to wait a week for the funeral. Her father had a stroke when told of his daughter's death and well, the family, not me, decided they could wait. That would also give us a chance to get the wounded on their feet and be able to attend the funeral also.

We made arraignments to fly our "family" from New Orleans to Clarksburg, West Virginia and have two Gray Line buses take them to Nestorville for the funeral. The team flew over the day before and went to the wake held at the church.

Emil wore his French Foreign Legion uniform with flashings from the 13th Demi- Brigade. He had on a green shirt with thirteen creases and a cummerbund wrapped around the waist, he looked very handsome, as if he could have stepped out of a movie. Patricia was with him, they made a very handsome couple. Patricia was dressed in a black dress with a veil covering her face.

When Emil and Patricia got out of the car, a sharp salute was rendered to the Marine and Naval Officers present who were classmates of Amber at the Naval Academy. They were surprised to see a French Foreign Legion uniform in the hills of West Virginia, but the salute was returned with great dignity.

There was a U.S. Marine Corp Honor Guard and Firing Squad from the Marine Barracks in Washington, D.C. as well. We saw their two busses as they came in from Washington. They parked just down the block from the church.

Bart and I decided to wear our uniforms also, Navy Chiefs. Dress blues with gold hash marks, white gloves with medals. We had them special made at a uniform shop in New Orleans for the occasion since neither one of us could wear the uniforms we had when we had retired twenty years before.

Samantha was able to walk for short distances with the aid of a cane and her husband. Bruce's strong arm was there for her. When they got to the gravesite, she was given a chair.

Sassy was still in a wheelchair, Stanley was with her, fussing like an old mother hen but she was doing fine. They rolled her up next to Amber's family. We had met some before when we were there a year or so ago. They came over and kissed her cheek and made her welcome.

Vinnie had the bandages taken off and he could see now, but he had to move slowly or he would have a headache. A very attractive nurse came with him to assure he was properly "cared for."

Bart and I rode together in the same van. Emily Masters decided that she had to come with us so she could "take care of Bart." When we arrived, I got out of the van first, helped her out and asked Emily to stand where she was for a moment as I helped Bart out. Bart was still a little sore. He put his hat on and started walking to the gravesite. Emily started to go with him, but I took her arm, had her on my left side as protocol dictated and said "Come with me, please."

When Bart took a few steps, the Marine Honor Guard was called to attention and the command "Present Arms" was given by a Marine Staff Sergeant in a manner that only a Marine can do. The senior officers rose to their feet, faced Bart and saluted.

Emily asked me very quietly. "Why are they doing that? Is he an Admiral or something? I don't understand Navy uniforms."

Bart walked up the three or four steps, turned and faced the Flag of the United States of America, saluted and went to the place he was directed. The Honor Guard was given the command, "Order Arms."

As Emily and I walked slowly up the steps, I explained to her, "Emily, see that medal he is wearing around his neck, on the blue ribbon?"

"Yes. It is beautiful." she said.

"Well, that is the United States of America's highest award. The Medal of Honor, he rates a salute even from the President of the United States." I said.

The two buses with family and friends from Louisiana rolled up and were unloaded a block away. When all the guests were in place, we noticed a procession coming up the paved road from the cemetery, where the funeral services were conducted in the small church in Nesterville.

The family had requested a private service. The procession stopped at the entrance gate and the cars with the procession proceeded into the cemetery. Everyone had arrived except one, Amber.

The thirty three pieces of the West Virginia Highlanders Bagpipe Band struck up a tune and stepped away smartly for the three hundred yard parade from the edge of the road to the grave site. They played "When the Battle is Over," Amber's favorite. The pipes moaning through the hills of West Virginia were beautiful to hear. This was a tribute to a warrior, and Amber was a warrior.

When the hearse pulled up, the Marine Honor Guard was called to attention. A lone piper on a small rise began playing "Amazing Grace." As Amber was taken to the grave site and placed on the straps that would lower her into the ground for the last time, the piper continued to play.

The Minister walked ahead of the casket as the Marine Pall Bearers carried the flag draped casket to the place designated and remained in place.

The Minister conducted a very good service and at the proper time the flag was drawn tight by the Honor Guard. As the twenty one gun salute was fired, the flag was presented by a Marine major to Amber's father, with slow ceremonial salutes as the lone piper continued to play. Amber's father never moved during the whole ceremony. The flag was accepted on behalf of the father by a woman who was unknown to us.

As the family filed away, I noticed the funeral director who had met the plane a week before, standing by the casket. I walked over to him, thanked him and handed him a card. I told him to make sure the bill was sent to me for payment in full. To my surprise, I was informed that the bill was already paid. In cash in fact, several thousand dollars by a strange man who came to the office that morning. "In fact, there he is over by that car." The funeral director pointed, it was our Mystery Man again.

As we talked to the funeral director, he did mention that he only had one strange request. "That was someone wanted a Teddy Bear placed in the casket with Amber. A small Teddy Bear, about three inches long, dressed as a Marine. In fact, the person that made the request was the nice Marine major there, who presented the family with the flag. Forget his name…Tommy something." he said.

"Did you do it?" I asked.

"Yes, I did. I put it in a place no one would notice, under the pillow. He was so grateful too, a nice young man." said the funeral director. "I told him it would be a closed casket funeral, but he insisted that it be placed under the pillow."

"Thank you, Sir" and we walked away and left the cemetery.

The next night, we all gathered at the Shadows for the last time as a "Team." We had a meal in the main dining room. Maria was there, presiding as she should have been. She was still not talking to me except in the line of duty.

The place where Amber normally sat was still there, but the chair was empty. All the glasses and plates were there, but no Amber, at least not in the flesh.

We closed the doors and had a meeting. It was decided that this adventure was over. I told them they were all still on the payroll as long as they wanted and that they still had a home and a place to stay.

However, it was decided that they had gotten, "It all out of their system." There just ain't enough crises to go around. We did what we did, and now it was over.

Samantha made it official that she was going to have a baby and if it was a girl, she would be named Amber and if a boy, she would name him Ames McGee. She and her husband would return to Powder Springs, Georgia, where he was a lawyer for the Coca- Cola Company, dealing with international sales and such.

They would leave in a day or two, they were in no hurry.

Stella asked if she could make an announcement. Everyone was trying to get into in a happy mood, after all the sadness of the last three weeks. Of course, everyone was shouting "Speech! Speech!" as she stood up. There were a few empty bottles of wine on the table by now.

"I have something to say that may shock all of you, especially Stanley and Robert, I have wanted to say something for thirty years and now I am going to say it." Stella said.

"Stanley, I am your birth mother." she said. You could hear the gasp and everyone turned to look at Stanley who was still in shock over what happened to Sassy and what a real live hero she was.

"What? What did you say?" he sputtered. "You are what?"

"She said she was your birth mother, Stanley. Now, go down there and give your Momma a kiss." Sassy said as tears welled in her eyes.

"Stanley, I have wanted to tell you all these years and now it is out." Stella shrugged her shoulders.

Stanley went to her and put his arms around her and they hugged.

Robert stood up shook Stanley's hand and said, "If you ever call me Daddy after we are married, I will bust you in the mouth." A big laugh was heard all the way to the kitchen. So much so, that the kitchen staff came out to see what was happening.

Robert stood up and said, "Well, we might as well make it official. Stella and I are going to get married. Don't know when, but we are." and a round of applause could be heard.

Patricia looked at Emil and smiled as if waiting for him to say something, but Emil had his hands on the table and was very still. "I wonder if she has her shoes off again, rubbing his leg." I thought.

"Charlie, I guess I am going into town in a few months and see if I can be a store keeper, you know. Emily has that big store to run, you know, since her husband passed on a couple of years ago…" He played with his food on the plate. "…and well, she did offer me a job. I need to learn a trade anyway." Bart said as another round of applause went up.

"He has to get well first. I have plans for him." Emily said, and then blushed at being so bold. She had never had this much wine before, maybe just a little sip of sherry at Thanksgiving, but never a whole glass. Still, she was having fun with us.

No one wanted the meal to be over, but is had to come to an end. All of us decided we would meet at least once a year, for the annual Boll Weevil Convention as we were going to call it.

Our flight crew, Steve, Rita and Eunice could not be there. They had to go back to Atlanta. I asked Steve to make sure I got a good itemized account of the trip for records. Shirley Guerra, my CPA was going to scream like a gut shot orangutan when she got the bill. Steve told me about his home office phone call. That there would be no paperwork, the flight ever happened, we never went anywhere.

"Okay, maybe our friends paid the freight, but what about the scar on Eunice's ass." we chuckled. "Tell her that never happened."

Geoff and Marlene would leave in the morning, flying back to Belize. Steve made arrangements for them to fly commercial first class on Continental Airlines.

We all hugged and promised to be at the next meeting. We shook hands like we were walking out the door, when in fact we were all going upstairs to our apartments for the night and would see each other in the morning for breakfast.

It has been two weeks since Amber's funeral. Everyone was gone, Emil and Patricia were still there. They had moved into the main house into three of the apartments which had been joined together. I was told they will need the room.

Robert found out he was cleared to go back to work for U.S. Customs, so he and Stella were going to El Paso where he will was reassigned to the E.P.I.C. Center. They were getting married in a few weeks. The ceremony would be held here and then, honeymoon for a week in Del Rio, Texas to meet some his family that did not come to the Shadows for the wedding.

Johnny Ramirez was going to take over the day to day operation of the ranch now. I made him a principle in the ranch. He would do a good job with this place.

The house would be closed down for a while until we decided what to do with it. I was on my way out the door with Juan, who is now my driver. We are going to Morgan City, Louisiana, to look at a house boat for sale.

Chapter 32

EPILOGUE

It has been a while now since we had our "trip" as we have learned to call it. We have been keeping in touch with the "old gang" for a lack of a better name.

I had the photograph of Amber Ames done in oil and hung it in the big entrance hall of The Shadows. It is a life size oil painting. You remember when we stopped in at the big hotel Marlene's folks run?

The newspaper folks in Belize City allowed us to use the photo. It was the one where the Brats were walking into the big party. Amber had the long black dress on that was split up the side. She looked beautiful, all of them did, and the artist did a good job. I look at that painting and smiled, what a woman.

Samantha had her baby or should I say babies, a boy and a girl. Amber Charlene McGee and Bartholomew Ames McGee, cute kids, smart as whips. They look like their mother. Lil' Bart's initials are B.A.M. so I call him "Bam

Bam." His mother cringes every time I do that. So I do not say it when she can hear. Bart says that he is his kid, she is just borrowing him.

Samantha is working at the Center for Disease Control (CDC) and is in contact with Marlene Albright almost every day or so concerning tropical diseases in children. In fact, they visit several times a year in Atlanta when Marlene comes to do her "big shopping"
as she calls it.

I asked Samantha at the last meeting if she was ready for another trip. She says she thinks about it and then remembers she has responsibilities now.

With Bruce in the Corporate Management, they are expected to entertain clients. She says that is boring. She has a hard time relating to a trip to the mountains as "big adventure." When she plays golf or tennis and people see her leg with the scar. She tells them it was a rock climbing accident. She says her husband has "respect" for her that other women can never imagine.

Sassy has her Arab horse farm. She says it is a straight business deal with Stanley. However, Emil and Patricia have seen them at the mall on the level below them while riding up the escalator. They were looking at wedding gowns in a window. Of course, nothing has been said…officially.

Robert and Stella came to visit not too long ago. They stayed here at The Shadows. They mentioned that Sassy and

Stanley went to Oklahoma to look at the Malloy Ranch. Her family ranch that was sold years ago to a corporate firm and it is for sale again. It was understood that Sassy gets that as a wedding present, but nothing is sure with those two. Stanley adores Sassy and I feel she loves him too, but after her last marriage, she is a little gun-shy.

Also, Sassy's daughter, I forgot her name, Becky I think, got married and just had a baby. So Sassy is now a grandmother. When I remind Sassy she is a grandma, she tells me she is not a "grandmother," she is a "recycled mommy."

Maria is gone. My lawyer Max Gurrera, got the tax issues straightened out in South Texas and now Maria has the family property back free and clear. The politicians also agreed to pay Maria for "her mental anguish" in turn for Max the Mouth Piece not turning over certain information to the IRS, not very ethical, but effective. Maria still has a company credit card, but she has never used it, even when I asked her to.

Emil and Patricia are married. Patricia's "husband" was found floating face down on the Mississippi River around the time we went on our trip to Peru. He got drunk and fell in the river, so I heard.

Emil has a green card now for permanent residence. Red Baxter and the Mystery Man got it squared away in about 72 hours once they got started. Funny how red tape can be reduced when you know someone and how to do it.

Emil decided to adopt the girls and that was taken of care too. The local judge was real receptive to the Mystery Man's "suggestion."

Patricia will have a baby next month. They are both working for the Boll Weevil Foundation. Emil was bringing in outside law enforcement agencies and training them. Patricia is almost finished with her two year college plan, straight "A's" all the way. She plans on a four year degree when the baby gets here. She will run the office now that Stella is gone. She still has to call Stella for "how do I do this" lessons, but she is a quick learner. She is a Girl Scout leader too, has all the little girls on the ranch as memebers.

"Big Bart" and Emily are running the Ace Hardware Store in town. Emily's daughters are going to take over the business soon. Bart said that Emily works him like a Hebrew Slave, wants him to be at work at the same time every day. They got married in a quiet ceremony about a year ago. They act like kids when you see them, great fun for each other. They come out for meals several times a month.

Pamela "Eunice" Bennett is now working for the Coca-Cola Company as an entrance level manager. A "number cruncher" in the Accounting Department, Purchasing Agent I think. Bruce wants ten more just like her. I saw her at a BRAT meetings as we call the annual gathering. Eunice was in two piece business suits, conservative hair style, but you can't hide that "drop dead" figure she has. I have been meaning to ask her about her scar.

And me? I bought an eight five foot cabin cruiser, 1920 old wooden hull model, the type with mahogany woodwork. It was rebuilt stem to stern and looks like something out of a 1930's movie. But it has all the modern goodies installed, such as big modern diesel engines. I even had a washer and dryer installed along with a microwave, satellite TV, air conditioned state rooms and modern communications gear. I guess I just want it to look old fashioned on the outside. Also has a three man crew.

I named it MY ANGEL. I keep it near Baton Rouge, Louisiana, and as I write this we are going under the big bridge at Baton Rouge, heading north on the Mississippi River, just enjoying the scenery from a different view.

Oops, there goes my cell phone. Patricia is calling on the "Bat Phone." "Charlie? Can you come to the office? I think it is important."